HEART JOURNEY

BOBBI BLANZY

ARPress
45 Dan Road Suite 5
Canton MA 02021
Hotline: 1(888) 821-0229
Fax: 1(508) 545-7580

Ordering Information:

Quantity sales. Special discounts are available on quantity purchases by corporations, associations, and others. For details, contact the publisher at the address above.

Printed in the United States of America.
ISBN-13:   Softcover   979-8-89330-133-5
                eBook   979-8-89330-134-2
Library of Congress Control Number: 2024901597

TABLE OF CONTENTS

CHAPTER 1

"We're losing her. Pressure's dropping under fifty." The voice of the anesthesiologist broke the sound of rapidly clicking steel instruments.

"There it is. I see it. Another bleeder." The surgeon pinpointed an area with the tip of his instrument. The surgical resident leaned closer to watch as the doctor deftly ligated the ruptured vein. When the bleeding was again under control, he asked, "What's her pressure now?"

"Pressure's eighty-six and rising."

Beneath the glaring lights above the operating table, Dr. Joe Travis raised his head. A nurse slapped a sponge into his extended hand. Already two and a half hours into the tedious surgery, there was no guarantee that this time would make any difference in the life of his patient.

On the other side of the table, the exhausted resident glanced up. "How many more times can we cut Mattie open? Pseudomyxoma is nasty. You know it's useless—"

"It's *not* useless. Where there's life, there's some hope." Joe's intense blue eyes burned into those of the weary resident. The surgery continued with no further exchange between the doctors.

At length, Joe Travis stepped away from the table. Stripping off his gloves, he took a moment, as always, to commend the members of his surgical team. "You all did an excellent job." Completely spent, he left the operating suite and headed for the recovery room.

* * *

Joe Travis shifted in the chair beside Mattie Walker's bed in a futile effort to make himself more alert. For hours after surgery, he had listened to the hushed voices and quiet footsteps of the ICU nurses making their rounds up and down the corridor.

The rhythmic beeping of the cardiac monitor began to lull him into an exhausted sleep when his patient moved. He pulled himself to his feet and leaned over the bed.

Mattie Walker slowly opened her eyes. "So," she drawled in a groggy voice, "I see you saved me again. How am I *this* time?"

"A little better than *last* time." The surgeon's hands closed around hers while his skilled fingers slipped neatly over her frail wrist and tightened across her pulse.

"Then God *wuz* with yo' hands, just like I tol' you He would be."

"Yes, Mattie, I believe He was. But neither of us could have done it without you."

A smile crossed her brown, weathered face. She struggled to focus somewhere past his shoulder, her leaden eyes heavy from hours of anesthesia. "What time is it?"

The young doctor glanced at the clock high on the wall. "A quarter after three . . . in the morning."

She closed her eyes, smiling again as she weakly gripped his hand in her own. "And I bet you's been here the whole time."

"Hazards of the trade, Mattie," he told her quietly. "Go back to sleep now."

* * *

The hospital's conference room was jammed with doctors, nurses, residents, and students, listening as the speaker ended the seminar.

"Anyone can be a tissue or organ donor. Old age or even history of disease doesn't mean you can't become a donor. And if organs or tissue can't be used in giving someone a second chance at life, scientists can use these vital parts for research.

"As members of the medical profession, every one of you has undoubtedly had the experience of attending patients who have been declared brain dead. And this, as you already know, is the crucial time factor for harvesting organs."

"But what about the donor *families*?" a voice called from the back of the room. "How can we avoid seeming so insensitive to what they're going through?"

"You would never ignore the grief of these people because this is a crucial time for them, too. But you *can* offer them this assurance: whether the individual has consented for donation or not would never affect the best care you would give to that patient. And donation procedures would not begin until everything possible had been done to save their loved one."

The young woman leaned closer to the microphone. "It has been estimated that over one hundred thousand children and adults are waiting and hoping for a chance to live a normal, healthy life simply because there are not enough available donors. Through a computer-based system, the distribution of donated organs allows for equal access to patients waiting for these much-needed transplants.

"I've carried a donor card for years. I can't urge you enough to do the same." She paused as she gazed over her audience. "Organ donation is the most precious gift you can give . . . because it means *life*. And there aren't enough *thank-you's* to go around when you offer a gift like that."

There was considerable round of applause as the woman sat down behind the podium. Dr. Benjamin Jordan, chairman of the surgical department at the Boston university teaching hospital, rose and stood behind the microphone. "I want to thank Ms. McCallister for coming to speak with us today. I've had the privilege of knowing her most of her life, and it's with a great deal of pleasure to me personally that she has accepted a position here at our medical center. Please make her feel welcome."

There was another round of applause as the speakers left the platform. Dr. Jordan accompanied the guest lecturer through the crowd as he made his way toward his daughter who was sitting behind a table in the back of the room.

"It was a wonderful speech," Callie Jordan proudly told her friend.

Beth McCallister smiled. "A little awareness goes a long way." Callie watched her father glance anxiously around the room.

"Where's Joe?" he demanded petulantly. "I asked him specifically to be here."

"I heard he was in intensive care most of the night, Dad," Callie explained.

Jordan's irritable expression lessened a bit. "I wanted you to meet my former prodigy," he told Beth, then, with a beaming smile, added, "Well, you can meet him tonight at the party."

Beth's expression drooped. Declining an invitation from Benjamin Jordan, or anything else he wanted, was not an easy task. "Thanks, Dr. J., but I'm exhausted. I'd really like to go back to the apartment. I have a lot of unpacking to do yet." She glanced at Callie for support.

"She is tired, Dad," Callie vouched for her friend. "She was on the red eye flight until early this morning. Let her have tonight off." Jordan made a reluctant face. "Drive carefully," he muttered.

As Beth disappeared through the conference room door, he dropped into a chair beside his daughter. "I think Bethie's going to like it here."

"So do I," Callie heartily agreed.

* * *

Beth McCallister drove down the dark expressway in her rental car looking for the sign that signaled her exit. Her eyes were heavy with fatigue from her late night flight from Charleston, South Carolina, the night before. In the past twenty-four hours, she had slept less than three.

She stifled a yawn, marveling she had gotten through the lecture at the hospital as well as she did. Now all she could think about was a hot bath and collapsing into bed. She speculated with disdain that the sheets were probably packed away in some box marked "Dishes." Maybe she shouldn't have declined Callie's offer to stay at the exquisite Jordan estate, but she was too tired to attend any parties tonight. As she drove, Beth pondered her growing up years with Callie.

Optimistic and lively, Beth had been involved in school clubs along with copious other activities. High school had afforded even more opportunities—senior class president, newspaper reporter, a veritable maverick for every worthwhile campus campaign that came along. As a result, she had attracted many friends, but none so dear as Callie Jordan.

Callie had been the shy one, devotedly trailing behind her buoyant friend, but Beth had not allowed popularity to overshadow her bond with Callie.

For Callie had been cheated of the opportunities that had come so naturally to Beth. At eight years old, Callie had contracted rheumatic fever, but the disease had been misdiagnosed. Years passed before extensive tests revealed that her heart valves had been significantly damaged by the childhood illness. She was a teenager by the time serious, disabling health problems began to plague her.

As a result, Callie was frequently in and out of the hospital for related heart problems. On one such occasion, when the girls were barely fifteen years old, Callie needed a transfusion to restore lost blood volume and correct some clotting problems. When it was discovered that the hospital's supply was almost depleted of Callie's uncommon blood type, Beth pleaded to be a blood donor for her. Benjamin Jordan, along with his physician partner, Beth's father, agreed to type and cross-match Beth's blood, finding her type to be remarkably compatible with Callie's. *Real blood sisters*, the girls had declared themselves after that. Consequently, they had enjoyed a union only real sisters might have shared.

After graduation, Beth left for college on the west coast while Callie enrolled in nursing school in Boston. The training was rigorous and took her longer than usual to finish, but she walked down the aisle on graduation day to receive her diploma. And no one, apart from Benjamin Jordan, was more proud of her than Beth.

Beth's eyes blurred with fatigue. She knew she wasn't far from the turnoff, if she hadn't missed it altogether due to her weariness. A sign ahead signaled "Bay" something. She drove on while, unconsciously, the sign evoked more memories.

For years, Dr. Benjamin Jordan and Beth's father, Dr. Alexander McCallister, had been surgical partners in a joint practice at the Boston teaching hospital. Every summer, the two families vacationed together at the ocean. Most of the trips had been quiet and uneventful. However, there was the one Beth would never forget.

* * *

The two girls jumped through the ocean waves, laughing and screaming in the surf. Beth had been having so much fun she had completely forgotten about Callie's heart condition. Diving into the waves once more, she surfaced, sputtering salty water. Then her own heart froze. She could not see Callie anywhere.

And then, in the distance, she saw her friend floating facedown in the foaming water. She swam against the current with all her strength until at last she reached her. She could hear Callie struggling to breathe as she dragged her toward the shoreline.

Tears rolled down Beth's cheeks as she held her friend on the sandy beach, praying while Callie gasped for air. "Callie, I'm so sorry," she sobbed. "I forgot to look out for you!"

People on the beach began to rush toward the two girls as Callie looked up at her friend. "Promise me, Bethie," she whispered, beginning to breathe a little easier, "promise we'll always take care of each other."

"Always," Beth reassured her as she brushed wet hair away from Callie's eyes. "We have promises to keep."

"Promises to keep." Callie repeated the words they had learned from the Frost poem in school, words they had adopted as their own creed.

* * *

But I have promises to keep and miles to go before I sleep, Beth remembered the words with pleasure.

It was only at the last second she realized she had fallen asleep; realized too late after she opened her eyes that the blinding white was not from foaming ocean waves, but from approaching headlights coming directly toward her. Swerving to avoid certain collision, she heard the frightful sound of splintering metal as her car crashed through the guardrail and plunged down the embankment below.

CHAPTER 2

Dr. Benjamin Jordan burst into the kitchen of his home to oversee the preparations for the annual spring dinner party given for his surgical residents. As Chairman of the Surgical Department at the prestigious teaching hospital, his yearly dinner parties had become something of a tradition.

"Is everything ready? They should be here soon."

"Everything's ready. We just have to light the candles." Maggie McCarran, the Jordans' cook and housekeeper for some twenty years, carefully finished arranging a platter of hors d'oeuvres before handing the tray to one of the extra hired girls.

"I don't know why I keep doing this," Jordan sighed heavily. "I suppose because my wife always thought it was a good idea."

Callie held the kitchen door open as Maggie went out with another platter. "It is a good idea, Dad. Your students work hard, and they need to see you in something other than your lab coat or scrubs. A smile on your face wouldn't hurt either."

Jordan put his arm around her. "Maybe I continue the tradition because you're such a gracious hostess. Your mother would have been proud of you . . . as proud as I am." She opened her mouth to speak but instead began to cough. He watched her struggle with the chronic respiratory ailment that accompanied her heart condition and then helped her sit down. "Are you having problems with that new medication Jeff Marcus prescribed for you?"

"No," she replied, her voice strained from the increasingly persistent cough. She looked up at him with a resigned expression.

"Dad, all these medications aren't going to be enough for the rest of my life. You know that as well as I do."

"Let me be the diagnostician, all right?" he said, seemingly impervious to the facts. She could feel the usual scrutiny more closely than ever. "You stay put until I think you can manage. Do you hear me?"

"Loud and clear." Callie sighed with reluctance at yet another paternal directive. "Will you at least let me know when Joe gets here?"

Jordan smiled as he leaned over the chair and kissed the cheek of his only child. "You care a lot about Joe, don't you?"

"Of course I do."

"Well, like I've always said, no man could be more perfectly suited for you than—"

"Dad, *please.*"

"All right," he said, straightening up again. "But I just can't imagine any man more ideally suited for you than Joe Travis."

"You mean ideally suited as *your* son-in-law, don't you?" The indignant look in her father's eyes immediately caused her to regret the statement, no matter how truthful. "I'm sorry, Dad. You know how important Joe's work is to him. He's perfectly content to be a bachelor."

"Maybe for now; however, *you* could change all that if—"

Maggie pushed open the door, ending the longstanding debate when she announced the arrival of the first guests.

Callie started to get up, but Jordan gently eased her down onto the chair. "You stay right there. Contrary to popular opinion, I *can* entertain, at least for a while." She watched the door close after him.

Callie lamented again the contentious remark she had made to her father concerning Joe Travis, knowing in reality the statement was only an abysmal expression of her own frustration. The sensitive subject left her ill at ease and was not something she could openly share with her father. Only Maggie was privy to her secret yearning. But tonight, she determined to confront that yearning. Maybe

Dr. Joe Travis would sit up and take notice of her, if she could just muster the courage to tell him how she really felt about him. For six years, she had languished in the shadows, enamored by the unpretentious young surgeon whose single-mindedness for his work left no time for anything else or any*one* else, for that matter.

* * *

The sideboards in the dining room were laden with mouth-watering appetizers, exquisite entrees, and beautifully arranged desserts. Polished silver complimented bone china serving pieces that surrounded a crystal punch bowl fountain. Six hired servants kept everything running smoothly.

After the meal, Benjamin Jordan circulated among his students with an ease he did not manifest at the hospital. A tall, stocky man, he carried a commanding demeanor and threatening glare. He was feared by his students for his scrupulous attention to detail and abhorrence for passivity in the area of medicine. Thus, he could relax only in a setting far removed from the corridors of the hospital.

Callie lolled in a wing chair near the entrance to the dining room at a modest distance from the gathering. Dressed in a pale pink gown, the rosy shade of her dress added no luster to the ashen color of her skin. Listlessly, she observed the students and their spouses until all at once her face brightened.

Eagerly, she watched as Dr. Joe Travis made his way across the room, stopping frequently to extend polite conversation to colleagues and students as he passed. A former resident under her father and now head of trauma surgery and critical care, Joe's extraordinary good looks were merely an added benefit to his remarkable surgical skills.

At length, he spied Callie at the far end of the room and slid into an empty chair next to hers. "You look beautiful tonight, Callie." She felt herself blushing. "Well, thank you. But unfortunately, your gracious comments don't excuse the fact that you missed dinner entirely."

He leaned toward her in a confidential manner, pulling uncomfortably at the tight bow tie that complimented an impeccably tailored black tux. "I fell asleep in my office. Was your dad upset?"

"Well, he didn't say much, but you know how he counts on you to be at these affairs. How's Mattie?"

"Stubborn as usual. And so far, holding her own."

Joe began surveying the crowd, conversing now and again with students who stopped to talk before turning back to Callie. "So why aren't you mingling?"

"You've known me long enough not to ask that. These are doctors, and they don't want to discuss nursing."

"Ah, but where would they be without their nurses? Remember my first surgery? I can't imagine having done it without you."

"You could have done it blindfolded and certainly without *me*." "Yeah, but I didn't *want* to do it without you."

She grinned as she watched him attempt to conceal the rumbling in his stomach. "I saved a plate in the oven for you."

"Cal, what would I do without you?"

"I hope you never find out." They rose together and made their way toward the kitchen. She opened the oven door and gingerly removed a warmed china plate filled with food and handed it to him. He barely had a fork buried inside the scalloped potatoes when the kitchen door burst open.

"Joe! What are you doing in *here*?" Benjamin Jordan's imposing presence demanded immediate attention. "I want you to come with me and listen to something. Harve Cleary has been working on a new surgical technique I want your opinion on. Callie, tell Maggie we're out of hors d'oeuvres, will you?" Before he could excuse himself, Joe's plate was again in Callie's hands as her father quickly ushered him out of the room.

Callie glared at the swinging door before reluctantly returning the plate to the oven. She leaned against the marble countertop, annoyed that her father had the audacity to whisk Joe away so easily. But her aggravation began to subside as she remembered Joe's flattering words regarding her presence at his first surgery. As she waited for his return, his reminiscing took her mind far away from the party.

* * *

Callie pushed through the swinging door and found Joe preparing to scrub for his first solo surgery. With his hands in the air, she watchedhim fumble in a restless attempt to dispense the soap.

"Well, I'm glad to see you're not nervous." Grinning, she squeezedthe soap onto his hands.

"Does it show that much?"

"Come on, you've seen Dad do this surgery a hundred times." "Even so, I don't relish the idea of your father watching me kill my

first patient." His smile began to fade as his blue eyes searched hers. "I can't let anyone know how scared I am."

"Who's going to know? The patient's asleep, and your secrets have always been safe with me." She watched the smile slowly return to his face. "You're going to do just fine. And not just this time, but many, manytimes."

Impulsively, he leaned over and kissed her on the cheek. "You don't know how glad I am you're going to be in there. And your cheek is no longer sterile."

He returned to the sink and began scrubbing again. As she stood watching him, she wondered if the aching in her heart would ever go away.

* * *

Her musing ended when Joe slipped back into the kitchen again. "Well, if you ever need prostate surgery, I'm your man."

His smile was intoxicating, and she immediately returned it. Then her expression grew more serious. "Joe, I . . . I need to talk to you—alone."

He glanced around the empty kitchen. "Is this alone enough?" "I'd rather go someplace where Dad won't be stealing you again." Then on second thought, she added, "But you haven't eaten anything."

"That's all right. If it's important to you, let's go."

They left the kitchen unobserved by the back entrance and walked down the hallway to her father's den. Joe pushed apart the double oak doors, and Callie followed him inside. To honor her wish for privacy, he pulled the doors together again.

She stood beside the fireplace. A vast library of medical books Joe had perused countless times lined mahogany shelves on either side of the stone hearth.

"You feeling all right, Cal? Are you having good response to the new medication?" he ventured, only guessing at her reasons for wanting a private audience.

Discussing her heart condition was not on her agenda tonight, though few knew her situation as extensively as did Joe. "I'm not responding as well as I should, according to Dr. Marcus. I've asked him not to be too specific with Dad, but there's not much you can hide from him." As a nurse, Callie's knowledge concerning her condition wasn't something she knew she could ignore, but she was determined to fulfill her mission tonight.

"Oh, Joe, I don't want to talk about my heart condition."

But for Joe, concern for her health took precedence. "What exactly did Marcus say to you?"

Callie hungered to tell him how she felt, to tell him how much and how long she had loved him. To that end, she hurried to give him an explanation. "He wants me to take it easier, maybe even quit working. But I don't want to quit working."

"What about cutting back on your hours? I could arrange that. You scrub with me more than anyone else does. Believe me, I see to that."

"That would be a possibility, except Dad would insist on knowing why." She turned away as a longstanding childhood anger aimed at her restrictive lifestyle rose inside her. "I'm just so tired of letting him run my life!" The gentle touch of Joe's hands around her shoulders fueled her with passionate courage. She turned to look at him once more. "I know he's spent years seeking the right 'cure' for my condition, and I can appreciate that, but what he will never understand is that I want to live my *own* way! He's controlled every facet of my life for as long as I can remember, even to the point of 'sanctioning' who I choose to fall in love wi—" Her eyes widened, and her face flooded with color as the unintentional words trailed into mortified silence, taking her conviction with them. She quickly looked away.

Joe's expression filled with sympathy. He had guessed by now that Callie had a secret, but he would never embarrass her by asking her to reveal it to him. He slipped his hand beneath her chin, turning her face toward his. "Believe it or not, I understand how you feel."

Her frustration mounted. The words . . . if only she could get the words out! She drew a nervous breath. There would never be a better opportunity than now. "Joe, I don't think you really understand how I feel . . . how I feel about—"

The carefully parceled words abruptly ended when one of the doors to the den slid open. "A thousand pardons for the intrusion, but ya're wanted on the telephone, Dr. Joe." Maggie McCarran cast a perceptive and apologetic glance toward Callie before quietly pulling the door closed again.

Callie waited patiently while Joe picked up the phone and answered questions regarding treatment and medication orders for one of his patients. She waited while his call was transferred to the intensive care unit, where he inquired about Mattie Walker's progress. Again, he proceeded to leave more orders with the nurses, all the while jotting down information on a pad of paper he kept inside his coat pocket.

As she watched him work, the very words she had spoken to her father began to haunt her. *You know how important Joe's work is to him. He's perfectly content to be a bachelor.*

Yes, she thought miserably as an even greater sense of longing overwhelmed her, *he's perfectly content.*

A full fifteen minutes had passed before Joe hung up the phone. When he turned away from the desk to resume his conversation with Callie, he found the doors to the den wide open, and he was alone in the room.

He sighed, stuffing his notes inside his coat pocket, hoping he hadn't hurt her feelings. He rose from the chair behind the desk and stood in front of the fireplace once more, contemplating their brief conversation.

A smile came to his face. So Callie finally had a love interest. He would never press her to know who it was. And Callie was right about her father. In his paternal endeavor to care for her, though understandable, he had assumed too much control. She was entitled to live her own life, to choose whatever man she wanted, and he would defend her right to do so.

However, beginning with the first year of his residency, Joe had learned early on that Dr. Benjamin Jordan was not a man one easily opposed.

* * *

Joe Travis knocked on the half open door, poking his head inside when he heard the familiar gravelly voice. "Dr. Jordan, you wanted to see me?"

"Joe, come in! And close the door." Dr. Benjamin Jordan returnedto his phone conversation. His broad shoulders and imposing formloomed behind his desk, a cumbersome piece of furniture that hardly took up space in the expansive office. In a sweeping gesture that matchedhis nature, he motioned for Joe to take a seat in one of the plush chairs opposite the desk.

A few minutes passed before Jordan hung up the phone. "Joe, I know a resident's time is precious, so I'll come right to the point," he began. "I want you to know I'm very impressed with your work."

"That means a lot coming from you, sir."

Jordan raised his hand for silence. "You have a natural instinct for diagnosis, an inherent ability for prognostication, not just a mechanical competence like some I've seen. You work hard. It's showing in your accomplishments."

Joe was unaccustomed to such words of praise coming from the man most of the residents and interns wanted to run from. "I appreciate that,Dr. Jordan, but I don't feel I work any harder than any other—"

"I also don't waste compliments on every young man who may havean interest in my daughter, either." In spite of the unyielding expression,there was obvious approval in his tone of voice.

Joe's eyes opened wider. "I beg your pardon?"

A hint of a smile appeared on Jordan's face. "You know I'm very protective of Callie. She's all I have since her mother died."

"I can understand that."

"Well, the fact is, I know you and Callie are close. She cares a lot about you. And it's possible that she may be ready to commit to something"—he stopped and looked hard at Joe—"that maybe you're not quite ready for." He leaned back in the immense leather chair and foldedhis hands across his big chest.

Joe had not been aware of this speculation. He looked again at thebig man across from him, choosing his words with careful consideration."Callie is a wonderful girl," he readily admitted, "and I do care about her, deeply. But right now I can't think about anything but becoming thebest surgeon I can possibly be. I hope you can understand that."

Joe watched as Jordan rose to his feet, warily scrutinizing him with penetrating eyes. He feared for what was coming next. "That is exactly what I hoped you would say." Joe slowly released a stifled breath. "Right now, losing your head to your heart would be foolish because you have the potential for becoming one of the best surgeons I've ever trained. But whether or not you ever become my son-in-law doesn't mean I'm going tolet up on you by any means."

Joe grinned as he rose to his feet. "No, sir, I wouldn't expect that." Jordan reached across the desk and squeezed his hand with sincerity.

"Whatever happens, I want you to know if I'd had a son, I would have wanted him to be just like you."

"I'm honored, sir."

"Now," Jordan resumed his customary authoritative air as he sat down once more. He opened a file in front of him and began shuffling papers. "I suppose you haven't had any dinner yet."

Joe could almost feel the thin, cash bare wallet buried in his back pocket. "No, I . . . usually don't eat supper on Tuesdays. I find every otherday works just—"

"Uh-hum," the perceptive surgeon interrupted without glancing up from the file. "Be at my house at eight sharp. I'm having a dinner party

for a few distinguished physicians that would do you well to make their acquaintance."

"I'll be there. And thank you." Joe knew he had been dismissed. But as he left the room, he felt the eyes of the great man following him even after he had gone.

* * *

Increasing commotion from the ongoing celebration interrupted Joe's reverie. He knew he should return to the gathering and apologize to Callie for their interrupted conversation. But for the moment, he paused to gaze at the elegant family portraits amassed on the wall above the fireplace.

Six generations of Jordans stared down at him in heavy gilded frames. Among them, of course, were the exquisitely painted portraits of Dr. Benjamin Jordan and his late wife, and their only child, Callie. This family, including Maggie, had become more important to him than they would ever realize.

Regardless of his brusque mannerism, Benjamin Jordan had demonstrated to Joe the sincerity of a real father. Jordan had given him far greater memories than the sorry ones left by his own father, an abusive alcoholic who had drifted in and out of his son's childhood. Joe had endured years of abuse from his father, beginning with neglect, at times turning to violence directed not only toward him, but his mother as well, and concluding with absolute silence.

Yet his mother had been a Christian woman. She had recognized the strong sense of self-determination in her son and had encouraged his independence. But at the same time, she strove to impress on him the value of relying on a loving God, despite the family's unfavorable circumstances, and the importance of maintaining a vital connection with One who would ultimately guide him the rest of his life. But the young Joe struggled to reconcile a caring heavenly Father with the cruel lack of sympathy and interest he encountered in his earthly father.

Yet there was nothing he wanted more than to please the man, but he could never satisfy him, drunk or sober, no matter what he did. Only in his mother did he perceive a semblance of the love she tried to convey. For her sake, he endeavored to accept the faults and failures of a selfish humanity.

Joe worked relentlessly to maintain a high scholastic average throughout his school years, continually bringing home grade reports with nothing less than As. Where his mother praised her son's efforts, his father largely ignored his accomplishments in favor of pursuing his own self-seeking interests.

But on a single occasion, he rendered one B. His father could do nothing but criticize the purported substandard grade. Joe said nothing, but the event was a turning point in his young life, a defining moment when he realized the only way he could avoid the continual disappointment would be to disregard it altogether. Emotional indifference provided a sanctuary from the father he could never please.

Eventually, the difficult years took their toll on his mother. She became chronically ill, and Joe spent the remainder of his teenage years caring for her. After her premature death, his father never returned, and Joe found himself on the brink of young manhood completely alone. However, by now, he had learned a hard lesson: survival meant depending on himself, a burden he unconsciously continued to carry into the present.

But Joseph Ian Travis resolved that injustice and rejection would not dictate the rest of his life. The helplessness he endured while tending to his mother's frail health merely fueled his passion to pursue his lifelong desire to become a surgeon—resolving as well to become everything to his patients his father had never been to him.

At the time of his mother's death, funds arduously set aside for his medical education had long been depleted. Consequently, Joe worked harder than most to make his way through medical school. An assortment of odd jobs helped with some of the expenses, though scholarships and loans became the primary source of meeting his ambition.

By the time his residency loomed before him, he was deeply in debt and equally discouraged. Though residency would provide him with some income, his earnings would never be enough to sustain him until he finished. After much deliberation and sleepless nights, a meeting with Benjamin Jordan would be unavoidable.

Dr. Benjamin Jordan had served for a number of years as chairman of the surgical department of the teaching hospital. Joe dreaded the confrontation with the feisty physician. But unknown to him, the renowned surgical professor had become well acquainted with the young doctor's remarkable skills in the operating room as well as his compassion at the patient's bedside. To Joe's amazement, Jordan offered not only to become his mentor, but agreed to help him financially through his last years of training. Though he had repaid the money long ago, Joe's allegiance and affection for the man steadily grew.

His hand passed over a small brass frame that held one of his favorite photographs. Few people were dearer to his heart than Callie Jordan was. Her shy nature and chronically ill health created in him a desire to protect her from the difficulties of the world, in much the same way he had tried to protect his mother. Yet Callie was the one to whom he instinctively poured out his problems. Afterward, he would berate himself for taking advantage of her gentle character. Never did he want to mar the innocence and simplicity that he loved most about her.

He worried about her increasingly problematic heart condition. As a doctor, he knew the odds of longevity for her were slim, especially if her condition continued to worsen, as it likely would. He could not imagine his life without her companionship.

He smiled as he wondered how Ben Jordan had ever misconstrued a romantic link between himself and Callie. Joe had always regarded Callie as the younger sister he never had. She was family—his family, if only by proxy. True, he had enjoyed a few minor relationships during his training, but concentration on his career had been his primary goal. Too much had been demanded of him through the years, too much time invested to allow any relationship to become serious. Now it had become way of life.

Sounds of the elaborate gathering grew more clamorous as strains of a familiar Irish tune began to waft through the air. Apparently, the festivities were beginning to liven up. Joe left the den and made his way toward the party once more.

* * *

The stringed ensemble had transformed its formal and measured pieces into a lively Irish jig. And Joe knew the change had come from the Jordans' headstrong housekeeper, Maggie McCarran.

With the floor to herself, she danced to the old Irish melody, fluttering her ruffled apron like a can-can girl. The now captivated guests stood on the sidelines, clapping their hands in time to her jaunty steps.

Callie stepped closer into the circle and marveled at Maggie's ability. Then she spotted Joe in the crowd, and wondered if he was remembering, as she was, Maggie's endeavor to teach him the simple folk dance for the first time.

* * *

"Oh, come on, Dr. Joe! It's time ya gave that noble brain of yours a rest! Let me show ya how to get the blood to really pulse through your veins!"

Maggie McCarran tugged at Joe's hand while he sat at the table in the Jordan's den, books and papers strewn all around him. "Maggie, I can't!" he protested, glancing at the study materials in front of him. "I've got an exam tomorrow. Dr. Jordan's exam! Do you have any idea what they're like?"

"No, and I don't expect to ever find out. I just know ya've been sittin' there with Callie for hours, your noses glued to those books, and it's high time ya took a break! Now let me show ya the jig I taught Callie when she was just a wee thing!"

"You might as well give in," Callie said, closing the textbook. "She's going to get you in the end anyway."

Joe sighed helplessly as he allowed Maggie to pull him from the chair. She pushed a button on the wall, and the room filled with music. Taking him by the hands, she began to demonstrate the simple steps to the dance. Almost at once, his feet were on top of hers, his attempt to mimic her steps awkward and clumsy.

"Maggie, this is ridiculous."

"No, it is not!" she declared. "Ya just have your mind on too many things!" Again, she tried to take him through the routine steps. But his self-conscious efforts came to a miserable halt when Callie began to laugh. "How can anybody be so adept with his hands and so clumsy with his feet?"

His deep blue eyes cut severely in her direction. "I don't operate with my feet."

Maggie glanced at Callie while still holding onto Joe's hands. "Callie, girl, come see what you can do. Your feet are younger than mine."

Willingly, Callie took Maggie's place. A rush of warmth spread throughout her at the touch of his hands. She felt her face begin to flush and looked away for a moment until Maggie started the music once more.

In half an hour, they were moving together in time to the music, while Maggie sat on the sofa, clapping out the rhythm as they circled the room. Callie knew she was becoming too winde, but did not want to stop.

Unnoticed, the oak doors parted, and Benjamin Jordan stepped inside the room, his overcoat wet with rain. He leaned against the wall, watching with obvious pleasure when Maggie saw him.

"Dr. J, you're home already! Would ya like a little tea before ya retire?" she asked above the clamorous music.

Without taking his eyes away from the handsome couple, he nodded. "That would be fine, Maggie, just fine. But what is all this?" he asked, nodding toward Joe and Callie.

"Oh, that! Dr. Joe's just takin' a little study break is all. I'll bring your tea to your room." Maggie left the den.

Joe and Callie laughed aloud at the far side of the room as the music ended. It was then they heard the single round of applause. "Beautiful! I had no idea you two were such delightful entertainers."

At the sound of her father's voice, Callie saw Joe's face turn red as they made their way back to the table. "We were . . . just taking a break, Dr. Jordan. We've been at it for hours."

"That's right, Dad," Callie agreed, out of breath as she took her seat across from him. "Joe's been doing an excellent job."

"Oh, I'm sure of that," Jordan said, with more than a hint of sarcasm in his voice. He folded his arms across his expansive chest. "I just didn't realize tonight was the grand opening of the Jordan School for Dancing Doctors."

* * *

The last of the guests were gone. Ben Jordan had been called to the phone, leaving Joe alone with Callie in the entry hall.

"Maggie was the sensation of the party," she said, attempting to make idle conversation. "Remember when she tried to teach you the same jig?"

The dimples in his cheeks deepened with his friendly smile. "I remember," he returned affectionately.

She looked down at the floor. "Joe, I'm sorry for sounding off in the den," she said quietly, regretting more than just her frustration where her father was concerned.

"Hey, if you can't sound off to me, who else can you to sound off to? Besides," he said as he put his hands around her shoulders and squeezed them, "I'm the one who should be apologizing to you for interrupting our conversation."

"It wasn't your fault. I understand."

"Well, tomorrow, we'll arrange for you to work part time. You can still scrub with me for emergencies when you're on duty. Then you can be a lady of leisure in the afternoons. How's that?"

She smiled. "I'd like that." As she studied his gentle expression, everything within her ached to confess how much she loved him. "Joe, there's something I want to tell you . . . something I've wanted to tell you for a long time." Gathering courage, her gaze wandered past the arched doorway toward her father on the other side of the living room. Still on the phone, his expression was attentive and approving as he discreetly observed them together. Callie couldn't hide her consternation.

"Joe, can we go out on the porch?"

As they opened the front door, Ben Jordan called from the living room. "Joe, wait a minute! You've got a stat consult. Auto accident to the ER in about fifteen minutes."

22

"I'm on my way." Instinctively, Joe felt for the keys in his pocket, but one look at Callie's dismayed expression stopped the search. "Cal, I'm sorry. You wanted to tell me something."

Once again, pressing circumstances stood in the way. "It can wait. You better go."

He leaned over and kissed her on the cheek. "I'll see to all the details tomorrow." He slipped through the open door and was gone. Alone in the entry hall, Callie watched from the window until

Joe's car disappeared around the curved driveway. She leaned against the door for a long time after turning out the lights.

CHAPTER 3

Joe Travis leaned over the stretcher in the recovery room and smiled as his eight-year-old patient's eyes flickered and then opened. Reaching across the metal side rail, he gently squeezed her hand. "It's all over," he whispered. "You came through like a real trooper. But your bike wasn't so lucky."

She wrinkled her nose and moaned in a groggy voice. "My new bike? It really got . . . messed up?"

"I'm afraid so," he returned sympathetically. "Trucks and bikes don't usually mix very well. You can always get another bike. But your mom and dad could never get another you."

She managed a sleepy smile. "I guess not."

Joe was amazed at her spirit, despite the pain he knew she was having. "When you're well enough, I'm going to kick you out of here, fast, and then we'll see about getting you another bike. Deal?"

She giggled and then groaned again. "You make it hurt more when I laugh."

He brushed the hair away from her face. "We're going to take care of that too." He took the chart a nurse handed him and spoke out loud as he pretended to write the order. "No laughing for twenty-four hours." She giggled again while he scribbled a postoperative medication order. "I'll see you later this afternoon. And remember, no laughing."

"Okay." She grinned affectionately at him as attendants wheeled her from the room.

The emergency surgery had taken up most of the morning. Joe walked out of the OR, rubbing the small of his back with his aching hands. He had had little reason to return home after the late hours he had put in tending to the emergency call last night after the party. Three hours of sleep on his office couch would have to see him through the rest of the day.

As he waited beside the elevator, he reached into his pocket, reassuring himself that his prized ticket to the basketball playoffs that night was still in place. But he knew he would never make the coveted game if he didn't begin his rounds right away, and then on to the ever-pending paperwork that waited in his office. His stomach growled from emptiness, but he would have to do without lunch.

The elevator opened on the ground floor. He hurriedly tried to pass through the emergency unit on his way to the records department when he was waylaid by a small, white-haired woman in dingy clothing and dirty sneakers.

"Dr. Travis, do you remember me? Do you?" The earnest, gap-toothed smile pleaded with him.

In spite of his haste, he stopped. "Of course I do. How are you?" She proceeded to tell him, though he had heard it all before.

She lived in a homeless shelter some blocks away from the hospital. In addition to the effects of advancing age and diabetes, her chronically high blood pressure made her a frequent patient in the emergency room.

He listened courteously, giving her his undivided attention. As she continued to pour out the same story, he began to walk her unsuspectingly back toward the waiting area. He helped her sit down, making small talk with her while he glanced at the numerous patients waiting to be seen. He knew she would have a long wait. "You just make yourself comfortable, and someone will be with you as soon as possible," he told her. He knew she only wanted someone to listen.

He nodded toward one of the nurses, waiting until she made her way in their direction. While the old woman engaged the nurse, he slipped away toward the records department to finish signing some patient charts and then headed for the elevator in a different direction.

Three floors later, he stepped behind the nurses' station. "I heard you were in surgery until quite late last night . . . again," one of the nurses commented without looking up from her work. "Do you think you can stay awake for the big game tonight?"

"I'm going to try." He sat down in front of the computer and began searching for test results on his late-night emergency patient. When he had found what he wanted, he rose from the chair and headed down the corridor.

He knocked on the open door. "Ms. McCallister?" The dark haired young woman looked up from her magazine as he walked in. "I'm Dr. Travis. I did your surgery last night."

"Oh, so you're the one!" Beth McCallister eyed him cautiously. "Are you really a qualified surgeon? You seem a little young to be so brilliant."

"Yes, as a matter of fact, I am . . . " His words came to a halt when he realized the twofold meaning of his answer. "Well, not brilliant, I mean, but . . . a qualified surgeon." In a hasty attempt to recover his dignity, he began to examine the stitches in Beth's forehead. "What do you remember about last night?"

"Not much. I understand I was pretty much out of it when I got here. That's too bad too." She sighed while he tilted her head toward the light for a better look. "I've been told I can carry on a conversation even when I'm unconscious, maybe even better when I'm unconscious."

He couldn't help but laugh as he marveled at her sense of humor, considering the headache she probably had. "Well, for someone who can break a windshield, you were fortunate to get away without a serious concussion. Are you sure you can't remember any details?" He motioned for her to lie flat so he could examine the abdominal surgical site.

"All I remember was how tired I was when I left here," she said, carefully easing herself into a prone position. "I must have fallen asleep at the wheel. The next thing I knew I was under some very bright lights."

He gingerly pulled the sheet back and lifted aside the hospital gown to continue his examination. "You say you were here, at the hospital?"

"Yes, I was giving a lecture late yesterday afternoon."

Joe finished his examination and then pulled the sheet up again. "Beth McCallister," he said, a smile touching his lips. "I was supposed to be at your lecture. You're Callie's friend, aren't you?"

"That's right." She looked up at him in astonishment. "And you must be Joe. Dr. Jordan was quite insistent that I meet you last night."

"Dr. Jordan is famous for being quite insistent." He helped her sit up again, then pulled a chair beside the bed and sat down. "I've heard a lot about you. You and Callie grew up together, isn't that right?"

"We sure did. I guess the only way we could have been closer would have been to be Siamese twins."

Joe returned her smile. "Callie tells me you're a counselor. Is lecturing about organ donation just something you do on the side?" "Well, it's more of a sideline," she explained. "I'm a grief counselor. I deal with a lot of accident victims and their families. As a result, I began to learn quite a bit about what organ donation can mean to a desperate family. When Dr. Jordan recommended me for a position here, he was anxious for the hospital staff to become familiar with the research I've done."

"Well, I think you're doing a fine thing." Joe stood up and pushed the chair back. "Looks like everything is just as it should be. Are you sure you aren't having any additional pain, aside from the incision?"

"Maybe a little. Is that unusual?"

He shook his head. "Not really. But let me know if you're having any discomfort."

"Oh, believe me, you'll know. I don't intend to stay confined to this bed very long. I was hired to do a job here, not take up bed space."

His growing attraction to her was irresistible. He had all but forgotten the game ticket in his pocket when he suddenly became aware that he was still smiling at her. "Well, I'll stop by again tomorrow."

"I'll look forward to it."

But as he left the room, tomorrow seemed a long way off.

* * *

Evening visiting hours had already begun by the time Callie Jordan entered Beth's room carrying a small suitcase, but she wasn't surprised to find that Beth already had a visitor.

"Callie, it's good to see you." Pastor Evan Richards rose from the chair beside the bed and extended his hand in welcome to his long time church member. "Beth and I were just talking about you."

Callie smiled at the young minister as she set Beth's bag on the bedside table. "I'm glad you could come and meet my friend so soon."

"Except I thought we might be on the same side of the bed," Beth remarked dryly. "I usually do my counseling standing up."

"Well, you don't look any worse for wear."

"That's what you think," Beth said, lightly tapping the thick white bandage that extended part way across her forehead. "I feel like a contestant in a Frankenstein look-alike contest."

The young pastor laughed as he pulled a chair over for Callie. They sat down together. "Dad was pretty upset when he found out you were the accident victim the ER called about last night after the party."

"Yeah, I got that impression when he came by this morning. So next time I'll know when to accept an invitation, no matter how tired I am." She glanced at the suitcase Callie had brought. "Did you find all my stuff?"

"I found everything except the robe. I guess you'll have to wear a hospital robe until I can find it."

"Well, I'm sure you girls have lots of catching up to do," Evan Richards said in a polite voice, preparing to excuse himself. "Beth, I know your work here at the hospital is going to be lifesaving for many people. And we both know Callie is a lifesaver from way back." Callie smiled. "Joe Travis was the real lifesaver," she said. She looked at Beth. "You were lucky he was on-call last night. He's probably the best surgeon we have here."

"You sound just like your dad. According to him," Beth said, raising her hands in feigned adulation, "there's no one else but Joe Travis."

"Well, I'm glad to hear that." A soft male voice sounded behind them.

The pastor and the two women turned at the same time to see the celebrated young surgeon leaning nonchalantly inside the doorway. Beth's face reddened. "How long have you been standing there?" "Long enough to find out what a fantastic reputation I have."

Grinning, he walked into the room.

"Joe, I don't believe you've ever met the pastor of my church," Callie began the introduction. "Dr. Joe Travis, this is Pastor Evan Richards."

He rose to his feet and accepted Joe's outstretched hand. "Callie's told me a lot about you."

Joe glanced artfully at Callie. "I fear all you heard may not have been totally objective." Amused, he watched her face blush.

"Well, I can assure you it was all quite complimentary." Richards reached for his coat draped over the back of the chair. "I'm afraid I'm going to have to get going. I have a few more patients to see." He shook hands with Joe once more. "Dr. Travis, it was a real pleasure meeting you. And Beth," he said, turning toward her, "I hope to see you in church soon. And I'm sure our paths will be crossing around here at some time or another."

Beth smiled. "I'm sure they will. Thanks for stopping by." After the minister left, Beth looked at again at Joe. "So tell me, Doctor," she began, "you never said when I can get out of here and start the job I was hired to do."

"I'm afraid you aren't going anywhere too soon. You just had surgery, and you need a little time to heal. Are you having any problems?"

"Not so far."

"Good," he returned. "I just wanted to make sure you were comfortable for the night." He walked toward the door then turned once more. "By the way, Cal, I made all the arrangements for you. You're officially my morning scrub nurse now. So don't stay out too late."

"I won't," she returned with more than appreciation in her voice.

The door closed behind him. "Such a handsome man," Beth remarked. "Is he always so genial too?"

"Most of the time," Callie readily admitted. "But he's not afraid to say what he thinks, particularly to the older, more conservative doctors. He's been in trouble with them more than once, especially where his patients are concerned. But that's because there's nothing he wouldn't do for his patients." She seemed distant for a moment as her mind wandered toward her heart. Intuitively, Beth noticed the change.

"Looks like there's nothing you wouldn't do for him, either." Callie cast her friend a piqued expression but without anger.

The subject of Dr. Joe Travis was too delicate, too private, something she could not divulge, even to Beth. "Joe's a good friend. He's always been there when I needed him." She rose from the chair. "I guess I better get going and let you get some rest. I'll see you tomorrow."

As she bent to hug her friend, Beth couldn't help but wonder if Callie's estimation of the handsome young doctor really did stop at friendship.

* * *

The wheelchair rattled noisily down the corridor the following afternoon, stopping outside Beth McCallister's room. Joe barely knocked before propelling the chair inside.

Beth's bored expression changed to dismay as she looked first at the chair and then at him. "Oh, not more tests," she moaned, sinking deeper into the pillows. "I haven't got anything left that somebody hasn't already taken or seen at least twice!" Then glancing at him from head to foot, she pushed herself up in the bed. "Green scrubs, white shoes. We're not going back to the operating room, are we?"

Joe laughed as he moved the chair beside the bed. "No, I just came from there. This is your first outing. And I'm driving."

"Is that so?" she asked, her interest peaked at once. "Then where is this little excursion to?"

He opened the closet door and pulled out the gangly hospital robe hanging inside. "You'll know soon enough. Now put this on and no more questions." Dutifully, she slipped into the unsightly robe. He helped her into the chair and then wheeled her out the door.

"You seem to prefer doing a lot of things for yourself," she commented as he pushed her chair down the corridor. "A lot of doctors would rather designate than do for themselves."

"I believe one should do for oneself as much as possible," he returned sardonically while rounding a corner.

"But as a busy surgeon at a large teaching hospital like this, how is it you're able to spend so much time with your patients?" She was glad he couldn't see the delighted smile creeping over her face.

"Well," he fumbled for words that eluded him, "you . . . make time for what's important. And I believe you'll find what I want to show you will be of some personal interest." He came to a halt in front of the elevator and pushed the button. The doors opened and he rolled her inside.

"Okay, I give up," she sighed as they descended to the ground floor. "What's this all about?"

"No more questions. Just sit back and enjoy the ride." He pushed her through the corridor of the emergency department and finally through the solarium. The sun felt good in the midst of the early spring air, together with the warmth of his hands as he gently tucked the robe more securely around her neck and shoulders.

They passed through a set of double doors and into the spacious, five-story office building adjoined to the medical complex. Ignoring her continuing barrage of questions, he said nothing until he stopped in front of one of the offices at the far end of the corridor. Then he waited until her eyes rose to the newly mounted metal plate on the door: "Beth McCallister, Grief Counseling."

He slipped the key into the door, opened it, and ushered her inside.

"Oh, my." Her hand rose to her cheek as she surveyed the spacious office for the first time. "I never dreamed it would be this nice." Richly paneled walls complimented a large window decorated with light colored draperies. Overhead cabinets and bookshelves provided ample storage space. A large oak desk with two burgundy armchairs in front graced the latter part of the room. A floor lamp was set beside a comfortable looking rocking chair in one corner.

Joe was pleased his mission had been such a success. "Dr. Jordan must think an awful lot of you." He helped her out of the chair, cautiously observing her as she hobbled across the room and sat down behind the desk.

"I can't get over this," she said, running her hands gingerly over the smooth desktop. But when she looked up, she found Joe shaking his head and grinning. "What's the big joke?"

"I just can't see anyone taking you too seriously in that robe."

She glanced down at her bedraggled appearance and then back to him. "You're right. I'm a mess." She sank back disdainfully into the chair.

Joe walked behind the desk and crouched beside her. "I didn't mean that the way it sounded. You're a far cry from a 'mess' in my opinion."

She pushed a mass of thick brown hair away from her forehead. "That's very sweet of you, even if is a matter of opinion, Doctor."

"It's Joe."

She glanced down at her bruised hands. "Joe," she repeated quietly. "That was my father's name. Joseph Alexander McCallister."

"Your father and Dr. Jordan had a joint practice for quite a while, didn't they?"

"Yes, they did. Callie and I couldn't have been more than five or six years old when they formed their partnership." She smiled, remembering. "My father was the complete opposite of Dr. J., very quiet and easy going. More than once people said that Callie and I were switched at birth, considering our fathers' personalities." Her jovial expression grew pensive before she continued. "My dad died shortly before he was planning to retire. Like Callie, I had no brothers or sisters, so you can see how much she and I depended on each other. It was hard leaving her when I went off to school, and she had to stay here because of her heart condition. I had every intention of coming back to Boston, but"—she shook her head—"when I was asked to organize a new counseling department at a prominent hospital in Charleston, South Carolina, I couldn't turn it down."

"So," he said, looking around the room, "this is coming home for you, isn't it?"

"Some homecoming." She shuddered as she considered again the terrifying car accident that could easily have taken her life. "Maybe coming back was a big mistake." She feared she was divulging more than she had intended. She pulled open an empty desk drawer and peered thoughtfully inside. A moment later, she felt Joe's hand slide over hers. She raised her eyes until they met his.

"Speaking for myself, I don't believe your coming back was a mistake." His hand slipped under her chin as her smile slowly returned. With his face only inches from hers, he felt an overwhelming desire to kiss her. He was sure he saw the same thing in her eyes as well.

What was he thinking? He was her doctor; she was his patient, and the ethics demanded by his profession forbid him to yield to such feelings. With passionate reluctance, his hand slipped away from her face as he rose to his feet. "I suppose I better get you back."

He helped her into the wheelchair once more. Outside in the corridor, he slipped the key out of the door.

"Joe?" Without reserve, Beth reached for his hand and looked up at him. "I really have been wondering if for some reason I wasn't supposed to be here. I hoped my coming back was God's answer to a prayer, not a mistake."

He smiled down at her as he squeezed her hand. "I'm sure God's bringing you here was in answer to many prayers. It was no mistake." At that moment, Joe's beeper sounded. He excused himself as he reached for the nearest phone in the corridor.

"I'm sorry, Beth, I'm needed in emergency," he told her on his return. "I'll send one of the nurses to take you back to your room."

As he hurried down the long hallway, he could not help but wonder if she was the answer to another prayer, an unconscious desire that he was only now beginning to realize.

* * *

Three hours later, Joe Travis trailed behind Dr. Benjamin Jordan through the emergency room. The two doctors stopped beside the nurses' station where Jordan picked up a chart and began scribbling notes.

Joe looked back when the door opened to the trauma room from which they had just emerged. Two orderlies discreetly pushed a covered stretcher toward the elevator. Jordan looked up from his writing and followed the younger doctor's troubled gaze. "Joe, we did everything humanly possible. I don't want you agonizing over a situation that was completely out of our hands."

Joe turned back to the desk. "You'd think we could have saved one . . ."

"Not in the shape they came in. Those boys never had a chance against that gang. All we can do now is leave it to the police and hope some justice can come out of it."

"Justice . . ." The mumbled word erupted with quiet vehemence as Joe ran his hand angrily through his hair.

Jordan continued writing. "I know how you feel, but you can't save the whole world. You've had a long haul today. Why don't you knock off for the rest of the night?"

Joe shook his head. "I haven't even finished rounds yet." Jordan made one more notation and then closed the chart.

"How's Bethie doing?" "All right."

"Well, when you see her, give her my best. And don't be too long. You need some rest." Jordan handed the chart to a nurse behind the desk and walked away.

Joe finished his own paperwork, then took the elevator to the fourth floor. When he noticed the door to Beth's room was open, on impulse, he walked inside.

"Hi," he said wearily, dropping into the chair beside her bed. "Hi, yourself," she returned, carefully pushing herself up in bed.

"I didn't have a chance to thank you for this afternoon. Seeing my new office was just the medicine I needed." When he offered only a wry smile, she realized something was wrong. "Joe, are you all right?" He glanced away for a moment before looking at her again. "Not really. I spent the rest of the afternoon losing patients in the ER."

She watched him with sympathy. "I'm so sorry," she said in a soft voice. "Is it something you want to talk about?"

"No, because I've never found an acceptable answer—" He stopped in midsentence when he noticed her open Bible on the bedside table. "Beth, how much do you honestly believe in the goodness of God?"

Immediately, she recognized a familiar dilemma in the terse remark, a quandary she had encountered often in her work. "You see too much unexplained suffering and death in your profession, and you wonder where God is sometimes. Is that it?"

Joe looked at her in wonder, as though she had interpreted what was in his mind before he had even formulated the allegation. "Yes, exactly."

"It's a valid question, Joe, one that many Christian physicians have struggled with. Was your experience in the ER today no exception?"

Morbid visions he could not erase rose like a storm in his mind. "We sent three teenagers to the morgue tonight, beat to pieces because of gang violence."

"Oh, no . . . "

He brushed aside his disheveled hair and drew a deep breath. "I wasn't two years into my residency when already I'd seen too much," he began, shaking his head. "I was delivering babies no bigger than the palm of my hand, born to drug-addicted mothers who only cared where their next fix was coming from. I'd treated and reported case after case of child abuse, spouse abuse, rape. I'd operated on mangled bodies pulled from cars hit by drunk drivers who simply walked away from the scene. Sometimes, I wondered why I ever chose to become a doctor. But that still didn't stop me from wanting to change every ugly thing I'd ever encountered, except I discovered I could change very little, if anything." Again, he glanced at her Bible. "My mother wanted me to believe in a loving God. But more often than not, reality tells me that He just isn't interested." He looked away, expecting a string of virtuous clichés he had heard a dozen times before, all intended to mollify his dispirited image of God.

"I know exactly how you feel, Joe. It doesn't make sense that God would allow so much suffering."

Surprised, his eyes rose to meet hers. "I never expected a response like that."

She smiled sadly. "Your picture of God is like that of so many people because Satan's prime objective has always been to warp His true character.

"You see pain, suffering, and death as few people ever will. And to you, it appears that God doesn't intervene because He doesn't care. But that's not true, Joe. He does care. And He is a God of love." She reached for her Bible, turned to a well-marked text in Jeremiah, and began to read. "I know the thoughts that I think toward you, says the Lord, thoughts of peace and not of evil." She closed the book. "That doesn't exactly describe an angry and disinterested God."

Joe shook his head. "I'd like to believe that, Beth, I really would, but it just doesn't add up to what I see here every day, or what I grew up with. To me, broken and mutilated bodies don't characterize love in any way, shape or form."

"That's because love demands freedom." "Freedom?"

"Yes, because real love comes with freedom to choose. You see, God lets us choose to love Him or not. If He forced us to love Him, that wouldn't be love at all because love doesn't come with control. But with that, freedom to choose comes risk, the same risk that's capable of creating mutiny. When we choose to go our own way, the result is selfishness. And it's that selfishness that results in what you see day in and day out as injustice and pain."

Joe stared at his hands as he contemplated her no nonsense explanation. No one had ever described to him the character of God in that way. Beth had given him the picture of a loving heavenly Father he had never had a real desire to know before now. "I still hate what I see."

"You always will because you're dedicated to preserving life." Then she smiled at him. "You're a complex, compassionate man, Dr. Travis. And I think you're a credit to your profession." She reached over and placed her Bible in his hands. "Making this a part of your life will only enhance your commitment."

Joe turned the book over and then rose to his feet. "I'll give it a try, at least for your sake."

* * *

Two nights later, Joe left Beth's room after another pleasant visit. Not only did he find her attractive and intelligent, but optimistic despite her uncomfortable circumstances and interrupted plans. She was easy to talk with, and he found himself confiding in her on a more personal level than was customary for him. His spare minutes throughout the day created opportunities (or were they excuses?) to stop in and see her.

Joe dropped into an empty chair behind the nurses' station, ready to begin the detested chore of dictating. Several nurses behind the desk greeted him.

"Good evening, ladies," he returned affably. "I'll be out of your domain as soon as I can."

"We'll let you know when you're in the way, Doctor," one of the nurses quipped. "By the way, Mrs. Matthews is requesting something for pain."

"When was the last time you gave her something?"

"She hasn't been given anything. There was no order for pain medication," the nurse explained.

Joe looked at her in surprise. "I didn't order anything for her?" "No, sir," she said, handing him the chart. He opened it, scanned it, and quickly scribbled an order for the needed medication and gave it back to the nurse. "She hadn't complained until earlier this evening. That's when we noticed the usual order was missing."

He went back to his dictation, disturbed that he had overlooked such a routine detail.

A few minutes later, the nurse returned. She waited until he paused in his dictation. "As long as we have you cornered, could you validate these additional orders you left unsigned yesterday?"

He checked through the added orders. He shook his head in agitation. "Why wasn't this brought to my attention earlier?"

"I'm sorry, Dr. Travis, I left them in your box, but you've been somewhat . . . preoccupied in 412."

Beth's room, he thought with acute embarrassment. Pretending to ignore the disturbing implication, he scribbled his signature on each form.

He returned to his dictation, seemingly engrossed with the work, but his mind was not there. How conspicuous had it been? he wondered. Had he honestly overlooked such routine tasks because of his growing attraction to Beth McCallister? If that was the case, what else had he failed to do, significant or otherwise?

Aware of a burgeoning conviction, he feared he was stretching what was supposed to be a professional relationship into something that should not—and could not—be.

CHAPTER 4

The next morning, Joe Travis walked behind the fourth floor nurses' station following an emergency surgery. Head nurse Jessie Gallagher greeted him. "I was just about to page you. Beth McCallister complained of some abdominal pain earlier this morning. She was also running a slight temp before breakfast of 101.2."

Joe reviewed her latest lab work, temperature, and pulse graphic sheet. "I better take a look at her."

"Hi," Beth greeted languidly when Joe walked into her room. "I hear you aren't feeling too well," he said, pulling the bedside table away. "Where's the problem?"

"I've got some pain right around here," she said, indicating an area of her abdomen.

"Well, let's take a look," he said. He pulled back the bed cover and gingerly began to palpate the tender area. He could see the pained expression increasing on her face, though she said nothing until he removed his stethoscope.

Joe pulled the blanket over Beth once more. "No bowel sounds this morning. I think we need to order a CT scan and another CBC." As soon as he uttered the words, he couldn't help but notice the worried expression on his patient's face. "Before you even think it, you are not a candidate for organ donation," he said with a grin.

"So what's wrong with me? Why would you order additional tests if you didn't think—"

"I didn't say what I was thinking, did I?" The dimples in his cheeks deepened with his smile, and she appeared to relax. "I just want to be sure you don't have something in your abdomen that needs to come out. This can happen after the severity of impact you had in your accident. Remember your spleen had a hematoma in it. It could be infected or leaking."

"So what if something is wrong? What happens then?" "We go back to the OR and take care of it."

Her anxious expression returned. "Surgery . . . ?"

In a soothing voice, he finished explaining the procedure to her. "Most of the time, your spleen can be repaired with fibrin glue and mesh. Sometimes, we have to take it out. If there's something else, like injury to your bowel, it can be repaired. Believe me, if there is something to correct and we left it untreated, you could have some serious problems."

A deep sigh escaped her. "And this is going to keep me in here even longer now, I suppose."

He nodded. "Probably so. But let me do my job and send you out of here in one beautiful piece, just the way you came in." At once, he realized his thoughts had slipped out with his words.

"You're quite the charmer, aren't you? I suppose if you told me it was time to have my head removed, I'd be obliged to say yes."

He grinned again. "Let's get all the results first, and then we'll decide what to do from there." He left the room and walked slowly back to the nurses' station. But an uneasy feeling began to come over him, and he knew exactly where it was coming from.

* * *

Joe flipped on the light to the viewing box behind his desk when the door opened, and Dr. Marsha Cundiff stepped inside. "Joe, you wanted to see me?" The sandy haired general surgeon closed the door behind her.

"Yeah, Marsha, can you take a look at this?"

The two surgeons began to study the x-rays. "Looks like the spleen is leaking from a hilar fracture."

Joe nodded. "That's what I thought. The white count is elevated, too."

Cundiff stepped away from the viewing box and sat down in front of the desk. "It'll have to be repaired, but it looks pretty cut and dry to me."

Joe flipped off the light and swiveled his chair around. "Will you do it?"

"Well, sure, but why don't you do it yourself?"

Joe hesitated. "Well, this doesn't exactly fall under the category of trauma surgery. And you've done a lot of these before."

"So have you," she maintained, but the grievous look on Joe's face persuaded her to ask no more questions regarding her colleague's reasons for not doing the surgery himself. "If you want me to do it, I will. Who's the patient?"

"Beth McCallister. She's in 412." He swallowed the rest of his reasons. "I'll let her know what's going on."

"That's fine, Joe. I'll put her on the schedule and call the OR crew in." Cundiff rose from the chair and left the room.

Joe leaned wearily against the back of the chair. Had he missed something, something that was going to send Beth back to the OR? Had his attraction to the young woman caused him to neglect what should have been obvious? Or was he being too hard on himself?

He would accept no excuses. Explaining the procedure to Beth had been the easy part. Explaining why he wouldn't be doing the surgery would be much more difficult.

* * *

"But I don't understand! Don't I have a choice? If I have to have more surgery, I want you to do it." Beth's usually cheerful expression had clouded with dismay and anxiety.

"Listen to me, young lady, you want the best, and Marsha Cundiff is an excellent surgeon. She's done hundreds of these procedures—"

"And you haven't? Why are you backing out on me? You're my doctor, not this . . . this Dr. Cundiff."

How could he make her understand without completely exposing the truth he could not divulge? She was so unreservedly charming, even in illness, which for Joe simply added to her attractiveness. Nevertheless, the conflict remained between what he felt for her and what his professional obligation demanded.

Joe pulled a chair beside the bed and sat down. "I am still your doctor, and I'm asking you to take my advice. Dr. Cundiff is the best surgeon for this job. Now are there going to be any more arguments?"

Disappointment overshadowed the anxious expression on her face. "But I know you. I trust you. Surely you don't underestimate the importance of trust." She suddenly felt confused. "Joe," she said at last, "are you refusing to operate on me . . . for personal reasons?"

Joe could not take his eyes away from her. He laughed softly, but the gesture was devoid of humor. "Well, maybe Dr. Jordan summed it up best when he said, 'Practice medicine with your head, not your heart.'"

A hint of a smile touched her lips. Maybe she was beginning to understand. "I appreciate his concept of objectivity, but what do you say? Does his philosophy extend to all your patients as well?"

Joe Travis had always been intensely conscientious of professionalism where his patients were concerned, and he suspected Beth knew beyond the shadow of a doubt it was indeed his own personal feelings that were creating the conflict. But his conscience compelled him to remain resolute.

"Beth, when a physician allows himself to get too close to his patients, he runs the risk of creating . . . certain problems, such as emotional dependency, loss of objectivity, sometimes even error in diagnosis. It's not always easy to divide yourself. But you have to do it." He paused for a moment. "For your own sake, I want you to trust me and believe me when I say that Dr. Cundiff is the best surgeon for this procedure."

There was no disguising her disappointment. She looked away, as though surrendering to an inevitable moment. "All right. If that's what you want."

"Beth, you don't understand—"

"Yes, I'm afraid I do understand." When she slipped her hand over his, he felt a rush of pleasure from her simple touch. "Let's just leave it at this. I appreciate everything you've done for me, but I especially appreciate making a new friend."

He squeezed her hand as he rose from the chair, taking her sad smile with him as he left the room.

* * *

A full moon had risen by early evening. Joe Travis leaned against the back of the swivel chair, staring down at the lights of the city through the large window behind his desk. Tonight, he could think of nothing but Beth McCallister as he had thought of little else since leaving her room.

He had found it impossible not be attracted to her. She was not only beautiful and charismatic but had caused him to rethink his misgivings regarding his perception of God. If He truly was a God of love, then what she had said about freedom and the risks it carried made perfect sense. Was there not some form of selfishness at the very core of most of the miseries he encountered?

But he had let his guard down as far as his feelings for Beth were concerned. He sensed a disturbing gap between what he expected of himself professionally and what he felt as a man personally. He knew there was no way he could open her up on the operating table, even for the simplest procedure. Neither could he ignore his most underlying fear: what if the conflict between his private and professional feelings in some way impeded his skills? There were valid reasons why doctors were trained to deal with patients from a detached perspective. And he would not put her at risk because of his vulnerable frame of mind.

Practice medicine with your head, not your heart. The concept had been indoctrinated into him throughout his training and beyond although he had refused to fully embrace the theory. But through the years, some transition had come. Yet at the time he had begun his residency, he had determined not to adhere to the businesslike system of treating patients.

* * *

"I'm sorry, Mrs. Lorna, but this surgery is for your benefit. If you choose not to have it, then it remains your problem, not mine." Dr. Doug Beecher slapped the surgical consent form on the bedside table. Then he walked toward the door, ignoring the aged, arthritic hand that tried to grab his starched white monogrammed lab coat. The haughty surgeon beckoned Joe to follow him. "Dr. Travis, I can't waste the rest of my time in here. We have other patients to see."

Joe looked down at the old woman in time to see tears welling in her pale gray eyes after Beecher left the room. Ignoring his superior's direct order, he pulled a chair beside the bed and sat down. Her mouth moved, but no words would come, the results of a stroke several months earlier. He took a tissue from the box on the table and wiped the tears away from her wrinkled cheeks. "You know, the surgery Dr. Beecher is recommending is quite common. And the results have been very good."

Again, her mouth moved in contortions as she struggled to get the words out. He pitied her frustration. With infinite patience, Joe waited for her to speak. "I . . . I'm afraid. I . . . don't like . . . that doctor."

Joe smiled at her. "His surgical ability is much better than his bedside manner."

There was a spark of life in the tired old eyes. Her twisted mouth fashioned into a grin as she gently poked him with a bent finger. "You . . . do it."

He laughed. "You don't want me! I'm not nearly as qualified as Dr. Beecher is. I might be able to assist. Would that be all right?" He squeezed her hand. "You'll be even more irresistible after the surgery, you know."

She produced a hoarse laugh. "All . . . all right, young . . . man. But only . . . only if . . . you're there."

He turned her frail hand palm side up, giving it a gentle slap. "Deal." She gestured toward the consent form on the table. Joe attached it to a clipboard and then slipped his arm beneath the pillow to raise her. With slow deliberation, she scrawled her signature with her good hand. "Now you get some rest," he told her, settling her against the pillow oncemore.

Calmness had come over the old woman by the time he left the room. It wasn't all that often that Joe felt at peace about his work. But today he knew he had accomplished something more important than getting a signature for surgical consent. Unfortunately, his sense of contentment was not to last long.

Later in the afternoon, he was summoned to Benjamin Jordan's office. This was nothing new, but he wondered why the urgency. He opened the door to his mentor's office, finding him seated stiffly behind his desk. A quick glance inside the room and he knew why. Doug Beechersat on the couch, his rigid expression more inflexible than usual. As Joe closed the door, Jordan nodded for him to sit down.

"Joe, Dr. Beecher has registered a complaint against you, but I wanted to hear both sides before recommending any action." Joe saw Beecher glaring indignantly at him. "Dr. Beecher tells me you're spending entirely too much time with any given patient. And this morning, I understand you remained behind to talk to an incoherent elderly womanwhen you were supposed to be on rounds with him. Is this correct?"

"Yes, I did stay to talk to her. She was frightened and—"

"And senile!" Beecher interjected. "She doesn't know what time of day it is. It was a waste of valuable time to sit and persuade her! And ifmemory serves me correctly, Doctor, when I was a resident, time was a commodity I didn't have much of."

Joe said nothing in the face of Beecher's abusive remarks. "Is this true?" Jordan asked.

"I didn't find the patient to be senile at all. In fact, she appeared quite lucid."

"And did she agree to the surgery?""Yes, she did."

"That has nothing to do with the fact that Dr. Travis is not utilizing his time to the maximum," Beecher claimed, incensed, as he bangedhis fist into his open hand. "He was assigned to me to learn, not to play nanny to an incompetent old woman! That sentimentality can be left tothe nurses."

A righteous indignation rose swiftly inside Joe. "It's my understanding that as physicians we're to treat the whole patient, not just the disease." "As physicians, young man, we also do not lower ourselves to the patient's level."

Angrily, Joe opened his mouth in rebuttal. However, a swift glance from Jordan's direction stemmed another opposing remark. As unpopular as Beecher was among the residents, he was still a superior. He swallowed his anger and said nothing more.

Jordan leaned against his swivel chair, folding his hands tent style across his expansive chest. "So you would recommend that Dr. Travis employ his time and judgment for the procedural aspects of medicine as opposed to the personal side. Remain more objective, more impartial."

"Yes, to say the very least. And the next time he's assigned to my service, I expect him to abide by my rules." Beecher rose to his feet, glancing once more at Joe. "He can practice emotionalism on his own time, not mine." The door closed with a thud as Beecher left the room.

Jordan looked hard at the young resident in front of him. "Beecher could make a lot of trouble for you, Joe, if you don't make an effort to stay on his good side."

Joe's restrained anger now grew explosive. "Why should I care about staying on 'his good side'? Beecher treats his patients with all the compassion of a snake!"

"How he treats his patients is Paul Martin's problem, not yours. You were assigned to him to learn surgery and that's all."

Joe sighed, openly venting his exasperation. "I went into medicine because I wanted to improve the quality of my patients' lives, not just cut them apart."

Jordan leaned across the desk. "I don't mean to dampen your enthusiasm, Joe. It's admirable and, at this stage of your training, very idealistic. But in day-to-day reality, you cannot emotionally attach yourself to every patient you treat! You'll never make it as a doctor." Jordan's penetrating eyes seemed to bore holes in the young man when he added, "You won't survive."

"I've heard this before."

"And you'll hear it again and again until you finally come to the conclusion that you must separate yourself from your patients! There's too much risk, to yourself as well as to the patient, if you get too close." The final words emerged in a slow, measured tone. "You're my responsibility, Joe. And I don't want to hear about this again. Do I make myself clear?" Joe got to his feet, the contentious expression still visible on his face. "Quite clear." But as he left the room, he carried his resentment with him.

* * *

Joe glanced at his watch. It was later than he thought. He would get nothing more done tonight. He slipped into his coat and pulled the door shut behind him, wishing home wasn't as equally lonely as the office.

* * *

Early the next morning, Joe walked down the dimly lit corridor, resisting the urge to call the nurses' station for information regarding Beth, when he heard his name paged stat. He rushed down the corridor to a telemetry room. A nurse leaned out the doorway. "Dr. Travis, it's Mattie!" she called in an urgent voice. "I think she's going into respiratory failure."

Joe raced into the old woman's room. He found her gasping for breath. In a single motion, he pulled the oxygen mask from above the bed and placed it over Mattie's mouth and nose, directing the nurse to adjust the oxygen to varying liters.

"We may have to intubate her," Joe said. "Let's get a blood gas on her, an EKG, and call x-ray for a portable chest. And I want a crash cart in here just in case." The nurse hurried from the room.

After placing a pulse oximeter in her earlobe, he began to observe the monitor strips. Moments later, the rattling wheels carrying the emergency equipment clattered through the door. The respiratory therapist began to draw the ordered blood.

Joe realized Mattie's breathing was gradually becoming easier. Her oxygen status had risen to near normal. Nevertheless, he removed the mask in preparation to slip the breathing tube into place, but he hesitated when Mattie rolled her head toward him.

"I don't understand why you keeps tryin' to save me unless my dyin' would make you look bad." The words came with breathy deliberation as her eyes slowly opened.

Joe sighed with relief as he dropped the tube onto the tray. "You're right, Mattie. Your dying would make me look terrible." He directed his attention to the nurse who had returned to the room.

"Keep the oxygen going for a while, but I want a report on that blood gas as soon as possible. Start her on a heparin protocol for a pulmonary embolus right away, and send her to x-ray for a chest CT."

He leaned over the bed, his hands dangling over the side rails. "How about hanging in there at least for the sake of my reputation?" She managed a hoarse laugh. "You is a real smart aleck, Dr. Joe.

If you was my son, I'd be obliged to smack you into shape fast." "What's the big idea of scaring me to death so early in the morning?"

"Now you knows I wouldn't do that on purpose, least not to you." Carefully, she folded her hands over her still mildly laboring chest. "It's awful to get old."

"It's worse not to."

She rolled her eyes in his direction. "Maybe," she said quietly. "But you wanna know somethin'?"

"What's that?"

"Dyin' can't be no worse then livin' a life that's no life at all."

He pulled a chair to the side of the bed, lowered the rail, and sat down. He studied her gentle, pensive expression. "Is that the way you see it, Mattie?"

"Sometimes." He continued to watch her carefully as she struggled with some effort for each breath. "I've lived a good life, a full life, and most of it's behind me now. But you is a young man, Dr. Joe. I wouldn't expect you to understand that like I does. For you, dyin' is losin'. But it just ain't that way for everybody."

He flexed his hands. "Seems to me giving up is the same as losing. You aren't telling me that, are you?"

She shook her head. "You has been a fine doc to me. But I leaves that up to the good Lord."

"But keeping you alive is what my job is all about. Besides, I'm not ready to let you go."

Again she laughed, a ragged and painful laugh. "Honey, when He sees it's my time to go, not you, not me, not nobody is gonna be able to do nothin'. And that's okay. But you just remember one thing." Mattie folded her brown, wrinkled hands over his. "The good Lord has seen fit to give you a set of fine, skillful hands. You give these hands back to the One who gave 'em to you in the first place, and you'll do all right."

"You don't have to worry about me, Mattie."

"Well, somebody should!" she declared weakly. "Here you is a fine, handsome young man. and you spends all your time hangin' around old ladies like me! Why, you hasn't even got one of your own."

He grinned. "Is that your recommendation? I need an 'old lady' of my own?"

She glared mischievously at him. "Well, it wouldn't hurt none." He leaned over and kissed her forehead. "You get a little rest so

I can stop by to argue with you later. In the meantime, I'd like you to wear this a little longer." His eyes twinkled as he returned the oxygen mask to her face before she could protest. "And don't worry. One size fits all."

He emerged from Mattie Walker's room and stopped beside the nurses' station. "Notify me right away if there's any change," he told one of the nurses. "And page me when you have the report of the CT scan and blood work."

He wondered if Beth was awake by now. He walked toward the surgery floor again, passing through the ward doors just as Dr. Marsha Cundiff emerged from one of the suites.

"Joe, your patient's doing just fine. The spleen had to come out, but there were no other injuries. She should be able to be released in a few days at most."

Joe felt a sense of relief wash over him. He extended his hand to his colleague. "Thanks, Marsha. I knew she was in good hands."

"So you want me to turn her back over to you now?"

"No," he returned in a somber voice. "If you don't foresee any complications, I'll just leave her on your service until she's ready to be discharged."

"Well, if that's what you want, Joe. But *this* one seems to be more than skin deep."

Joe could feel the color rising in his cheeks in view of his colleague's insightful remark. With an impish grin, she waved him on and walked through the door to the surgeons' lounge.

Joe stood alone in the corridor, wrapped in a jumble of feelings he did not know how to separate. Then he walked slowly out of the OR.

When he got to his office, he pushed open the door and stepped inside. The waiting room was empty as he passed through into his private office. Immediately, his eyes trailed to Beth's Bible that lay on the corner of his desk. He opened it up to the last place he had stopped reading, surprised he had actually read so much in only a few days.

With the book in his hand, he turned around and walked toward the door. It would be easier if it were back in Beth's room before she woke up.

* * *

Three days after her second surgery, Callie drove Beth home from the hospital following her discharge. Together, they walked into Beth's disheveled apartment and glanced around.

"Are you sure you've got enough stuff?"

"I know, it's a mess," Beth sighed. "I spent less than one day in here before I wound up in the hospital. I thought moving would force me to get rid of a lot of stuff, but it didn't."

"I can see that." With no need for invitation, Callie plunged into an attempt to make the place more presentable. A few minutes later, Beth walked out of the kitchen with two cups of hot tea.

Callie watched Beth grimace as she bent over to set the cups down. "So how's the incision?"

"Which one? They're both painful." Gingerly, Beth sat down in the chair, handed Callie her cup, and then picked up the other for herself.

"Didn't Joe leave you a prescription for postoperative pain? He rarely releases any of his patients without giving them something."

"Joe didn't release me," Beth returned in a mildly indignant tone. "I didn't even see him after the surgery. All I found was my Bible on the bedside table."

This was news to Callie. "Oh, I see," she said quietly. "And you didn't want to stay with Dr. Cundiff?"

"I wasn't given a choice." She still felt an acute disappointment that Joe Travis had mysteriously become so distant with her. That had not been the image she had gleaned from Callie or from her own initial experience with him. Something had sent him packing and in a hurry. Now her frustration was turning into an angry quest to know why.

"I know you think a great deal of him, Cal, but I just don't understand why he was so engaging and friendly at first and then just dropped me in another doctor's lap. It's like . . . something scared him, and he ran." She set her cup down. "I don't know what I did, but I think the least he could have done was tell me he didn't want to treat me anymore."

Callie's even-tempered expression changed quickly. "Joe wouldn't do that," she returned defensively. "He would never just walk out on one of his patients."

"Well, that's exactly what it appears he did to me." Though Callie said nothing more, Beth knew she had trampled on hallowed ground where Dr. Joe Travis was concerned.

An awkward silence came between the two young women. But as abruptly as the silence came, so did Beth's memory of the day Joe had taken her to see her new office. He had been so attentive, so caring, that she could not resist being drawn to him. Now in shame she glanced at Callie. Her friend's dismayed expression matched her own. "Maybe I just envy you," Beth said at last. "I wish he'd given me the chance to know him like you do."

Gradually, a smile covered Callie's face, and in a matter of moments, the gesture was returned. Very few disagreements had ever come between the two friends, and those that had, had not lasted long.

But now, a new and troubling thought occurred to Callie. There was something unexplainable about Joe's peculiar dismissal of Beth as his patient, an act completely out of character for him. Had yet another obstacle emerged to prevent her from telling him how she felt, one far more threatening than she had thus far imagined?

Even if Beth wasn't aware of it, had Joe's commitment to her friend gone beyond a professional relationship?

CHAPTER 5

Joe stood beside Mattie Walker's bed two weeks later, his fingers idly tapping the release form lying on the bedside table. "You know I'm not very happy about this, don't you?"

"Yes," she said doggedly. "But you has done everything you can think of for me, and now it's time to let me do some of my own thinkin'." She tried to glare at him, but the glimmer in her eyes gave away the façade. "I has been gone from my family too long. They's things I need to do, things I need to take care of myself."

"Mattie—"

"Dr. Joe, my mind's made up. You knows how stubborn I canbe, *almost* as stubborn as you."

"No, Mattie, he still holds the world's record for that." The voice came from Callie Jordan who had suddenly materialized in the doorway of the room.

Mattie began to laugh. "Now this girl knows what's she's talkin' about! Callie, you tell him. I need to get *out* of here."

Callie glanced at Joe and then looked at Mattie again. "What's the hurry, Mattie? Is anything wrong at home?"

The old woman settled herself against the pillows once more. "No," she returned in a compliant voice. "I just wants to get my affairs in order. It's important to me. I just can't see why the good doc here don't understand that."

Joe sighed wearily. "All right, you win. But the *minute* you start to have any problem—"

"I know what to do." She looked at Callie. "Now get him out of here. They's no proper way for me to get dressed while he's standin' there gawkin' at me."

Joe feigned a hurt look, then squeezed her hand. "I hope I don't see you any time too soon. But is it okay if I miss you?"

"You can do that. Now go on."

Joe waited outside the door while Callie finished attending to Mattie. A few minutes later, she came out of the room.

"She certainly has a mind of her own," Joe commented gruffly as they walked down the corridor together.

"That she does," Callie agreed. "Maybe that's why you have so much respect for her."

Joe grinned. "Maybe that's why." They continued down the corridor together. "So tell me," he asked, trying to sound casual, "how's Beth doing since her surgery?"

"She's doing remarkably well. In fact, she started workday before yesterday. Haven't you seen her?"

"Well, no," Joe fumbled for words, "not since I turned her over to Marsha Cundiff."

"And she wasn't too happy about that," Callie murmured quietly, instantly regretting the unintentional slip.

Joe grimaced. "Did she . . . tell you that?"

She hesitated as an uncomfortable feeling arose inside her. "Why don't you find out for yourself?"

Joe began mumbling more excuses as they continued down the corridor, unaware that Callie's pace had begun to slow. When he realized she wasn't beside him, he turned back in time to see her slump languidly against the wall.

Immediately, he was beside her. "Take it easy, Cal," he said, putting his arm around her drooping body. "Are you having any chest pain?"

She looked up at him, her eyes filled with anxiety. "A little." She struggled to catch her breath, her hand tight against her laboring chest. The words came in breathless spurts. "I'll . . . I'll be all right. I guess I'm just . . . more tired than I thought."

Joe didn't like the sudden pallid color of her skin or the beads of sweat that had broken out on her forehead. He watched her closely, ready to call for a gurney and a portable oxygen tank at any moment. "I want to take you over to see Jeff Marcus."

"No, Joe . . . please. I'll be . . . all right. Just let me . . . let me sit down a few minutes. I'll be okay," she pleaded.

Against his better judgment, he agreed, supporting her body against his own as he attempted to guide her down the corridor, but the endeavor was useless. Moments later, she collapsed in his arms, and he lowered her to the floor.

"I want an oxygen tank and a gurney, stat!" he called over his shoulder in a loud voice, outraged with himself for not heeding the obvious warning signs.

At once, an orderly and two nurses pushed a gurney through a small number of gathering onlookers. Joe scooped Callie's limp body into his arms and hoisted her onto the stretcher while one of the nurses strapped an oxygen mask over her ashen face. Immediately, they propelled the gurney into a waiting elevator.

As the doors opened on the ground floor, Joe began issuing orders to the oncoming emergency room team.

"Call Dr. Marcus!" he shouted to a nurse as he raced beside the gurney toward the cardiac room. "And Dr. Jordan too. And make sure there's an available bed in CCU just in case."

Once inside the cardiac room, Joe lifted Callie from the stretcher onto the exam table. He grabbed a stethoscope and listened to her heart. The pulsing sounded weak and erratic. He increased the flow of oxygen and then ordered an intravenous line and labs while a nurse began hooking her up to the cardiac monitor.

A few minutes later, the door opened, and Dr. Jeff Marcus, chief of cardiology, hurried into the room. Joe recounted to him the events of the episode as they watched the tracings of her low blood pressure and slow heart rate scrolling across the multicolored screen.

The door opened again, and a nervous Benjamin Jordan approached the table. *"Callie,"* he whispered anxiously, taking his daughter's small hands into his as he leaned over to look at her. He glanced up at the two attending doctors. "How bad was it this time?"

Marcus took over while Joe drew Jordan away from the exam table, explaining what had occurred in the corridor. With restless anticipation, Jordan kept glancing back at the table where the cardiologist and team of technicians and nurses worked over Callie. "Jeff's with her now," Joe offered reassuringly. "She's in good hands."

Moments later, Jeff Marcus turned away from the table and approached Jordan. "Her condition's not good, Ben, but it's also not as bad as I thought it would be. She must be developing acute valvular failure. Still, I'd feel better after seeing her catheterization results. We might not be so lucky next time," he added quietly. "I want to admit her right away." He handed Jordan the results of the lab tests. Jordan studied the numbers and nodded. "Yes, by all means, admit her now." He handed the results to Joe and then stood beside the table, tenderly stroking the cheek of his only child.

✳ ✳ ✳

Joe waited until Callie had been taken to the cardiac care unit before leaving the emergency room. He had felt a greater measure of anxiety for Callie's condition then he had been willing to express in front of Ben Jordan.

It was obvious the progression of Callie's illness had deteriorated over the past few months. Joe realized she was going into heart failure quite rapidly. The cardiac episodes were increasing in intensity as well as frequency, and everyone left him more ill at ease than the time before.

When Joe reached his office, he called the CCU to check on Callie's condition. Her blood pressure had stabilized, and she was no longer in pain. Her heart catheterization had been scheduled for the following morning. He felt a measure of relief knowing she was in the care of an expert cardiac care team.

Joe sat down behind his desk and contemplated the pile of paperwork his secretary had prepared. But his thoughts, far from the work in front of him, now returned to Beth McCallister. She had not been off his mind for one day since he had signed her over to Marsha Cundiff.

He knew he had mishandled the situation. There was no way he could justify his action without putting into plain words that it was his own professional objectivity that had prevented him from treating her any further because he knew he was falling in love with her.

Absorbed in his thoughts, he looked up, startled to discover Dr.

Paul Martin, chief of staff, standing in front of his desk. "Didn't your mother ever teach you to knock?"

"I beg your pardon, but I *did* knock," Paul said. "Where were you?"

Joe glanced down at the paperwork beneath his hands and shook his head. "Lost."

"Patient going bad on you?" Paul asked as he sat down on the edge of the desk.

"No . . . I went bad on a patient." "What are you talking about?"

Joe knew if he could confide in anyone, it would be Paul Martin. With doleful eyes, he looked up at the older man. "I think I'm in love with one of my patients. A former patient, but a patient, nonetheless." He braced himself for some reaction, but when there was none, he continued. "I knew I was spending more time with her than was necessary. What I didn't realize was that . . . my work was beginning to suffer because of it." Again, he wrestled with the notion that he had inadvertently brought about her need for a second surgery. He drew a deep breath. "I guess I realized too late what was happening."

Striving to conceal a smile, Paul studied the humbled young man in front of him. "So while you were performing surgery, she was stealing your heart."

Paul's candid remark transformed Joe's self-admonishment into an attempt at convincing explanation. "Listen, I knew what I was doing, not that I intended for it to happen because I know all about ethical obligation." His self-defense came to a halt when Paul began to laugh. "I fail to see what's so amusing."

"Oh, I'm sorry, Joe. I don't think it's amusing. I think it's great." "What?"

"I think it's great," Paul repeated. "Just look at yourself. You have no family to go home to, no wife, no children because you married your career!" He shook his head in wonder. "You're a fine doctor, Joe, and an excellent surgeon, but it's high time you found a life outside this hospital." His eyes gleamed with mischief as he rose from the desk. "Do I . . . happen to know the lady?"

Joe raised his eyes. It was all out in the open now. What did he have to lose? "It's Beth McCallister."

Paul grinned. "Then go to her. Find out for yourself if what you have now is better than what you've been missing."

"I can't."

"Why not?"

Joe drew a deep breath. "I'm afraid the lady is rather angry with me and has every right to be."

Paul listened to the brief, self-denouncing details. "Well then, I'd say at best you owe her an apology."

"Yes, I do." Joe sighed heavily, leaning across the desk. "And I'll give her one, just as soon as I find enough courage."

* * *

It was a few minutes past eight the following morning when Joe walked into the cardiac care unit. "Callie slept well last night, Dr. Travis. No complaints," the dayshift nurse informed him.

"I'm glad to hear that." Joe scanned the latest lab results, peered at the telemetry screen, and then glanced at his watch. He wanted to see Callie before she had to go to the catheterization lab.

As he made his way down the corridor, he noticed another early morning visitor emerging from Callie's room. His steps came to a halt when he suddenly realized Beth McCallister was walking straight toward him, unaware that he was directly in her path. At length she looked up and, somewhat startled, came to a stop in front of him.

"Well . . . Dr. Travis," she offered in a reserved tone. She glanced back toward Callie's room. She had no intention of letting her friend overhear anything unfavorable regarding the hallowed name of Dr. Joe Travis.

"Hello, Beth," he said, nodding hesitantly. "I must say you've made a remarkable recovery. You look wonderful. How have you been?"

"I've been doing very well, thank you. Dr. Cundiff has been taking good care of me." She glanced at her watch while moving past him. "And now if you'll excuse me."

"Beth, please," he interjected quickly. She stopped and looked at him squarely in the face. He could feel the color rising in his cheeks. "I admit I deserved that. What you deserve is an apology for my not giving you a complete explanation for why I couldn't take you back as my patient."

"Well, I appreciate your owning up to that much, but frankly, I don't feel I need another explanation." Once more, she started to walk past him when he caught her by the arm. When she offered no resistance, he guided her into an empty room.

She stood facing away from him. Nevertheless, he was determined to continue. "No, you don't need another explanation," he agreed. "What you need are the plainspoken facts."

Her interest peaked at his admission, and she turned to look at him.

"Beth, the practice of medicine is a peculiar thing," he began.

"It connects people in the strangest ways, but in spite of that connection, it's important for doctors to remain impartial, to keep their feelings separate from their work. In your case, I found I couldn't do that."

The expression on her face began to soften. "You couldn't?" "No, I couldn't. I couldn't separate my professional obligation from my . . . personal feelings. As your doctor, it was my responsibility to keep our relationship on a professional level. But as a man." He paused, pretending to study his hands before gaining enough courage to look at her again. "I found I couldn't do both. You see, it's not an ethical practice of medicine to allow one's self to get into such a . . . predicament."

Her eyes grew hopeful. "Predicament?"

He could no longer hide his grin. "It is highly frowned upon," he said as though quoting from a medical textbook, "for the surgeon to fall in love with his patient."

"Joe . . . "

Without another word, he drew her toward him, put his hands around her face and kissed her. "Now tell me, Ms. McCallister, do you think it's too late to put this . . . predicament . . . back on a strictly professional level?"

She grinned. "Much too late."

CHAPTER 6

A week later, Callie sat on the veranda outside the hospital cafeteria, having returned to a restricted work schedule only the day before. The weather was cooperating beautifully on this late spring day, too beautifully to stay inside. However, her luncheon engagement had not been as accommodating as the weather. She had been waiting almost an hour for Joe.

The sun had slipped a little more toward the west when he finally slid his lunch tray across the table. He pulled up a chair and then glanced down at her empty plate with some disdain. "I thought you were staying later to have lunch with me."

"I thought that too, an hour ago."

He glanced hastily at his watch. "Cal, I'm sorry. I didn't realize it was so late. I got held up in recovery."

"I can't believe it."

He grinned in spite of her sarcasm while squeezing a slice of lemon into his iced tea. "Cal, I've got something to tell you."

"Something good?" "I think so."

"I'm sorry I'm late!" Beth's high heels clattered to a halt on the white cement floor. She dropped into a chair beside Joe, then leaned back, and looked at Callie. "Say, you look familiar, but—"

"You can't place the name," Callie finished in a droll voice. They giggled like schoolgirls, remembering an old maxim from childhood.

"Somehow, I thought your moving back here meant we might *see* each other every once in a while. I didn't know you'd just be another name on a door."

The wind brushed at Beth's chestnut colored hair. "Well, for one thing, your father never mentioned the endless hours to this job, and most of the time, you're in surgery all morning with the good doctor here, then you're gone! And by the way, do you feel as good as you look?"

"Yes, much better. Dr. Marcus has adjusted my medication, and Joe has adjusted my schedule. So how did you happen to find us?"

"Oh, *I* found her starving on the fourth floor and felt sorry for her," Joe cut in. "Cal, I thought I knew everything there was to know about you, and here I find you've failed to tell me about your childhood friends." Though his words were directed to Callie, his attention was riveted on Beth. Callie watched with mild surprise as he squeezed Beth's hand. Whatever the dilemma had been after Beth was discharged from the hospital, it certainly appeared to be resolved now.

"I've told you about Beth before." The inflection in her voice waned as the same uneasy feeling began to seize her.

Again, Callie watched Joe squeeze her friend's hand with more than obvious pleasure, still never taking his eyes away from her. "Well, you didn't tell me how fantastic she was and is."

"All right, enough!" Beth laughed, pulling her hand away. "Let's eat."

At that moment, Paul Martin appeared beside the table. "Joe, I'm sorry to track you down at lunchtime, but it's Mattie Walker. They just brought her into emergency. Looks like she's hemorrhaging again."

"Oh, Joe," Beth began anxiously, aware of his affection for the old woman.

Joe pushed his chair away from the table and began to run, with Callie trailing behind him.

* * *

Two hours later, the doors to the emergency room burst open as Joe Travis made a hurried exit through them. In frustrated haste, he made his way down the corridor, longing to leave the grim scene behind him as he slammed through the door into the unoccupied doctors' lounge.

Sinking onto the couch, his head slid miserably into his hands. Failure was something he had never come to terms with, somethinghe had never been able to accept. The trust he formed with his patients meant everything, and for him, failing was a miscarriage of that sacred obligation. Yet he could not help but wonder if the science of medicine had increased the quality of Mattie's life or, in reality, had he only allowed it to add quantity to her already numbered days?

Lost in self-condemnation, he was unaware of quiet footsteps taken toward him until he felt a hand gently touch his own. He lifted his head to see Callie easing down beside him, her face a mirror of his own miserable thoughts. His head slipped into his hands again. "Don't say it," he muttered angrily. "I don't want to hear it."

"*Don't say* that you gave Mattie months of life that she never would have had, had it not been for you? *Don't say* that you made her life tolerable because she wasn't in as much pain as before? *Don't say* that you understood her situation enough to allow her the dignity to prepare for her own death? She knew what the odds were every time you took her into surgery. No one likes the idea of losing a patient, least of all you." Her voice trembled with emotion as she added, "But at least for you, it's something personal, not something you distance yourself from."

Joe raised his head once more and saw the sympathetic tears that glistened in Callie's eyes. Until this moment, he had desired no words, no exoneration for his failed endeavor to preserve Mattie's life any longer. Yet because of Callie, he began to feel some of the burden beginning to lift. Only she could break barriers he was secretly tempted to erect to escape the grief that was an endemic component of his profession.

He reached for her hand and squeezed it. "How is it you always know how I *feel*, no matter what I *say*?"

"Because there's no one harder to forgive than yourself. And I know you've never been one to forgive yourself, even when you aren't to blame."

He rose to his feet and looked at her one more time. "Sometimes, all I can see is what I can't change. *You* see so much more." He left the room, his courage strengthened to face the grieving family.

Callie stared at Joe's empty place on the couch. She knew there was but one way she would ever see Joe Travis, the only man she would ever love.

* * *

Mattie Walker's funeral was a quiet affair. The family exchanged consolation with Joe and Callie and extended their gratitude to them after the service.

It was almost dark by the time they returned to the hospital. Joe dropped Callie off beside her car in the parking lot and then walked the rest of the way to his office.

After returning some phone calls and checking the next day's schedule, he stood in front of the mirror in his waiting room, retying his tie. All at once, he sensed he was not alone. He turned around and glanced toward the open door. "Callie, I thought you'd be home by now."

There was some reticence before she spoke. "I just . . . wanted to make sure you were okay."

"I'm all right," he said in a quiet voice. "I appreciated you going to Mattie's funeral with me. It wasn't something I was relishing doing alone."

"Mattie meant a lot to me too," she empathized with him. "But I just thought it might do you good to think about something else." "Oh, yeah?" he asked with a hint of intrigue in his voice as he slipped into his suit coat. "What did you have in mind?"

Once more, she struggled for courage to tell him of her feelings, but her shyness and inexperience in the art of romance precluded words she longed to express. Maybe in the cheerful atmosphere of a familiar restaurant, she might feel more confident. Nervously, she cleared her throat. "Well, I thought maybe you'd like to escape to some place a little less sterile . . . and have dinner with me."

He reached for her hands. "Your offer is generous, Cal, but unfortunately too late."

"Too late?"

"Well, as it happens, I have an invitation from Beth to see what kind of cook she is." He grinned mischievously. "Should you prepare me for something I might not know?"

The same unsettled feeling came over her once again. "You're . . . going to Beth's?" she asked, trying to disguise the dismay in her voice.

Still grasping her hands, Joe gently pulled her down beside him on the couch, but one look into his eyes, radiant despite his weariness of soul and body, told her there was no need for explanation. "Cal, I've never known anyone like her! That was what I wanted to tell you at lunch the other day. She makes me feel so alive! And after what we go through here, day after day, it's so rejuvenating just to be with her. Can you understand what I'm saying?" There was a lilt in his voice she hadn't heard for a long time.

Her fixed smile camouflaged the despair that railed inside her. She had to ask, though she didn't want to know. "Do you love her?" "Yes, Cal, I do." His voice was soft and, for Callie, painfully sincere.

Irrepressible tears welled in eyes he couldn't see in the light that shown behind her. Words of love she had dreamed of hearing would never be spoken to her.

She rose to her feet, knowing she had to escape his presence before her tears demanded an explanation she was too ashamed to give. "Then you better not keep her waiting."

"You're right." He rose easily beside her. "At least let me take you back to your car," he offered. "You must be exhausted. It's been a long day for you."

She shook her head. "No, I'll . . . I'll be all right. You go on. I'll lock up."

He placed a fond kiss on her cheek. "You really do look beautiful. It's a shame you can't dress like that for surgery." With a playful wink, he was gone.

She listened to the echo of his footsteps in the empty corridor, the doors to the elevator as they opened and closed. And then all was silent.

She glanced around his familiar office. Leather-bound books and medical journals lined mahogany shelves on one wall, pictures and diplomas hung in neat rows along another, and his electric razor sat on top of the windowsill behind his desk. Here was the only place that Joe Travis would ever belong to her, a bleak world where elements of pain and suffering had actually brought her joy and completeness. Slowly, her hands rose to cover her face as hot, stinging tears began to flow down her cheeks. Joe's happiness would never depend on her. And now that very happiness she drew from him, though in secret, had turned to hopelessness.

* * *

The remainder of the carefully prepared dinner lay cold and forgotten on the table. The candles had dwindled to almost nothing as Beth and Joe curled on the couch together, listening to quiet music in the background.

Joe brushed lose strands of hair away from her forehead. "The fettuccini was wonderful."

She leaned away from him with a shocked expression. "Fettuccini? Is *that* what you thought it was?"

"Long, white, flat noodles in Alfredo sauce? Yes, that's what I thought it was."

She shook her head in amazement. "And I thought it was macaroni surprise."

He laughed softly as she rested her head against his shoulder again. "I shudder to think what kind of meals I might come home to with you in the kitchen."

She looked up at him once more, but her genial expression had sobered. "I'd take good care of you," she whispered. Once more, she laid her head against his chest.

Strands of her sweet-smelling hair fell lightly through his fingers while an intense longing for her burned within him. He wished he never had to consider dividing his life between personal desire and professional obligation, but devote all of it to her. Yet he knew that was an absurdity.

At the time he had entered medicine, the altruistic endeavor was the single, most important factor in his life, so how could he ask her to share a life that would demand a part of him from which he could never be free? Would she not need him as much as his patients would need him, even if the reasons were not the same? He pulled her closer. He had never felt so torn between two worlds, one whose grueling struggle had taken years to accomplish, and the other he so effortlessly longed to embrace.

He took her face into his hands and kissed her with a passion unlike any he had ever known before. "Do you have any idea how much I love you?"

"I think so. I hope so."

Tenderly, he caressed her face as he considered his dilemma for the hundredth time. "Can you be satisfied with that, knowing how much I love you, for a little while longer?"

"I love you, Joe. And I'll be content with whatever you ask of me, for as long as you want."

He kissed her again, with a growing conviction that he could not spend another day of his life without her.

CHAPTER 7

"Dr. Joe!" Two frail arms reached toward Joe Travis as he walked into Cory Robinson's room. He took the child's small, thin hands into his own and squeezed them. "It's on the table," he whispered excitedly. Joe picked up a piece of paper saturated with crayon coloring. Then he looked again at the eager face of his little patient.

"It's the most beautiful picture I've ever seen," Joe declared, doing his best to achieve the maximum in enthusiasm. He sat down on the side of the bed and listened while his young patient explained every line and curve of the drawing he had made exclusively for his favorite doctor.

"You *will* put it on the wall in your office, won't you?" Cory asked.

"Oh, yes," Joe reassured him, "right where I can see it every day.

Now let me have a look at *you*."

Cory Robinson had been a peritoneal dialysis patient for most of his eight years of life. Symptoms of polycystic kidney disease had become evident early in his childhood, resulting in more hospitalizations than he could remember.

However, several weeks earlier, Cory had been the victim of a car accident. His injuries had forced Joe to remove one of his deformed kidneys. In addition to the nephrectomy, he had also removed his spleen, and now he worried about the danger of strep infections and subsequent renal failure.

And the remaining kidney was already becoming progressively worse. Joe knew the child was nearing the critical point where transplant would be his only alternative. But suitable donors were scarce and, as Cory was adopted, the family members, though tested, had been ruled out as possible contributors, so the wait went on.

The door opened, and Janet Robinson walked inside the room with Beth McCallister beside her. Janet stood next to her son and smiled down at him. "So you finished it," his mother said proudly. "You're going to be quite the artist when you grow up."

Cory glanced curiously at Beth and then to his mother. His eyes seemed almost too big for his small, emaciated face. "No, not an artist," he said soberly. "I'm going to be a surgeon, like Dr. Joe."

Joe grinned. "I'm honored." He motioned for Beth. "Cory, this is Ms. McCallister."

"Hi, Cory," Beth greeted. "I've heard a lot about you." "Is she your special friend you were telling me about?"

"She sure is," Joe returned. "Ms. McCallister knows a lot about what it means to replace worn out body parts with new ones. Remember?"

"You mean like the new kidney you told me I need?"

"That's right," Beth answered. "Mind if I sit and chat with you while Dr. Joe and your mom take a walk down the hall?"

"Okay," he said amiably. He scooted over to the side of the bed so she could sit down beside him.

Joe pulled the door shut as he and the boy's mother stepped into the corridor. "Beth has worked with quite a few transplant recipients and their families," Joe explained. "I hope she was able to answer any questions you might have had."

"Yes, she was a tremendous help," Janet Robinson returned. "And I appreciate that she's taking time to explain things to Cory." Then she came to a stop and looked directly at Joe. "It's not looking good for him, is it?"

"I wish I could tell you differently. I'm surprised his remaining kidney has lasted this long."

"And you're thinking a transplant might be his only chance?" Her voice was steady, but tears glistened in her eyes.

"I believe a transplant would be his *best* chance. But in the meantime, we'll keep him on peritoneal dialysis until we see some more improvement." The woman brushed away tears beneath her eyes as Joe slipped his arm around her. "Let's don't lose hope. God knows what Cory needs more than we do."

"I wish I could be as sure of that as you are," she wept quietly. "It's just so hard watching him get weaker and weaker every day. He knows he can't do what other children can do. He misses his school friends, and he gets so lonely."

"Well, I'm ready to do something about that. Cory's already missed a lot of school. I'd like to arrange for a tutor so he can begin catching up to where he should be. Right now even homework might look good," Joe said with a grin.

Immediately, the mother's face brightened. "Oh, Dr. Travis, that would be wonderful."

At the nurses' station, Joe reached for the phone and called Callie. "Cal, see how soon you can make arrangements for Cory Robinson to have some tutoring in the children's ward. I'll be back in the office soon."

* * *

Callie Jordan stopped at the fifth floor pediatric nurses' station to finish making tutoring arrangements for Joe's young dialysis patient. She seated herself behind the tall counter and began filling out some forms, unaware that Joe and Beth had stepped off the elevator. She glanced up from her work just in time to see them walk past the desk.

Callie rose to her feet. From behind the counter, she watched as they walked down the corridor together, watched as Joe pulled Beth closer to his side, their faces bent confidentially toward one another. To Callie, they smiled at each other like a pair of conspirators. She watched as he pushed open the stairwell door at the end of the hallway where they disappeared from her sight.

Slowly, she sank down onto the chair once more. A miserable jumble of hurt and resentment rose inside of her. She felt like a jealous schoolgirl, but this was Beth! How could she ignore that Beth had been her lifelong friend, her constant companion through childhood, never once neglecting her when others had benignly abandoned her because of her restrictive illness? Beth meant everything to her, had done everything with her, knew everything about her.

With the exception that they were both in love with the same man.

How could she ever reconcile this miserable twist of fate? Callie's love for Joe Travis had been her solitary secret apart from Beth. She could not deny that her devotion to him, a love she had cherished for years, was as real as anything had ever been in her whole life.

Just as she also could no longer deny that Joe's obvious love for Beth was just as real.

She looked down at the forms once more, but the words on the papers had begun to blur.

* * *

Joe returned to his office to finish some paperwork, but twenty minutes later, the work still lay on the desk behind him as he gazed absently out the window.

"Joe, you look like a man in love."

Startled, Joe turned away from the window to find Dr. Rick Stuart strolling toward his desk. "Won't you come in?" Joe remarked with good-humored sarcasm.

"Okay, I think I will," Rick said, sliding into a comfortable chair opposite the desk. He pushed a manila envelope toward his colleague. "There's the ER reports you wanted."

"Thanks." Joe placed the envelope on top of the growing stack of papers. "*Man in love*," he repeated. "What made you say that?"

"Oh, I don't know," Rick returned. "You just seemed kind of lost in thought, and thinking about some beautiful woman is sure a nice way to be lost. So what *is* on your mind? Anything wrong?"

"I've . . . got a case I can't seem to stop thinking about." He knew Cory Robinson was not the only cause for which he could not stop thinking about. Maybe it was time for a second opinion. "Rick, mind if I ask you a personal question?"

"Not at all."

Joe extended his folded hands across the desk. "What happened between you and Connie?"

It was obvious from the declining expression on Rick's face that the subject of his failed marriage was not easy to discuss. "It wasn't Connie's fault. I never blamed her, not once."

"Then what caused you to break up?"

Rick took a deep breath and slowly blew it out his cheeks. "I was in my last year of residency when we got married. And I made a promise to myself that after that grueling year was over, I would settle into a practice of my own, and Connie and I would make up for all the time we were missing because of my education.

"But after that year was over, I got even busier trying to establish a decent practice. It took more time than I ever imagined. I was practically living at the hospital. Connie used to joke that my real address was the emergency room.

"She wanted a home and kids—and a husband. But family life was almost nonexistent for me. We got to the point where we never talked, never even argued. I wasn't home long enough to have a good fight with her!

"And then one day . . . she just wasn't there anymore." He leaned forward in the chair and studied Joe's troubled expression. "I loved Connie, but she deserved more, a lot more than I was either able or willing to give her. She thought she was marrying a man, not a hospital." At that moment, Rick's beeper sounded.

"I'm sorry, Rick."

"I'm sorry too," he returned dolefully after shutting off the beeper and reaching for the phone on Joe's desk. "Sorry I didn't warn her what life as a doctor's wife could be like. I could have prepared her, but I didn't. At the time, all I could think of was, *I don't want to lose this woman.* And ultimately, I did just that." He returned his beeper call and then replaced the phone. "I've got a case," he said, rising to his feet. "How about lunch tomorrow? One o'clock?"

"Yeah . . . that'd be fine."

After Rick left the room, Joe glanced out the window once more and shuddered inwardly. If only Rick hadn't confirmed everything his conscience was already telling him.

* * *

The next day, Beth McCallister hurried down the sidewalk in front of the hospital. "Callie!" she called. "Wait up!" Earlier that morning, she had seen Callie outside one of the OR suites and had tried to talk to her, but Callie had mumbled something about being late and quickly excused herself. Her hasty retreat seemed almost deliberate to Beth. It had been weeks since they had talked, and now she was beginning to worry that something was really wrong. Callie's feeble health was always in the back of her mind.

Callie stopped and waited as Beth ran breathlessly in her direction. "Hey, what's been going on with you?" Beth asked when she caught up with her friend. "I haven't found a minute that you aren't either preoccupied or gone."

"I'm sorry, Beth. I've just . . . been busy, that's all. We've had a lot of emergencies in the past few weeks."

The two young women began walking toward the parking lot. "Joe mentioned that. He's pretty worn out at the end of the day too." Callie stared straight ahead until Beth put her hand on her arm, and they came to a stop. "Cal, are you all right? You aren't having any kind of trouble, are you?"

Callie shook her head and managed a smile. "I guess I'm more tired than I want to admit, but I'm okay."

"Joe wouldn't let you overdo it, would he? I mean, you *would* tell him if something was wrong, wouldn't you?" Her words were gentle as well as sincere.

"I'm okay, Beth. Really I am."

Beth sighed. "All right, I believe you." She hoisted her shoulder purse a little higher as they started toward the parking lot again. "Cal, has Joe told you anything about us?"

"A little. Why do you ask?"

"Because . . . I think he's going to ask me to marry him, sooner or later." The announcement, though inevitable, came like a stab wound to Callie. "I have to leave for Chicago tonight for a conference. Maybe being apart for a little while will give him some time to come to a decision."

Callie came to a stop. Painful as it was, she had to know. "And if he asked you?"

Beth looked at her friend squarely in the face. "I'd say yes in a heartbeat." Her expression became radiant as she took Callie's hands into hers. "Oh, Cal, I've been dying to tell you about this! Joe is such a private sort of man, and you've known him so much longer than I have. I just don't know what's troubling him! He seems to need a lot of time and space before making up his mind." She shook her head and grinned at her long time friend. "Can you picture *him* pouring all this out to someone?"

He would tell me, Callie thought.

"I would never push him," Beth continued, "but it's so hard waiting, so hard to know what he's really thinking about. I suppose all I *really* know is . . . I'm in love with him."

The knot in Callie's throat grew tighter as she silently concurred with that of her own feelings. She wanted to turn and run but knew she had to reply in some manner that would preserve the truth, yet safeguard her secret.

"Joe . . . Joe isn't an easy man to figure out," she said at last. "He's intensely committed to his work, and he's fiercely loyal to what he believes in. He's worth the wait." The tears were coming too quickly now. She pretended to glance at her watch. "I have to go . . . " Her voice was a strained whisper as she turned and hurried off in the direction of her car.

Beth stood on the sidewalk in the mid-afternoon sun, watching as Callie disappeared among the mass of cars. Her first inclination was to go after her, but for now, she glanced at her own watch and realized she still had things to take care of in her office before going to the airport. Reluctantly, she turned and began to walk toward the hospital again.

Callie was unhappy about something, and Beth determined she would find the underlying cause of whatever the problem might be.

CHAPTER 8

Joe replaced the phone, satisfied the plans he had made were nearly perfect. The time and place had been arranged. Now all he needed was the lady.

Ten minutes later, he leaned against the open door of Beth's office, amused as he watched her try to cram a file folder into an already overstuffed drawer. "Need any help?"

"No, I don't need any *help*," she repeated in frustration, not bothering to turn around, "because I'm going to make this *fit*."

Joe walked over and put his arms around her. "Forget that," he whispered, turning her toward him before ardently kissing her.

"You can make me forget just about anything—except you." "Good, let's keep it that way."

Self-assuredly, he leaned forward for another kiss when Beth pulled herself out of his arms. "Joe, I'm worried about Callie," she announced flatly.

He straightened up, making no pretense to hide the displeasure of his rejected overture. When she failed to acknowledge his obvious discontent, he pushed the file drawer shut and leaned against the cabinet. "What makes you say that?" he sighed, resignedly folding his arms across his chest.

"I saw her this afternoon. She isn't herself, Joe. I know something's wrong."

"Well, *what's* wrong? Is she not feeling well?"

Beth wasn't about to divulge the confidential details of her conversation with Callie. But neither could she ignore her uneasy feelings about her friend. "I don't think it has anything to do with her heart. She just seems . . . depressed. Sad. Have you not noticed it?"

"Well, now that you mention it, I suppose she's been a little depressed, maybe a little more quiet than usual. I also know *because* of her heart condition, she has good days and bad. Her mental health is naturally going to be affected to some degree—"

"Joe, this isn't some objective clinical evaluation I'm asking you to make! We're talking about Callie!"

Joe's affection for Callie was as unfaltering as ever, but his thoughts were preoccupied with his plans for a romantic evening. "You're right. I didn't mean to sound so impersonal."

For some reason, his mind trailed back to Dr. Jordan's annual dinner party earlier in the spring, and he remembered the brief talk he and Callie had had in the den that night. Several times, she had tried to tell him something, but their conversation had been interrupted, and he had never thought about it again until this moment. She had become agitated when she spoke of her father, mentioning something about the control he continually exerted over her. He had also guessed that she had a romantic interest, though he had yet to observe her with anyone. Had Ben Jordan put a stop to that too? Now he could only speculate the reason for her unhappiness. "My guess is it's her father."

"You may be right. Callie really gets frustrated with his constant overprotection. She's a grown woman, and he still treats her like a child. She's hated that ever since we were kids."

"I think he's so afraid something might happen to her when he's not around that he goes overboard. He'd never forgive himself. He means well, but it makes her feel like an invalid."

"That's it then," Beth concluded. "I dearly love Dr. J., but I'll have to talk to him because Callie won't stand up to him." When Joe began to laugh, Beth's confident expression waned. "Why are you laughing?" she demanded.

"Because 'having a talk' with Dr. Jordan is about as effective as putting a Band-Aid on a severed limb."

"Well, that doesn't mean I'm going to say nothing simply because—"

"Simply because *he is her father*," Joe finished in a measured tone as he put his hands on either side of her taut shoulders. "It's their business, Beth, not yours and not mine. Callie can work this out herself."

"But why should—"

This time he deliberately pulled her toward him and kissed her. "Leave it alone. Now listen to me. I just made a reservation for two at one of Boston's finest restaurants tonight. And all I'm asking for is your sincere, undivided, adoring attention."

Beth's indignation faded into dismay. "Have you forgotten I have to leave for Chicago tonight?"

He dropped into the chair behind her desk. "I forgot all about it," he sighed. He picked up a pencil and drummed it dismally on the desktop, wondering which of them had had to break more dates lately, him or her. "Well, can I at least take you to the airport?"

"I was hoping you'd volunteer," she returned. She reached beside him to pick up her purse when he pulled her down onto his lap. She put her arms around him and laid her head against his shoulder. "I *hate* being away from you."

"I hate it too," he told her, pulling her closer.

* * *

It was late by the time Joe returned home after taking Beth to the airport. He unlocked the door and turned on the lights inside the foyer, still despondent over his spoiled plans. He wandered into the kitchen and rummaged through a scanty assortment of groceries looking for something to eat, though he really didn't feel like eating. Most of all, he didn't feel like being alone.

He closed the cabinet doors and leaned against the counter. He thought about the dinners he and Beth had prepared together and the contented evenings that had followed. Yet tonight, even the quietude away from the hospital merely reinforced his feelings of isolation apart from her.

His conversation with Rick Stuart several days earlier continued to trouble him. Rick had been a good friend and colleague for a number of years. Yet Joe could rarely recall associating with him outside of hospital functions, realizing the time-consuming hours Rick put in at the hospital matched his own, and by Rick's own admission, he conceded his marriage had failed because he had allowed his work to come before the woman he loved. His marriage had become another statistic. Joe could not fathom doing that to Beth.

So why was he allowing one man's experience to preclude his own? Statistics were only numbers. Was spending the rest of his life alone somehow superior to taking a risk?

* * *

Joe walked into his outer office after a fitful night's sleep and picked up the mail from his secretary's desk. Listlessly, he scanned hospital announcements, postoperative reports, a letter of appreciation from Cory Robinson's mother. Dropping the rest of the unopened envelopes on the desk, he felt his energy level at an all time low. He wished he had no decisions to make today, no responsibilities, nothing that required anything he had to put forward.

His bad mood increased when he opened the door to his office and found more work piled on his desk. There was a half written article he had begun a week ago, reports to be read, consultation letters to write, orders to update.

The phone began to ring before he sat down. Fifth floor nurses' station, his secretary, Kate, informed him from the door. With uncommon irritability, he picked up the phone. "No, I'm *not* going to increase the dosage until I see the last test results," he snapped. "And until that happens, I don't want to hear about it again." He dropped the phone roughly.

"What on earth is wrong with you?"

He glanced up as Paul Martin walked through the door of his office. "Nothing's wrong," he mumbled.

"Oh, sure, sure," Paul indulged him as he sat down. "Has Beth had the privilege of seeing this side of you yet?"

"She's out of town," he returned in a sullen voice, probing through the pile of papers for anything that demanded his immediate attention.

Paul nodded knowingly. "That would explain a lot."

Joe looked at his old friend, fully aware of his colleague's inventive endeavor to obtain the reasons behind his ill temper. "All right," he surrendered, ending the quest. "What is it you *really* want?"

"Well, initially I came by to tell you the committee meeting has been postponed for today. But frankly, I'm more curious to know why you're so upset this morning. Did you and Beth have a fight?"

"No, nothing like that." "Then what's bothering you?"

He shook his head, leaning wearily against the back of his chair. "Paul, did you ever have any real doubts before you married Sarah?" Paul's white eyebrows rose in new interest. "Well, I suppose every man has *some* doubts before he gets married. About the only thing I *didn't* doubt was how much I loved her. I figured the rest of my qualms would just somehow fall into place as long as we understood each other."

"Understood each other," Joe repeated thoughtfully. "How do you mean?"

"I mean that Sarah knew the routine of a doctor's life long before we got married. Her father and grandfather were both doctors. So right from the beginning, we agreed that *my* work, however hectic and time consuming it might become, had nothing to do with how I felt about her. Oh, there were plenty of missed dinners, holidays spent alone, vacations canceled or cut short, but Sarah understood the most important thing in my life was her, above everything else. She appreciated that my work was important to me, but she understood it was only *part* of my life. She was *all* of my life."

Joe's anxious expression began to relax. "I never thought about it that way."

"Well, I suppose I was lucky," Paul said, leaning forward in the chair. "Not every woman could be as understanding as Sarah, though she did have a temper the color of her hair. And sometimes, she vented it on me with a vengeance, I suspect mostly out of frustration.

"But then we'd plan some time alone together. We'd go up to the cabin whenever we could, or sometimes we'd just turn the ringer off the phone at night."

"That was all?"

"Pretty much." Paul's eyes twinkled as he got to his feet. "Listen, your patient load is pretty light right now, and you haven't had a real vacation for some time. Why don't you take a few days off? I'd be glad to take care of your patients just to see you get away for a while."

"You mean now, today?"

"Sure! It's summer! Go up to my cabin and do some fishing." His discerning eyes narrowed on the younger man's surprised expression. "It's my guess there's a great catch out there waiting just for you."

* * *

The sun was slipping toward the west as Joe set his hastily stuffed travel bag behind the door of the conference room. Standing out of sight against the wall, he could see Beth behind the podium, nearing the end of her afternoon lecture. Following a brief question and answer session, she brought the proceedings to a close with the offering of a short prayer.

He stepped into the corridor as people began to leave, leaning against the paneled wall behind the door until the room had emptied. Then he heard the familiar clatter of high heels coming toward him.

As Beth walked through the door, he reached out and pulled her into his arms. A startled gasp escaped her lips. "Joe! What on earth are *you* doing here?"

"Well, I realize I missed most of the lecture, but I did catch the question-and-answer session. And I have a question," he said matter-of-factly.

"You still haven't told me what you're doing here," she said, scarcely concealing the delight of having him beside her.

"I told you," he said again, "I have a question."

"And so naturally you flew all the way to Chicago. And what *is* your question?"

He put his hands around her shoulders, his voice soft with hopeful expectation. "What would be the prognosis if I asked you marry me *right now?*"

Her eyes widened. "*Joe . . .*"

He glanced around, not wanting to attract any undue attention to his most private moment. He ushered her to a quiet corner, his buoyant expression changing to one of genuine concern. "Beth, it's important to me that you understand what being a doctor's wife would involve. It would have a thousand drawbacks. There'd be demands on me that I wouldn't have any control over. I have obligations that I'm sworn to uphold. And you'd have to realize my time would *always* be torn between home and the hospital."

Her expression transformed into an amused smile. "Are you forgetting I grew up with exactly what you just described?"

"Maybe so. But that would have no reflection on how much I love you."

"You make this sound more like a proposition than a proposal.

Which is it?"

He took a deep, nervous breath. "It's a proposal . . . but not exactly the way I rehearsed it."

Immediately, her arms encircled his neck. "Oh, Joe, proposition or proposal, you know the answer is yes!"

He pulled her closer. "I just want to be with you the rest of my life," he whispered, "starting right *now.*"

She took a step back. "Are you really serious? I have two more days at this conference."

"Details," he said, rolling his eyes and shaking his head. He glanced around the elegant lobby. "I wouldn't think of stopping you from your conference, just . . . interrupting it a little. Paul Martin has generously given me a few days off, and I think in that length of time we could find a justice of the peace and have some semblance of a honeymoon until I can arrange one that you really deserve. In the meantime, we can save the expense of two rooms because I'm not leaving here without you. Are you with me?"

She shook her head and laughed. "Yes, I'm with you forever and ever!"

When they reached the front desk, she put her hand on his shirtsleeve. "Joe, did you really come all the way to Chicago just to ask me to marry you?" she asked expectantly.

"Well, that and one other thing," he said as he began thumbing through a phone directory. "Paul thought it was time I went fishing."

CHAPTER 9

From far down the corridor, Callie could hear the prattle behind the OR desk before she even saw the cluster of nurses.

"Well, she certainly must have had something the rest of us missed," one nurse was commenting.

"Like you had a chance to begin with?"

"Well, it won't be the same for me," another returned. "Now I can't even *dream* any longer."

Callie ignored the customary gossip gathering as she stepped behind the desk area. She sat down and reached for Joe's schedule. At once, she noticed all of his follow-up surgeries, including his call schedule, had been altered with replacement surgeons. *Why would he change the schedule without telling me . . . ?*

"Say, Callie, you'd know!"

Still puzzling over the schedule in her hands, she asked absently, "Know what?"

"Is it true about Dr. Travis?"

"Is *what* true?"

"That he got married!"

Callie's breath caught in her throat, and her chest tightened as she turned to look at her coworker. "Where did you hear that?" The words tumbled from her lips as though they had come from someone else.

"Well, it's all over the hospital, but Casey overheard Dr. Martin telling your dad about it."

The clipboard slipped out of her hands. "I . . . I really don't know." Without another word, she rose from the chair and vanished at a run down the hallway.

* * *

Sunlight crept along the windowsill outside the hotel suite where Beth and Joe had spent their first two days as husband and wife. Lazily, Joe opened his eyes and glanced up at the ruffled canopy above them. *This may be elegance, but it's definitely not a man's bed*, he thought.

But no matter. He pulled a still sleeping Beth closer. "Do you know," he whispered as she began to awaken, "if I could stay like this forever, I think I'd be the happiest man alive."

She rested her head on his bare chest, her eyes still closed. Just the warmth of him next to her seemed as essential as breathing. "And if I thought I could *keep* you like this forever, I would. But if I remember correctly, I was duly warned that being a doctor's wife was not all fancy hotel suites and beautiful canopy beds."

He propped himself up on his elbow and gazed down at her. "Well, enjoy it while you can, lady, because I'm not letting you out of the contract." He kissed her passionately. "Now did you have any more remarks on the subject before I take you to breakfast, Mrs. Travis?"

"Just one thing, Doctor," she said gravely. "Was going out to breakfast every morning part of the deal?"

* * *

By early evening, Callie stood alongside Maggie McCarran, dicing an onion as though she had a score to settle. The kitchen door swung open, abruptly ending a sober conversation between the two women the moment Benjamin Jordan entered. He crossed the gray stonefloor to lift the lid of a steaming pot, ignoring their hasty retreat into silence. "I'm starving, and I've got a ton of work to do tonight. How much longer until dinner?"

"About half an hour," Maggie informed him officiously. "And you'll wait, patiently, just like the rest of us."

A mumbled rejoinder followed as he helped himself to some carrot sticks. "I suppose you heard about Bethie and Joe," he said with pretended annoyance. "Paul Martin told me this morning. And I know news travels like wildfire down those corridors." He picked up a few more raw vegetables.

Maggie cast a quick glance at Callie and watched as she turned her head aside. "Yes, Callie was just tellin' me about it," she said in a quiet voice, putting a ladle into the soup. "I suppose there must be somethin' excitin' about eloping," she finished with a sigh.

Jordan caught her gaze and walked over to his daughter. She began vigorously chopping another onion. Her red-rimmed eyes did not convince him her tears were due solely to the onions. "Callie? You feel bad that Bethie didn't tell you before?"

"She didn't have to tell me anything," she answered quickly, chopping frantically on the onion.

Her father slipped his arm around her shoulders and squeezed them. His brusque mannerism became quite the opposite when dealing with Callie. "Was there . . . maybe a time that you were hoping the same thing might happen between *you* and Joe?" he ventured in an unusually gentle voice.

Callie dropped the knife with a thud and turned angrily in the direction of her father. "I believe that was *your* dream, Dad. I'm sorry if I haven't produced a suitable son-in-law for you yet, but even*thinking* that Joe Travis would ever . . . would ever . . . " The broken words ended in a muffled sob. She fled through the doors and up the long staircase. Throwing open the door to her room, she fell across the bed and wept as though her heart would break.

* * *

There was no consolation for Callie's misery, in spite of the subdued apology she made to her father the next morning. Maggie had come to her room late in the night and offered the single listening ear to which Callie could unburden herself. But the insightful and loving housekeeper could do little to soothe the wound Callie felt so deeply.

Three days later, alone in an empty surgical suite, Callie mechanically prepared for the first surgery of the day, merely going through the motions as she arranged instruments and checked equipment.

As she worked, an endless vision of her best friend married to the man she adored burned like wildfire in her mind. Beth had only known Joe for a few months. She had known him for years. And in no time, the signs had all been there. Yet ignoring the inevitable had been easier than facing it. Now there would be no escaping it.

She felt like a trapped animal. How could she possibly continue to work beside Joe Travis day after day while trying to conceal an emotional struggle that raged inside her? Jealousy seemed secondary in comparison to her real frustration, a frustration of feelings never made known.

For years, she knew Joe's affection for her had been like that for a younger sister. Yet she had continued to hope that someday he might see her differently. Now it was too late, and it would be up to her to find a way to live with the agony, and pretend it didn't exist.

Outside in the corridor, she could hear the commotion of doctors, nurses, and technicians coming onto the surgical floor. Then without warning, the door swung open.

"Cal, I've been looking all over for you!" The sound of Joe's friendly voice brought fresh tears to her eyes, and she was too ashamed to turn around and acknowledge his presence. "I guess you heard the news by now." He came up behind her, gently grasping her shoulders. "Cal?"

Something snapped inside her at the touch of his hands. Turning fiercely in his direction, the amicable expression on his face quickly waned. "Why didn't you have the common decency to tell me that you and Beth were going to get married?" she spurted angrily, her voice raspy from days of weeping. "Why did I have to hear it from a bunch of gossiping OR nurses?"

"Cal . . .I'm sorry," he tried to apologize, stunned by her baffling reaction. "I know it was sudden. I didn't think. Cal, I thought you'd be happy for us. I don't understand why you're so upset—"

"And you never will!" She buried her face in her hands and burst into tears he could not understand. When he tried to draw her toward him, she tore herself away and fled from the room.

* * *

It was already dark when Beth heard the sound of Joe's car in the driveway. She hurried to light the candles on the dining room table. This was an evening of celebration, their first real dinner at Joe's home—now their home—as husband and wife.

She quickly smoothed over the black lace dress he had bought her in Chicago as the front door opened and shut again. Hidden from view, she leaned alluringly against the wooden archway that led into the dining room, waiting for him to walk past her on his way to the kitchen. But after several minutes, her husband did not appear.

Feeling foolish, she walked into the living room. There she found him slouched in a chair beside the fireplace. She stood behind him and put her hands on his shoulders, feeling the tenseness in his muscles. She would not press him for an explanation.

"Dinner's ready," she told him quietly.

He reached up and grasped the hands that rested on his shoulders. "Whatever it is smells wonderful." Still, he did not move or offer an account for his silence.

She crouched beside the chair. "Joe, what's wrong?"

When he turned to look at her, she could see the concern in his expression. "I found Callie in the OR today to tell her we were married, but she said she'd already found out from 'a bunch of gossiping OR nurses.' She was pretty upset with me."

Beth drew a quick breath. "Oh, Joe, I was afraid of that. She must be so angry with me!"

Joe shook his head. "She's angry with me, not you."

"You don't understand," Beth said, rising to her feet. "When we were just kids, Callie and I used to spend hours planning our weddings right down to the *I do's*. We vowed that we would be each other's maids of honor. And I didn't keep that promise."

HEART JOURNEY

"You were kids, Beth! She couldn't possibly be holding that against you."

"Maybe not that part," she continued, "but as far as she must be concerned, I ran off and got married without even telling her. How would *you* feel?"

Joe pulled her down onto his lap and began absentmindedly stroking the black lace of the dress he had yet to notice. "I understand what you're saying, but we have our *own* lives to live now. If she needs someone to blame, let her blame me. But I'm not sorry I went to Chicago and married you, however impulsive it may seem to *anyone*. Are you?"

Beth looked into the reflective blue eyes that still captivated her. "Of course I'm not sorry. But I can't be content as long as I know I've hurt Callie."

"I don't want to feel I've hurt Callie either," he said, pulling her closer. "Why don't we go and talk to her?"

Beth shook her head. "No, it would be too awkward for her if both of us went. This is something I need to do alone. Callie and I go back a lot farther than you and I do."

* * *

Maggie McCarran stood in the entrance hall of the Jordan house, searching through her purse. Morning sunshine streamed through the windows behind her. "Well, they just aren't here. Where would I have laid me house keys?" She looked at Callie once more. "I do wish you'd change your mind and go shoppin' with me. Ya've been cooped up in this house for days, and ya need to get out and do somethin'! Moping isn't going to change a thing."

"I'll be all right, Maggie," Callie contended. "Besides, I'd . . . I'd really rather be alone."

Maggie shook her head. "I still say it's not good for ya. But ya've always known your own head." She sighed disparagingly. "Now if ya happen to find me house keys . . . "

"I'll put them in your room." With an anxious smile, Maggie left, and Callie closed the door behind her.

She began to climb the long, winding staircase back to her room. Almost a week had passed since she had had the miserable encounter with Joe in the OR. Beth had tried to call her every day since, but Callie could not bring herself to face either one of them, alone or, worse, together. At least she had stopped crying. What she needed now was time to think, time to think of a way to reevaluate her life that would never again embrace idealistic thoughts about Joe Travis.

The sudden ring of the doorbell interrupted her train of thought. Halfway up the stairs and already winded, she turned and made her way back down to the entry hall. As she pulled the heavy door open, she wondered what Maggie had forgotten to tell her now. "Callie, please let me come in. I *have* to talk to you." Beth stood on the veranda, nervously clutching her shoulder purse, her eyes pleading with her friend. "*Please.*"

Callie hesitated for a moment and then stepped back to allow Beth to enter. "Cal, let me say this before I lose all my courage," she continued in one breath. "I *know* you're angry with me, and you have every right to *be* angry! This may sound like an excuse, but I didn't have any idea that Joe was planning to come to Chicago to propose. But when he did, it was just . . . just like a dream, a whirlwind, and before I knew it, we were standing in front of a judge—"

"Beth, really, this is none of my business."

"But it's *my* business when I've hurt my best friend!" Beth's eyes glistened with tears. "When I thought about all the hours we used to spend as kids planning our weddings, promising to stand up for each other . . . well, I just didn't plan for it to turn out this way." She reached for Callie's hands. "Joe told me what happened in the OR. All I could think about was how disappointed you must have been, finding out the way you did. And I'm so sorry!" she whispered anxiously.

Callie pulled away from Beth's hands and leaned against the staircase railing. Gazing into the innocent face of her friend overwhelmed her with guilt for her jealous anger. Beth had no more idea than did Joe what her outburst in the operating room had really meant. "You don't have anything to apologize for," she said at last, gazing down at her feet. "I'm the one who needs to apologize, especially to Joe."

Beth wrapped her arms around her friend and held her tightly. "Callie, you mean so much to me. And to Joe too. But you already know that."

Gradually, Callie embraced Beth more firmly. Beth had done nothing overt to win the love of Joe Travis. Nevertheless, Callie knew she could never regard her friend in the same way again. Her feelings would remain helplessly unchanged. With tears in her eyes, she prayed again for a peace that eventually might expunge the anger and resentment.

"Want to go into the kitchen and make a pot of tea?" Callie asked in a tenuous voice.

"Oh, yes!"

As they walked toward the kitchen together, Callie knew what she had to do, something drastic, something that would require far more courage than she had ever had to marshal before. Because nothing but time—and distance—would heal the pain of surrendering her cherished dream.

CHAPTER 10

Joe hurried down the corridor on his way to grand rounds when he heard the booming voice of Dr. Benjamin Jordan booming louder than usual. He rounded a corner to find his former mentor wagging his finger in the face of a pale looking intern.

"I've *never* seen a worse case history in my entire life! How do you think for *one minute* you'd be able to make any *kind* of proper diagnosis—"

"Dr. Jordan, you're going to be late for grand rounds." With quiet subtlety, Joe attempted to rescue the hapless young doctor. Jordan turned, his face discolored from anger. Past Jordan's shoulder, Joe could see the relieved look on the intern's face.

"What time is it?" the professor demanded.

"Almost nine o'clock. You have several cases to present, don't you?" he reminded him.

"Yes . . . yes, I suppose I do." Joe eased him away from the young man though Jordan continued to rave as they walked down the hall. "When I tell him to take a patient history, I expect him to get every possible detail! This is the third time—" The tirade came to an abrupt halt when Joe pushed open the door to the doctors' lounge and ushered him inside. "What do you think you're doing?" Jordan snapped.

"I'm going to check your pressure for starters." "You most certainly are not!"

Nevertheless, Joe ignored the customary obstinacy while escorting the petulant older surgeon to a chair where he compelled him to sit down. With reluctant indignation, he allowed Joe to check his vital signs. "So are you taking your blood pressure medication every day like your doctor ordered? Or every day or so?"

Jordan slumped in the chair as Joe wrapped the cuff around his upper arm. "I'm taking it," he barked, "when I think about it."

Joe pumped air into the cuff while placing the end of his stethoscope in the bend of his mentor's arm. Then he slowly released the valve. "Well, 220 over 100 convinces me you're telling the truth." He rolled the cuff back up and replaced it on the counter. "You can't fool around with that pressure of yours. You know what's at stake."

"Yes, and I don't need you to remind me!" he snarled. Jordan rose swiftly to his feet when a sudden sharp pain, one he had experienced more often than he liked, stabbed at the center of his chest. Immediately, he staggered. Joe grasped his arm in an effort to steady him.

Jordan managed to mask the pain as he voluntarily sank into the chair once more. He leaned forward and rested his head in his hands for a moment while waiting for the pain to subside. Only now was he aware of Joe's anxious voice repeating his name while the younger doctor's hand rested on his back.

Benjamin Jordan had no intention of allowing Joe—or anyone else—to suspect that something might be out of the ordinary as far as his health was concerned. As a result, he decided to confess his legitimate concern about Callie. "Oh, Joe, it isn't you," he said with a sigh. "It's Callie." The tough exterior began to melt into feeble resistance at the mention of his only child. "She suddenly thinks she has to leave home."

Stunned, Joe eased himself into the chair next to his "Leave home?"

"She wants to be on her own. She wants to live her own life," he finished in a mockery of his daughter's words.

More than a week before, Joe had disclosed only to Beth the details of Callie's angry encounter with him in the OR. Though he knew Beth had already spoken to her, Callie had not mentioned any plans to leave. He had said nothing when she had not reported for work as her heart condition frequently required more rest than Callie was sometimes willing to give to it. Yet even though Ben Jordan's announcement did not come as a complete surprise, still Joe felt pangs of guilt that he could neither explain nor understand.

All at once, he was aware that Jordan had been ranting on while he had been lost in thought. "She's never been on her own before!" Jordan was declaring. "I've always been there looking out for her! What about her heart condition?"

Still convicted that he was somehow responsible, Joe sought consolation for his former mentor as well as himself. "She's lived with it all her life. She knows what her limitations are. But are you sure this is what she really wants?"

Jordan took a deep breath. "I don't know," he said miserably. "Maybe it is." Jordan leaned against the back of the chair. He glanced thoughtfully at Joe. Trying to piece together Callie's impulsive desire to move away led his thoughts to her outburst in the kitchen the day Paul Martin told him of Joe's elopement with Beth. He recalled how distraught she had become when he'd brought up the young doctor's spontaneous marriage.

Of course, that was it. Jordan cursed himself for his ignorance. Callie would never admit it to him, but why else would she have been so ambiguous about her behavior, veiling herself in her room for days afterward? Callie evidently could not accept a marriage between her best friend and . . .

"Think it would do any good?"

Jordan's eyes rose as he became conscious of Joe's voice once more. "Think what would do any good?"

"If I talked with her?" Joe repeated words Jordan had not even heard.

"Yes . . . yes, it might," he agreed idly, trying to redirect his thoughts. "She's always taken a lot of stock in your opinion. But remember you've never had a daughter. And you don't always know what you're talking about, Doctor."

"You got me on that one."

There were more times than not when Jordan had difficulty maintaining his paternal brusqueness with the handsome young doctor. "I . . . guess I never got around to congratulating you . . . and Bethie."

Joe grinned as he pulled out the cuff again. "No, you never did. But thank you anyway." He took Jordan's pressure a second time. "190 over 98. Better, but still—"

"I know, I know," he growled irritably, struggling out of the chair. He glanced at his watch. "Now look what you've done. You've made me late for grand rounds."

* * *

It was late in the afternoon as Joe drove up the long, winding driveway to the Jordan estate. He pulled to a stop and climbed out of the car. The oppressive summer heat from the hot paved road engulfed him like an oven.

He stuffed his sunglasses into his shirt pocket, gazing for a moment at the exquisite fifty-two-room mansion, perched majestically on top of the hill. The house had been occupied by six generations of Jordans. Callie and her father marked the last of the clan.

Maggie greeted him at the door. After a polite exchange of words, she showed him into the den and then knowingly excused herself.

Joe walked across the room and stood beside Benjamin Jordan's desk. The afternoon sun poured through the handsome arched floor-to-ceiling window, bathing the room in a golden glow. He glanced around the familiar room, at the heavy damask draperies, the dark antique furniture, the Oriental carpets, thinking how unpretentious Callie was by comparison.

He had been relieved when Beth had come to see Callie, but she obviously had said nothing to Beth about plans to leave Boston. He determined to find out what her reasons were for wanting to leave the only home she had ever known.

"Joe?" He turned and saw Callie standing unobtrusively in the doorway. He walked toward her and squeezed her hands, though her eyes remained fixed on the floor. Her appearance troubled him. She looked pale and more frail than usual. "Joe, I'm . . . I'm sorry aboutthe way I behaved in the OR. I had no right to get so angry—"

"You had *every* right," he interjected softly. "It was never my intention for you to find out like that. Forgive me?"

With a sense of guilt, she dropped his hands and turned away. "Joe, *please . . .* " Stubbornly, he turned her toward him once more.She looked into his face only to see what she had always seen. He cared— he would always *care*—and even though it was touching, it was all she would ever have. "I really am sorry," she uttered in an anxious whisper.

The dimples in his cheeks deepened with his smile as he drew her toward him. "That's enough apologizing." His unaffected smile changed to mock severity as he lifted her chin. "This is me, remember? Save those polite platitudes for people you don't know so well. And in the meantime, you can tell me what all this talk is about leaving."

She turned away and sat down on the sofa. "It's . . . not just talk, Joe. It's high time I took charge of myself. As much as I love my father, he's protected my every move for too long. You know what I'm talking about. Getting *out* on my own is the only way I'll ever have a *life* of my own." She looked away, masking tears that would demand more explanation.

Joe knew that he, too, had been guilty of a strong compulsion to protect her, almost as much as Ben Jordan had. He sat down beside her. "You never mentioned leaving to Beth. When did you decide all this?"

Her expression was one of resignation, of unspoken surrender to inevitable circumstances. "I . . . I've been thinking about it for a while now," she said, averting her eyes. "If I'm ever going to do something about it, I'm going to have to do it now. I don't expect Dad will ever understand, but I knew if *anyone* could"—she paused, looking at him once more—"it would be you."

Knowing Ben Jordan for as long as he had, Joe understood all too well. Yet he suspected there was more to her decision than the simple explanation she had offered. "I *do* understand. No one has the right to tell you how to live your life, but don't underestimate your father. He has a right to care about you too." His fingers stroked her cheek. "I just want you to be sure this is what you really want."

Callie knew it was not a question of want, but one of necessity. She needed a life of her own, not a longing that would never be satisfied. "It's what I really want."

"But where will you go? What do you plan to do?"

"I've been making arrangements to work at the same hospital Beth was at in Charleston. I'll be in the OR there."

His expression waned. "How soon until you leave?" "Maybe a week or so."

"And there's no chance of persuading you otherwise?" When she shook her head, he got to his feet and pulled her up beside him. "All right," he said, still unconvinced as he draped his arms across her shoulders. "But I want you to know I don't ever expect to have another scrub nurse as good as you." He watched the bare hint of a smile return to her face.

They walked together to the entrance hall. Standing beside the door, Joe looked at her again, his expression sympathetic but sober. "Cal, tell me just one thing. You've known a lot of residents and interns through the years. Haven't you ever considered getting married and having a family of your own?"

If he had stabbed her in the heart, the irony would have been no different. She glanced down at her feet. There was no way she could look at him while offering any kind of truthful answer. "I guess," she began, hesitating, "I guess you might say the right one just never proposed."

"Well, when the right one does," he said, gently lifting her chin with his hand, "he's going to be one lucky man." With a kiss to her cheek, he opened the door and was gone.

Through the window, Callie watched as his car slowly disappeared around the curved drive. The idea of leaving the only home she had ever known to strike out on her own was terrifying, but there was no other way she knew how to live with the hurt. This way there would be no need to pretend.

But the emptiness would be with her for a long time, maybe a lifetime.

CHAPTER 11

Two paramedics pushed the gurney through the ambulance bay entrance and hurried toward the resuscitation room. The child of only nine years seemed lost in the huddle of emergency personnel as the transfer from gurney to resuscitation table was swiftly completed. A mass of hands began untangling the tubes and wires that connected the young boy to what life was left in him.

There was no movement from the unconscious child as a nurse quickly began cutting away the torn and bloody clothing. As Joe Travis directed the emergency proceedings, he knew immediately that the child had lost a massive amount of blood. The abdomen was tight and distended, and the skin, covered in wet and dried blood, was a pale white. He was going to need more help. The call went out.

Intravenous lines were established as the boy was connected to the ventilator. Blood was drawn for type and cross matching while a Foley catheter was put in place. Antibiotics were administered in preparation to go to the OR. Orders were given for x-rays.

While he worked, Joe listened as one of the paramedics provided the accident report. "The child was unresponsive during transport, maintained shallow breathing and thready pulses. We couldn't get a blood pressure at one point. Pupils were fixed and dilated. Most of the injury was sustained to the cranial region. The parents were notified by the police and are on their way now."

Joe's heart wanted to break as he realized the little boy's chances were slim at best. Nevertheless, he had a job to do; emotions had to be set aside. He and the members of the highly skilled trauma team were the boy's solitary hope. "How did this happen?"

"Hit on his bicycle by a drunk driver."

Anger surged through him. *Treat the injuries now, deal with the anger later*, Joe reminded himself as he continued working.

The door opened, and Joe was relieved to see Rick Stuart enter the room. While a nurse helped Rick into a pair of gloves, Joe quickly gave him the details of the accident.

"Is he ventilating?" Rick asked the nurse at the head of the table who was pumping oxygen into the child's lungs.

"Yes, both lungs equally," she returned.

Joe finished taping the chest tube in place when he glanced at another nurse doing chest compressions. "Any pulses yet?"

The nurse shook her head. "What there is, is barely palpable."

Joe exchanged an anxious look with his colleague. Both knew the boy's chance of survival was almost nil. Nevertheless, Joe's sense of urgency to save his young patient became even more compelling. "Where's that lateral of the neck?" he shouted.

In minutes, a technician slapped an x-ray onto the viewing box and flipped on the light. Rick and Joe stepped up to the box. "Neck's broken in two places, right here at C1 and C2," Rick said quietly, outlining the area with his gloved hand. "There's not much we can do now. You better call it."

Joe turned and looked down at the small, ashen face. Though he knew further effort was futile, his patient was still only a child. A pronouncement of death was the part of his job he hated most.

He glanced once more at the x-ray on the viewing box. "All right," he sighed with reluctance. He called for a halt to the resuscitation. "But keep him on the ventilator until I talk with the parents and the transplant team." Wearily, he straightened his aching back beside the table and commended the team members. "You did everything you could."

* * *

After the team left the room, Joe leaned despairingly against the steel counter. He watched as nurse Jessie Gallagher began to clean the blood from the child's face for the sake of the parents who would see him soon.

What justification was there in a child's death? he thought angrily. What possible excuse was there? The responsibility of informing the parents of the fate of their child would fall to him.

And what then? How were they expected to pick up their lives after such a pointless slaughter? How would they make sense of a tragedy of this magnitude, while just down the corridor, the inebriated driver waited in a drunken stupor for a few stitches to his forehead?

The door opened, and a floor nurse poked her head inside. Joe watched as she glanced with cool indifference at the child, then grimaced at the sight of the blood soaked sheets and instruments strewn about the counters and floor. "Dr. Travis, gunshot wound to the chest. Should be here in just a few minutes." With another sidelong glance, she pulled the door shut.

Jessie stopped her work and watched as he turned away. "Dr.

Travis, are you all right?" There was no answer. "Joe?"

He turned and glanced again at the doomed child on the stretcher. "Why are we expected to be so impartial, so dispassionate, to separate ourselves from one tragedy just so we can be objective enough to go on to the next one?" He shook his head in anger. "Can you do it?"

"Not in a million years." Jessie turned back to the child.

Joe anticipated his next task with dread. He had perhaps five minutes to spend with two grieving parents to explain what had happened to their boy. "Jess, when you're finished, find my wife and ask her come down here as soon as possible." The nurse nodded.

Joe stood beside the boy and squeezed the motionless hand. *Dear God,* he prayed in silence, *give me the words to say, and if there's any justification in this tragedy, please show me what it is.*

* * *

Beth Travis hurried down the corridor, the heels of her shoes clattering against the hard linoleum. As she entered the emergency department, she found her husband coming out of another trauma room. "I got your message. What happened?"

Joe explained the situation as they walked quickly down the hall. "The parents are devastated. They need your special kind of comfort, Beth. I wish I could be there to help you, but—"

"I know. It's all right."

Joe left her outside the private waiting room where the parents were and then turned and hurried back toward the trauma room from which he had just emerged.

Beth paused for a moment, routinely praying for words as she opened the door. "Mr. and Mrs. Garrett?" Two grief-stricken faces turned toward her. "I'm Beth Travis. I'd like to help you."

* * *

An hour later, Beth quietly stepped out of the waiting room. At the far end of the corridor, she could see Joe giving orders to one of the nurses behind the counter.

He glanced in her direction as she began to walk toward him. Even from a distance, he could see the mental exhaustion on her face that came from dealing with bereavement.

In the middle of the darkened corridor, she eagerly came to him, finding solace that only his arms could provide. When he lifted her face toward his, he saw her red-rimmed eyes, knowing the comfort she offered had come fully from her own heart. "The parents are with the boy now," she told him. "And they're willing to donate his organs."

"How did you manage that?"

"What else is there when you've lost everything? I told them about Cory. At least now, there's some reason for them to go on."

Joe smiled down at her. She was truly the miracle in his life. Was she also part of the miracle for Cory? "You may be the answer to a prayer." He turned his attention back to the nurse.

A commotion at the far end of the corridor caught their attention. Two police officers emerged from a treatment room with a stumbling drunken man handcuffed between them. Joe bristled with anger at the sight. Instinctively, he started toward them until he felt Beth's hand grasp the sleeve of his coat.

"Don't do it, Joe. What good would it accomplish?"

Astonished, he stopped and turned to face her. *She knew exactly what his intentions were.* Only then did he allow his wearied expression to expose the passionate anger he had concealed until now. "Oh, I don't know. It might do *me* some good . . . "

"*No.*" Her usual sympathetic attitude swiftly changed to vehement opposition. "No matter how you feel, it's not up to you to pass judgment on what he did. He has to spend the rest of his life trying to find a way to live with what happened tonight. Right now, Cory Robinson and that boy's parents are your greatest concern. They need you—calm, compassionate, and in control. Sooner or later, you'll have to find forgiveness, because if you don't, it will ruin the rest of your life."

The intrepid words reached deep into his anger. He remembered the prayer he had uttered before going to see the parents. *If there's any justification in this tragedy, please show me what it is.* He wanted to believe there was no rationalizing the death of any innocent victim, but it was *not* up to him to pass judgment on another. That judgment belonged to God. He thought about Cory Robinson and suddenly realized that God might indeed be showing him that He alone could bring about a miracle in the midst of an inexcusable tragedy.

Once more, Joe turned his attention to the nurse. "Notify the transplant team. If the kidney's a match, then it's a go. I'll be in OR Three, and I want to know *stat.*" Immediately, the nurse began to carry out the orders.

He squeezed Beth's hands before leaving for the operating room. "I love you, Beth Travis."

For the first time on that long night, a smile came to his face.

* * *

It was dawn when the transplant team wheeled Cory Robinson into the recovery room.

Still in his scrubs, Joe walked down the dimly lit corridor after surgery on the gunshot victim he had seen in the ER. He wanted to be sure Janet Robinson had received word that Cory had successfully come through his operation.

As he neared Cory's room, he heard voices coming from inside. He paused beside the door, then stopped and marveled at the sight within.

Beth sat beside the parents of the dead boy, their hands clinging to Janet Robinson's as stories of their children spilled back and forth. The room overflowed with a multitude of emotion, desperate feelings finding release amid the joy of one and sorrow of another. Beth glanced toward the door and, seeing Joe, slipped away unnoticed into the corridor.

"How's Cory?" she whispered.

"He's stable. I understand the tissue match was excellent. I wasn't sure how much longer he could keep hanging on."

"Don't forget, where the ability of a surgeon ends is where God and His miracles begin," she reminded him.

Joe put his arms around her. "I think *you're* some kind of miracle worker too, Mrs. Travis."

Beth grinned. "Not me. The real miracle workers are in there," she said, nodding in the direction of the two families. "What they're doing right now is the first step in healing, for all of them."

"I think I'm beginning to believe in miracles myself." He pulled her toward him and kissed her. "Somehow, I knew marrying you was a good idea. Let's go home."

CHAPTER 12

Callie Jordan waited impatiently inside Dr. Stephen Lewis's office. She glanced toward the large windows behind his desk where far in the distance she could see foaming white waves breaking onto the shore.

The door opened, and the young cardiologist went directly behind his desk. Callie knew from the look on his face the news wasn't good. "Callie," he began, "your echocardiogram is indicating that the ace inhibitors just aren't giving your heart enough push. Consequently, your heart failure is becoming unresponsive to your medications. But from your symptoms, you knew that too, didn't you?"

"Yes," she agreed quietly. "I also know I'm just about out of options."

The young man with the boyish face studied her carefully, taking mental note of the increasing bluish tint around her eyes from lack of sufficient oxygen. "As a nurse, I'm sure you're familiar with the progressive symptoms of failure—shortness of breath, fatigue, syncope, diaphoresis. And you've done exactly what you should so far as rest, exercise, and diet are concerned. Do you wear a heart failure bracelet?"

She pulled up her sleeve in answer, exposing the dangling bangle. "For longer than I care to remember."

Lewis glanced down at her chart once more, then walked around his desk and stood in front of her. "I understand you had rheumatic fever as a child, but the symptoms were misdiagnosed."

"That's right."

Lewis shook his head in pity. "That was an unfortunate error, Callie. But you know sooner or later, your best option is a transplant." "And that's miracle surgery, especially finding a proper donor," she said dolefully. Then her face brightened a little. "But I keep reminding myself that 'with God, all things are possible.'"

Lewis was amazed at her attitude despite her dismal prospects. He could not help but smile. "Callie, you moved all the way to South Carolina knowing your condition wasn't good. It seems to me it would have been so much easier for you to stay in Boston with your own cardiologist to look after you. What caused you to leave?"

Her expression began to wane. "I've lived in Boston all my life and I . . . I just needed a change of scenery."

The doctor sensed that was not all there was to it. But his interest concerning her was solely professional, and he reminded himself again that her personal life was none of his affair. "As things stand right now, I'm afraid you're going to have to take it easier. I hate to think of losing you at the hospital. It didn't take me long to discover what a good scrub nurse you are from the few times you've assisted me. You've only been here, what, a few months?" She nodded. "Well, you'll need to cut back on your hours. Can you afford to do that?"

"According to you, I can't afford *not* to."

He felt a growing appreciation for her. "I don't want you to lose hope, Callie. You have a lot of courage. I admire you for that."

"It's not *my* courage," she said plainly. "I have to believe if God has a reason for me to live, He'll provide a way. But I do have one request of you."

"Name it."

"That what we discuss stays strictly between us." "Done," Lewis said.

* * *

A distress signal sounded in Joe's mind as he replaced the phone. Snatching his jacket off the hook beside the door, he walked quickly through his outer office and hurried across the parking lot to the hospital.

Dr. Rick Stuart met him beside the nurses' station in the emergency room. "Do you know a Mrs"—he looked again at the name on the chart—"Elizabeth Adams?"

"Yeah," Joe said, "she's been admitted a number of times with acute pneumonia. I've seen her on several occasions. She's back with it again?"

"Yep, and she's asking for you. And she refuses to see anyone else *but* you." Joe's gregarious colleague grinned as he handed him the patient's thick chart. "Do you have time to take a look at her?"

Joe took the chart and smiled. "She's a very special lady. I'll make the time."

He pushed open the door of the exam room. "Lizzy, I thought we kicked you out of here for good the *last* time. Are you back to see more of our class act?"

"I can't seem to stay away from you, Dr. Travis," she returned in a raspy voice. "You're just too charming to leave alone." The rest of the words came in soft, breathy spurts.

At seventy-one, Lizzy Adams had more exuberance than the majority of patients her age whom Joe had treated, but today, her usually bright demeanor had been replaced with a pale, bluish appearance, and it was obvious she was having difficulty breathing. She began to cough.

"How long have you had that dry cough?" Joe asked, slipping the stethoscope into his ears.

"About a week," she answered in a feeble voice.

He listened intently to the increasing congestion in her lungs and then pulled the stethoscope away. "Lizzie, why didn't you come in sooner?"

She struggled for breath between bouts of coughing. "I was hoping this time, it might go away on its own."

"Well, not this time," he gently admonished her. "And not last time or the time before that. Lizzie, you can't mess around with this stuff. We're going to get some x-rays, and then you're going to have to be admitted. Today." She nodded in compliance. "But you need Dr. Wellington. He's the pulmonary specialist around here, and he's the one—"

"No, I want you, Dr. Travis. I don't want anyone else." "*Lizzy* . . ."

But she remained adamant.

Joe pulled the stethoscope from around his neck. "All right. It's a little unusual, but so are you." He grinned appreciatively.

Two hours later, Joe scanned the x-rays, confirming his diagnosis of pneumonia in both lungs. Then he went to ICU to Lizzie Adams' room. Intravenous lines dripped antibiotics into her veins, while nurses tried to make her as comfortable as possible. But as she struggled for each breath, it was apparent the effort was causing her to become weaker.

With growing concern, Joe leaned over the bed to examine her once more. He knew she would need to be placed on a ventilator again. Then, as though reading his mind, he heard her whisper, "Dr. Travis, no ventilator this time . . . please."

"Lizzie, I know how much you hate that, but it may be our only option if your breathing doesn't improve soon."

Her eyes remained fixed on him. "Please . . . no ventilator," she whispered again.

Joe straightened up beside the bed. How could he make such a promise? Her life could well be on the line without the dreaded procedure. She could die, and he would be responsible. He put his hands around hers and squeezed them. "Lizzy, you have to understand—"

"Dr. Travis . . . please . . . promise me."

Joe looked down into the anxious eyes. His heart melted. *Lord, it's up to You*, he prayed silently. "All right." He turned when a nurse came in. "I want her on continuous oximetry," he told her, charting the orders as he spoke. "If there's any change, call me."

* * *

The shrill ringing of the phone jarred Joe from a restless sleep. Before he could move his hand toward the night table, Beth had reached for the phone. He looked at the bedside clock. Dawn was an hour away.

He could hear her mumbling something into the receiver before turning toward him. "Joe, it's Mrs. Adams. She can barely breathe. They're afraid she's going into respiratory failure."

He took the phone and spoke to the nurse. "Get a portable chest x-ray and a blood gas, stat. I'll be right there." Five minutes later, he was dressed and kissing Beth good-bye.

* * *

Benjamin Jordan marched down the corridor of the medical complex, lost in thought and muttering to himself. In one hour, he was due to meet with the hospital board regarding more budget cuts. He was well aware of the possibility of losing much needed financial support for new programs, if certain funding wasn't met, and soon. If that didn't happen, Joe's proposal for a new physician's assistant training program would be shelved yet another year.

Jordan had promised to bring the innovative proposition to the Board at the next meeting, but remembered only this morning that Joe had all the files. Annoyed at his own negligence, he headed toward the younger surgeon's office for the needed documents.

He was met with silence after knocking on the locked door to Joe's office. His aggravation grew as he turned away. Then he saw Paul Martin striding down the corridor. "Paul!" he hailed his colleague. "Where's Joe? Why hasn't he come in yet?"

Paul Martin was all too familiar with the irascible nature of the petulant professor. He smiled as he purposefully slowed his pace. "I believe he's in ICU, Ben," he said as he came closer. "I understand he's been with a critically ill patient since early this morning."

Ben muttered something, then turning on his heels, stomped off in the direction of the intensive care unit. "And you have a nice day too," Paul called after him.

* * *

The nurse glanced up from her work just as Benjamin Jordan marched up to the nurses' station. Her only greeting was a familiar glare over the counter. "Good morning, Dr. Jor—"

"What room is Dr. Travis in?"

She looked at the patient roster beside her. "He's with Mrs. Adams, room four," she returned in a compliant voice. Jordan mumbled an expletive under his breath as he turned to make his way down the corridor to the designated room.

The door was shut, and he could hear nothing coming from the other side. He glanced impatiently at his watch and then pushed the door open, ignoring any privacy on behalf of the patient. Then, just as abruptly, he came to a halt inside the room.

Morning sunlight spilled across the bed where Jordan saw the young doctor sitting, his patient's hands clasped tightly in his own. Jordan could see the peaceful expression on the woman's face. Her eyes were closed, but a hint of a smile touched her lips. Whispered words drifted back to the older man, and he realized at once that Joe was praying.

"In Your healing hands, Father . . . watch over your servant, Lizzie . . . Thy will, not ours. Amen."

Jordan knew if he had never witnessed the source of Joe's strength before, he was witnessing it now. Embarrassed, he stepped outside the door, letting it close soundlessly behind him.

He walked more slowly down the corridor. For the first time in all the years he had known Joe Travis, he almost envied him a faith that had obviously become so great a part of his life and work. There must be some comfort, he reflected, in not depending solely on one's own understanding. Emotional strain was an unceasing factor in any surgeon's life. Surely, it had taken a toll on himself. Yet for Joe, turning that tension over to a higher being was something of value that seemed to sustain him, just as that same trust had always sustained Callie and his own wife.

Jordan shook his head in doubt by the time he approached the nurses' station. Faith in God was fine, but it was a crutch for which he had never felt the need. If he had not considered it necessary before to depend on a power beyond his own ability, what need was there for it now? No, all the deity he had ever found necessary laid within the established realm of medical science.

He leaned against the counter in preparation to leave a note for Joe. "What's the problem in room four?" he asked out of curiosity.

The nurse stood up and looked at Jordan. "It was the most remarkable thing I ever saw. Mrs. Adams has been admitted repeatedly with pneumonia, but she's deathly afraid of the ventilator. Last night, her condition continued to deteriorate until we finally had to call Dr. Travis. We had the ventilator in her room before he even got here because we knew he had to order it. But instead, he asked if any of us would stay by her bed and *pray* with her, and in half an hour, she literally began to breathe more easily. He's been with her ever since."

Jordan heard footsteps approaching from behind. He turned to see the tired, young doctor come to a stop beside him. Joe respectfully greeted his former mentor as the nurse placed Lizzie Adams' recent lab results on the counter in front of him.

"Looks like you won't need the ventilator for Mrs. Adams after all, Dr. Travis."

Joe smiled as he examined the results of the blood gases. "Not this time. She's going to be just fine without it."

"I never would have believed it if I hadn't seen it for myself," the nurse remarked. "I didn't think she'd make it through the night. And certainly not without a ventilator."

"Well, she *did* make it, but she wasn't alone." "She's lucky to have you for her doctor."

Joe returned the lab results to the admiring nurse. "Thank you for saying so, but actually I did very little for her." Then he turned his attention to Benjamin Jordan. "I'm sorry, Dr. Jordan, were you looking for me?"

Jordan had almost forgotten his mission as he was still trying to grasp the nurse's remarkable story. He looked at Joe with indignant eyes as they walked out of the ICU together. "How can you say you did 'very little' for that woman? She was obviously in dire distress, and *you saved her life!* You talk as if you left her completely alone!"

Joe came to a stop as the two men approached the entrance to the intensive care unit. "Not alone," he said with a smile, "just in better *hands.*"

* * *

Callie dropped the half-read letter on top of her kitchen counter.

Weather, work, hospital gossip, and general news from home was always a welcome inclusion in Beth's faithful correspondence. But when the news turned to her friend's picture perfect life with Joe Travis, this Callie could not endure. She had hoped against hope that leaving Boston meant leaving the pain. But all she had really left was her heart, after she thought she had packed everything.

Callie's own letters home were filled with nothing but cheerful news about her life in the beautiful, historic city of Charleston, her work at the hospital, her new associations. Never did she mention the rapid deterioration of her heart condition, that her doctor had insisted she cut back on her working hours, that her lifestyle, as restraining as it was in Boston, was becoming even more restrictive in Charleston. These things she would have longed to confide, but she would not risk having her father discover how serious her circumstances were actually becoming.

Tears came to her eyes as she glanced once more at the letter from Beth. Though she loved her friend, she could not forget that it was Beth who had unwittingly taken away from her the only thing she had ever wanted as badly as living a normal life.

CHAPTER 13

Autumn's colors were fading, and summer was only a pleasant memory. Cooler days had brought showers of falling leaves, a welcome change from the oppressive months of humid summer heat.

Joe stood beside the picture window in the living room, sipping contentedly on a steaming cup of tea. A smile edged at the corners of his mouth as he watched Beth painstakingly dig hole after hole to plant daffodil bulbs.

She wiped her forehead with the back of her gloved hand, then patted the earth securely over the last bulb. Struggling to her feet, she brushed the dirt from her jeans and walked toward the house.

Inside, a fire crackled in the fireplace, a warm and welcome alternative to the cold and overcast autumn afternoon. Joe turned when she walked into the living room. "Want a cup?" he offered, raising his mug in her direction. "I think there's some hot water left in the kettle."

She looked at him in mock severity, her mouth set in a firm line, her hands resting squarely on her hips. "Do you mean to tell me, Joseph Ian Travis, that because this is your day off, you've just been standing there at the window, watching me do all the work?"

"I wasn't just *standing*," he countered. "I was *admiring*."

She drew a deep breath. "Lucky for you I planted the last bulb. But just remember, those are *my* flowers you'll be enjoying in the spring."

He set the mug down on the table and took her into his arms. "I'll never forget."

"That's because I won't *let* you forget," she finished for him.

* * *

The intercom page sent Dr. Stephen Lewis racing down the corridor toward the emergency room. The call rang like doomsday in his mind—Callie Jordan had collapsed outside the OR. Her condition was worsening more rapidly than he had anticipated. He had hoped for her sake that her illness would not interfere with the upcoming holidays.

Beads of sweat had begun to band on Stephen's forehead as he burst through the exam room door, finding a rapid response team surrounding his patient on all sides. A nurse had already begun an IV, feverishly pushing medication through the hastily placed line. A resident stood by, ready with the defibrillation paddles. The screen on the cardiac monitor flickered with tracings of her sluggish electrical rhythm.

Stephen watched as the nurse continued with concentrated effort to restore Callie's breathing and heart function. His eyes remained glued to the cardiac monitor, mentally willing it to show a return to normal sinus rhythm.

With help from the oxygen, the ashen color of Callie's face slowly began to return to a pinkish hue. At length, the heart rate picked up and she started to cough. Stephen called a halt to the bagging, realizing she was breathing once more on her own.

Her eyes fluttered open as she gradually became more alert. He brushed strands of hair away from her forehead and smiled down at her. "So what's the big idea? If you wanted some time off, you could have just asked."

Callie found Stephen's quiet humor reassuring. He lifted the oxygen mask above her face. "I'm sorry," she mouthed the words.

"Oh, it's okay. I just happened to be rushing in this direction anyway. Aren't you lucky I once ran in a marathon?" He squeezed her hand and then turned to the resident. "Admit her to CCU. I'll be up in a few minutes to leave orders. And call my office to get her father's phone number—"

A slight tug on his sleeve interrupted his instructions. He looked at Callie again. The expression on her face grew more anxious as she shook her head *no.*

He took her hands in his own and squeezed them. "Callie, your condition requires me . . . " But he couldn't bring himself to finish the statement—not right now. "It's only fair to let your dad know what's going on, don't you agree? We've kept quiet until now."

She shook her head again as she struggled for breath and coughed. Her eyes pleaded with his.

"All right," he conceded. "I couldn't break a promise to you, even if I wanted to." He turned again to the resident. "Take her on up. I'll be there in a few minutes." His hand slipped away from Callie's as the attendants pushed the gurney through the door.

Alone in the exam room, Stephen leaned against the counter, gripping the cold metal edges. He took a deep breath. He hadn't had the courage to tell her how critical her condition had become, that he was prepared to put her on the transplant list as soon as he went upstairs to the cardiac unit. He closed his eyes and shuddered, still amazed she hadn't died on the stretcher. He feared he was losing his objectivity because the very thought of losing her . . .

He opened his eyes and looked down at his hands. They were still trembling.

* * *

Beth and Joe sat together on the couch in front of a crackling fire. Beth curled up beside her husband while Joe's head rested lazily against the back of the couch, his eyes closed in comfortable drowsiness. The dining room table was laden with dirty plates, goblets, and casserole dishes.

"Do you think I fixed enough food, Joe? It just didn't seem like so much after I got it all on the table. I hate to think I'd disappointed Paul."

"You fixed more than enough, and I'm envisioning leftovers for at least a week," Joe returned, eyes still closed. He squeezed her shoulder. "You did a beautiful job preparing your first Thanksgiving dinner. Paul was *not* disappointed. In fact, I think we sent him staggering out of here."

She settled comfortably against his chest once more. "I wish Dr. J. could have come. I hated to think of him spending a holiday alone since Callie couldn't be here. Did he ever tell you *why* she wasn't able to come home?"

"Nope, just that she was working and didn't feel she should take time off so soon after starting a new job."

Beth sat up and turned to look at her sleepy husband. "Joe, I haven't heard from Callie in weeks. Every time I've tried to call her, I can't reach her. She's never home. It's as though she wants nothing to do with any of us anymore."

Joe opened his eyes and took a deep breath. "I know how much you and Callie enjoy worrying about each other, but did it ever occur to you that maybe she's trying—even a little too hard—to make a life of her own? She has new friends, a new job, a lot more independence since she's not under the thumb of her father. Leave her alone for a little while."

"That seems so cruel."

"It's not cruel. Callie's experiencing autonomy for the first time in her life. She's not deserting you or me or her father or anyone else she cares about. She just wants to establish some independence."

Beth sighed wearily and tucked herself into Joe's arms once more. "I hope you're right. This is a side of Callie I've never seen before. And I can't help—"

"Worrying about her," Joe finished. "Enough is enough. Now how would you like to go and get a Christmas tree this weekend?"

"So soon? It's only Thanksgiving."

"I know. But as a kid, I didn't get to do much Christmas celebrating, and this is my first Christmas with my first girl. What do you say?"

Beth looked up and kissed him. "I say all right. You're buying."

* * *

Stephen Lewis walked into Callie's hospital room a week later with several boxes tucked under his arm. By some miracle, she had continued to rally from her near-death experience but had remained in the cardiac care unit on *status one*. The struggle to keep her stablewould go on until a suitable heart donor could be found.

Callie pushed herself up in bed when Stephen set the boxes on the bedside table. "What's this?" she asked, intrigued.

"I thought that since you were stuck here through Thanksgiving and won't be able to go home for Christmas," he said while opening the larger of the two boxes, "I might bring Christmas to you." He pulled out a little artificial evergreen tree and placed it on the table in front of her.

The improvement in her spirit came quickly. "Oh, Stephen, how thoughtful!" she exclaimed. "But you didn't have to go to all this trouble."

"Oh, yes, I did," he said, pushing the smaller box toward her. "It's also my job to make sure you keep a good attitude while you wait for a heart." Like a little girl, she opened the box and peered inside at the colorful array of ornaments, tinsel, and strings of tiny lights.

"I *have* been depressed," she said at last. "Missing Thanksgiving was bad enough. But Christmas is an awful time to be in the hospital." "And waiting is the hardest part. But in the meantime, we can do our best to make a real Boston Christmas in Charleston."

With a sad smile, she glanced at the vivid rays of sunlight streaming through the window beside the bed. "Can you make it snow too?"

"For you, I wish I could." Then his mood became more somber. "What did you tell your dad?"

"Just that I couldn't get away to come home."

Stephen shook his head. "Callie, how long are you going to put off telling him?"

"As long as I have to," she contended. "Please, Stephen, I know what I'm doing. You don't know my father like I do. He was all set to come out here, but I managed to convince him to stay home and go on with the usual plans."

Stephen sat down on the edge of the bed. "What are the *usual plans?*" he wanted to know.

She settled back against the pillows. "As long as I can remember, Dad's always hosted two elaborate parties every year for his students, one in the spring and the other at Christmas. He'd never admit it, but the reason for the one at Christmas is not exactly in keeping with his time-honored image."

Stephen grinned. "And what is that?"

"Dad knows how financially strapped most of his med students are, especially at this time of year. Some of them can't get away from the hospital to be with their families, and most of them can't afford the luxury of an elegant Christmas dinner. So he opens the door for any or all of his students to come to our house and have the grandest meal of their lives. Traditionally, they bring a little gift to show their appreciation." She smiled as she remembered. "To this day, Dad's kept every single gift his students have given him through the years."

"Sounds like your dad is a pretty impressive fellow."

"He is," she returned quietly. "He really is." Together, they delved into the box and began bringing out lights and decorations to adorn the little tree. "This will only be the second time in my life I can remember a Christmas with no snow."

"*No snow,*" Stephen repeated thoughtfully, passing her a string of lights. "I can only remember one Christmas in my life when there *was* snow. I was only nine or ten years old at the time and my grand-parents were living in Vermont . . . "

But her attentiveness to Stephen's story ebbed away as memories of another Christmas, a very special Christmas, crowded into her mind, a Christmas that for her didn't necessitate the traditional mantle of snow.

* * *

Maggie McCarran walked into Callie's bedroom just as the frustrated young woman thrust her hairbrush down on the dressing table. "Callie, girl, what's come over ya?"

Callie eyed herself with disgust as she looked into the mirror. "There's only so much you can do with limp, dishwater blonde hair!" she cried miserably.

Maggie stood behind the chair and quietly reached around her for the hairbrush. Methodically, she began brushing at the girl's wispy hair. "So you're afraid you're not goin' to look just right for Dr. Joe tonight, isthat it?"

Callie caught Maggie's knowing smile in the mirror. "You don't think anyone else knows, do you, Maggie?"

Maggie set the brush down and began twisting the delicate strandsof hair into a stylish French braid. "No, 'tis still a hallowed secret betweenyou and me," she said in the same hushed voice she had used to calm Callie's fears when Callie was a child.

From the mirror's reflection, Callie watched as Maggie worked. "It's just that this is his first Christmas here and I . . . I want everything to be just right for him."

"And it will be. Ya have nothin' ta worry about." She turned Callie'shead to one side as she continued with the braid. "Besides, with that beautiful red satin gown you're wearin', no one would notice if you werebald!"

Callie smiled. "Do you think Joe will like it?"

"He'll love it." Maggie continued to prattle as she deftly worked her way toward the end of the braid. "Funny there's no snow now. Coldenough to freeze my bones together, it is, but not a flake o' snow."

"I can't even remember one Christmas without snow. It doesn't really seem like Christmas without snow, does it, Maggie?"

The housekeeper put the final touches on Callie's now fashionable hairstyle. "The tradition of snow is nice this time o' year, but 'tis n't snowthat creates the real spirit of Christmas," Maggie commented sagely as sheapplied a little hairspray. "Christmas is all the love you can muster insideyour own heart . . . and then give away." She gently patted Callie's hair. "All done."

Callie admired the restoration of her hair. "Oh, Maggie, thank you!" Then through the open bedroom door, the two women heard the doorbell chimes. Callie pushed the chair away from the dressing table. "Do you think it's Joe?" she asked breathlessly.

"Only one way to find out."

Maggie left the room to answer the door. Callie listened from the top of the staircase until she heard the door open and then the sound of Joe Travis's friendly voice. With one last anxious glance in the mirror, she hurried out of the bedroom and with nervous poise made her way down the stairs.

Maggie had already taken Joe's coat and left the grand entrance hall as Callie descended the last few stairs. Smiling, Joe took her hand as she reached the last step. "Callie, you've never looked more beautiful. That dress is magnificent."

"I'm glad you like it." She felt her face flush as she withdrew her hand from his. "Would you like to go into the living room? I'm sure you know everyone."

Together, they walked into the elaborately ornamented room where small groups garnered among the exquisite furnishings. A sixteen-foot tree, garishly decorated with years of memorabilia and hundreds of tiny colorful lights, rose like an icon in front of the massive north windows. Genuine pine garland with red velvet sashes festooned the mantle and each icy windowsill. The air was filled with music, and the fragrance of scented candles mingled with the delicious aromas beginning to waft from the dining room.

Maggie bustled about the room, collecting coats and scarves from other newly arrived guests. It was then that Callie caught a glimpse of Joe's waning expression as he watched the housekeeper take a small gift from each visitor and place it on an antique table near the tree.

Callie knew Joe's financial resources had been meager at best. Though he had been to the Jordan estate many times since beginning his residency, this was his first Christmas with them. Now she could only imagine his humiliation from his lack of knowledge in bringing even a token gift, considering the high regard she knew he held for her father.

Sensing his acute embarrassment, she placed her hand on his arm, stroking the sleeve of the worn suit coat she had seen countless times before.

"It seems a little cold in here. Would you mind if we went into theden?" He said nothing as he trailed behind her.

In the smaller, more hospitable room, the fire crackled and hissed, offering warmth and intimacy that was absent in the rest of the house.

Decorated garland with tiny white lights draped the mantle above the fireplace while a matching lighted wreath hung on the stonewall above. Beneath, flickering candles of red and gold bestowed a shimmering radiance on a collection of miniature antique toys—a baby carriage, a teddybear, a turn of the century bicycle, and a wild stallion, whose celebratedcoming out was but once a year.

A smaller and less garish looking Christmas tree stood some feet apart from the fireplace. Red and gold bows perched among the fresh-smelling pine boughs, twinkling lights, strands of polished beaded garland and shining glass ornaments.

Callie noticed the tension in Joe's face beginning to ease apart fromthe crowd. Still, he remained quiet as he stood in front of the hearth, seemingly lost in contemplation of the beautiful decorations. Yet her heartbroke for him. How long would he have to struggle? She had often heardher father remark that with Joe's surgical aptitude and natural talent, hewould never remain impoverished a day in his professional life.

With these thoughts in mind, she glanced down at the shimmering evening dress. She thought about the hours that she had spent trying to perfect her appearance, mostly to be pleasing and noticeable to Joe. Yet now as she stood beside him, realizing his shame over the lack of a little gift, she felt as ostentatious as one of the gaudy ornaments hanging on thetree. Her superficial desires seemed shallow in light of the real disparity.Joe's wounded sense of worth was all that mattered.

At length, he glanced away from the fire and turned his attention toward the lavishly decorated floor-to-ceiling window. Through the icy glass only the faded green of the shrubbery offered a contrast to the frozenground outside, now spread barren and brown. "I . . . thought it usuallysnowed around Christmastime in Boston," he remarked awkwardly.

"It usually does," she returned and then, remembering her conversation with Maggie, added, "But with or without snow, it's still Christmas." He began to shake his head disparagingly. "Callie, I wish I'd known about the

gifts. There's no one I admire more than your father. No one has been better to me than he has. And here I am, without a single token of appreciation! If only—"

With boldness uncommon to her bashful nature, she reached down and slipped her hand into his. "The gratitude you feel for my father doesn't come packaged in a gift. It's in your heart. He knows that."

Slowly, his hand tightened around hers. The anxiety in his face began to relax into a dimpled smile. "I guess you're right. Thanks for reminding me." With a last squeeze to his hand, she walked toward the double oak doors. "Where are you going?" he asked.

"Upstairs to put on something a little more comfortable and a little less pretentious." She paused beside the door. "Maybe it'll snow next year."

* * *

"Callie, are you all right?"

Callie turned her head toward Stephen, suddenly realizing she had not heard a word of his story. "I'm sorry. I guess I wasn't paying very good attention."

His expression was full of understanding. "That's okay. I'm not the greatest of storytellers. Let's see how your tree looks." He bent down and pushed the plug into the wall socket, then sat down beside her to admire the tiny twinkling lights.

Callie smiled. "It's beautiful, Stephen. Thank you for being so considerate. Now please, tell me your story again."

At that moment, Stephen's pager began to beep. He stood up and shut it off. "*You* were just saved by the bell," he said with a grin, reaching for the phone beside the bed. "Next time, you might not be so lucky."

After Stephen returned his call and left the room, Callie leaned against the pillows and looked at the little tree. Bittersweet thoughts of Joe came back to her as she imagined him and Beth spending their first Christmas together. She envisioned them decorating their tree, wrapping gifts for each other, celebrating not only the season, but also their love.

Without warning, a miserable combination of fear, frustration, and jealousy produced a well of tears in her eyes as she thought about their happiness and her insurmountable problems. She had never felt so alone or frightened. There was no one here to whom she could unburden herself, no one who understood how deep and complicated her pain really was.

Weeping, she thrust her hands over her face and began to pour out her heart to God, knowing that He alone could give her the peace and courage she so sorely lacked.

# CHAPTER 14

"The roses are gorgeous," Beth Travis told her husband over the phone. She dropped the long white flower box on the floor. "But what's the occasion?"

"Does there have to be an occasion?" Joe propped his feet up on the desk while balancing the phone against his ear. "I just miss you." She sighed heavily. "At least you won't be on-call on next weekend. It's our first Christmas together, and I don't intend to celebrate that alone."

"I won't let you celebrate alone, and that's a promise," he assured her.

"Which reminds me of another promise, a very gracious promise I made to you when we got married, that I'd understand perfectly when you got tied up for days at a time. Well, I'm not feeling so gracious anymore."

"I tried to warn you about being a doctor's wife." "A little late now, wouldn't you say?"

Joe leaned his head against the back of the soft leather chair. "I have a few more rounds to make, and then I'm out of here. Except I'm not sure how fast I'll make it home," he said, glancing uneasily out the windows behind his desk. "It hasn't stopped snowing all day." "Well, be careful and just remember, I'll be right here, pining away for you."

He grinned again. "See that you do. I'll be home soon." Joe heard the click of the receiver. He replaced the phone, stood up, and slipped into his lab coat before pulling the door shut behind him.

* * *

A cold winter darkness had settled long before Joe finished his rounds. As he walked down the corridor toward the elevator, he heard the last thing he wanted to hear—his name being paged over the intercom.

"Dr. Travis, emergency room, stat. Dr. Joe Travis . . ." He groaned aloud, knowing he had no choice.

Forgoing the expected wait in front of the elevator, he rushed down several flights of stairs to the ground floor and made his way toward the emergency department.

He spotted Dr. Rick Stuart amid the trauma team members, hunkered over a near-lifeless body on the stretcher. Rick seemed relieved to see him. "He's bleeding into the chest. I could sure use your help."

"What happened?"

"Work accident," he explained. "Fragment injury, close to the heart."

Joe began to assist with the rest of the examination, concurring with Rick that the young man's probability of survival was slim. At best, it would take hours of surgery just to offer him that much. Joe glanced across the table at Rick, convinced his colleague was reading his thoughts. "Joe, I know you aren't the only trauma surgeon here. But you're the one I'd want in an emergency."

The two surgeons quickly finished their assessment. "Notify the team and the OR, stat," Joe instructed a nurse.

"I'd like to assist," Rick offered.

"That's fine. I'll go see the family, then meet you upstairs."

Joe tried to disguise his wearied expression as he walked into the waiting area. A nurse pointed out a noticeably distraught young woman sitting alone, nervously pulling at her hands. As Joe approached, she rose to her feet. "Mrs. Carson? I'm Dr. Travis. We'll be taking your husband to surgery in a few minutes."

"Will he be all right?" came the inevitable anxious question. "There's not much I can tell you right now," he said with tenderness. "He's bleeding internally, and his chest injuries are quite severe. But I promise you, we'll do all we can for him." When the woman visibly began to tremble, Joe eased her into a chair. "Is there someone you can call, someone who can wait with you?"

Anita Carson shook her head. "No . . . no one. We only moved here a few weeks ago, and we . . . we really don't know anyone."

He squeezed her arm. "Let me see what I can do." He knew time was running out for her husband, and he had to hurry. He stopped beside the nurses' station and motioned to nurse Jessie Gallagher. "Jess, who's on-call in the Counseling Center tonight?"

Jessie ran her finger down a list of names on a clipboard. "Beth," she said simply.

"Call her for me. Tell her I'm going to be tied up in surgery for the next few hours and ask her to come down and talk with Mrs. Carson." He started down the corridor. Then, suddenly remembering, he stopped and called to Jessie once more. "And tell her to be careful."

"I will." Jessie picked up the phone as Joe disappeared into the stairwell, taking the steps two at a time.

* * *

Beth tossed her purse across the seat and pulled the car door shut, shivering in the bitter cold as she turned the ignition. The wiper blades brushed aside the powdery snow from the windshield as she began to back down the driveway.

Street lamps along either side of the wide, deserted street made the heavily falling snow appear more like thick fog. She had come home from work only a few hours before, yet traces of her previous tire tracks were already gone. The wind had picked up, and now the blowing snow made driving more difficult. Snowplows had come down the road an hour earlier but had done their work practically for nothing.

Beth glanced at the dashboard clock as she eased the car onto the main road. She had sensed an urgency in Joe's message regarding the frightened wife of his critically injured patient. Somehow, she would have to hurry to get to the hospital. She pressed down on the accelerator a little harder.

* * *

Three miles down the expressway, the driver of a tractor-trailer fought to keep his huge rig centered in the right lane. Snow was falling fast, and whiteout conditions made visibility almost impossible. The truck radio blared with the latest blizzard warnings, which now included directives from the state police to clear the roads of all vehicles but emergency ones.

All at once, the driver realized the truck was sliding toward the median. Impulsively, he applied the brakes, which sent the huge rig skidding out of control. With a wrench to the steering wheel, the truck continued to swerve, hit the median, tipped, and finally jack-knifed across both northbound lanes of traffic. The driver, now unconscious and bleeding, slumped against the broken window, oblivious to the freezing air pouring in around him.

In minutes, cars, trucks, buses, and vans tried to skid to a halt to avoid collision with the crippled rig. But the crunch of steel against steel pierced the cold night air as one vehicle after another began to pile up.

* * *

The tedious surgery proceeded at a painstaking pace as the surgical team completed the third hour in the operating room. Exhausted, Joe tilted back his aching head. "I think we're about ready to close," he said at last. "What's his pressure?"

"126 over 64," the anesthesiologist informed him. "Incredible," Rick said, glancing across the table at Joe. "I never

would have believed it."

Joe shook his head. "It's still going to be a long night, and there aren't any guarantees he'll make it."

"But he wouldn't even be *alive* if it weren't for you."

Joe glanced up at his appreciative colleague, ready to refute the admiration he found more discomforting than complimentary, when a gowned nurse entered the operating room and stood inside the door. "Dr. Travis, Dr. Martin wanted to know how much longer you'll be."

"We're almost through."

"I'll tell him. He'd like to see you as soon as you're finished." "All right." Joe sighed wearily as he looked at his colleague across the table. "Is this night ever going to end?"

Rick's eyes crinkled under his mask. "You go see what the boss wants. I can finish closing."

Joe found the nurse in the outer room and pulled off his mask. "Where is Dr. Martin?" he asked in weary annoyance as he began to strip off his gown and gloves.

"He's in trauma room three."

A few minutes later, Joe stepped out of the elevator and walked toward the trauma room. The last thing he wanted was another emergency. What he really wanted was a hot bath, a warm bed, and the loving arms of his wife.

He pushed open the door, finding the older surgeon and a nurse standing on either side of the gurney. When the handsome whitehaired man glanced up, the expression on his face was overwhelmingly grieved.

A feeling of dread began to engulf Joe as he approached them. As the nurse stepped aside, he caught a glimpse of the patient. Then his dread turned to horror—he was looking at Beth.

Her head was swathed in bandages, her body punctured with tubes and intravenous lines, her breathing sustained only by means of a respirator. Paralyzed with disbelief, Joe stood helplessly by as the horrifying moment froze forever in his stricken mind.

Paul moved beside the distraught young doctor. "It happened on the expressway about two hours ago," he explained as gently as possible. "There was no way we could tell you since you were in surgery."

In stunned silence, Joe reached out a quivering hand and touched Beth's face. Blood had been cleaned away from deep lacerations left unstitched. He lifted her eyelids, exposing a fixed, unresponsive stare.

"The EEG?" His voice trembled in a hoarse whisper. "Joe . . . there's no brain activity."

He closed his eyes as he turned away. All that he had been taught as a doctor stood between himself and his wife. There was no need for exhaustive studies, no need for detailed prognosis. Her injuries far exceeded his means to save her.

But he wasn't ready to give her up. Not yet. Had Beth not told him once that where his ability as a surgeon ended was where God and His miracles began? Yes, that would be his hope. Still, he had to do all that lay within his power, however futile.

With renewed resolution, he turned toward Beth. "I want a complete cranial, CT scan, perfusion scan, another EEG—"

"Joe," Paul said quietly, his hand gripping Joe's shoulder, "she needs a miracle . . . not more tests."

His strained composure began to unravel as a frenzy of injustice tore him apart. He glanced fiercely in Paul's direction. "She's my wife! I want everything possible to be done for her!" Yet he could not ignore the truth. As his conviction weakened, he sank onto a stool beside the gurney and dropped his head into his hands. "I can't lose her, Paul . . . I can't."

Paul motioned to the nurse to leave the room. After the door closed, he put his hand again on Joe's shoulder in a hopeless effort to comfort him. "You know there's nothing more we can do for her." Slowly, he lifted his head and looked at Beth once more. He wrapped her motionless fingers around his own and pressed them against his cheek, now visibly wet with tears. "Don't ask me to play

God and pass some kind of judgment on her. Not now."

"All right," Paul said at last. "She'll have everything she needs."

* * *

Alone in the hospital chapel, Joe Travis wrestled with agonizing questions. Never in all the years he had practiced medicine had he faced a struggle of such personal enormity.

Why was his beloved wife lying upstairs in a hospital bed at the point of death when she had been en route to minister to another human being in need? Why would God have allowed this to happen, when Beth had dedicated herself to His service, to see to the welfare and healing of others? And most terribly of all, how . . . *how couldhe live with what he had done, knowing he was the one responsible for calling her out on a night like this?*

He buried his face in his hands as he struggled to accept what he knew as a doctor, yet desperately wanted to reject. He yearned for comfort, to cry out for help in the most inconsolable hour of his life, but it was a cry that could neither be answered nor comforted.

Never had he known a love like the one he shared with Beth. Long days at the hospital found him counting the very hours until he could be with her again. He pictured her as she must have been earlier that afternoon, busy with preparations for their first Christmas together. He imagined her in the kitchen, trying to plan dinner to be ready when he told her he would be home. How many times had he disappointed her? Nevertheless, she still greeted him with loving arms when he finally got there, and he had not yet been able to take her on a long-promised honeymoon.

Innumerable times, he had drawn upon her faith, particularly when his was running low; how much he had gleaned from watching her and praying with her. Because of Beth, his conception of God had changed dramatically, and he had come to depend on a divine power far outside of himself. Daily, he had observed how her trust in that same power sustained her decision-making ability to console and counsel the grieving people with whom she dealt.

No one had ever completely fulfilled his life as Beth had done. Now the mere thought of living without her was more than he could bear. For years, he had seen calamity touch the lives of his patients, and though it was lamentable, it was simply an unpleasant fact. Yet now that a cataclysm of this magnitude had touched *his* life, it had become a tragedy beyond description.

"Dear God," he prayed, more from despair than faith, "don't take her away from me . . . please don't take her away from me!

There's nothing I can do for her. I'm only a man, a tool in Your hands. But You . . . You can heal where I can't even help . . ."

The grief-stricken words came to a halt when he heard someone slip into the pew behind him. A large hand grasped his shoulder. "Joe,

I . . . I'm so terribly sorry." The voice belonged to Benjamin Jordan. "If there's anything I can do to help . . . "

Numbly, Joe shook his head. "There's nothing you can do.

There's nothing anyone can do."

Jordan struggled for words that invariably eluded him. "Joe, you know I've never put a lot of stock in . . . God . . . maybe because I've never seen a miracle. But if there is a God—" His words fell short when Joe turned around. For the first time, he saw the young man's face wet with tears.

"I know there's a God," Joe repeated almost in a whisper. Then cursing himself for his weakening faith, he added, "I'm just not sure where He is right now." He turned around again, gripping the pew in front of him as he leaned his head against his hands. Moments later, he heard heavy footsteps going toward the door.

Joe had no idea how much time had passed since he had stumbled through the doors of the little chapel. Now, as though lifting a great weight, he pulled himself to his feet.

Making his way toward the door, he stopped when he noticed a small plaque he had never read before. A brass wall lamp cast a dim light on the simple words:

Believe in the sun even when it is not shining, Believe in love, even when you are alone, Believe in God, even when He is silent.

Never had he felt so alone, and never had God been so silent.

CHAPTER 15

Dr. Stephen Lewis walked into Callie's room. When he sat down on the edge of the bed, she turned her face aside but not before he saw the outline of tears traced on her cheeks. "Callie, I know how difficult this is for you."

"And I know you're doing all you can."

He squeezed her hand, and she turned to look at him. "You're going through a lot right now. For most people, the waiting is worse than the surgery."

"I can understand that now. At least with the surgery comes hope."

"Have you talked to your father yet?" She shook her head. "How much longer are you going to put off telling him where you are?"

"I know him, Stephen. I know what he'll do. He'll drop everything just to come and sit here. He doesn't need to do that kind of worrying, and I don't need to watch it."

"Don't you think he has a right to know where you are? No one can be sure how long you'll be here. He's bound to find out one way or another." He squeezed her hand again. "Would you like me to call him for you?"

Callie looked miserable. "Not yet, Stephen. Please."

* * *

Early morning light filtered through the blinds in Beth's room.

Slumped across the edge of the bed, Joe Travis gradually awoke to the sound of water gurgling through the ventilator tubing and the steady beep of the cardiac monitor. The pervasive odor of antiseptic filled the room.

He lifted his head and focused bleary eyes on the motionless form of his wife. Then pulling himself out of the chair, he checked the ventilator, trach tube, IVs, and nasogastric tube. He watched while the same tracings moved steadily across the multicolored screens.

The door opened, and Dr. Harry Jamison, Beth's primary physician, quietly entered the room. "Morning, Joe," he greeted in a benevolent voice.

"Harry," he returned dully, accepting his colleague's outstretched hand. Joe moved past him and stood idly staring out the window through the blinds, waiting while Jamison made an identical check of the life support mechanisms.

Jamison had not yet confronted Joe with regard to Beth's continuation of life support. On her admission, he had privately received word from Paul Martin that Joe was in no frame of mind to make any decisions yet; thus, he had not pressed him.

At length, he turned away from his patient. "Everything's running normally, Joe. But what about you?"

"What about me?"

"You haven't left this room for days. Is there anything I can do for you right now?"

Joe was touched by the man's compassion and insight, a quality that he saw in too few of his colleagues. "I appreciate that, but no. Thanks anyway." The two men shook hands once more before Jamison left the room.

Joe sat down in the chair next to the bed. He laid his head beside Beth's and closed his eyes, stretching his hand toward hers until he grasped the limp fingers in his own. "Beth . . . can you ever forgive me?" he whispered. "I need you so much. Don't you know how much I need you?"

* * *

Ben Jordan sat behind the desk in his office, a stack of paperwork before him, and no motivation to begin the task. His mind was on Joe Travis and a loathing for himself because of his inability to express his heartbreak to the young man who had been as close to him as a son.

Benjamin Jordan had been a surgeon for over thirty years. In spite of his arrogance and overbearing nature, patients and students held him in high regard because somewhere beneath the no-nonsense exterior, they sensed he cared about them.

But he had no ability to show the affection he felt. He had trained his students to implement total impartiality toward their patients, not disinterest, but objective detachment. He wholly supported the concept of patient objectivity for obvious clinical reasons, but deep down, he knew a large component of the principle stemmed from his own inadequacy. Now he felt that helplessness more acutely than ever before as he considered the tragedy Joe was facing.

Maybe he would talk with him tomorrow. Yes, tomorrow, he would go to Beth's room, and one way or another, Joe would know he was hurting for him as much as any father could hurt for his son.

* * *

Night had fallen when Paul Martin stopped inside the doorway of Beth Travis's room. He paused to listen while Joe spoke poignant words of encouragement into his wife's unhearing ears. He listened to the sound of his voice, a voice contrived with hope and expectation.

Day after day, Paul's heart was torn as he observed the devotion of the young doctor at her bedside. The windowsill and table were laden with flowers he had brought her, and Christmas cards from friends and colleagues adorned the wall opposite her bed. A large poinsettia sat in one corner of the room.

Buoying himself, Paul stepped into the room. Joe rose from the chair beside the bed, his hand still grasping the limp one that lay in his own. "Paul's here to see you," he whispered into an unconscious ear.

Dutifully, Paul stroked the pale, sunken cheek. "We're praying for you, Beth, every day." Then he glanced across the bed at Joe. "Can I see you for a minute?"

Joe turned toward the bed once more and kissed Beth on the forehead. As usual, he paused for a moment afterward, waiting, hoping for any sign of response. When there was none, he followed Paul into the corridor.

"If you're worried about my schedule—"

"That's all been taken care of," Paul interrupted. "What I'm worried about is you."

"I'm all right."

"You're not all right. You're exhausted. You've hardly left this room aside from your on-call duty. No one expects you to be here at all hours of the day and night."

Joe leaned against the wall and closed his eyes. There was no use pretending. "Paul, I need to be here. If I left now and something happened—"

"If you left now, you'd have to go home and think. And you don't want to think about the inevitable."

Joe's wearied face took on an angry expression. "I know what the odds are," he returned defensively. "I also believe that miracles do happen."

"Yes, miracles do happen," Paul agreed. "But how long do you think Beth can go on waiting for a miracle God may not see fit to send?"

Joe drew a deep breath. "Somehow, I thought you'd see things a little differently than most."

Paul hesitated for a moment. "I'm not trying to discourage your faith, Joe. I just want you to prepare yourself emotionally for whatever decisions you may have to make for Beth. Fatigue is wearing you down. It can impede your judgment. And you may not be as prepared as you need to be when the time comes . . . " He could not bring himself to finish what he knew needed to be said.

"You're telling me to let her go. You want me to give up on her.

I won't do it."

Paul shook his head. "I'm not telling you that, Joe. That's something you're going to have to decide. I'm only asking you not to overlook your own health." The unyielding expression on the younger man's face did not change. With a sigh, Paul turned to leave. "I'm going home. I'll be there if you need me."

"And I'll be right here," Joe returned.

*　*　*

Benjamin Jordan walked with determined steps toward the intensive care unit, propelled not only by his conscience, but for his tremendous affection for Joe Travis. He felt a strong sense of need to do something, anything, for the young man whose life had, with no warning, been turned upside down.

Once inside the unit, he sat down to check Beth Travis's file. Hoping against hope for better news than he expected, he scanned the nurses' notes. Almost every entry was the same—patient remains comatose; no change.

A feeling of cowardice overwhelmed him as he left the nurses' station and walked down the corridor toward Beth's room. Memories stalked his mind. As a young intern, he had walked these same steps, experienced the same pain, yet in another time. Nevertheless, he could not think about that now.

He came to Beth's room, pausing just outside the door. He could see Joe sitting on the edge of the bed, brushing strands of dark hair away from her closed eyes. He lingered in the doorway before coming into the room. "Joe?"

The young man turned. Jordan was stunned at the bleary eyes and several days' growth of beard that greeted him. A forgotten tie hung loosely around the open collar of Joe's wrinkled shirt. In spite of his bone weariness, Jordan watched as he respectfully rose to his feet.

"Dr. Jordan, come in."

Jordan made his way to the bedside. He had not seen Beth since the night of the accident, and now he hardly recognized the young woman he had known since her childhood. Already, her appearance had altered considerably. The bones of her still-bruised face were more prominent, her cheeks hollow and sunken, the skin stretched a shiny white across her wasted body.

How has Joe held up this long? Jordan wondered in amazement. "Well, I . . . I just wanted to stop by to . . . Joe, if there's anything you need, anything at all . . . "

An indulgent smile creased the dark circles beneath Joe's eyes. "I appreciate that, Dr. Jordan. I'm fine. Really I am."

With a slight nod of acknowledgement, Jordan left the room and hastily made his way down the corridor.

* * *

"Stephen, it's beautiful. Thank you." Callie Jordan let the expensive silk scarf drift through her fingers after pulling it out of the elegantly wrapped gift box. "How did you know I love scarves?" "Lucky guess," Stephen said with a grin. Yet the gift was more significant than his naïve smile suggested. For after her surgery, Callie would welcome the scarf to conceal the long scar she would carry from that day forward. But for now, the expression on the young doctor's face carried nothing but optimism. "You can wear that your first night out of here."

She smiled in a contrived act of reassurance for his sake. He didn't seem to mind her growing dependence on him. She had never anticipated being in the hospital during Christmas. Yet so far, Stephen had managed to help her endure the lonely holidays, the first ones she had ever spent away from home.

She knew she couldn't put off telling her father much longer about her increasingly critical condition. She regretted not heeding Stephen's advice to tell him at the time of her admission weeks before. Telling him now seemed almost cruel.

Stephen sat up in the chair and leaned toward her. "Can I guess what you're thinking about?"

"Probably. And I suppose I should get it over with." "Would you prefer if I did it for you?"

"No. Hard as it is, it would still be better coming from me." She struggled to take a simple breath, but the effort was becoming progressively more difficult.

CHAPTER 16

Joe slumped in the chair beside Beth's hospital bed, his head cradled in his hands.

As the endless days and nights had passed, expectation had slowly given way to resignation, anticipation given to despair. Joe Travis struggled with a burden heavier than any he had ever borne.

He had become oblivious to the activity around him—the constant presence of the nurses, the drone of the machines, the friends and colleagues who stopped by to offer comfort. Christmas had come and gone without his awareness.

A slight knock on the door startled him as he looked up and watched Evan Richards step inside.

"Joe, please forgive me for not coming before now. I was out of town visiting my family and only found out last night what happened." The words came quickly and earnestly.

Joe rose from the chair. "I'm glad you're here now."

Evan stood beside the bed and, without hesitation, reached down and took Beth's hands in both of his own. Joe admired his straightforwardness, grateful that he was not repulsed by the deteriorating appearance of his once-beautiful wife.

Evan bowed his head and began to pray quietly while still holding Beth's limp hands. When he finished, he gently placed them at her sides once more before turning his attention to Joe.

They sat down in two chairs near the window. The frosted edges of the pane framed swirling snow flurries that spun from a gray sky. "Joe," Evan began, "you can take comfort knowing that Beth is experiencing no pain. She's not hurting, she's not worrying, she's not distressed with decision making."

Joe marveled at the young pastor's insightful parallel of Beth's cataleptic condition with that of his own conscious suffering.

Richards continued. "The one I'm really concerned about is you."

Joe looked at the man incredulously. "I'm not the one who needs prayer, Evan."

"You are just the one who needs prayer, Joe. You're the one who's bearing the brunt of this. And I believe you're the one, too, who might be questioning why God would allow something like this to happen."

It seemed as though Evan Richards could see to the very back of his mind. Yes, he had done nothing but question why God would permit this tragedy, had done nothing but blame himself for it ever having happened in the first place. He questioned if he even believed any longer, questioned if he even wanted to believe any longer.

"Then tell me why, Evan. Why would God allow this?"

Richards gazed out the cold window for a moment before answering. "I can't tell you that, Joe. I can't tell you because I'm only a man, like you, not an all-knowing God, but I can tell you that you must cling to the faith you have, even if you feel there's not much of it left. God has a purpose.

"From the Bible what agony did Job go through that you haven't felt yourself? And he questioned God. But he also clung to his faith when he declared, 'Though He slay me, yet will I trust in Him.'"

Despite the sincerity of the words, anger surged inside of Joe. He looked hard at Richards. "At least you aren't afraid to admit you don't have the answer. But you talk about purpose. What possible purpose could be served by this?" He lowered his voice. "Beth was on her way to the hospital to minister to a woman in need that night! She was on her way here, driving through a blizzard, because I—" A confession of his deepest guilt almost escaped in the midst of the angry words, but he said nothing more, only leaned against the back of the chair and watched as another dismal night drew on.

Evan understood the bitter conflict going on inside his friend as he glanced at Beth's unmoving form. "Did you ever observe Beth at work with the people she dealt with?"

"Yes, many times."

"And do you recall how she handled such sensitive situations?" Joe was silent, remembering the times he had watched her at work, remembering the tender compassion she had displayed, yet at the same time, daring to have the gentle courage to say what had to be said. "Beth had the gift of giving herself to others, wholly and completely, without a thought for herself. It was her life," Joe finished in a quiet voice.

"And even now," Evan added, "she can do the same thing. I believe that's something she would want to do. Something she would want you to allow her to do."

Letting Beth go was not a new deliberation for Joe, yet it was something he had been unable to bring himself to act upon. What was he really waiting for? Medical miracles that were well beyond his ability to accomplish? Divine miracles that in all probability were never going to occur?

As a doctor, he knew her time was running out, but as the man who loved her, how could he let her go?

* * *

Evan Richards had gone, yet Joe could not remember his leaving. He could not escape their conversation, could not escape the guilt he felt so intensely, could not escape the questions that had riddled his mind for almost two weeks, questions for which there were no simple answers.

How much longer could he—or should he—keep Beth alive by artificial means? Was he simply postponing death or prolonging a hopeless existence? In his own practice, he had struggled with these questions before, but never on an emotional level such as this.

What was the real purpose of medical care? Was he selfishly clinging to her not only because he loved her, but because it was his own stubborn nature not to give up? If that was the case, then how much consideration was for himself and how much was for Beth?

But of all the uncertainty with which he struggled, none was worse than this: who was he to play God, holding her life in his hands? Could he let her go and live with that decision the rest of his life? And where was God, the God who continued to remain so distant and silent?

With every glance at Beth, memories of his mother came to his mind. Her loss had prompted Joe to become more determined than ever to be the best physician he could possibly be. He wanted to be the one who could defy the odds, at least with the help of God. But where was that help . . .

"Any change?"

Joe lifted his head and saw Paul Martin standing inside the doorway. He leaned forward and let his head sink into his hands once more. "No."

Paul gazed with pity at the helpless young woman. He stood beside Joe, resting his hand on the young man's shoulder. He didn't know himself how much longer he could endure seeing his friend in the throes of such agony. What he had come to say had to be said. Now he prayed for the right words.

"If I were Beth," he began gently, "before I was subjected to any more procedures, any more intubations, any more tubes and needles, I think I would choose death over this kind of existence. Even if her respiratory function returned to normal, I don't believe she would want to live like this."

Deep inside, Joe believed it too. All the neurological tests had confirmed the same diagnosis—irreparable damage to the brain stem. For all intent and purpose, Beth had died on the road on her way to the hospital. Her heart merely continued to beat.

Joe rose from the chair and stood beside the window, gazing up at the night sky in a futile attempt to banish tears that welled in his eyes. "She's not just another patient, Paul. *She's my wife!*"

"Even so, you're clinging to emotion rather than reason. You're *feeling*, not *thinking*. And you have to *think* about Beth." her!"

"I *am* thinking about Beth! I can't think of anything else but "But you're allowing *how you feel* to postpone making a decision for her."

Joe turned around, the stricken look on his face pale from weeks of exhaustion. "I was trained to be a *healer!*" he cried, thrusting taut hands outward in frustration. "How am I supposed to accept what I *can't do?*"

Suddenly, he began to weep, and Paul knew he had reached the breaking point. Joe stumbled toward him, and the older man seized the trembling young doctor in a tight embrace. He struggled to steady his voice. "Reconciling the facts with how you feel is the hardest part of this profession, my friend."

Joe was beyond any sense of indignity as he openly wept, clinging grimly to the older man. Time and again, he had drawn upon Paul's counsel and direction throughout their professional association. But never had he been so grateful for the personal solace offered by his superior, an empathy he had longed to experience with his own father.

At length, he pulled away, awkwardly wiping away the tears from his face. "Paul," he began in a hollow voice, "how do I *know . . .* "

Paul's eyes trailed to Beth's gaunt figure. "Joe, from my own experience I've come to believe that when it's a question of how to cure, how to correct a problem, or how to improve the quality of a patient's life, *that's* when we do what we're trained to do. But when there's no more curing to be done, no possible way to improve on life, that's when we have to let go, and leave that decision in God's hands."

"God's hands," Joe repeated, his voice trembling with anger this time. "What kind of God would allow this kind of suffering? What did Beth ever do to deserve this?"

"You're asking the wrong question, Joe. God isn't sitting in judgment, deciding whom He's going to punish or reward. He's right here with us, ready to help us cope with our tragedies, if we can just get beyond the anger. You're frustrated that God hasn't answered your prayers in the way you expected Him to. Now is the time to ask that His will be done."

"His will? Can you honestly tell me this is His will?"

Paul understood the anger, the grief, the bitter feelings. "No, I can't tell you that, but I *can* tell you that faith isn't merely accepting the good that God sends. It's accepting what He sees *fit* to send. Sometimes, trials come into our lives for reasons known only to Him, but He doesn't leave us to struggle alone with them. He *will* restore us, Joe. And in spite of everything that's happened, remember, only God can bring a miracle out of a tragedy. Beth loved you, but this isn't what she'd want, not for herself, and definitely not for you."

He watched as Joe turned away, knowing he had yet to say the hardest words of all. "Beth lived by the creed she taught others, and she was willing for her own organs to be donated when the time came. But you know as well as I do that time is running out for that option. *Do you intend to honor her wishes?*"

Wearily, Joe rested his head on his arm against the cold window. "The papers have all been signed."

Surprised, Paul realized Joe had already made the heartbreaking decision, his argument apparently directed more toward himself than toward Paul. "I'll take care of the arrangements." The older man looked tenderly at Beth once more. The tears in his own eyes weren't there for the first time. "If you can take any comfort at all, remember what you're allowing her to do is the answer to someone's prayer."

Joe turned to look at Paul once more. "If that's true . . . what's the answer to mine?"

* * *

Joe eased himself onto the side of the bed after Paul left the room. As he gazed at Beth's face, the older man's words sank deep into his mind. *She wouldn't want to live like this.* Though he knew it was true, he steeled himself against the accursed words—words that condemned him to a life without her.

Dyin' can't be no worse than livin' a life that's no life at all, Mattie Walker had once told him. He picked up Beth's hand and folded the motionless fingers over his own. This was no life for her. But what would the rest of his life be without her?

Tears slid from his closed eyes as he carefully put his arms around her. With a deep, shuddering breath, he kissed her for the last time.

* * *

Ben Jordan walked as if in a daze down the hospital corridor after leaving his office. Callie's phone call a few hours earlier loomed monumental in his mind. *Transplant list. She had been placed on the transplant list and had not told him until now!* He shook his head, trying to absorb the inevitable, but still shocking news and subsequent explanation her cardiologist had offered shortly afterward.

As he approached the nurses' station at the end of the corridor, he could see Paul Martin leaning over the desk. "Have you notified Dr. Stuart to take any calls for Dr. Travis tonight?" Paul was asking the nurse behind the desk.

The woman replaced the phone in her hand. "I haven't been able to locate him yet."

Paul sighed heavily. "Keep trying."

As the nurse picked up the phone once more, Paul turned toward a wide-eyed Jordan. "Joe consented to discontinue Beth's life support tonight."

"Is she . . . ?" He couldn't bring himself to say the words. "Preparations are being made for organ donation right now." "Where's Joe?"

"I'm not sure. He was with Beth until a short while ago. I . . . don't think he wants to be around when they actually take her into surgery."

Jordan's mind was reeling as he tried to marshal his thoughts. "Paul, I . . . I have some urgent business to attend to out of town. It's imperative that I leave right away."

"Is there anything I can do?"

Jordan straightened his shoulders. "No . . . no, I don't think so." He turned to leave and then paused, looking at Paul again. "Just take care of Joe."

As he hurried across the parking lot toward his office, he shuddered at the prospect of what was going through his mind. What he had to do, he had to do at once. Time was of the essence and it was quickly running out.

CHAPTER 17

Joe Travis wanted only to escape. Distraught with grief and overwhelmed by weeks of exhaustion, personal devastation superseded his normal sense of responsibility. He had to escape. Somewhere. Anywhere.

Blindly, he made his way through the maze of corridors until he came to the lobby and pushed open the heavy glass doors. A blast of arctic cold stopped him outside the entrance to the hospital. Snow was falling, and he cursed the elements of nature that he held accountable for his shattered world. Then he began to walk, faster and still faster until at last he broke into a frenetic run down the snow-covered sidewalks, his sole destination to be as far from the misery of the hospital as he could get.

He kept running, past darkened buildings, past lone street lamps that cast pale streams of light across deserted streets, past rows of magnificently decorated houses, past snow-laden trees and hedges. The sound of his shoes crunched on frozen slush and new fallen snow. A dog barked somewhere in the distance.

He kept running. He could hear the sound of firecrackers far off in the streets. Church bells began to toll a haunting midnight hour. Only now did he realize it was New Year's Eve.

Exhaustion had left him unprepared for reality. For all his knowledge as a doctor, for all his experience and skill, how could he accept that he had been powerless to save the one person he loved as much as life itself?

He had clung to the hope that maybe, *maybe*, God would provide the miracle he had been incapable of achieving. But there had been no miracle. *Oh, if only he hadn't called her out that night!*

As he ran, Joe Travis became certain of one thing: his wife would be alive tonight if it had not been for him. Now as never before, he felt the terrible burden of blame resting solely on him.

Stumbling through tears that blinded his eyes, he came to a sudden stop beside a tree. With outstretched arms, he leaned heavily against it, breathless as he panted the frigid night air. And then, exhausted, he sank to his knees in the snow.

He buried his face in his hands as a paralyzing awareness of what he had done overcame him. Wrenching sobs tore from his throat. Never in his life had he felt such emptiness. *"Oh, God, how could You let this happen?"* he cried angrily through clenched fists covering his face. *"How do You expect me to go on without her?"*

In foolish expectation, he looked up at the night sky. Glistening flakes of snow fell in dreamlike fashion around him, indifferent to his suffering as they melted with the tears on his face. In complete despair, he cried aloud, "What more do You *want* from me?"

And then, in the midst of his anguish, the piercing sound of his beeper erupted inside his jacket. The shrill noise in the cold night air jarred him back to his senses and at the same time unleashed an escalating rage deep inside him.

For all his pain and agony, someone needed him. Though his private world was in ruins, he could not even be left alone to grieve. He was still expected to play the part of the healer, in spite of his own loss and despair.

He struggled to his feet and reached inside his coat pocket. Unable to restrain his anger, he grabbed the small black instrument and hurled it through the freezing air until the intruding mechanism fell lost somewhere in the deepening snow.

He leaned his back against the tree and closed his eyes. His life was out of control. For him, everything that mattered had died with

Beth tonight. His faith in God, even his confidence in his own abilities, began to disintegrate into a burgeoning anger—an anger of injustice he could neither endure nor understand.

Suddenly, he became aware that he was shivering. In his haste to leave the hospital, he had forgotten his overcoat. He glanced about him and realized for the first time he was several miles away from the medical complex in a deserted park somewhere within the city.

Wearily, he began to trudge in the direction of the hospital once more.

* * *

Snow was falling heavily when Ben Jordan boarded the private chartered airplane. As the plane roared into the frozen night, he settled against the back of the seat, but he could not settle his thoughts so easily.

* * *

"I'm afraid she's nearing the end stages of congestive heart failure," Dr. Stephen Lewis had explained to him over the phone earlier that evening. His voice had evinced as much caring as proficiency.

"Then she really doesn't have much time left, does she?" Jordan asked.

"No, sir, I'm afraid she doesn't. She's in good physical condition, butshe won't survive much longer without surgery."

At that point, Jordan had shielded his misty eyes. "I can't believe she never told me . . . she never told me how bad her condition had become!I had no idea you'd placed her on the transplant list."

"I'm sorry you had to find out so late," Lewis had said with empathy. "It was Callie's wish that you not be told. She was only trying to spareyou the worry of knowing."

Jordan read more than concern in the young man's voice. "And without the surgery, she has no chance whatsoever?"

"In my opinion, no chance at all." "And the tests have all been completed?""All the preliminary ones . . . "

* * *

Ben Jordan jolted awake when the plane began its descent into Charleston. He glanced out the window, watching as the runway rose to meet the wheels of the small craft until it finally taxied to a stop.

An hour later, he pushed through the doors of the hospital's cardiac care unit. He crept to his daughter's bedside. "Callie? Can you hear me?"

Callie slowly turned her head toward the familiar voice. She tried to acknowledge him with her eyes above the oxygen mask. She blinked blearily from the heavy sedation she had been given.

"You're going to be all right," he whispered, squeezing her hand. "I've taken care of everything."

He heard footsteps and turned around to see a wearied looking young man walk into the room with a stethoscope slung around his neck. Extending his hand, he said, "You must be Dr. Jordan. I'm Stephen Lewis."

"I'm glad to meet you, Doctor." Jordan was amazed as he shook hands with the young surgeon. His youthful appearance didn't coincide with his unprecedented reputation.

Lewis leaned over the bed to check his patient once more, speaking to her in soft, reassuring tones. When he straightened, he motioned for Jordan to follow him outside to the nurses' station. "I can only imagine how you feel right now, but thanks to you, I believe she has a good chance."

"What sacrifice would you not make for your only child?" Jordan put his hand on the young man's arm. "Whatever it takes . . . do it."

A nurse behind the desk answered a ringing telephone and then nodded at Lewis. "The team's ready, Dr. Lewis. They're standing by in OR Three."

Lewis clasped Jordan's hand. "I'll see you right after surgery."

* * *

Benjamin Jordan paced the long corridors of the large, unfamiliar hospital, glancing frequently at the clocks mounted high on the walls. Stephen Lewis had invited him to observe Callie's surgery from the dome, but Jordan had declined. Now as he turned another corner, he found himself once again outside the operating rooms.

He paused near the entrance doors to the surgical suites. Nurses clad in green scrub gowns passed him. Technicians pushed equipment down the hall. Surgical personnel passed back and forth through the double doors.

Yet for all his expertise with hospital protocol, Benjamin Jordan felt completely out of place. He was a surgeon of remarkable ability, but here he had no reputation, no mark of recognition. To those who benignly passed him on either side, he was merely an unrecognizable outsider in a world beyond medicine.

He felt a helpless sense of insignificance, alone and dependent on strangers, while the last member of his family lay on an operating table behind the gray steel doors. As never before, Benjamin Jordan understood what a source of comfort Joe Travis had been to his patients and their families.

Though his mind was set on the progress of his daughter's surgery, he could not stop thinking about Joe. Some nine hundred miles away, the young man he had taken to his own heart years earlier was in the throes of the worst tragedy he had ever encountered. He could not help but wonder if Joe's faith in his God was deep enough to sustain him through such a crisis. He knew the emotional bond between Joe and Beth had been especially strong. How would the loss of such a union affect the rest of his life?

Jordan was unsure how he would face the young surgeon when he returned to Boston. He turned away from the operating room doors, trying to put a stop to the disquieting thoughts he could not ignore.

He turned to pace down the long corridor again when the steel doors opened. He looked back in time to see Stephen Lewis emerging. His green scrubs were visibly wet with perspiration, but his steps seemed almost lively in spite of his weariness. When he spied Ben Jordan, he hurried to catch up.

Stephen put his hand on his shoulder before he could utter a word. "She came through just fine, Dr. Jordan. Everything looks good."

Jordan breathed a sigh of relief as he humbly grasped the young surgeon's hand. "I . . . I don't know how to thank you."

With an unassuming smile, Lewis asked, "Would you like to see her now, or would you rather wait until she's back in CCU?"

"Oh, no, I'll . . . I'll wait." He slowly withdrew his hand. "Thank you. Thank you again." It had been many years since Jordan felt tears welling in his eyes. Excusing himself, he turned and walked quickly down the corridor.

* * *

A full moon had risen and dazzled in a ghostly whiteness outside the window of the cardiac care unit where Benjamin Jordan dozed in a chair beside Callie's bed. The ventilator hissed softly, the cardiac monitor beeped methodically, all reassuring sounds as he drifted in and out of sleep.

Stephen Lewis walked past the nurses' station toward Callie's room. Less than twenty-four hours had passed since the surgery. Once outside her room, he paused in the doorway. His heart was touched as he observed Dr. Ben Jordan at his daughter's bedside. For the moment, he couldn't envision him as a distinguished professor of surgery but simply a father encumbered by worry for his only child.

Lewis gowned in customary sterile attire, then walked to the bed to examine his patient. As Jordan struggled to a sitting position, Callie's eyes slowly fluttered and opened. Stephen looked down at his patient, his own eyes crinkling with a hidden smile beneath the protective mask. "It would appear that I came by right on schedule." "I believe you did, Doctor," Jordan answered under his own mask. He squeezed Callie's hand.

Lewis glanced at Jordan. "How soon do you suppose it'll be before she begins instructing us about patient care?"

CHAPTER 18

Paul Martin closed the front door to Joe's house after thanking the caller for another prepared dish of food. He set it among countless others that would remained untouched on the kitchen counter.

Friends and colleagues at Beth's funeral earlier that afternoon had filled the small church almost beyond its capacity. Despite the bitter cold, most of the mourners had been present at the cemetery. Later, some had stopped by the house with food and offerings of sympathy to Joe once more. Now all was quiet but for the sputtering and crackling of burning wood.

Paul returned from the kitchen to find Joe sitting, just as he had for the past few hours, hunched forward in an armchair beside the fireplace. The light from the flames flickered across his expressionless face, but Paul saw the suffering in his eyes.

He sat down in the chair next to Joe, from whom there was no movement except the occasional clenching and unclenching of his fists.

"I don't think I can handle this." Joe fought to keep his voice steady as he uttered the wrenching words. A part of himself had been buried alongside his wife on the iron gray afternoon. With her had gone the joy of his life, his shared future, and a faith expelled by an escalating anger. Only loneliness, inexpressible grief, and unanswered questions remained behind.

Paul sighed with understanding. "I didn't think I could handle it at first after Sarah died either."

Joe looked away. "What did you do?"

Paul leaned against the back of the chair and watched the flames. "I cried—a lot. Oh, I was able to put on an acceptable front when I had to be around other people. But when I came home at night, it was the same thing all over again." He looked at Joe, whose face was still turned aside. "I couldn't see it then, but I know now that by allowing myself that time to grieve, to release those feelings when I was alone, actually helped me to heal."

Joe's shoulders heaved once, and then he was still. "If I only hadn't asked that she come in that night," he said in an agonized whisper. Then in a more audible and angry tone, he added, "As long as I live, I'll never forgive myself, *or God.*"

"Joe, you can't blame yourself for Beth's accident any more than you can blame God for what happened."

"Oh, no?" Joe turned sharply to look at him. His eyes were wet. "Where was He when Beth was *dying*? I *begged* Him for a miracle, and what did I get? *Nothing!* He left me alone as surely as He left Beth alone to die."

Vividly, Paul remembered his own struggles but knew a debate was not what the grieving young man needed. He watched as Joe turned away again. "You know," he began quietly, "there's something that makes us want an explanation for everything that happens. Especially as doctors, we want to justify the causes and cures of the diseases and injuries we're faced with day after day.

"But no matter how hard we try, there's no easy way to justify death, and that's exactly what Beth's work was all about. She didn't try to explain it or make excuses for it. But she did offer the next best thing—*hope*—life for others after the death of one. Think of the miracle of life Beth's organs have already given to others."

Joe sat motionless, his eyes fixed on the fire. "*Love one another as I have loved you; greater love has no man than this, that he lay down his life for his friends.*" The verse Evan Richards had quoted in reference to Beth's bequest had merely created more turmoil in his already ravaged thinking.

"Joe," Paul continued, "what you expected and what God saw fit to allow has left a tremendous breach in your thinking. You feel alienated and alone. As abandoned as you feel right now, you need to ask Him for enough faith to *believe* that He had a purpose for permitting Beth to die. And maybe more often than not, faith means having to accept what we *can't* understand, but that doesn't mean He's forgotten you or left you alone. He's there."

Joe rose from the chair and leaned against the mantle, resting his head on his arm as he stared into the flames. "I left my wife's funeral today trying to *justify* why I had to lose what I loved the most." Then he turned to look at Paul. "Am I expected to *praise* God for taking Beth away from me with some kind of . . . broken hallelujah? I can't do it. Neither can I accept the 'loving God' you're so willing to defend as one and the same." Again, he turned back to the fire. Paul leaned forward, dropping his hands between his knees. "I remember thinking like that after I lost Sarah. The pain I felt was so intense, I was convinced I could never trust God again. But Joe," he added gently, raising his head, "God isn't punishing you. And even though we may question why God permits certain things to happen, He's the One—*the only One*—who can and will override that kind of pain with mercy." Paul gazed again at the fire, remembering. "It took me a long time to accept that idea, until someone reminded me of something." Warily, Joe turned and looked at him once more. "Even thorn bushes are covered with roses."

* * *

Callie Jordan was moving slowly across the floor of her hospital room when Stephen Lewis appeared in the doorway. "Not too fast," he cautioned, smiling at her.

"Fast is out for me," she said as she reached the chair. He helped her sit down. "It's been almost a week. How am I doing?"

"I don't think I've ever seen anyone doing better than you are.

Another week, and we can take those wires out of your chest." "That'll be a relief," she said. "But all these tests—blood tests, x-rays, EKGs, ECGs—they're wearing me out."

He crouched beside the chair. "All necessary things we talked about. We have to monitor you very closely for any signs of rejection or infection." Then he grinned. "But I intend to send you *running* out of here."

She returned his smile and then looked down at her lap. "I've been doing a lot of thinking."

"About what?" he ventured, though he could guess the answer. She looked up at Stephen. "I knew a transplant was the only thing that was going to save my life, but I can't stop thinking that some family somewhere is grieving over a death that *I've* benefited from. I feel almost selfish. Do you find that strange?"

"No," he said quietly, "not at all. But remember, as hard as it is to accept the fact that yes, someone died, at least this way, the family can find comfort knowing that their loved one is still giving life." He squeezed her hands. "You don't need to feel selfish."

"But I still feel so sad."

"Depression is a common side effect. You'll get past it in time." "Someday, I hope I have enough courage to find that family and thank them. Do you know who the donor was?"

"No, I don't know. In some cases, the family might choose to contact you, and then it would be up to you to respond or not. And then in other cases, I've found that it's best *not* to know. Just accept that God has given you a second chance and go from here."

He rose easily to his feet when Ben Jordan appeared in the doorway. "How's my girl doing, Steve?" Jordan strode confidently into the room and shook Stephen's outstretched hand.

"So far she's a model patient. She'll need her first biopsy soon.

But I honestly believe she's going to be fine." "Thanks to you," Callie told him.

Lewis grinned. "Well, if you'll both excuse me, I have *sick* people to see now." He shook Jordan's hand once more before leaving the room.

"A fine young man," Jordan commented as he pulled a chair beside hers. "You were lucky to have someone like him."

"Yes, I was," she returned in a quiet voice. She smiled as she reached over and grasped her father's hand. "Now what about you?

How long do you think the hospital can stay in one piece with you not there to run things?"

"Not long," he said with some contrived arrogance. "But I'm not about to leave until I'm sure you're all right."

"Dad, you heard Dr. Lewis. I couldn't be in better hands. And besides, I know he's going to keep me here until he's positive there no immediate risk of rejection, and then I have to start cardiac rehab. Now please think about yourself. I bet you've concocted an agenda that's a mile long."

Jordan grinned, squeezing her hand tighter. "You do know your old dad, don't you? Yes, yes, I guess I do have a few things that need to be attended to."

"Then go back to work, where you belong."

His pale gray eyes met hers. "And what about you? Where do you think you belong now, baby?"

For the first time since the surgery, Callie allowed her thoughts to consciously return to Joe, and then to Beth, and finally to the life she was determined to lead apart from them. "I'm going to stay right here, at least for the time being. When Stephen thinks I can go back to work, I will. In the meantime, I feel very confident having him so close by. And so should you."

Jordan's paternal anxieties began to relax as he listened to his daughter's logical sense. He would have gladly welcomed her home to recuperate under his supervision, but if she came home, she would learn of the tragic death of her friend. It was a wonder she still didn't know, and right now, he wanted nothing in her life that would cause her any undue alarm. Eventually, she would have to know, but not now. At least not until she was stronger.

"Well, in that case, I suppose I could make a return flight reservation pretty soon. Would that ease your mind?"

"I think it would ease *your* mind," she returned affectionately.

* * *

Two days later, Benjamin Jordan settled back into the cushioned seat of the airplane that would fly nonstop to Boston. As the jet gained altitude, he unbuckled the cumbersome seatbelt and leaned forward to pull a magazine out of the seat pocket in front of him, but the periodical slipped from his grasp when a sharp pain seized the middle of his chest.

This time, the pain was severe enough to cause him to groan aloud before he could stifle it. He felt a cold perspiration break out on his face and neck, while the painful spasm traveled down the muscles of both his arms. A sensation of dizziness rocked him as he leaned back against the seat once more. He could do little but struggle for breath.

A moment later, he realized a flight attendant had come to the empty seat next to his and had begun to loosen his tie and unbutton his shirt. Just before the attendant pulled down the portable oxygen mask from overhead, he caught her hand in midair. "It's . . . all right. I'm all right."

"I'm sorry, sir, but you seem to be having some trouble. Would you like me to see if there's a doctor on board?"

Jordan closed his eyes while his head rested against the back of the seat. "No . . . *I'm* a doctor . . . and I'm all right." He waited another moment before opening his eyes to find the flight attendant still beside him. "I know what I'm doing," he assured her. "Just . . . let me rest." He closed his eyes again. In time, he heard the attendant move out of the seat.

Angina, he persuaded himself. He reached inside his coat pocket and pulled out a small bottle of nitroglycerin tablets. With a shaking hand, he put one under his tongue.

But deep down, Benjamin Jordan suspected something more than angina. He knew he could no longer postpone the cardiac workup he would have to have. The attacks were increasing in severity each time, but he would not have the testing and lab work done at his hospital. Maybe somewhere outside of Boston, but *not* at his hospital. He would not risk jeopardizing his position merely because of symptoms he could manage on his own.

His hand was still shaking as he fumbled for another tablet and slipped it under his tongue.

* * *

Maggie McCarran opened the door of the car while her boss set his suitcases on the floor of the backseat.

"How was the trip, Dr. J.? And more importantly, how's my Callie girl?" Maggie anxiously wanted to know. "Ya know, ya might have called more than once," she finished in a scolding voice while settling herself behind the steering wheel.

Jordan crawled into the passenger seat and pulled the door shut as they prepared to leave the airport. "Callie's just fine, just fine. She's in the care of a very capable cardiologist whom I wouldn't be afraid to trust my *own* life to. Now let's go. I've left enough work for an army of doctors to attend to."

As Maggie pulled out of the parking lot, Jordan wearily laid his head against the back of the seat. Unconsciously, he rubbed his hand across his shirt and took a deep breath. His chest still felt tight after the incident on the plane.

* * *

The next morning, Benjamin Jordan replaced the phone in his office, confident that his appointment under a pseudonym at the small hospital some fifty miles outside of Boston would guarantee his anonymity. As soon as he had results from the cardiac testing and bloodwork, he would begin his own treatment.

For now, he rose from the soft leather chair, slipped into his lab coat, and made his way out of the medical complex. He straightened his tie before stepping through the wide glass doors to the entrance of the hospital. With nervous anticipation, he scanned the passing faces of patients and medical personnel as he walked toward the elevator.

He stepped inside and the doors closed. He had yet to see Joe Travis since his return from Charlest on the day before. Considering the grim circumstances, he was sure Paul Martin had made certain that Joe would take much needed time away from the hospital. Joe needed that time to pull his emotions together, he reasoned. Jordan admired the young man's fortitude, yet no one could expect him to return to work so soon after.

The elevator doors opened. Jordan strode out into the corridor and cast a quick glance in the direction of the nurses' station, only to spot the young surgeon in his scrubs writing orders at the counter.

Immediately, he wanted to retreat into the elevator, but it was too late. The doors closed behind him. He moved aside as two orderlies pushed an empty stretcher past him. *How was it possible that Joe had returned to work so soon after Beth's funeral? What could he possibly say to him?* He was not prepared for a spontaneous meeting. With faltering steps, he made his way toward the nurses' station.

Joe glanced up as Jordan approached. The wearied expression on the young man's face told him what he was already sure of. "Joe," he fumbled for words, "I'm truly sorry I wasn't able to—"

"I have a scan I'd like you to look at," Joe interrupted without emotion. "Come by my office as soon as you can, will you?"

"Of course, right after grand rounds." Jordan sighed with concealed relief. "What do you suspect?"

"I can't be sure, but it looks likes early stages of pulmonary carcinoma. That's always been your forte."

"I'll be there in an hour."

Joe stuffed the pen into his front pocket and walked away.

* * *

In years past, Benjamin Jordan would have felt at ease walking into Joe's office unannounced, but today, he knocked gingerly on the door and waited.

After a brusque verbal acknowledgement from the other side, he went in. He found the younger man hunkered over files and papers that swathed his customarily organized desk. "Joe, you have that CT scan?"

Joe turned the computer monitor so both could view the screen at the same time. Jordan stepped up for a closer look. Using his pen as a pointer, Joe outlined the area of abnormality within the lung section.

"I think you're right. It definitely looks like the beginning of mesothelioma," Jordan agreed. "Have you scheduled a PET scan?"

"Yes, first thing in the morning." Joe turned aside, pushing away some papers on his desk until he found his schedule. He studied it for a moment. "If the scan proves positive, he'll need athoracotomy as soon as possible. I just don't know where I'm going to fit it in."

Jordan looked away from the screen and glanced wide-eyed at the agenda in Joe's hands. "Joe, how is it you have such a heavy schedule? You have enough procedures here for two surgeons!"

The mordant expression on Joe's face remained unchanged as he continued to examine the schedule. "I can handle it."

"Well, obviously not, if you can't even find the time to fit in a simple lobectomy that may need immediate attention!" Jordan's old self was returning without his realizing it. "Why in the world would you make such a schedule for yourself? It's ridiculous!"

"Ridiculous?" Joe exploded. "What else have I *got*?"

An immediate and awkward silence filled the room. Jordan was not prepared for the young man's unexpected hostility, with such animosity never before directed at him. When he found his voice, it was remarkably calm. "I'm sorry, Joe. I know how difficult things must be for you right now. If you'd like me to do it, I'd be glad to arrange it."

Joe's rueful eyes rose to meet Jordan's, merely acknowledging the offer with a nod in the direction of his former mentor.

Jordan waited while Joe copied down the patient's name, code, and telephone number on a piece of paper and then left the room. But along with the information, Ben Jordan carried a conscience that silently screamed inside him.

CHAPTER 19

Benjamin Jordan sat hunched over his desk. Through the window behind him, trees swayed in the cold February wind while snow flurries swirled from an iron gray sky.

With the door locked, he read again in detail the results of his cardiac testing several days earlier. Nuclear scan, EKG, echocardiogram, stress testing, bloodwork, and cardiac CT scan indicated serious blockage of the main artery and two smaller branches.

He suspected the results would not be good, but in fact, they were much worse than he had anticipated. The cardiologist had tried to persuade him to check into the hospital right away, but Jordan had declined. He could treat his condition his own way.

* * *

Lizzie Adams had been waiting almost an hour past her scheduled appointment time. When Joe walked into the exam room, he sat down on the stool beside the examination table where Lizzie sat. There was no customary apology for the delay as he began to review notes from her last hospitalization.

Lizzie had heard that he had lost his wife several months before. Now she longed to offer him some personal comfort, just as he had done for her the last time she had been in the hospital. Never would she forget that extraordinary night when she had clung to Joe's hands while he prayed for her recovery. Finally, she broke the uncomfortable silence.

"Dr. Travis, how have you been?"

Joe stuffed his pen into his lab coat pocket as he closed her chart. "Have you been having any discomfort, Lizzie? Any pain in your chest or trouble breathing?" Either ignoring her gesture of consolation or oblivious to it altogether, he seemed to want only to get on with the purpose of her visit.

"No, so far so good." Lizzie observed for the first time his isolated disposition. She took deep breaths on command as Joe listened to her chest sounds. "Well?" she remarked with optimism. He made no comment as he pulled the stethoscope away from his ears, slung it around his neck, and began writing notes. She waited until he had closed her file before trying to return to conversation. "Does everything sound all right to you?"

"Yes, everything seems normal," he returned with brusque politeness. "But the first sign of trouble you begin to experience, you don't delay. You get yourself to the emergency room."

She watched as he left the room. In the past, she had taken pleasure in spending a few minutes alone with him in conversation. He had always gone to such trouble to answer her questions and offer reassuring explanations. He had been so easy to talk with, so willing to listen, so kind and encouraging.

But as she slid off the table and picked up her purse, she was sadly aware that her beloved doctor was no longer the same man she had once known.

* * *

The entire month in the OR had been unusually hectic.

Benjamin Jordan slumped in an overstuffed armchair in the surgeons' lounge, too weary to walk across the parking lot to his own office.

As he sprawled in the chair, he began to think about Joe once more. He had passed him several times in the corridors throughout the day, but the young surgeon appeared as he always appeared anymore—

preoccupied, hurried, seemingly unaware and disinterested in those around him.

Jordan had been discreetly observing Joe, watching for noticeable signs of grief in the young man. He knew the process of grieving was difficult, yet was something that would bring about healing. However, he saw none, but what he did see alarmed him.

For years, Benjamin Jordan had secretly admired Joe Travis's unimpeded ability to convey compassion toward his patients even though Jordan himself supported the rationale that sympathy did not lend itself to the making of a good surgeon. He contended rather that emotional indifference, objectivity, was essential to meet that end. However, during the years that Joe had been under his mentorship, Jordan had never been able to persuade him in regard to that theory.

Jordan could well remember times when he had frequently reprimanded the young surgeon for spending countless hours with his patients, to the point that he feared for Joe's health. But the order had gone unheeded. Joe had continued to spend his time not only imparting valuable medical skills, but also conveying a gentleness that Jordan himself had never been able to render.

But no more. Now Dr. Joe Travis regarded his patients as anonymous, almost faceless individuals with whom he was no longer willing to risk emotional identification. In the two months since Beth's untimely death, Joe's tender compassion had gradually been replaced with calcifying ritual. Though Jordan knew his former protégé would care for his patients with competence and unparalleled skill, Joe's approach had become analytical and businesslike.

To those who had not known him before, he seemed unapproachable, but Jordan knew differently. He knew an anger seethed within the young man, an anger that masked itself in overwork and reserved formality, and Jordan understood from bitter experience that Joe's withdrawal was merely a way to suppress the guilt and grief that eventually would have to be dealt with.

His troubling thoughts were interrupted when the door opened and several surgeons walked in. Joe entered a few minutes later, saying nothing as he sank into a nearby chair.

"Tough day?" Jordan asked without moving.

Joe's penetrating eyes glanced in his direction. "Every day's a tough day."

As Jordan observed the wearied young man, a surge of pity overcame him. Not for the first time did he lament the fact that he would likely never again be close to Joe as he had been years before, even months before.

And he recognized the camouflaged pain. "What happened, Joe?" He waited, saying nothing more but kept his eyes fixed on the young surgeon.

After some tense moments, Joe ran his hands despairingly through his hair. "Twenty-eight years old, mother of two, and there wasn't anything I could do but close her up." His voice carried a bitterness that was becoming all too common.

"That's hard," Jordan said with unusual sensitivity. "Everything inside you wants to do whatever's necessary to save a life, but there are times you have to force yourself to *accept* the fact there's simply nothing you can do. The circumstances don't always take into consideration how you feel."

Joe's wearied expression met that of Jordan's. In the past, he would have anticipated a relentless checklist of surgical procedures, not empathy. "That's strange advice coming from *you*," he said with subdued contention.

"Maybe," Jordan agreed. He waited a moment until the room emptied before continuing. "But the more I observe, the more I have to accept that I can't *do* everything. I can't *be* everything." His voice was barely audible when he added, "And I can't undo what's already been done."

Joe's embittered expression faded briefly into clemency. "I've never known you to talk like that before."

Jordan uttered a mild oath. "There are a lot of things you don't know, Joe. In spite of everything you've been through, you still haven't experienced it all." He pulled himself out of the chair. "Why don't we go over to my office for a while, and I'll give you a lesson you've never had before."

* * *

Joe sat down on the couch in Jordan's office and watched as his former mentor slouched in the big leather chair behind his desk.

He had not noticed before now, but the older man had gained weight in the past few months. Joe didn't like the ashen color of his face, and he was equally concerned when Jordan unlocked a drawer and pulled out a flask of brandy and a shot glass. After filling the glass, he gestured toward Joe, but Joe refused as well as declining to offer admonishment for the alcohol.

Jordan seemed more relaxed after a second drink. "I've been watching you these last few months since Bethie died." Joe's mouth tightened as he glanced away, but Jordan would not be dissuaded. "And watching you has been like a rerun of a miserable time in my life I would just as soon forget, let alone *talk* about. I've never told anyone this before, except my wife. But when I was a young man, long before I was married, I had an experience that was not unlike the one you're going through right now."

Touched, Joe looked into pitying eyes he had seldom seen before. With some effort, Jordan continued, "When I was a resident at this very hospital, I acquired a young woman for a patient who had been admitted with what was believed to be aplastic anemia. But all too soon, I realized she was quickly becoming more than just a patient. I found myself falling in love with her." He seemed distanced for a moment, lost in remembrance. "I knew my superiors would never accept it, and I couldn't risk jeopardizing the residency I had fought so hard to get. But I didn't want to lose her either.

"The more I saw of her, the more I realized how serious my intentions were becoming. And to my joy, I found she felt the same toward me, believe it or not." His eyes glinted with amusement. "We even managed to keep the whole thing a secret while she was in the hospital.

"Then shortly before she was to be discharged, an appalling discovery was brought to my attention." For a moment, Jordan looked away. "One of my superiors came to me and took me into the lab. There he showed me something I had only seen in textbooks. The bone marrow indicated she was approaching advanced stages of acute myelogenous leukemia."

Joe could see the increasing anguish in his eyes as he continued to recall the incident. "I blamed myself for overlooking the diagnosis, though I was never held accountable for it, but the worst part of it was that I couldn't bring myself to tell her. I was actually grateful when her case was turned over almost immediately to an oncologist. After that, I saw her as little as possible and *hated* myself. Nurses would tell me she was asking to see me, but I always made sure I was too busy. I couldn't face her, or her illness.

"Eventually, she was transferred to another hospital that specialized in cancer therapy. Months later, when I learned she had died, I locked myself in a janitor's closet and cried like I'd never cried before in all my life."

At length, Jordan leaned over the polished desk, giving a hard stare to the young man across from him. "When I realized I couldn't forgive myself for my guilt, I determined I would never fall prey to that kind of suffering again. I threw myself into my books and clinical rotations and research like I'd never done before. But I discovered a brain without a heart is really nothing," he mused caustically.

"I guess what I'm trying to tell you is this: for whatever it's worth, don't make the same mistake I did. Protecting myself from feelings that were too hard to deal with has amassed years of shutting out the emotional needs of everyone around me, patients *and* family. By carrying the burden of guilt for not standing by that girl, for not facing her illness with her *and* the pain I found so crippling, I accepted all the self-deprecating consequences that went with it. I allowed that incident to transform me into someone I never intended to become."

A tender chord struck somewhere beneath Joe's own pain as he considered what Ben Jordan had arduously revealed to him, compelling him to come to his mentor's defense. "But you're no less a fine teacher and surgeon because of it. Nothing you could have done would have . . . saved her." He stopped; the point had made it home. "No, nothing at that time would have saved her," Jordan repeated. "But I've never forgiven myself for not staying by her when she needed me. So instead of facing up to my weakness, my . . . inability to deal with emotional situations, my guilty conscience, I chose to spend a lifetime compensating for it by developing strategies to safeguard myself." For the first time, there was an audible tremor in his voice. "Joe, you *are* what I *was* thirty years ago. And I'm telling you now, *don't* spend a lifetime as I've done protecting yourself from pain. Accept what you can't do and forgive yourself! And if you can find it in your heart . . . *forgive me*." With that, Jordan rose from his chair and brushed past Joe, walking quickly out of the room.

Joe sat alone for a few minutes, wondering. After all Ben Jordan had done for him, for what would he ever have to forgive him?

CHAPTER 20

Winter in the coastal city of Charleston, South Carolina, had been anything but what Callie Jordan had been accustomed to.

Three weeks after her surgery, Stephen Lewis had condescended to discharge her as an outpatient, with strict instructions regarding diet, exercise, and cardiac rehabilitation. She had spent the first three months of her recuperative time faithfully following his orders.

The early April morning was cool. As she took her morning walk alongside the ocean, she pulled the scarf Stephen had given her a little tighter around her neck to conceal the scar she would carry the rest of her life.

A breeze rustled through the live oaks, palmettos, and evergreens. Daffodils and tulips had come and gone, and now blossoms of lavender, magenta, and salmon from southern azaleas spread like a carpet coloring the landscape. Pink and white dogwoods bloomed everywhere; wisteria draped fragrant blue flowers over century old stone walls.

In all directions, Callie saw people walking along the beach, reaching down for shells, some brave enough to put toes in the water. She could not help but think about her father and Maggie, all the people she had known and loved. Charleston was indeed a strikingly beautiful city, but she missed Boston and everything that made it home.

But that was in the past, and what was in the past would have to remain so. At least here, she could live her life without longing for something there that she could never have.

So maybe the time had come to begin that life.

And the place to begin was to return to work, to be useful and of value to others, something that would take her mind off of herself. And once more, Dr. Stephen Lewis was the one making it possible.

As she walked, she smiled to herself as she recalled the day he had come to her room, less than two weeks after her surgery, with an offer she had hardly expected.

* * *

Callie had no idea Stephen Lewis had been standing in the doorway of her room until she heard him knock lightly on the door. She turned away from the window as he came inside.

"I can tell you're getting pretty bored," he remarked with a boyish grin.

"Is that what comes with feeling better?"

"I suppose there are drawbacks to becoming healthy again."

She laughed as she made her way to the chair beside her bed. "I guess I shouldn't complain. But the routine is getting a little tedious. Do you know how many tiles are up there?" she asked, gesturing toward the ceiling.

Stephen sat down on the bed across from her. "One hundred and sixty-two."

Her eyes widened. "You're close. How would you know that?"

"You aren't the first one to ever occupy this room, but I'm not here to discuss ceiling tiles. I've come with a proposition for you. Something you can think about when you get really bored."

Her expression brightened. "And that is?"

Stephen drew an obvious deep breath. "Would you consider going to work for me in my office when you feel you're up to it?"

"Are you serious?" A smile tugged at the edges of her mouth.

"Well, of course, I'm serious. You're doing remarkably well. And even though you're not going to be up to full speed for a while after I release you from your little asylum here, I figure if you were working for me, you could just about pick the hours that would suit you until you felt you were ready for full time work again. You're not going to find that in *the OR. And being an office nurse is not quite as rigorous as a surgical nurse. This way, I could keep a better eye on you if you were right under my nose. What do you say?"*

Callie had never known anything but the OR, yet the offer intrigued her. "I say it's definitely something to think about."

"Good." Stephen rose to his feet. "Now I won't worry about your being bored. You have something to think about." Just as abruptly as he appeared, he disappeared into the corridor, returning with a rattling wheelchair in front of him. "You're also due in rehab right now. Would you like a personal transport downstairs?"

She shook her head in amazement. "Who could decline an offer like that?"

* * *

Callie came to a stop and looked out across the water. Stephen had done so much for her. Now he had not only offered her an ideal working situation but had given her the go ahead to begin any time she felt she was ready. Maybe working with him was just the right medicine she needed.

Stephen Lewis, she concluded, was definitely in the life-saving business.

* * *

"Now, Callie, are you sure it's not too soon?" Benjamin Jordan asked her brusquely over the phone. "What is Lewis telling you?"

"He suggested I start with a few hours a week and then see how it goes from there."

"Callie, I don't know—"

"Dad, I'm not a fragile little girl anymore, and I *wish* you'd stop treating me like one. Sometimes, I think Joe was the only one willing to recognize that."

In the hasty, unguarded moment, her thoughts turned to Joe Travis as she had not permitted them to for a long time. She had been careful never to ask about him or Beth when she spoke with her father, and he in turn had never volunteered information. Letters from both of them had ceased months before. She never asked why. "I'm sorry, Dad," she said in a more apologetic tone. "A lot has happened to me since I left home. I've had to become more independent than I ever believed I could be, and I want to be part of a world that up until now I've only been able to observe. Can you understand that?"

For a moment, there was silence at the other end. "Yes, baby, I can understand that. If you feel like you can handle it, then you do what you think is best. I suppose working for your own cardiac surgeon can't be all bad."

* * *

Stephen had been overjoyed by Callie's decision to work with him. "Now I want you to do only what you feel you *can* do to start with," Stephen cautioned the day before she was to begin. "I won't have you overdoing it."

"So the rule is *do as you say, not as you do*," Callie returned with an emphasis on the word *do*.

Stephen grinned. "Are you going to get belligerent with the boss even before you start?"

"Would it change anything?" He laughed. "I guess not."

Callie was amazed at the level of activity in Stephen's busy office. Her return to work began with two days a week, but as the weeks passed and her duties became more numerous, she gradually began to increase her load.

Predictably, Stephen hovered over her like a mother hen. "Callie, don't you think it's about time to take a break?" he would inevitably ask her, almost to her embarrassment, when he poked his head into the receptionist's office.

"I will, when I get tired," she promised matter-of-factly.

Feigning satisfaction, he would leave to go to another exam room, but she could almost feel his scrutiny of her even after he had gone.

But for Callie, returning to work was better therapy than all the medication she would have to swallow the rest of her life. Just the daily routine of patient care, putting charts together, filing, sending lab reports to Stephen's colleagues, or entering data into the computer told her for the first time she was actively pursuing a life of her own, one that did not involve something—or someone—she could never have.

Stephen was in his private office early one morning when he heard a soft knocking outside the door. He was pleased to hear Callie's quiet voice on the other side. "I just wanted to tell you Mr. Grayson is in room two. I've already drawn blood for a drug level."

Stephen was at the door by now and opened it wide. "You can come in, I'm not hiding . . . " And then, "Callie, what have you done to your hair?"

Where a fine, poker-straight length of dishwater blonde had always hung limply about her shoulders, now tight, bouncy curls of bright blonde hair enveloped a smiling, but slightly anxious, face.

"I got a permanent yesterday," she returned in a hasty voice as though if she didn't say it quickly, she wouldn't be able to say it at all. "I've never done this before. Do you . . . like it?"

Stephen took a step back to take in the full picture. "You look completely different. I'm not sure I would have recognized you, at least from the back! But yes," he added with a grin, "I think I like it."

With his affirming words came another smile. "I'm glad. And I don't need to take a break . . . yet."

* * *

Paul Martin walked unannounced into Joe's office and found him, as expected, hunched over reports and papers that covered his desk. "Might I ask if you've had any dinner?"

Joe glanced at his watch. "No, I haven't. I guess I didn't realize how late it was." He shifted one stack of papers for another and then returned to the chart in front of him.

Paul sat down on the edge of the desk, fishing for amiable conversation with his reluctant colleague. "Ben Jordan told me Callie's doing beautifully since her surgery."

For a moment, Joe's interest was piqued. He glanced up from his work. "What surgery?"

"Callie had a heart transplant, several months ago," Paul remarked with surprise. "Ben told me shortly afterward. I thought surely he had told you too."

Joe appeared thoughtful for a moment and then shook his head with an air of indifference. "No, he didn't. I'm glad she's doing all right." He continued writing.

Paul stood up. "Well, it's my guess you've missed more than just dinner. And there's a new restaurant along the waterfront I've heard great things about. I may not be much to look at, but I *am* good company, and I *am* starving. Come on, Joe, it's spring! What do you say?"

Joe continued with his writing. "Thanks anyway, but I've got a lot of work to do."

"*Joe . . .*"

The younger doctor's steel blue eyes met Paul's intuitive gaze. "Don't say it. I've heard it all before."

"Well, maybe you need to hear it one more time," Paul blurted out. "When you're not in the OR, you're sequestered in this office at just about any given hour of the day or night. I know you're avoiding going home. I know how difficult it is facing an empty house too. But hiding behind a sixteen-hour workday isn't the answer. Life *does* go on. It's been almost five months."

Joe slammed down his pen on the desktop. "I know to the *minute* how long it's been!" He ran his hand irritably across the back of his neck and then slumped against the chair. It was a moment before his repentant eyes met those of his colleague. "I'm sorry, Paul. I know you mean well."

Paul knew when he was beaten. With reluctance, he turned and walked to the door. "Sure you won't change your mind?"

Joe sighed wearily. "Yeah . . . I'm sure." He watched as Paul closed the door behind him.

Joe turned and looked out the window. A streak of lightening flashed across the evening sky, followed by a low rumble of thunder in the distance. He returned to the open file in front of him and then slammed it shut.

* * *

Joe Travis couldn't remember the last time he had been home.

The front door closed behind him with a hollow, empty sound as he flipped on the light in the foyer. He shook his overcoat free of the spring rain that had begun to fall on the way home from the hospital and then draped the wet coat over a hook.

An eerie sense of abandonment was his only welcome inside the darkened living room. The silence throughout was almost palpable. The house felt cold and uninviting, and a stale, wintry air permeated the rooms. What had once been a refuge of warmth and intimacy now seemed just a collection of dark corners and empty space.

He pulled open the draperies and stood in front of the expansive picture window. He watched as an occasional car drove slowly past, its headlights reflecting like mirrors on the wet pavement of the wide street.

Through intermittent streaks of lightening, he could see the withering remains of spring daffodils in the front yard, daffodils Beth had planted. The ghostly memory rose in his mind as he remembered standing at the window one cold autumn afternoon watching her, on hands and knees, arduously digging hole after hole to plant the bulbs that in the spring would bloom into her favorite flower. What had she told him? *Just remember, those are my flowers you'll be enjoying inthe spring.*

But she had never seen them. He drew the curtains together once more.

He tossed his jacket and tie over the back of the couch before dropping wearily into a chair. Across the room, he could see the dim outline of the fireplace, a gaping hole in the semidarkness. It seemed an eternity had passed since he had felt the warmth of a fire. As he stared at the crumbling, half-burned logs, a smoldering vision of the very last fire he had made seemed to rise straight out of the ashes.

* * *

He had just put another log on the fire when the front door opened, and a gust of cold air surged across the room. He turned to see Beth struggling in the foyer trying to balance shopping bags and packages in her arms.

"I didn't think you'd be home until late," she said, out of breath as Joe took the last of the packages from her hands.

"I finished earlier than I expected and thought I'd come home and take care of you," he said, helping her out of her coat.

"I thought it was my job to take care of you."

He grinned as they walked into the living room together. "You forget I took care of myself for a long time before I realized what I was missing. I was quite independent, you know."

"Well, I'd just as soon you forgot how 'independent' you once were and let me convince you otherwise." She leaned forward and kissed him.

He sat down in one of the chairs near the hearth and pulled her down on his lap. "You can spend the rest of your life doing just that."

"I think I will." She snuggled deeper into his arms and together they watched the fire for a long, long time.

* * *

He closed his eyes in an effort to suppress what he did not want to feel, but the feelings, once set into motion, were not so easily dismissed.

He longed to look into her eyes once more, to reach out and hold her, to feel her inside his arms, to wake up in the morning and find her next to him. She was his reason for living; she was the one to whom he had pledged his life and love.

He could sense Beth in every room, an undeniable presence if only in the sanctuary of his mind. He could hear her puttering about in the kitchen and could almost smell the delicious aromas that filled the house when he came home. As they would eat together, he would tell her what his day had been like, divulge to her in unguarded detail his ideas and dreams. And then later, he would lie down beside her in front of a languishing fire, reveling in the greatest contentment he had ever known.

But now, the scattered ashes only reminded him of what once was and could never be again.

Enough. Seizing the arms of the chair, he opened his eyes in an endeavor to halt the painful reverie. He knew fatigue was wearing down his emotions as well as his reasoning. Maybe a hot shower and a decent night's sleep would make a difference.

He pulled himself out of the chair and went into the bedroom, but as he opened the closet doors, a lingering scent of perfume drifted into the stale air, and without warning, he realized he was staring at Beth's garments that he had never removed.

The simplicity of her clothes hanging next to his, as though nothing had ever changed, struck with far greater impact than the subtle reminders earlier. Impulsively, he reached out and stroked a dress he had bought her in Chicago, a silk blouse he had loved, a sweater she had never worn, as if in touching them some semblance of the past might comfort him.

But there was no comfort. The unwary moment proved more than he could stand, and with impassioned vehemence, he slammed the doors shut.

He lay down across the bed, burying his face in his hands as the intensity of his unleashed emotions became more than he could bear. The echoes and the emptiness, combined with the dreary sound of the rain striking the windows, served only to increase his loneliness apart from the woman he still loved, the woman he still reached out for in the night.

Paul was right. He had indeed stayed away to avoid what he knew deep down he could not endure. He could not escape the phantoms that held him captive in this house. For here, his protective façade had weakened, and the pain had seeped through. Tonight had only been another obstacle he had failed to conquer.

Joe Travis was a man with no beliefs, not living, but simply trying to survive in a pressurized world of his own making. As he drifted into an exhausted sleep, his last thoughts as always were of Beth. Though there was no way he could ever forget, in truth it hurt too much to remember.

* * *

Morning light filtered through the bedroom curtains. Joe awakened to the soft chimes of Beth's antique clock. Fully clothed, he lay sprawled across the bed in the same position in which he had fallen asleep the night before.

He pulled himself off the bed, showered and shaved, and then drove to the hospital. As he walked through the doors of the emergency department, a nurse ran toward him. "Dr. Travis, you're needed in the cardiac room right away!"

He quickly followed her into the room. There he saw the rapid response team skillfully performing their duties around the unconscious patient. One of the nurses had finished cutting away the man's clothes, exposing his huge chest while another made connections to the cardiac monitor. Intravenous lines were already in place. The resident, hunkered over the victim, was breathlessly counting off cardiopulmonary compressions.

Joe maneuvered past the response team members. As he approached the table, his breath caught in his throat when he glanced down at the ashen face of Dr. Benjamin Jordan. "How long?" he asked in disbelief.

"About four minutes," the resident said, puffing, but not missing a beat. "Dr. Marcus is on his way."

Quickly, Joe stripped away his jacket, rolled up his shirtsleeves, and asked the resident to step aside.

The door burst open again, and Dr. Jeff Marcus, chief cardiologist, rushed into the room. At the same time, another nurse jerked the stethoscope from her ears. "I can't get a pressure."

Marcus glanced at the cardiac monitor. The line was flat. "Full arrest! Give me the paddles."

Joe stepped away from the table as a nurse extended the defibrillation paddles to Marcus. Quickly placing them in position, he called, "Clear!" The current from the electric shock convulsed the patient, but the monitor showed no returning heart rhythm. "Again. Clear!" he shouted. Jordan convulsed, but there was no cardiac response.

Joe steadily increased the voltage as Marcus continued to repeat the procedure, each time with no success. Marcus called for a syringe of epinephrine. Joe watched as the cardiologist administered the stimulating drug into the IV line and then glanced disparagingly at the monitor.

Twenty minutes passed. Marcus repeated the procedures again and again. Finally, he looked across the table at Joe and then down at Jordan. With resignation, he announced in a quiet voice, "We've lost him."

"No!" Startled, Marcus looked up when he heard Joe's adamant voice. With dogged determination, Joe turned his attention to one of the nurses. "I want a transvenous pacemaker set up *now*."

Though skeptical, Marcus acknowledged the order with a reluctant nod, and the procedure cart was brought to the table.

A nurse slipped sterile gloves over Joe's hands. With skilled precision, he made a small opening in the chest wall and deftly threaded the subclavian catheter into the vein leading to the heart. He then eased a pacing wire through the catheter while the nurse attached the pacer wires to the pulse generator.

Impatiently, he watched the monitor for electrical capture. As the minutes passed, he could feel the pressure in the room intensifying. "Come on, come on!" he muttered with urgency. Beads of sweat banded on his forehead as he grew more distressed, glancing first at Jordan, then to the monitor and then at the clock, methodically ticking away precious time without mercy.

But no heart spike was seen.

As he began to adjust the equipment, a hand clamped over his wrist. "Joe, there's too much damage to the muscle," he heard Jeff say. "It's over."

"It's not over," Joe declared stubbornly. go."

"Joe, it's *over*," Jeff repeated with quiet persistence. "Let him Unseen tears burned in Joe's eyes. Reluctantly, he withdrew his hand, stripped away the bloody glove, and slammed it into a waste can. He looked down at the pallid face of Benjamin Jordan once more and then sank into a chair on the other side of the room.

* * *

The giant lights were dark now. Only a bluish tint from the corridor cast a pale glow through the open exam room door. The stretcher was gone, the instruments put away. The room was quiet once more.

Joe leaned heavily against the counter, staring idly at the drawers, stainless steel trays of instruments, vials of medicine behind glass doors. He had no idea how much time had passed; he only knew he had no will to move. The colorless face of his beloved mentor would not cease to haunt him. The nightmarish scene played repeatedly in his mind as he duplicated every procedure, every order given, every decision that had been made.

"Joe, I heard what happened. I know you did all you could." Behind him, the voice of Paul Martin was soft and sympathetic.

Without turning around, Joe spread his hands to either side of the steel counter. "All I could," he repeated. "The man's dead, Paul."

Paul understood the misery Joe was going through, an agony of blame every conscientious doctor took upon himself. "Losing a patient isn't something any of us ever get used to," he said gently, "let alone a colleague and friend. It's just something we have to try to understand. I know what Ben meant to you. I also know how difficult it is for you to accept defeat, but sometimes, there's no other choice. And in Ben Jordan's case, there was no other choice. Ben knew he was pushing himself too hard. He should have retired years ago."

Joe turned around. Paul was moved when he saw the younger doctor's stricken face. "Is that what I'm supposed to tell Callie?"

"No, of course not. Joe, I know how you feel, but you aren't to blame."

"Can't you understand?" he snapped in a sudden blaze of anger. "I don't want to *feel* anything."

"It isn't a crime, Joe."

"Then let's just say I've learned that *feelings* only get in the way of what I have to do." He quickly brushed past Paul and disappeared down the hallway.

* * *

For Joe, the rest of the day passed like a jumbled mass of disconnected events. After long hours behind his desk, he stepped outside his office into the dimly lit corridor. His effort to bury his sadness in his work had been to no avail. He could not escape the paralyzing effects of grief.

Leaning against the wall, he closed his eyes. He sensed a heaviness, an air of composed misery in the darkened corridor. He could almost feel the darkness pressing down on him. Somehow, night always seemed to bring its own punishment.

Then from far down the hallway, he heard the sound of hurried feet, and someone calling his name. He opened his eyes and saw Callie Jordan rushing down the corridor toward him.

Having only known her in sickness, he was amazed at the changes that had taken place since he had last seen her the summer before. Even from a distance, it was obvious the gaunt features no longer existed. The pallid color of her skin had changed to a healthy hue. The languishing invalid was gone. Her restored health had created a striking difference.

She was out of breath by the time she reached him. She accepted his outstretched hands and, for a moment, appeared more controlled than he would have expected. But as her eyes rose to meet his, the years of acuity between them began to dissolve the outward calm. "He's really gone . . . isn't he?" With the spoken words came an onslaught of tears.

Her weeping rendered in Joe a barrage of crushing guilt. His arms encircled her as he propelled her out of the corridor and into the privacy of his office. Still weeping, she covered her face as he put his hands around her trembling shoulders. "Callie, I did everything I could, everything I knew to do; it just wasn't enough. Can you ever forgive me?"

Slowly, her hands withdrew from her tear-streaked face, her expression incredulous as she gazed at him. "How could I ever blame *you*?"

He reached out and drew her toward him, and willingly, she surrendered to the solace of his arms. Compelled to comfort her, he tenderly kissed the top of her head, her forehead, her cheek. And then, seized by the complexity of his own grief, he lifted her face toward his and began to kiss her with a passion he had known only once before.

In that reckless moment, there was no other thought, no other person in the world. As his arms tightened around her, Joe's nightmare of pain and despair began to fade into tranquility he had almost forgotten. He felt a mesmerizing sense of contentment as the turmoil inside him slowly ebbed away. For the first time in months, he understood how oppressive his loneliness had been, and he longed for it to end.

Then, with sudden intensity, Callie's unconscious resistance snapped into place. A tiny gasp escaped her lips as she struggled to free herself from his arms. "Joe, what are you *doing*? What about Beth?"

Suffocating silence filled the room as his hands slipped away from her. With the innocence of her stunned remark came all he needed to know—Callie's allegiance to Beth would never allow for unfaithfulness to her. "You don't know, do you? Your father never told you."

"Told me *what*?" Then her eyes widened in terrifying awareness. "Is something wrong with Beth?"

Joe's face paled. His entire demeanor transformed into something she could not understand as a frightening stillness settled around them. His body grew taut, his hands clinched at his sides.

Panic seized her. "Joe, what's wrong with Beth? If something's wrong, I need to—"

"Beth is *dead*, Callie!" The ghastly words pierced the silence with blistering intensity.

She shuddered while her hand, trembling, rose to cover her gaping mouth. "*What?*"

At once, he realized the cold callousness of his words, and he was mortified by his unbridled behavior. He took a step closer, his hands extended toward her, ready to offer what meager reparation he could. "Cal, there was . . . an accident—"

"And no one told me? Why didn't someone tell me? Why didn't you tell me?" Joe's hands fell to his sides as she shook her head in frantic disbelief. "*How could you*? How could you *do* this to me? You're the only one who never treated me as if I would break! *You were the one I trusted!*"

The angry words dissolved into broken sobs. Her father was gone, her friend was gone, and all the tender utterances in the world were at best only meaningless clichés. Sweeping past him, she wrenched open the door and fled down the empty corridor.

CHAPTER 21

Joe Travis slumped in the leather chair behind his desk. He stared outside the windows, lost within his own miserable thoughts. The painful scene with Callie hours earlier had painted an indelible picture in his mind.

How could I ever blame you? Callie's innocent words echoed repeatedly, painfully. But for Joe, there *was* no one else to blame. His conduct toward her, his insensitive disclosure about Beth, his helpless endeavor to save Benjamin Jordan's life, all magnified in his already guilt-stricken mind.

He knew Callie had come to him seeking comfort, to share with him a common bereavement, but he had been unable to offer the consolation she sought. Instead of conducting himself in the role of older brother and protector as he had done so conscientiously through the years, he had merely added his own abiding pain to hers, a pain attributable to the bitter and lonely months he had suffered without Beth.

No one could understand that kind of emptiness. For what had begun as an unconscious endeavor to protect himself from further pain had in reality become something entirely different. He had cloaked himself behind an emotional mask for so long that it had grown to a perfect fit.

Then with no warning, Callie had reentered his life, and in one unguarded moment, he had relinquished the mask, but in the letting go, he feared he had used her. And maybe he had, in a blind and selfish attempt to escape the demons of loneliness and loss.

Yet there was something in that impetuous kiss he knew he would not soon forget. In frustration and misery, he dropped his head into his hands as he contemplated how much Callie Jordan must truly hate him.

* * *

Maggie McCarran wrapped her arms around Callie. Two hours earlier, a taxi had driven up the driveway, and she had watched through the window as the disheveled contents spilled from the backseat.

She had expected as much. What she had not expected was that Callie had first gone to the hospital in search of Joe and from there had found out about Beth. Her heart ached knowing the girl not only had the grief of her father to bear, but now added grief for the loss of her friend.

Tears rolled down Callie's cheeks as she leaned against the trusted housekeeper. "Maggie, why didn't anyone tell me? Why couldn't I know?"

"Your father wouldn't permit it," she answered softly, smoothing Callie's hair away from her forehead. "He was always s'worried about ya, he simply forbid your findin' out. I had no choice but to abide by his wishes."

"*Oh, Maggie . . .* " Callie wiped her eyes with the back of her hand. "For as long as I can remember, I wanted to be like Beth, *but I just couldn't.*"

Maggie hugged her tightly. "If you had made yourself a carbon copy of Bethie, we wouldn't have had our Callie."

Callie appreciated what Maggie was trying to do, but a wretched sense of guilt was beginning to overshadow the grief. And no one but Maggie would understand why.

She sat up and wiped her eyes again. "For a while, I was almost *glad* Beth stopped writing because . . . because it was so hard reading about all the things she and Joe were doing together, all the things they were planning." Shame prevented her from continuing, and she buried her face in her hands again. "But I never . . . *never* wanted—"

"Oh, Callie, of course ya never wanted anything to happen to Bethie!" Maggie finished in a soothing voice, pulling the girl into her arms once more. "And *I* know all the reasons why it was so hard for ya. But ya just can't imagine how hard it's been on poor Dr. Joe. He took it so badly. I think your comin' home will be a real comfort to him."

But Maggie did not yet know all that had occurred in Joe's office. Now as she rested her head on Maggie's shoulder, Callie squeezed her eyes shut in a futile endeavor to eclipse the painful scene. "I'm not so sure, Maggie," she said at last.

* * *

A steady rain was falling as mourners for Dr. Benjamin Jordan began to leave the cemetery. Joe Travis stood in the drizzle searching the faces that passed him on either side. He had not seen Callie since the day she had fled his office.

And then he spotted her among a few remaining people near the casket. With head down and lost in her own grief, he watched as she turned away and walked toward him, unaware of his presence.

"Callie?" She stopped and looked up. Rain slowly trickled down her face and hair. "May I take you home?"

Without hesitation, she nodded her head. He pulled her coat closely around her shoulders as he guided her in silence across the rain-soaked grass.

Inside the car, Joe slipped the key into the ignition, then paused before starting the engine. "Cal, I didn't mean to hurt you." He stared straight ahead, his hands gripping the steering wheel as he pushed the words forward. "I loved your father like he was my own dad, and I was devastated when I couldn't save him. After he died, I went over every move I made a thousand times, just trying to be *sure*." His hands grasped the wheel tighter for a moment. "But taking advantage of you wasn't the way to deal with my own grief."

"I was hurting too you know." Her voice was gentle with no hint of reproach. In surprise, he turned to look at her. "When you told me about Beth . . . it was more than I could take." She stared down at her hands. "I know by not telling me, Dad was only trying to protect me. But this time, it made things worse."

"I'm sorry, Cal. I guess I'm just as guilty as he is." Through the windows of the car, he glanced uneasily at the marble tombstones and crosses that glistened in the drizzling rain. "I *hate* this place. I haven't been back since . . . " He turned to look at her again. "I don't want you to be alone today."

"I don't *want* to be alone," she said.

* * *

By early evening, the Jordan house had emptied of friends and colleagues who had come from the funeral to express condolences. The house was quiet except for the monotonous sound of the rain that continued to strike the windowpanes.

Joe pulled the sliding oak doors together as he joined Callie in the den. The fire he had built earlier warmed the room with a gracious ambiance that sharply contrasted with the dampness felt throughout the rest of the house.

"Thank you for staying," Callie said as he sat down beside her. "I could never have stood this by myself."

"I wouldn't have been anywhere else."

His hand tightened around hers, and with his touch, her eyes began to fill with tears once more. In a single motion, he drew her toward him. She laid her head against his chest, finding more comfort in his deep and steady breathing than in all the sympathetic words that had been offered her. Tenderly, he stroked her hair until her weeping ceased.

At length, he rose to tend the fire. Callie watched as he placed another log on the dwindling embers. Idly, she studied the thin blue stripe of his dress shirt, the tie that now hung loosely around his neck, strands of light brown hair that brushed against his open collar. Though still strikingly handsome, it was evident he had aged since she had last seen him. His statuesque features had a tired, bleak appearance. And she knew why—too many cruel circumstances involving life and death decisions, both personal and professional, had taken a heavy toll.

"I don't know how I could have made it without your father." Joe broke the quietude as once more he seated himself beside her on the couch. "He could be so tough on me, so demanding, but he gave me everything he had." He glanced around the familiar room, always his favorite. "He opened this house to me, and it's been my place of refuge ever since. I'll always be indebted to him."

Callie smiled at Joe's touching tribute to her father. "You know as far as Dad was concerned, you were the son I was supposed to be." He glanced at her again, a slow smile covering his face as he reached over and flicked one of her curls. "I'm glad you weren't a son." Then he leaned toward the fire once more. "When do you have to go back?"

She imagined his voice carried a hint of longing. "I have a return flight at the end of the week. But I've been thinking about . . . coming home," she added with some hesitancy. "There's so much to do, what with settling Dad's affairs and all." She waited, wondering if there would be any response from Joe with regard to her faltering announcement.

"You mean . . . you'd consider moving back to Boston?"

"Well, maybe—that is, *if* I could get my job back in the OR, and *if* I had a good recommendation from somebody who might be interested in getting his old scrub nurse back. Only this time, a little healthier."

He squeezed her hand. "I guess I didn't get around to congratulating you on your surgery. And right now, I can't think of anything I'd like more than getting you back in the OR—*beside* the table, not *on* it."

Despite the cold rain and deep sadness shared by both of them, they laughed.

CHAPTER 22

Stephen Lewis looked like he had lost his best friend.

"Are you sure this is what you want, Callie? I mean, if it's a case of needing more time . . ."

Callie sat beside him on the couch inside his office. "It's not just that, Stephen. I don't know how long it's going to take to bring my father's work and estate to a close. It could take a *very* long time, and that wouldn't be fair to you. And Boston is my home, and I miss it." She smiled when Stephen affectionately squeezed her hand. She had become truly fond of him. "And I'll miss you too."

Callie's announcement had not come as a surprise but left Stephen feeling disheartened nonetheless. However, that was his problem, and he would not burden her with personal feelings now. "You haven't even been here for two months, but you've become such a valuable part of this team, Callie. The staff loves you, the patients love you, I—" The fragmentary sentence came to an awkward close as he glanced down at their joined hands.

"I feel bad about this, Stephen. I feel like I'm letting you down after everything you've done for me. There's no way I can ever adequately thank you."

"You don't owe me any thanks. Just stay in touch. Promise me that."

"I promise."

He knew there was nothing he could say that would persuade her to stay. Slowly, they rose to their feet and walked to the door, his hand still clasped firmly in hers. Only with great reluctance did he let go of it.

* * *

Stephen insisted on seeing Callie off at the airport a week later, with scores of promises that her job would be waiting for her should she ever wish to return.

As she left him in the waiting area while walking to her gate, she could see him growing smaller and smaller in the crowd of people. One last wave, and he was out of her sight altogether.

In a short time, she was settling back in her seat as the plane began its ascent. There was no doubt she had mixed feelings about what she was doing. With her father's death had come more changes in her life than she had ever imagined.

She was sure she was leaving something—and someone—that offered her more sanctuary than to that which she was returning. Maggie, of course, was thrilled that she had decided to come back to Boston. What sense would there be in leaving the trusted housekeeper to wander alone around that huge house?

And unquestionably, there was her work at the hospital, but aside from that, would there be anything else waiting for her when she got home?

* * *

Callie spotted Paul Martin waving his arm high above the heads of other passengers in the airport terminal waiting area. When she caught up to him, he wrapped her in a fatherly hug. "I bet you're glad to be home."

"It wasn't easy telling everyone good-bye, but it *is* good to be home." She glanced warily past Paul's shoulder. "I thought maybe . . . Joe would come with you."

"No, I'm afraid he couldn't get away, Callie."

She looked at her watch. "He's not still at the hospital, is he?

Did he have an emergency?"

"No, not exactly." Paul understood her bewilderment but hesitated to explain. He said nothing more as he picked up her carry-on bag, and they began to walk through the airport terminal.

"Paul," she said, "I didn't press him, but Joe never mentioned Beth once last week. Is he coping without her?"

Paul sighed resignedly. "He copes by working. He doesn't want to think about what his life is like now, so he deals with it by . . . by not dealing with it."

Callie's expression grew anxious. "But doesn't he talk with *you*?" "He doesn't talk with anyone. Joe has become a very angry man, and no one is exempt from that anger."

"I can't believe that. You can't be talking about the same Joe I know," she countered.

Paul shook his head sadly. "I'm afraid you're going to find a lot of things that aren't the same with Joe anymore."

* * *

Maggie McCarran was beside herself to have Callie back again. "I didn't know what I was going ta do ramblin' around in this gargantuan house all by meself," she confided to Callie over breakfast the next morning. "Before, there was no *end* ta what I needed ta do when your father was alive. And now . . . " Her voice trembled as she reached across the table and grasped Callie's hands. "Oh, Callie, I'm just s'glad ya decided ta come home!"

Callie squeezed the devoted housekeeper's hands in return. "I don't know what's going to happen, Maggie," she said at length. "All I *do* know is that nothing is going to be exactly like it was. I'll go over to the hospital soon to see what has to be done in Dad's office. After that, I just don't know."

* * *

Two days later, Callie walked across the hospital parking lot and through the doors of the adjoining medical office complex to her father's vacant office. Despite the dismal journey down the corridor, she felt strangely comforted by the familiar sights and sounds, and she was grateful she would be returning to work soon.

Reaching the office, she unlocked the door and stepped inside. Her eyes roamed the large, handsome room. Nothing was out of place, except Dr. Benjamin Jordan's conspicuous absence.

She walked across the floor and stood beside his treasured antique desk. Lost in reverie, she ran her fingers lightly across the polished wood, remembering a time long ago when she could barely see over the edge. How unthinkable that her father was no longer a part of this room, no longer there to occupy the big swivel chair.

Somewhere in her sadness came thoughts of Joe. Surely by now, Paul Martin had told him of her return, but there had been no inquiry, no phone call, no visit.

Paul's disclosure at the airport had left her feeling disturbed and anxious for him. Yet in spite of the ominous foreboding, the thought of being with him once again in any respect was cause enough for her. The tender comfort he had offered her the day of her father's funeral was still with her, and she longed for another quiet and gentle time with him.

Then from the hallway, she heard the sound of his voice. Eagerly, she stepped out of the office and saw him standing, in surgical scrubs, with a nurse at the far end of the corridor. But moments later, her enthusiasm to see him came to a sudden halt.

"This isn't the medication I ordered," she heard him snap.

The woman began to apologize. "I'm sorry, Dr. Travis. I don't know how it happened, but I'll have it changed right away."

"Have it changed right *now*. And I don't *ever* want to see a mistake like this again. Do you understand me?"

"Yes, sir."

Callie watched as he scribbled a new medication order and then shoved it into the nurse's open hands. Quickly, she stepped back into her father's office, unseen as he walked past the open door. A series of rapid footsteps followed as the chastised nurse hurried to correct the erroneous medication.

Had Paul been right? Was no one exempt from Joe's anger? Callie simply did not want to believe it. With a sense of sadness, she closed the door and locked it.

* * *

Several hours later, Callie had finished sorting through the first of numerous filing cabinets in her father's office. The scene she had witnessed between Joe and the nurse still troubled her. The only way she knew to deal with Joe's uncharacteristic behavior was to deal with it head on. However, her courage to confront him was dwindling.

She locked the door behind her. For now, the easiest thing would be to continue down the corridor and head straight out the front door, but her steps seemed to compel her to turn the corner until at length, she found herself standing in front of Joe's office.

The door was closed. She could hear nothing, no voices coming from the other side. It was getting late, long past office hours. *Whatdid she think she could possibly say to him that would make any difference?* Nevertheless, she was convinced that Joe was hurting, and she would allow nothing, even his anger, to prevent her from reaching out to him.

She put her hand on the doorknob, almost praying it was locked, but it opened with silent ease.

On the other side of the room, she could see the door to Joe's private office partly opened. A narrow thread of light spilled across the carpet. From where Callie stood inside the doorway, she could discern the backs of a man and woman hunched forward in front of his desk. Immediately, she began to withdraw until the man's anxious voice broke the silence.

"But, Dr. Travis, you haven't told us. Will she . . . *will she* be all right?"

Callie stopped, listening intently for the customary reassuring words, words she had heard countless times before, words that had come from the heart of a man who cared so much.

But she was disappointed. "Mr. Morton, as I told you before surgery, your daughter sustained a lot of internal injury. There's not much we can do right now but wait."

The man appeared to be wiping his eyes. "You know, we . . . we lost her a long time ago. It's been two years since she ran away from home. We never gave up searching for her but finally came to realize there was nothing more we could do. It was a friend here," he said, indicating the hospital, "that recognized her and called us." The woman squeezed the man's hand in hers. "All we want is to tell her how much we love her and want her to come home." His trembling words came to a halt. "I'm sorry. I don't usually do this." His hands rose and covered his face.

"There's nothing more I can tell you at this point." Callie heard Joe say in an officious voice. "She's still in recovery, but you can wait in her room."

Callie was riveted to the spot where she stood while she continued to listen, appalled and dismayed, to Joe's terse and unfeeling remarks. Her mind reeled, remembering the hundreds of surgeries he had performed, some of them hopeless, the majority of them brilliantly successful. She had come to believe a kind of magic lay within his hands, a gifted, healing touch that miraculously made everything all right.

Yet even though the hands still worked the same skillful magic, the touch had been replaced by insensitive routine. The healing of the injury might take place, but there would be none for the soul.

Suddenly, Callie felt a hand gently grasp her shoulder from behind. Startled, she turned and looked into the troubled face of Paul Martin, into the same troubled expression that mirrored her own. Embarrassed and almost numb from what she had just witnessed, Callie could only stare into the older man's discerning eyes.

They stepped into the corridor, after which Paul soundlessly pulled the door shut behind them. "I know, Callie. Now *you* know too."

* * *

"Joe, I've seen it myself." Seated behind his desk, Paul Martin jerked his glasses off, his face set like a marble stone, while Joe leaned back in the chair and listened with impassive interest. "You do everything within your power to avoid any kind of personal involvement anymore.

And where it shows is in your attitude of indifference toward your patients and their family members. The Morton girl is just another case in point."

At the mention of his patient's name, Joe's emotionless demeanor changed to provocation. "Since when has it become policy to eavesdrop on my private conversations with family members?"

"It hasn't, and I apologize for the accidental intrusion. I was on my way out last night when I happened to see Callie outside your door, and both of us overheard—"

"*Callie*? What was *she* doing there?"

"She told me she'd come down to talk to you, but after overhearing your curt explanation to the Morton girl's parents, she left. Joe, that girl's been gone a long time. She hasn't seen how emotionally detached you've chosen to become."

"Emotional detachment doesn't make me less sensitive to the needs of my patients," Joe contended, "only more impartial. There's nothing wrong with that."

"All the impartiality in the world doesn't compensate for a lack of empathy," Paul argued. "The textbooks may not reiterate it too often, but our profession calls for *more* than medical expertise. It calls for caring and understanding for how the patients and their families feel. It's that bond, that trust we form with them, that goes a *long* way in the healing process."

Joe leaned back against the chair, crossing one leg over the other. "Save this for the residents."

Exasperated, Paul leaned forward. "What makes you think it's some sign of weakness anymore to admit that you may have feelings too?"

"How I *feel* has nothing to do with my ability to treat my patients."

"It's not your ability that's in question." Paul slipped on his glasses. "Joe, some scars aren't visible, but they're still there, just the same. I know you lost the woman you loved, and you've had a lot of mental anguish because of it. No one expects you to be stronger than the rest of us, only human, *like* the rest of us."

"I haven't got time to listen to this." Angrily, Joe rose from the chair and made his way across the room.

Nevertheless, Paul's final words stopped him at the door. "You have many gifts, Joe. No one is sorrier than I am that compassion isn't among them anymore."

CHAPTER 23

Callie Jordan had spent most of the week in her father's office, sorting and boxing personal belongings in a poignant attempt to bring thirty plus years of service to a close.

Today, as she hoisted another box of books to the top of the desk, she glanced toward the open door in time to see Joe Travis walk by. He had yet to acknowledge her homecoming. Callie suspected he was aware that she had overheard his conversation with the Mortons. For that alone, she understood why he might not be in any frame of mind to welcome her back. She knew she owed him an apology, but her courage had failed in approaching him.

She picked up a roll of tape to fasten the box shut when she heard a slight knock on the opened door. "Are you receiving visitors?" The voice was calm, yet carried a hint of nervous anticipation.

She looked up to find Joe lingering inside the doorway, impeccably dressed in a dark blue suit and white tie. A half smile came to her lips. "You don't need an invitation."

He walked over to the desk, running his hand thoughtfully across some of the stacked textbooks. "This must not be very easy for you," he said quietly.

"No, it's not," she returned, shaking her head. "But better to be busy doing something, even as unpleasant as this than to sit around and brood."

Joe said nothing with regard to her intuitive remark. "When are you coming back to work?"

"Monday. You still want me?"

"Callie . . ."

She could not stand the uncomfortable reserve between them, but Joe didn't seem to be aware of it. She glanced down at the box again when she heard utterances of an awkward apology.

"I'm sorry I didn't call you when you got back. I've been . . . really busy. I'm glad you're home." He glanced at his watch. "I've got to go. I'm late for a meeting. Maybe we can have dinner one night." "I'd like that. You can wear that suit," she said with an approving nod, trying to ease the tension once and for all.

Joe nodded in accord, then turned and left the room.

* * *

The OR was no less demanding than Callie had remembered.

Three days following her return to work, her hands were busy setting up for a late afternoon emergency laparoscopic appendectomy. She had checked and rechecked her instrument tray when she suddenly realized she had forgotten a retrieval bag for the pending surgery.

She walked out of the OR suite into the supply room where she noticed two scrub nurses, their heads bent toward each other, deep in conversation. Callie ignored them as she began searching the shelves for the needed item, when she happened to overhear bits of their hushed discussion—a disreputable exchange concerning Joe.

As soon as they saw her, they quickly separated and left the room. Hurt and angered, Callie reminded herself she had a job to do, found the needed item, and went back to the OR.

Shortly afterward, the double doors swung open, and the stretcher came through with the patient, a child of ten, victim of an auto accident. She leaned over the gurney and spoke to him, squeezing his hand reassuringly as the anesthetist began to administer the sleep rendering drugs.

A moment later, Joe entered the operating suite, gowned and gloved, his preference now being to wait until his patients were draped and asleep before coming in. Thus, he had only to contend with the procedure and could disregard the individual beyond the anxious stare.

Callie took her place beside Joe, listening to the soft hissing of the machines that made the single audible sounds. With skill and proficiency, she assisted as he made the customary three incisions into the abdomen and then deftly inserted the camera for the appendectomy. The surgery proceeded quickly and uneventfully. Only necessary words were exchanged.

For the majority of Joe's surgical procedures, Callie had long been adept at anticipating what he would ask for, but today, as her thoughts wandered to the scandalous discourse between the two scrub nurses, her emotional state left her distracted.

Callie knew that where her coworkers merely saw an angry and impatient man, she saw much more. She could see plainly that Joe had turned his despair and resentment over losing Beth onto himself. However, the private pain he wrestled to keep within had succeeded in pushing her farther away, rendering her helpless to try to alleviate his grief.

It was true that since her return, the emotional changes she saw in Joe were almost more than she could tolerate. Her heart broke as she realized the gentle and compassionate man she had once known had become lost to her, lost somewhere in a bleak world to which he had succumbed.

She despised the callous reputation he had acquired, the prisoner of gossip he had become, the angry man whom Paul had affirmed. Oh, how she mourned the loss of his kind and sympathetic nature . . .

"Callie!" Jolted out of her rueful preoccupation, she realized Joe was preparing to close the incisions. Quickly, she reached for a pair of suture scissors, but in her haste, the instrument slipped from her hand, clattering loudly to the tile floor.

She looked at Joe. Choleric eyes matched scathing words that had never before been directed at her. "It's a good thing we're almost finished so you don't wind up *killing* this child with your inattention. Don't *ever* let that happen in my OR again."

Mortified, Callie watched as every member of the surgical team turned to look at her. Burning tears welled in her eyes until she could hardly see. She promptly handed Joe another pair of scissors. When he had finished suturing the last incision, he made one final check on the boy and then left the room.

An awkward silence followed as the child was wheeled out to the recovery room. Callie tenaciously busied herself until she was the only one left in the OR. Tears she had managed to hold back now fell freely down her cheeks.

As she left the operating room suite, she knew without a doubt that Paul Martin had been right. *No one* was exempt from Joe's anger.

* * *

In the waiting room adjacent to the OR, the mother of the young appendectomy patient clung to Joe's hands while the quiet, nervous father looked on. "Will he be all right?" the universal words spilled out.

He could feel the woman's hands tightening around his own, and he wanted to retreat, to withdraw from the clutching fingers and fretful eyes. But this was part of his job. "He's going to be all right. He's awake and in recovery right now. You can see him as soon as he's back in his room."

"Will there be a scar? Will he have a scar the rest of his life?"

Some scars aren't visible, but they're still there, just the same. As Joe regarded the woman's worried face, the heated encounter in Paul's office several days before came back to him.

There had been a time when he had once touched these families, gazed into their eyes with pity and compassion and understanding, put a comforting hand on their shoulders in a genuine effort to impart to them some his own strength. He remembered praying with them, assuring them they were not alone, would *never* be alone. He had willingly done all within his power to console them, taking their telephone calls day and night, celebrating in their joys and sharing in their sorrows. Always, he had tried to impress on them that God knew what was best in every situation. Because in spite of everything, he had believed that "all things worked together for good."

What excuse was there for what he had just done to Callie in the OR? Where *had* his compassion gone for which Paul had expressed such grief?

"Dr. Travis? The scar?"

The anxious sound of his name suddenly brought him back to the present. "The scar will fade in time. Now if you'll excuse me." He gently pried the mother's hands away from his, then turned and walked away.

* * *

Night had drawn on like a black curtain as Joe trudged through the door of his outer office. The appendectomy had been his last surgery, but he had been on a quest of a different kind since then.

Walking through the outer office to his private office, he pushed the door open and turned on the light. And then he saw her.

Callie Jordan sat on the couch, her knees drawn up under her chin, her head on her arms. Relieved, Joe leaned against the doorjamb, sighing heavily. "I've been looking everywhere for you." When she said nothing, he crouched on the floor in front of her. Whatever she was prepared to say, he knew he had coming. "Cal, I'm sorry about the OR. I was completely out of line."

"No," she said, her voice trembling as she shook her head, "you were right. The OR is no place for daydreaming."

An admission of blame was the last thing he was expecting. With her self-admonishment came an even greater loathing for himself, too much like the day he had so rashly kissed her. He put his hands around hers, gently coaxing her to look at him, convinced she had every right to despise him.

At length, she lifted her head, her face streaked with tears, but instead of justifiable anger, he saw only unspeakable sadness. His head drooped to avoid the heartrending expression. "All I've done is hurt you since you came back."

"Yes, you've hurt me . . . but it's *yourself* you've hurt the most!" In sudden urgency, she grasped his hands as fresh tears began to slide down her cheeks. "Can't you see what you're doing to yourself? You're still the same gifted *surgeon* you always were, but you aren't the same *man* anymore!"

Her tender appeal touched his heart as nothing had before. He knew she was right. He wasn't the same man he had once been. He no longer knew who he was, only that he detested who he had become. *A brain without a heart is really nothing.* Ben Jordan's insightful words came back to him with more significance than ever before.

Slowly, he rose to his feet. "I know I've been unfair to you. But whatever I've done to you can't compare with what I did to Beth." He turned back to his desk. "She's dead and all because of me."

Stunned, Callie looked up. "How can you possibly say that?" "Because I *never* should have let her leave the house that night!"

She shuddered as his fist came down violently on top of the desk. "*I* was the one who had her called to come to the hospital that night! It's *my* fault she was trying to get here in a blizzard!" His voice began to tremble. "It should have been me . . . *it should have been me . . .* "Callie rose from the sofa and came up behind him. "*Joe . . .* " Touched beyond reason, her arms encircled his quaking shoulders while she gently laid her head against his stooped back. "Oh, Joe, it wasn't your fault!" she whispered in earnest. "It was an accident! You *can't* punish yourself for something you had no control over."

Like a child, she led him away from the desk and back to the sofa, sitting down close beside him. He slumped forward and dropped his head into his hands.

"I can't live with this anymore. I'm so tired." His voice, weary and disheartened, faded away as he lifted his head and looked at Callie. His face was streaked with unleashed tears, his eyes desperately searching hers for some kind of answer for which he had none. "Cal . . . what's *happened* to me?"

He sank to his knees in front of her and crawled into her open arms. Bowing her head over his, she held him as something precious she longed to protect. "You're angry, Joe. And that's *all right*," she whispered, "but be angry with the circumstances, not with people who only want to help you! This afternoon, *I* was the object of your anger, but the one you're really angry with is *yourself*. Beth's death was an accident. It wasn't *your* fault, and it wasn't *God's* fault."

Still, Joe clung to her while she talked. "You've been hurt, and nothing is ever going to change that, but carrying this kind of guilt isn't going to change anything either. Beth wouldn't want that, and God doesn't *expect* that.

"But even though you carry a scar, you don't have to carry the pain." Lovingly, she caressed strands of his hair. "You can ask God to take away that pain by simply asking Him to give you forgiveness, even forgiving yourself. Forgiveness makes it possible for you to get on with your life. Resentment will only hold you back. Joe, you're fighting against something that you can't *hope* to win without God's help. And He's the *only* One who can heal you and make it possible for you to love again."

Once more, she thought about the reprehensible transformation that not only threatened to destroy his career but him as well. "I've known you a long time, Joe. I've seen for myself how guarded you've become. You're afraid if you surrender to the grief, it'll overwhelm you. But if you can just allow yourself the privilege of feeling, the healing will come."

For all his sorrow, for all his anger, resentment and guilt, no counsel offered to him had seemed as clear or as uncomplicated as the simple words Callie had uttered. "I was afraid to let anyone get close to me because I didn't want to be hurt like that again." His voice was muffled, his head still buried in her lap.

He bitterly regretted his lashing out at her in the operating room, realizing the scope of his guilt and grief had gone far beyond punishing himself. He pulled himself up and sat beside her. "Can you ever forgive me for humiliating you in front the entire OR staff? When I realized out of *my* anger I could hurt *you* and still in return you give me nothing but love and understanding . . . " His eyes met hers as his words trailed away. "Forgive me, Callie . . . please."

A smile crept over her face as she gently brushed strands of hair away from his eyes. "Of course I forgive you."

They talked far into the night. Every repressed emotion spilled over as Joe stumbled through his anger and rebellion, his resentment and regret, his paralyzing guilt and grief, until finally coming to a resignation he had been incapable of accepting until now. With Callie's understanding came a freedom he had not known for months, a liberation from a self-imposed loneliness he had endured for too long. And then, for the first time in a long time, he knelt with her, and together, they prayed.

Though she doubted in her own ability to mend the deep wound made by the premature death of her friend, Callie was sure of one thing: when Joe Travis allowed God to free him of his pain, she was convinced he would put himself once more in the hands of the only One who could truly heal his broken heart.

* * *

Morning light crept beneath the drawn curtains in Joe's office. Sprawled across the couch, he awoke and looked at his watch. He didn't remember falling asleep. He lifted his head and glanced around the room, but he was alone.

He struggled to a sitting position when he noticed a covered tray on his desk. Pulling away the cloth, he discovered a complete breakfast awaited him. He opened the note: "Breakfast is on me. Dinner is on *you*. Callie."

It had been a long time since he'd had any surprises and an equally long time since he had started a day smiling.

* * *

An hour later, Joe hurried down the corridor to catch up with Callie just before she got into the elevator. He could not help but notice her sleep-deprived eyes. "Breakfast was wonderful," he said with a grin as the elevator doors closed behind them. "And dinner is anywhere you want to go."

"It may cost you."

He lightly kissed her cheek. "Just name your price. I owe you more than I can ever repay." The doors opened, and they stepped out onto the patient floor. "I won't be long," he said softly. "Wait for me." Callie stood beside the nurses' station while he wrote orders and checked reports for some postsurgical patients. He seemed relaxed and calm this morning, friendly and considerate to the nurses.

His charting finished, Joe came back to where Callie stood waiting for him, and together, they walked down the corridor toward the OR. "Cal, I had an idea. How about taking a little time off?"

"Joe, I just came back. I don't see how I could ask for any time off yet."

He waved his hand. "That doesn't matter. What *does* matter is this," he said, coming to a stop and resting his hands on her shoulders. "Would you consider going away with me for a few days up to the mountains? Paul Martin's had a cabin up there for years he keeps telling me is mine any time I want it. There's a resort nearby."

"Oh, Joe, it sounds wonderful, but"—she shook her head— "you know how people around here talk—"

"Let them talk," he returned deviously. "Let's give them a real scandal."

"*Joe . . .*"

He laughed at her childlike innocence as they walked into an empty scrub room. There he stopped her again and turned her toward him. "I mean to be strictly honorable, Ms. Jordan. I thought if I stayed in Paul's rather rustic cabin, you might enjoy a lovely room with a view at the resort." He looked at her in earnest. "I *need* some time away from here, Cal. And I'd love to spend it with you."

"Well, in that case, Dr. Travis, I'd be more than happy to help nurse you back to health. When do we leave?"

CHAPTER 24

The drive into the mountains two weeks later was rejuvenating for both Callie and Joe. As they turned off the expressway and followed the two lane roads, they talked with the natural ease they had always enjoyed before. But Callie would not let herself be deceived. She knew that healing for Joe would not happen overnight. Letting go would take time.

They found Paul Martin's cabin first. Situated neatly at the end of a tree-lined dirt road, the small log home nestled unpretentiously among a cluster of evergreens. The scent of pine was strong, and a stream meandered lazily through the woods behind the house. The beauty of the forest was breathtaking, the air crisp and fresh.

Joe pulled his bags from the trunk of the car and dropped them on the porch in front of the door while he searched his pockets for the key. At last, he pushed the door open, and they stepped inside.

Callie's eyes opened wide as she surveyed the long abandoned living room. Thick dust gave a gray covering to the wood floor and furniture. "How long do you suppose since anyone's been in here?"

"Years, I'd say. I just hope we're alone in here," Joe returned cautiously, scanning the room for signs of uninvited life.

"Maybe if Paul knew the shape this place was in, he wouldn't have been so generous with his offer." Warily, she pulled open a closet door, found a broom shrouded in a dusty cobweb and began to sweep. It was almost dark by the time they drove to the lodge where Callie would stay. They ate supper in the large, beamed ceiling dining room, afterward taking a walk around the premises until at length they stood beside Joe's car.

"Are you sure you want to stay in the cabin?" she asked him. "Maybe they have available rooms here."

"I'll be fine," he reassured her. "We did a great job cleaning up." Then he grinned. "Maybe *that* was Paul's original idea, and we fell for it."

* * *

In the morning, Joe met Callie for breakfast in the lodge's dining room. Afterward, they drove into the nearby town and bought food for their time spent at the cabin.

Callie was in the kitchen putting away the groceries when she heard the front door bang shut. "I think we can survive a week on this," Joe called from the living room as he brought in the last of the bags.

"I think we could survive a *month* on this," Callie answered, surveying the abundance of food spread across the countertop. She reached up to put a box inside one of the overhead cabinets when something soft and swift skittered across her hand. Instinctively, she screamed and jumped back, whirling unintentionally into waiting arms behind her. She looked up into a dimpled face smiling down at her.

"Make a friend?" "That's not amusing."

"I wasn't trying to be amusing," he countered. "This is life in the woods."

She scowled. "Well, that kind of life can stay *out* in the woods." "Funny, I never thought you to be the kind that was afraid of mice."

She rolled her eyes. "I hate mice, spiders, and snakes. But not necessarily in that order."

Joe laughed. "You never would have made it in research."

Only now did Callie realize Joe had been holding her tightly in his arms the whole time. She felt her face begin to grow warm.

"You . . . better let me finish putting this stuff away before it spoils." Gently, she pulled herself away.

But as she did so, there seemed to be some resistance from her protector.

* * *

The cottage was charming, despite its rustic character. Joe even took pleasure in pumping gallons of rusty water from the hand pump at the sink. He found an axe in a shed behind the cabin and chopped enough wood to build a fire in the fireplace after supper that evening before taking Callie back to the lodge.

"You ever been canoeing?" he asked her as they walked down the hall to her room.

"I'm a city girl, Joe. What do you think?"

She handed him her room key, and he slipped it in the lock. "I think it's about time you tried it. There're miles of beautiful lake out there. What do you say? Tomorrow?"

"If you do the rowing, I'll beat time."

The dimples in his cheeks deepened with his smile. "Guess that makes me the galley slave." She grinned. "See you for breakfast?"

"I'll see you for breakfast."

He opened the door for her, leaving the key in her hand. He waited until she was safely inside before going back to his car.

* * *

A brilliant red sunrise began a warm and windless day. The lake was calm, and Callie enjoyed watching Joe propel the canoe through the still water. As they rounded each bend in their excursion of the lake, she took notice of everything around them—the plunging of the paddles dipping and rising in the water, the chirping of the birds, the mournful sound of the breeze passing eerily through the trees along the shoreline.

They ate a picnic lunch along the water's edge and, by mid-afternoon, had explored much of the eight-mile lake and several of the walking trails. But late in the day, as they turned the canoe in the direction of the lodge, dark clouds began to veil the sky. A strong wind came up quickly, causing the tranquil lake to churn and whip into small waves.

"Joe, we're never going to make it back before this storm breaks!" Callie called over the wind.

"We'll make it over to those trees, but I'm afraid you're going to get wet before we get there!"

They paddled hard toward the water's edge. Once in the shallows, Joe slipped over the side and hoisted the canoe as far onto shore as he could. Callie stumbled toward him in an effort to get out of the teetering boat, but Joe feared she would never make it without falling.

"Callie, take my hand!" he yelled above the rising wind. She grabbed it, and he pulled her toward him just as the sky broke loose. Rain assailed them as they bolted for the trees.

The rain fell harder as they scrambled for shelter below the swaying pines. They crouched beneath the thick branches, huddling close to the trunk of the tree. Joe wrapped his arms around Callie, tucking her head under his own as a bolt of lightning exploded over the lake, followed by a peal of rolling thunder. He could feel her shaking, maybe more from fear than being wet.

The wind shrieked through the trees, sending sprays of leaves, twigs, and pine needles through the air. The lake churned in front of them, with miniature waves washing end over end onto the shoreline.

Joe lifted Callie's chin and looked at her. Rain trickled in steady rivulets down her face. "You okay?" he shouted above the wind.

"I'm fine!" He was sure he saw a certain amount of apprehension in her eyes, but at the same time, a smile crept over her face. "If we ever do this again, let's check the weather report first!"

The muffled sound of his laughter drowned in the wind and rain as he tucked her head under his own once more.

* * *

Callie stepped out of the bathroom, almost lost inside the ample terrycloth bathrobe, an amenity provided by the lodge. Her wet hair was wrapped in a large white towel.

Joe turned away from the window and grinned at her disheveled appearance. "Feel better?"

"Much. Is it still raining?"

"Well, the moon's definitely not out," he answered without enthusiasm, glancing at the tiny rivulets of water weaving paths down the glass. "At least the wind died down some."

"Well, you got us back in one piece," she added optimistically. "I never would have dreamed you could row that fast. You didn't need me to beat time after all."

He turned away from the window and sat down in a chair near the fireplace. "What you should do is beat *me*. I'm really sorry, Cal. I never gave a thought that the weather would turn bad. It was so beautiful this morning! That brilliant red sunrise—"

"*Red sky at morning, sailors take warning,*" she admonished as she sat down on the floor next to him.

"*Red sky at night, sailors delight,*" he finished the adage. With a mischievous grin, he pulled the towel off her head and began towel-drying her hair.

"Joe, you've been in those wet clothes for hours. Don't you at least want to take a hot shower?"

"So I can put them on again just to drive back to the cabin?" He pulled the stuck wet shirt away from his chest. "I'll be all right. If I catch my 'death of cold,' I know what to do. I just feel bad for putting you through that storm."

"You want to know something?" she said, smiling up at him. "In spite of the storm, I had a wonderful time. I think I could even get used to living in the country. What about you? Would you miss the city?"

"You mean the traffic, the noise, the sirens, the stress, the ER?" He shook his head, stretching back in the chair. "I'd miss being a doctor. But not life in the city. In fact, I might even enjoy being a country doctor."

"And you'd make a good one. Your patients would appreciate you."

He leaned forward and looked down at her. "Cal, I hope you know how much I appreciate you. This trip has been wonderful for me. I would never have enjoyed it as much if I'd come alone." He paused and looked searchingly at her. "Somehow, you've always been there just when I needed you the most."

"Joe . . . " she began, faltering for words she could never say aloud, "*I've* needed you more than you ever thought you needed . . . " Embarrassed by the impulsive pronoun, she quickly tried to make a correction. "I mean *we* . . . Dad and I."

He reached down and squeezed her hand. There was no need for words. He always knew when to come to her rescue.

Joe glanced at his watch. It was late, and he was sure Callie was exhausted. "I guess I better go and let you get some sleep." He rose to his feet and pulled her up easily alongside him.

As he affectionately squeezed her shoulders, a strong desire suddenly overcame him, an intense longing not to be alone this night, a need to stay just where he was. He knew he should leave, knew all the reasons why he should leave, except for the one reason that eluded him. *Was it the late hour? Too weary to drive back to the cabin? His imagination? Could it be possible, after all the years he had known her . . .*

His hands tightened around her shoulders. Undeniably, he knew he must not linger. He leaned over and kissed her cheek. "I'll see you in the morning."

The door closed with a quiet thud behind him.

* * *

He didn't realize until now how worn out he really was.

Joe pushed open the door to the cabin. Stepping into the darkness, he fumbled for the wall switch and flipped it on. The soft light from the wagon wheel chandelier dispelled the shadows in every corner.

He went into the bedroom, kicked off his shoes and stretched out, face up, across the bed. His clothes were still damp, but he was suddenly too tired to change them.

He stared up at the ceiling, cradling his hands behind his head, and listened to the rain. Usually, he enjoyed the comfortable sound of a rainstorm, but tonight, it was a lonely sound.

He thought about the fierce afternoon storm he and Callie had been caught in, how they had crowded together beneath the trees not only for shelter but for mutual reassurance. Holding Callie next to him had been so comforting, so calming. And he began to wonder if he had felt something more for her than brotherly protection.

He closed his eyes. He was tired. Not just physically, but tired of being alone, and tired of facing the tempests in his life alone. How ironic that Callie seemed to be protecting him now just as he had tried to protect her through the years.

His thoughts moved from the day's events to a wordless prayer. Gradually, he had begun to find himself in prayer again, slowly beginning to trust once more, consciously willing to put the past behind him. But his life still had missing pieces. There were gaps in a future he was not yet sure of.

At length, he drifted off to sleep, listening to the lonesome sound of the rain softly striking the windowpanes.

* * *

A steady rain fell all night. Morning ushered in a thick fog that lingered like a ghostly figure over the lake, but by early afternoon, the sun came out.

Joe slept late and didn't get to the lodge until almost noon. After lunch with Callie in the dining room, they set off by foot down an old mountain path close to the hotel, dodging puddles of water that had collected during the night. Occasionally, they passed other hikers, most of them campers at a nearby campground.

They hadn't gone far when a distant scream pierced the air. Joe glanced quickly at Callie and then set off at a high speed run toward the sound.

He found himself on the outskirts of the campground where he soon discovered the source of the anguish. In the distance, he could see a dark haired woman leaning over a young child, sobbing as she rocked him back and forth in her arms.

Out of breath, he came to a stop beside her. "What happened?" The woman was obviously too distraught to explain. A bag of marshmallows lay scattered across the ground next to a smoldering fire. Beside the fire were several long, metal spikes, evidently used as spears with which to toast the marshmallows.

But one was coated in bright red blood several inches from the tip. Joe guessed the child must have been running with the spike and had slipped on the muddy ground, stabbing himself somewhere in the chest, but the woman clung to him so tightly he could not see where the wound was.

"Oh, please help him!" she sobbed. "Please!" By now, other campers had begun to gather.

Joe tried to pull the woman away from the child, but in her agitated state of mind, she refused to let go. "I'm a doctor. I think I can help him," he said in a gentle, but compelling, tone of voice. With assistance from another camper, Joe managed to pry the woman away from the boy in order to examine his injury.

Callie had arrived by now. She tried in vain to extract the story from the mother while Joe ripped open the child's blood-soaked shirt. "Cal, there's no time for that," he said with quiet urgency. "He's barely breathing. We've got to get him out of here, *fast*."

A man stepped forward. "You can put him in my car. I've been fishing up here for years. I know where to take him."

Joe pressed his keys into Callie's hand. "I'll take the boy and go with him. You follow in my car with the mother." In a single movement, Joe scooped the child into his arms and ran with the man toward his station wagon.

* * *

The two vehicles came to a screeching halt in front of an older two-story house that served as the doctor's office and home in the nearby town. A weather beaten sign bearing the name "Edgar Caviness, M.D." swung lazily on two rusty chains from beneath the porch roof.

The driver of the car pushed open the dilapidated screen door as Joe rushed inside with the child in his arms. Dr. Caviness, clearly past the age of retirement, led the way to the one examination room. Joe laid the boy on the table, unaware until now that his own shirt was covered in blood. Callie stood by the mother inside the doorway while the distraught woman continued to sob.

With no time for introductions, Joe briefly gave the doctor his assessment of the child's condition. The older man slipped his stethoscope into his ears, watching the steady trickle of blood that ran continuously down the left side of the chest. The boy's skin was cool to the touch, his eyes unresponsive to light.

Caviness pulled the stethoscope away from his ears and glanced resignedly across the table at Joe. "There's no heartbeat," he said as quietly as possible, shaking his head in dismay. "It was a gallant effort, Doctor, but I'm afraid we're too late."

"No!" the mother screamed as she pulled away from Callie. Callie struggled to hold her back from the examination table. "Do something! Do *anything!* Don't let my boy die!" she sobbed. "*Please don't let him die . . .*"

Callie's eyes met with Joe's, her eyes pleading with his. It was out of character for him to give up without a fight, and she knew it, regardless of how impossible the situation appeared.

Joe turned back to the doctor. "I want the biggest needle and syringe you've got, a scalpel, and a retractor."

"I don't *have* a retractor. This isn't one of your fancy city operating rooms," he returned in a terse voice. With a nod of his head, he gestured toward the sobbing mother, still tight in Callie's embrace. "Doctor, really, this woman has been through enough."

"Just give me what you have," Joe commanded quietly. "What I want to do may not matter one way or the other, but at least let me try."

Reluctantly, the older doctor collected an assortment of instruments and placed them on a sterile towel beside the table.

With skilled precision, Joe inserted the needle through the boy's chest cavity. Immediately, he began suctioning blood through the syringe. As the pressure surrounding the heart was alleviated, the organ began beating once more.

"Callie!" Joe called. She released the mother to the doctor and then came beside Joe. "I'm going to make an incision here," he said, pointing to an area near the entry wound. He glanced anxiously around the room. "But I need something to retract the ribs while I find the hole in his heart."

"Will these do?" she asked, holding up her hands.

Joe was impressed with her acuity. "How long can you hold on?"

"As long as I have to." Caviness showed her where to wash up, then opened a pair of sterile gloves and slipped them onto her hands. Joe made the incision, and then Callie slid her hands inside, gingerly pulling apart the ribs. With the heart exposed, he found the small puncture and pinched it shut with his fingers. Deftly, Joe sewed the perforation closed with a suture needle, finally allowing Callie to release the ribs.

"We're going to have to airlift him out of here. Where's the nearest place a helicopter can land?" Joe asked the older doctor as he placed sterile gauze over the chest incision, carefully taping down three sides to allow air to escape.

"In town, about three miles down the road. We had to airlift a cyclist out of here just last summer." Caviness hurried into the next room to make arrangements over the phone.

Callie began to wrap the boy with blankets to keep him warm while Joe went to the sink to clean up. But the child began thrashing about on the table. "Callie, keep him still," Joe cautioned over his shoulder while he washed. "I don't want him moving any more than possible."

A few minutes later, Joe and Caviness loaded the boy into the back of the driver's old station wagon. Callie crawled in the back to monitor the child while the doctor assisted the mother into the front seat. Joe stuck his head through the rear window and checked his patient one more time. "Stay with him, Cal. I'll be right behind you."

"See that you *are*," she said with apprehension. The car sped away in the direction where the helicopter was to meet them.

Joe turned to get into his own car when Caviness stopped him, placing his hand on his arm. "Doctor, I know you're in a hurry, but I just want to tell you . . . " he hesitated, "I just want to tell you that was some of the finest work I've ever seen. Out here, there's not much call for the kind of skills you have. But that boy would be on his way to the morgue right now if it weren't for you." He extended his hand. "You and your wife make a wonderful team."

Joe opened his mouth to correct the man's misunderstanding but instead accepted his outstretched hand and squeezed it. "Thank you, sir. I appreciate all your help." He climbed into his car and drove off, leaving a spray of gravel behind him.

* * *

Joe arrived just as the helicopter was making its descent onto the parking lot where the boy would be transported to Boston. A gathering throng watched as paramedics slid the child, now conscious and crying, into the chopper.

Callie's arm encircled the mother until the helicopter lifted off and was out of sight. Then, amid the scattering crowd, she spotted Joe shaking hands with the driver, who had generously agreed to take the mother to the hospital.

Joe reassured the woman once more as he helped her into the man's car and then watched as the vehicle quickly disappeared around the bend in the road. Draping his arm around Callie's shoulder, he guided her across the parking lot until they came to a stop beside his car.

"Do you think he'll make it?" she asked.

"I'm not sure, but I think he's got a fighting chance."

Callie shook her head wearily as she slumped against the door of the car. "That was too much like work."

"You were terrific," he said, grinning admirably at her. "You knew just what to do, and you handled that poor woman with perfect control."

Callie glanced down at the ground, embarrassed and self-conscious of the praise. "I didn't feel in perfect control. Besides, you were the one who saved his life."

Gently, he lifted her face toward his. "*We* saved his life."

Joe watched as her smile slowly returned, but this time, he saw something else, a familiar expression that he recognized but could not explain, again drawing him to her in a way he had never been drawn before. Her eyes, wide and imploring, appealed to him, but without insistence.

Tenderly, he put his hand against her cheek. "Callie . . . " But something held back the elusive words as his hand slipped away. With a vague sense of reluctance, he opened the car door. "Let's get some dinner."

* * *

Callie lay awake a long time that night, thinking about the child she and Joe had ministered to earlier in the day. She fully believed God had led them just where they were needed and at the exact time they were needed. She was sure the boy would survive. Joe's skills had been unparalleled in bringing him back from the very brink of death. She thanked God for allowing them to be part of such a miracle.

She wondered what Joe was thinking about right now. She brushed her fingers across her cheek, remembering the gentle touch of his hand. She thought about the restless but tender expression on his face the previous night just before he left her room. *Had* something genuine passed between them? She struggled to dismiss the appealing notion. There had been too many disappointments through the years.

She glanced at the clock beside the bed. It would be dawn in a few hours. She imagined Joe sleeping peacefully in Paul's cabin, far away from the wail of the ambulance sirens, the telephones, the life-and-death decisions, the trauma she faced every day.

And she was glad.

* * *

Callie descended the staircase the next morning and found Joe already waiting for her in the lobby.

"Did you sleep well?" he asked as they walked into the dining room for breakfast.

"Did you?"

"Not that well," he said with a grin as they seated themselves at a table near the windows.

She nodded in agreement. "I suppose you had the little boy on your mind too?"

"Not entirely," was all he said.

CHAPTER 25

Two days later, Paul Martin gingerly clapped Joe on the back as he walked into the doctors' building. "I wanted to be the first to congratulate you! I understand the boy you sewed up is doing just fine. You were a real hero."

Joe shook his head, disregarding the unwelcome praise as they walked down the hall together. "Callie and I were just in the right place at the right time. That's all there was to it."

"Well, according to the mother of the boy, that's not all there was to it. She was quite grateful for everything you did." They stopped when Paul put a firm hand on Joe's arm. "I hope you take the time to stop by his room and accept her esteem—humbly, of course." Joe recognized the artful command and nodded a grudging consent as they began walking again. "So," Paul continued amiably, "how'd you find the cabin? I haven't been up there in years, you know."

"You don't say?" Joe returned sardonically, coming to a stop beside his office. "You'll have to tell me about it sometime." Grinning, he went inside, leaving a bewildered Paul standing outside the door. Joe dropped into the swivel chair behind his desk and dismally surveyed the accumulation of mail and messages. Though arranged in orderly piles by his secretary, Kate, it still meant hours of sorting and decision-making.

But for now, he decided to forego the inevitable task. Turning around, he leaned against the back of the chair and gazed out the window. The morning sun dazzled against the walls of the adjoining hospital and other buildings that surrounded the university campus.

Though looking, he was not really seeing. In his mind stretched the mountains, the lake, the old stone lodge, the cabin, the forest trails. Something was happening to him. For the first time in months, he was beginning to awaken with a sense of purpose, with reason to be content, as he had not been since Beth died. He had found cause to laugh again. Even his work, though never mundane, had taken on a new kind of challenge. Gradually, he found himself looking ahead, with less resentment for what had been left behind.

And he knew what the sustaining influence was behind all the good that had come to him—Callie Jordan had somehow begun to transform his life at a time when it had become all too complex.

With a reluctant sigh, he turned around and began to sort through the work on his desk.

* * *

"Mrs. Morales? Do you remember me? I'm Joe Travis. I—" "Yes, yes! Dr. Travis!" The dark haired Latino woman sprang to her feet when Joe entered her son's room. "You save my boy's life. I ask that nice Dr. Martin to please send you here. I wanted to thank you with all my heart for what you did."

Embarrassed, Joe accepted the woman's outstretched hands. "I'm glad I could be of help." He stopped beside the bed and smiled down at the boy. "And how are *you* doing?"

"Fine now," he said.

The door opened, and to Joe's relief, Callie walked in. Juanita Morales hugged her. "How are you?" Callie asked brightly. "Is everybody treating you okay?"

"Everybody treat us just fine," she said. Then, stepping back, she grinned at both of them. "You make good team," she said, beaming with affection.

Joe remembered the same words from Dr. Caviness. After a few more minutes of what seemed like endless accolades, he excused himself and Callie. They walked down the corridor and through the front doors, crossing the parking lot. A few minutes later, Joe opened the door to his outer office. Kate was on the phone behind her desk.

She balanced the receiver against her ear while handing him a stack of calls awaiting him. Joe took them into his private office with Callie following behind him.

She watched while he flipped through the seemingly endless messages before dropping them onto his desk. "It's my guess you'll be ready for another vacation in about a week, right?" she asked knowingly. "I think I will too."

Joe looked at her appreciatively. "You can't leave me now. We 'make good team,' remember?" His expression was full of affection as he came closer and put his hands around her shoulders. "And you know something? I really think we do."

His eyes searched hers for but a moment before he drew her toward him and tenderly kissed her. This time, there was no impulsiveness, no reckless desire borne of a grieving heart, only a gentleness Joe had almost forgotten. As his hands slipped away from her face, he asked, "Will you have dinner with me tonight?"

She smiled. "All right."

* * *

The candlelight in the restaurant flickered unevenly across Joe's pensive face. Callie watched as he toyed with the half-eaten food on his plate. He had been unusually quiet throughout the entire evening, preoccupied to a greater extent than she had ever seen before.

"You've hardly touched a thing," she said at last, breaking another long session of silence. "I always thought you liked this place."

"I do. It's fine."

She rested her chin in her hand. "Oh, I see. *That's* why you've eaten so much."

"Yes, exactly."

She leaned toward him. "I know when something's bothering you. Is it a patient?"

"No, it's nothing like that." He laid down his fork and looked at her. "It's you."

"*Me?*" She sat up again.

His hand reached across the table and closed around hers. "Cal, I'm not sure what I would have done without you through the years. You've been my friend, my colleague, my confidante, but things don't always stay the same."

She gave him a friendly smile. "Nothing could ever change between us."

"They already have, Cal. They changed for me a long time ago. I just didn't realize it." He glanced away before looking at her once more. "My life fell apart after Beth died, and I forgot the way things used to be. You've helped me remember who I was, who I used to be. But I can't be that person . . . without you."

She watched the candle's wavering reflection in his eyes. "You've always been so strong, even in the worst of times. I've always . . . admired you for that," she returned with carefully chosen words. "I never thought of you needing *me*."

"Well, I do need you. I was so full of grief and anger after Beth died, I didn't think I could ever love anyone again, even *want* to love anyone again. But *you* told me God could make it possible. And He has." His hands tightened around hers. "I love you, Cal. And I want to ask you to be my wife."

His simple proposal restored the secret desires she had struggled to put behind her since his marriage to Beth. Yet his words and actions of late had been no secret, no flight of her imagination.

Nevertheless, instead of the joy she had always anticipated, she felt a sense of disillusionment. For Callie was no longer the naive and helplessly dependent young woman who she had been before. Selfreliant and no longer constrained by her poor health had been cause for her to reevaluate her life and purpose. Though she had been devastated by Joe's marriage to Beth, it had prompted an independence she had been forced to accept.

But there was no denying that she still loved him, and she was sure there could be only one reason why he might suppose he was in love with her now.

"Joe, Beth hasn't been gone a year yet, and I know how lonely you've been."

He shook his head. "That's not why I want to marry you. And it's not an answer." His gentle expression pleaded with her. "Cal, is it so difficult to think of me as . . . something more than an old friend?"

Oh, if he only knew! Even now she was too ashamed to admit the love she had always had for him, too ashamed to admit she had never stopped loving him even after his marriage to Beth. "No, of course not," she answered at last.

For a moment, his gaze rested on their joined hands. "Then . . . are you saying you don't think you could ever love *me*?"

Her mind reeled for an honest answer in light of the awkward question. "No . . . I'm saying I'm no substitute for Beth."

His expression grew incredulous. "Is that it? You think I'm looking for some sort of . . . replacement? Cal, be fair! Don't condemn me without a trial. It's *you* I want."

"I'm not condemning you. But consciously or unconsciously, I could never live up to your expectations of her."

"I don't expect you to be Beth!" he declared in disbelief. "Cal, I didn't realize what you'd come to mean to me until after your father died. That night when you came to my office . . . " He looked away, ashamed, remembering. They had never spoken of the impetuous incident apart from the funeral. "I thought I kissed you out of my own grief. It wasn't until later that I realized how I felt about you went much deeper than that. I loved you then, Cal, and I love you now."

An uncomfortable silence fell between them. Callie glanced away to escape the compelling blue eyes on the other side of the table, but memories of Beth were not so simply avoided—growing up together, all the firsts they had shared, the girlish secrets between them. They had been as close as sisters. Callie had so wanted to be like Beth, but she wasn't like Beth. She wasn't beautiful, she wasn't clever and amusing, she wasn't engaging, strong, and full of spirit.

But she loved Joe Travis with a love like none she had ever known before.

Yet an angry jealousy had developed when Beth unwittingly surpassed her in the most private sphere of her life. Now that Beth was gone, she feared she was unintentionally being persuaded to play the part of the second wife—the second wife who could never hope to receive the same love as the first.

"Joe," she ventured timidly, "are you sure you aren't resolving to settle for someone who can make it easier for you to forget?"

His eyes betrayed unquestionable disappointment. "That's not the way it is, Cal. *I love you!* What can I do to make you understand that?"

"You don't have to do anything." Looking away, she added timorously, "You've always meant everything to me."

"Then what are you saying?"

"I'm only asking you to think hard about what you really want.

You asked me that once, remember? You wanted me to be sure."

He remembered. He had come to her father's house before she left Boston, only days after he and Beth had been married. "Yes, I suppose I did." He wouldn't pursue it any further. She meant too much to him. "All right," he conceded. With no more words, he rose from the table. He drew back Callie's chair as she stood up, and they made their way in silence out of the dining room.

As Callie followed Joe outside, her mind carried her back through the years she had known him, through the same years she had loved him. Filled with jealousy and disappointment after he had married Beth, eventually sheer loneliness for him had replaced the envy. Beth had not only become his wife but his confidante, and he no longer had the same need for her.

Gas-lighted lamps flickered across the parking lot where they lingered beside Joe's car. He stared down at the pavement, then looked at her. "Callie, I wouldn't do anything to spoil the relationship we've had all these years. I want you to know I love you, but I won't bring it up again, at least not until you want me to." Saying no more, he opened the door and helped her into the passenger side.

Both remained silent as Joe drove down the highway. Staring at the dark road ahead, illuminated only by the headlights of the car, Callie began to think about the events that had played out in their separate lives. Each had lost something of themselves that could never be recovered. Each had felt the effects of loneliness and separation.

In spite of his declaration, Callie knew how much Joe had loved Beth, a love not so easily forgotten, and now she wondered, could she live in the shadow of the woman he had first loved? Could she be content to be settled for instead of chosen? Had he proposed to her out of love or loneliness?

But given the love she had cherished for him for so long, what of it really mattered?

"Joe . . . would you want to live in your house or my father's?"

He glanced at her in surprise, momentarily taking his eyes away from the road. "What?"

"Would you want to live in your house . . . or my father's?"

He eased the car to a stop alongside the darkened road. The smile on her face was all the answer he desired. "It makes no difference to me as long as we're together." With inexpressible joy, he drew her into his arms. "Say it, Cal," he whispered. "Tell me what I want to hear."

At last, she uttered aloud words she had only dared to express in her dreams. "I love you, Joe. I love you, and there's nothing I want more than to be your wife."

He drew her closer and kissed her. "I don't want to wait long, Cal. I want to marry you soon. *Very soon.*"

"We can see Pastor Richards if you'd like." "That's what I'd like."

Callie put her arms around him. She knew nothing but the passage of time would resolve her unsettled feelings. But as she clung to the only man she had ever loved, every anxious thought vanished in the light of the happiness that finally lay within her reach.

CHAPTER 26

The warmth of the afternoon sun filled the late summer air. An assortment of wildflowers, scattered across the spreading lawns, fanned lazily in the breeze. Chickadees and cardinals sang from branches of hundred-year-old trees.

"What are you thinking?" Joe pulled Callie closer beside him as they surveyed Benjamin Jordan's historic property.

Her eyes wandered over the daunting exterior of the old mansion. "When I was a little girl, I was sure I really lived in a castle." Joe smiled in amusement. "Now I'm wondering if we could ever make it a little less . . . *austere*." She turned to look at Joe. "Are you sure you'd be happy living here?"

"Cal, this is your home. It's been in your family for generations. We can make it *our* home until we decide something else. And this way, we can keep Maggie on." Joe walked a few yards away from her. "Besides, it's big enough for all of us."

"It's big enough for a dozen of us."

He turned and grinned at her. "Okay, if you want a dozen kids, that's all right with me."

She felt her face flush. "Joe, I didn't mean . . . "

He came back, locking his arms around her slender waist. "I want a family, Cal. I want to come home to you and my own family. I've been alone too long, and I never want to be alone again." He cupped his hands around her face and kissed her. Then he glanced at his watch. "We're going to be late getting out to Paul's, and I'm supposed to introduce Dr. Rainer tonight."

* * *

Paul Martin's housekeeper opened the wide front door. The social gathering was well under way as Callie and Joe stepped into the foyer. Before they could lose themselves among the guests, Joe felt a familiar hand grasp his shoulder from behind.

"I thought you promised me you wouldn't be late." Joe turned to see Paul Martin's gaze bearing down on him.

"I'm sorry. Is it too late for the introduction?"

"Not quite. I just wanted to give you a hard time." Paul grinned as he winked at the young woman who clung to Joe's arm. "Callie, will Joe's introduction of Dr. Rainer make you uncomfortable?"

"Because he's taking my father's place? No, of course not."

A few minutes later, Paul brought the festive affair to a halt after motioning for Joe and Callie to come to the front of the room. Dr. Bob Rainer, a tall, distinguished looking man with graying temples, stood beside Paul as Joe commenced his unrehearsed speech.

"It was my privilege and good fortune to have been associated with Dr. Benjamin Jordan for many years, both personally as well as professionally. I know Dr. Jordan's passing has been felt by all of us, especially myself and Callie." He squeezed her hand hidden behind his suit coat. "But tonight, it's my pleasure to introduce to you the man who will be taking Dr. Jordan's place as chairman of the surgical department. Please welcome Dr. Robert Rainer."

A round of applause filled the room as Dr. Rainer made his way to the front. Joe extended his hand in welcome to the new department chairperson while Callie intuitively stepped back, but Joe gently urged her to stay beside him.

Rainer's speech was brief and well received. Afterward, Joe introduced him to Callie. "Dr. Rainer, I'd like you to meet my fiancée, Callie Jordan. Dr. Jordan was Callie's father."

Rainer clasped her hand in both of his. "I'm very happy to meet you, Ms. Jordan, and please accept my condolences. I only knew your father by reputation." She returned his cordial smile. Rainer glanced again at Joe. "And you say congratulations are in order? How soon?"

"In a few weeks."

"Well, many, many congratulations," he said once more.

At that moment, Paul approached them. "Bob, there's a number of people I'd like to introduce you to when you're free."

"Of course," Rainer returned graciously.

"And, Joe, may I speak with you for a minute?"

Joe and Paul stepped apart from the gathering when Rainer turned to Callie again. "Ms. Jordan, I wonder if it would be possible for you to bring me some of your father's accounting records for the department? I'd like to see some figures for the past, oh, five or six years. I didn't realize you had a wedding coming up, so your time is probably quite limited. Would it be asking too much to bring them by my office sometime this week?"

"No, not at all."

"Fine, fine, and thank you." He turned and disappeared into the crowd.

* * *

Joe eased the car to a stop in front of the Jordan house. He pulled Callie toward him, tenderly brushing aside loose stands of hair from her forehead. "I'm afraid I'm not going to see you for the next several days."

"Why not?"

"Paul asked me tonight if I'd take his place as a presenter at the surgical conference in San Francisco. He can't get away, and he needs me to go." He sighed heavily. "I'd much rather be here with you, believe me."

"When do you have to go?" she asked, not even trying to hide the dismay in her voice.

Joe's face mirrored her disappointment. "Tomorrow."

She leaned against his chest, despite the encumbrance of the leather bucket seats and gearshift. "Why did I ever get involved with surgeons and their schedules?"

She sat up when Joe pulled back. "And what does that mean?" he asked in mock derision.

A grin spread across her face. "It means I'll miss you. I'm tired of hearing my own echo in that great big house," she said, nodding toward the looming stone mansion beside them. "That place is just too big for Maggie and me."

He tilted her face toward his and kissed her. "That's all going to change soon." He got out of the car and opened the door for her, then walked with her to the house.

They stood on the brightly lit veranda. "You know Maggie is leaving in a day or so to take care of her sister."

"I don't like the idea of you being out here by yourself all that time."

"I don't like it either, but I'll be all right."

An impish mix of anticipation and mischief crossed Joe's face. "If we got married tonight, that would solve everything."

She smiled, then reached up and kissed him goodnight, a simple act she still could not take for granted. "You're tempting, but we're going to do this right."

* * *

Maggie McCarran hung up the phone. "Me sister's having her surgery day after tomorrow," she told Callie the next morning. "I'll have to leave this afternoon. Are ya sure you'll be all right if I go stay with her until she's on her feet again? It'll be a few weeks for sure."

"Maggie, don't give it another thought!" Callie exclaimed while removing her mother's wedding gown from the back of the bedroom door.

Maggie grimaced. "But the weddin's coming up so soon, and I don't want ya worrying that I won't get your mother's dress altered in time."

Callie smiled as she slipped into the gown. "You've been pulling off miracles for me as long as I can remember. Now I'm not worried and not another word about it!"

With that, Maggie made a quick tuck in the antique lace and inserted a straight pin. When Callie twisted a little to the left, Maggie promptly repositioned her. "Now hold still, or I'm liable to be stickin' *you* with these pins!" She shook her head. "You must be even smaller than your sainted mother because it looks like I'm goin' to have to take this in more than I thought."

"But you *can* do it, can't you, Maggie? I've always imagined being married in my mother's dress."

"That I know ya have," Maggie returned. "Don't ya worry. It'll be fine. No matter what, I'll be back in time to put the final touches to it." She turned Callie toward her to continue with the alteration. "How I wish your father had lived to walk ya down the aisle to Dr. Joe. How proud he would have been! And what a *ceremony* it would have been! And it wouldn't be at that darlin' little church, either. Nothing less than the National Cathedral would be my guess."

"You're right about that," Callie sighed wistfully. "For Dad, it wouldn't have been just a ceremony; it would have been a coronation." She began to smile. "Remember how Beth and I used to go up to the attic and pull out Mother's gowns and play in them? But we never touched her wedding dress. It was like . . . like there was something revered about it."

Maggie pushed in another pin. "I imagine your father would have had more than a few words to say to the two of ya if he'd caught ya up there."

"And what about you?"

"Ha!" Maggie laughed. "Don't be thinkin' I didn't know what ya two were doin', at least most of the time! Now hold still for one more minute, and I think we've about got it conquered." The housekeeper put the last pin in place.

Callie slipped easily out of the dress. "I never thought this would happen to me."

Maggie smiled while she laid the flowing gown across the bed. "I know ya didn't, but sometimes dreams do come true."

"But as much as I dreamed about it, I always knew it was just a dream. Even now, I find myself lying in bed at night and hearing Joe ask me to marry him over and over! Do you think that's silly?"

"No, I do not think it's silly," Maggie repeated. "Ya've been so in love with him for so long it only seems right that you're going to have your grand day at last. And Callie girl," she said softly, taking Callie's hands in her own, "ya don't know how grateful I am that you and Dr. Joe want me to stay on. I'm proud to take care of the both of ya."

Callie hugged her with deep affection. "We wouldn't have it any other way. You know that."

Maggie dabbed her eyes with her apron. "But didn't ya even consider livin' in Dr. Joe's house? It's a fine house in a lovely neighborhood."

"Joe's never said it, but I suspect there're too many memories in that house for him."

The housekeeper's observant eyes narrowed on Callie's. "And what about you? Are there too many shadows of the other wife for you too?"

Callie was silent for a moment. "I'm afraid there will *always* be those shadows for me, Maggie. It's something I'm going to have to learn to live with."

The telephone began to ring. Maggie picked up the bedside phone while Callie got dressed. The conversation was short and to the point, and a moment later, she replaced the receiver. "That was Pastor Richards," she said. "He wants to meet with you and Dr. Joe as soon as possible to finalize all the arrangements."

"I'll call him," Callie assured her.

The two women left the bedroom and began to descend the long staircase together. "Ya never told me how the party went at Dr. Martin's house last night."

"Dr. Rainer seems very capable," Callie told her. "Joe thinks he'll do a good job, which reminds me," she said as they reached the bottom of the stairs. "I promised I would bring him some of Dad's old accounting records. I don't remember seeing any financial files when

I was cleaning out his office. Do you have any idea where they might be?"

"I suppose everything that's *anything* is most likely locked in your father's desk or one of those file cabinets in the den. I can help ya look for them."

"No, no, you have enough to do getting ready to leave today. I'll look for them as soon as I get home from work tonight."

* * *

Callie was late getting home that evening. She dropped her purse on the deacon's bench in the entrance hall, then read the note Maggie had left on top of the neatly stacked mail beside the phone.

"Dr. Joe called; arrived safely and will call soon. You know where to reach me if you need me. Maggie."

Callie smiled at the note, pleased that, in spite of his schedule, Joe could be so considerate. She sorted through the mail, then dropped the envelopes on the table and went into the den to search for the records Bob Rainer had requested.

She sat down behind her father's antique desk and unlocked the drawer. Inside were countless files, most of them recent, some yellowed with age. She sighed deeply, recalling her father's refusal to throw anything away.

She began to sort through handfuls of documents for the accounting records when one file caught her full attention. Her name was written on the tab, scrawled in her father's familiar handwriting. She could not imagine what it was.

Curiosity caused her to set aside the rest of the charts as she placed the mysterious file on top of the desk. Opening the folder, she carefully scanned the papers until a terrible reality began to dawn on her.

With trembling hands, she lifted one of the documents out of the folder and stared at it in wide-eyed horror. "*It's not possible . . .*" she whispered aloud, her voice quivering on the edge of panic. "*It can't be possible . . .*"

The document slipped from her grasp, scattering with the others on the floor as she thrust her hands over her face.

CHAPTER 27

Paul Martin's friendly smile invited Callie into his spacious den early the following morning. One glance at her bleary eyes confirmed what he had suspected from her phone call the night before. "This must be pretty serious for you to come all the way out here," he said as they sat down together. "We could have talked in my office."

"I know," she returned quietly. "It's just . . . it's not something I could talk about at the hospital." He watched her pull some papers from her purse. He couldn't help but notice the trembling in her hands as she passed them to him. "I found these last night in my father's files. No one else has seen them."

"No one—*no one* meaning Joe?" She nodded as he took the papers. Paul slipped his glasses out of his shirt pocket. She watched his amiable expression begin to wane as he perused the documents. After a few minutes, he removed his glasses and tucked them into his shirt pocket once more. "Do you intend to show this to Joe?"

Callie's eyes widened with disbelief. "How can I? What do you think it would do to him?"

Paul's expression sobered as he glanced down at the papers and then back to Callie. "I'm not sure. But how long do you think you can keep this to yourself?"

"As long as I have to, as long as it matters—"

"What matters," Paul interrupted, "is the degree of Joe's involvement."

She looked down at her hands, too ashamed to lend voice to the unutterable truth. "How can I ever face him, Paul? How can I ever look at him again . . . knowing what I know?"

"But you can't hide this from him either. He has a right to know.

Callie, what exactly are you afraid of?"

She could almost feel Paul's gray eyes staring straight through to her miserable thoughts. She shook her head. "I don't want to lose him," she admitted softly. Then, lifting her head, she repeated with more intensity, "I *can't* lose him!"

Tears burned in her eyes as she buried her face in her hands. Moments later, she felt Paul's fatherly arm tighten around her shoulders. "Callie, I've known you a long, long time," he said in a soothing voice, "and I know you'll do what you think is right. But remember, Joe deserves what's right, too."

* * *

Callie drove home after leaving Paul's house, grateful that today was her day off. She was in no frame of mind to be at work.

At the end of the winding driveway, she parked her car and then walked toward the empty house. Her only consolation was that Joe would be out of town until tomorrow. At least that would give her a little more time, time to try and recover from what she could not accept as fact, time to decide what course of action she should take.

She pulled open the front door. Inside, the house felt so vacant with Maggie gone. She dropped her purse on the table in the foyer, then wandered down the long hallway. She stopped in front of the den where the two doors remained flung apart in her haste to leave the room the night before.

She stood looking inside. The chair behind her father's desk was pushed aside; the charts and papers she had begun to sort were scattered across the top, just as she had left them. A file drawer was still open, jutting out like a gaping tongue that threatened to divulge a deadly secret.

She closed her eyes, wishing she could pull the doors together and seal forever the revelation that loomed menacingly over her future. If only the dilemma could be solved so effortlessly.

Could she lock away forever what she had discovered inside this room?

* * *

The next morning dawned hot and muggy following another sleepless night. Summer's oppressive heat matched Callie's mood as she drove to the hospital.

Her mind seemed a complete blank. She could not come to a decision, could not make a choice as a result of what she had painstakingly divulged to Paul Martin. At least, she still had a little time. Joe would not be home until that evening.

And then, she suddenly remembered her father's empty office. If there was anything more to be found, that would be the only other place to look. Somehow, she would have to find time to search there, and she would have to do it today.

She walked out of OR Three after a routine surgery when she heard her name called from behind the nurses' station. "Callie, phone call for you."

She hurried down the corridor and reached across the counter for the telephone.

"Ms. Jordan, is there any way I could interest you in a gourmet cafeteria lunch this afternoon?"

The unexpected voice immobilized her. "Joe?"

There was a slight hesitation on the other end. "You sound a little panicked, Cal. Have you been seeing someone else in my brief absence?" Joe's deep and even voice, normally so comforting, now created within her an absurd anxiety.

"Where are you? Aren't you still in San Francisco?" she heard herself breathlessly asking the question.

"I'm on my way to the hospital right now. I was able to catch the red-eye flight last night. I was hoping to at least have lunch with you. Can you get away?"

Her mind was reeling. She couldn't—didn't—want to see him right now. She had always been an open book to him when he suspected something was wrong.

"I'll . . . I'll try, Joe."

"Okay, I'll meet you around one thirty. I'm supposed to be at a conference this afternoon, so I haven't got a lot of time. But I missed you, and I love you," he added quietly.

Before she could formulate an excuse, he had hung up.

She returned to the OR, forcing herself to consciously attend to her regular operating room duties until she was free by noon. When she finally slipped away, she hurried downstairs to her father's empty office. As she slid the key out of her scrubs pocket, she was grateful the lock had not yet been changed. She opened the door and stepped inside, carefully locking it behind her.

She glanced around the room. It was almost empty now, the books, boxes, and personal items having been removed in preparation for Dr. Rainer's arrival. Thankfully, the filing cabinets she had not emptied still stood in place.

She pulled open the first drawer and meticulously began to delve through each file.

* * *

Joe sat alone at a table in the hospital cafeteria, glancing at his watch for the fourth time in the past half hour. He was due at a clinical conference in twenty minutes, and there was still no sign of Callie. He drummed his fingers impatiently on top of the table while continuing to scan the faces coming and going in the crowded room. He checked his beeper again, but there were no return numbers. He had called his secretary twice, but there were no messages. It wasn't like Callie to break a date without getting some kind of word to him, even if he was in surgery.

Ten more minutes passed before he rose from the table. He could not be late for the conference. After the meeting, he would have to make third floor rounds with the medical students. Maybe after that, he could find out what was going on.

* * *

The clock high on the wall above the third floor corridor read four thirty in the afternoon. A group of medical students surrounded a weary Joe Travis as they reviewed the treatment plan for the last patient.

Joe happened to glance up when he spied Callie passing the nurses' station. Quickly excusing himself, he caught up with her, reaching for her arm as she swept past him. He pulled her to a stop, turning her toward him. "Hey, where *were* you? I waited in the cafeteria almost an hour."

Callie looked away from the penetrating blue eyes. "I'm sorry, Joe, I . . . got tied up."

He couldn't help but notice the over-sensitive tone of her voice. "It's all right," he returned quietly, guiding her toward the elevator at the end of the corridor. "I was just hoping for a passionate welcome home from you." The dimples in his cheeks faded with the teasing smile that was not returned. "Couldn't you have left a message with Kate? What were you doing anyway?"

They came to a stop in front of the elevator. "Joe, I just couldn't get away! Why are you questioning me like this?" Callie was growing increasingly agitated as she smacked the *Down* button with her hand.

He stood back and looked at her, astonished by her overreaction to a simple inquiry. She suddenly seemed more like a stranger than his fiancée. Nevertheless, maybe to her his concern did sound like an interrogation. "I'm sorry, Cal, I didn't mean to come across like that. Accuse me of being selfish and wanting to keep you all to myself." She glanced away, her expression never changing. In spite of everything, he persisted. "Let's have dinner someplace nice tonight—"

"Joe, I can't make it."

His expression fell as abruptly as her words. "Why not?" "I . . . I just have too much to do tonight."

"But we haven't had any real time together in days."

"I can't help it, Joe. Please try and understand." The elevator doors opened, and people began to file out, cutting short a probable argument. Callie saw it as a way of escape. "I'm sorry I've got to go." Hastily, she stepped inside.

The doors closed before he could say another word.

* * *

Callie leaned against the wall inside the elevator. A sense of deceitfulness seized her. She knew her awkward excuses would not satisfy Joe but would merely provoke him out of genuine concern to question her even more.

But she did not trust herself with the answers. She had always been far too vulnerable where Joe was concerned. A look in his eyes, an expression on his face, the mere touch of his hand could be enough for her to confess whatever was on her mind. No one could draw her out as easily as he could.

The doors opened on the ground floor, and she stepped out of the elevator, but she could not leave her misery behind. The search through the remaining files in her father's office had produced nothing more.

Callie had never been anything but completely truthful with Joe; she had never kept a secret from him, except for the years of love she had cherished for him. Could she do the same now? Because if he knew what she carried inside her, their relationship could be destroyed for all time.

* * *

It was dark when Joe turned the lights off in his office. With Callie's decline of his dinner invitation, he had decided to work late. The OR had been comparatively quiet, and the temporary lull would at least give him some time to catch up on work he had left piled high on his desk.

But there was no lull from his growing concern about Callie. He could not understand her peculiar behavior in the corridor earlier that afternoon. Why were women so secretive when men were typically so open? He knew in two lifetimes he would never have the answer to that one, and thus resolved that whatever was wrong, he would be patient until she either worked it out for herself or came to him on her own.

He pulled the door shut. He was tired and hungry and wished he could enjoy a late supper with Callie. He pulled out his cell phone and then glanced at his watch. It was later than he thought, and he stuffed the phone back into his pocket.

He walked past Paul Martin's office and saw a light coming from beneath the door. He knocked quietly before stepping inside, finding Paul hunched over a stack of papers.

Paul looked up when Joe entered the room. "You think you're the only one to burn the midnight oil?" the older man quipped.

Joe grinned and sat down in front of the desk. "Never. But why are you here so late?"

Paul slipped his glasses off and leaned back reflectively in the chair. "I'm honestly too tired to explain." Then he pushed the papers aside and looked at Joe. "Well, all right, it was supposed to be a big surprise, but at least this way, you can appreciate me even more."

"What are you talking about?"

"A few of your esteemed colleagues, myself included, would like to celebrate your forthcoming nuptial by having a little party at my house." He reached for an empty styrofoam cup teetering on the edge of his desk and looked inside. "However, contributions have been a little slow coming in."

The dimples in Joe's cheeks deepened with his smile. "Very funny. But I'm honored, nonetheless."

"We thought you would be, so I figured if I didn't get through this stack tonight, I might just find myself absent from the festivities in my own house. The plan is for Saturday night. Would that be good for you and Callie?"

The smile on Joe's face waned slightly as he leaned a little closer to Paul's desk. "After today, I'm not sure."

"A doctor's work is never done." "It's not that. It's Callie."

Paul said nothing, only waited for Joe to continue.

"She acted as if she wasn't glad to see me today. She made excuses for not wanting to have dinner with me. When I tried to get her to tell me that something was evidently upsetting her, she denied that anything was wrong. But Callie's always been a terrible actress." "Did you really press her about it?" Paul asked with reservation.

Joe shook his head. "I didn't want to do that. I just hope whatever it is, she'll eventually come to me about it. What do you think I should do?"

"I think waiting for her to come to you is *exactly* what you should do."

Joe sighed. "The waiting game. I'll never get used to it. In any case," he said as he rose to his feet, "I'm sure she'll be pleased knowing that our friends have thought about us"—he paused, picking up the empty cup—"so charitably."

* * *

Joe turned into his driveway and shut off the ignition. In the peaceful silence of the car, he let his thoughts drift over the past few months. Callie had brought more happiness into his life than he had ever hoped for since Beth died, and he would not risk letting that slip away. Despite the late hour, he would call her as soon as he got inside. At any rate, he had to be sure she was all right.

But a cold sensation gripped him as he stepped out of the car.

Was it possible that Callie was having second thoughts about their upcoming marriage?

CHAPTER 28

Callie Jordan wandered through the halls and rooms of the great house, finally coming full circle beside the grand staircase. She sank down onto the bottom step. She hated being alone—alone with her thoughts—and wished Maggie was there. She missed the sound of her comfortable chatter.

And the empty house only intensified her loneliness apart from Joe. She had succeeded only in aggravating and avoiding him. Yet she had to come to terms with her dilemma before he began asking questions she didn't want to answer.

She dropped her head into her hands. Tomorrow evening, she and Joe were to meet with Pastor Richards to finalize the arrangements for the wedding. Yet how could she keep pretending nothing was wrong, all the while knowing . . .

The phone began to ring. There was no need to look at the caller ID; she knew it was Joe. *How could she love someone as much asshe loved him, and at the same time despise herself just as equally?* How long could she evade him? And how long before he would demand an explanation, an explanation she could neither bring herself to give, nor expect him to understand?

At length, the phone stopped ringing, and she lifted her head from her hands. *No more*, she concluded. She would not do this to herself or to Joe. She *would* do whatever it took to become Joe Travis's wife because that was all she had ever wanted. She would simply find a way to live with what she knew, and no one would ever be an accomplice to her knowledge, with the exception of Paul Martin. She would allow nothing to separate her from the only man she had ever loved, or ever would love.

She rose from the step and wearily trudged up the staircase toward her room. Before she reached the second landing, the phone was ringing again.

* * *

"I was worried about you last night. Why didn't you answer the phone?" Joe leaned across his desk, waiting for some response while he gripped the receiver in his hand.

"I was tired, Joe, really tired," Callie tried to answer with some measure of honesty. "I didn't mean to worry you." Feigning all was well was not as easy as she had thought.

Joe ran his hand through his hair while he drew a deep breath. His resolve to be patient with whatever her predicament was fading fast. "Cal, I haven't *stopped* worrying about you since yesterday. If anything is wrong, why won't you let me do something to help?"

"Why do you assume that something's wrong?" she countered abruptly. When silence met her unconvincing challenge, she added, "I'm sorry. I didn't mean to sound like that."

"I know you didn't," he returned in a soft voice. "But I've known you a long time, Cal. Do you really expect me to believe that nothing was bothering you yesterday?"

"Yes, I do," she replied feebly. Then in an attempt to change the subject and stifle the uneasiness in her voice, she said, "Pastor Richards is looking for us tonight."

There was an audible sigh from Joe's end. "I can't make it tonight. Can you go without me?"

"I can just cancel it."

The very notion that she was so willing to rescind their appointment with the pastor disturbed him. But this wasn't the time to confront her with more anxious feelings. "Cal, the wedding's getting too close to postpone this. We decided to keep it simple. You can work out the ceremony with him, and I'll go along with whatever you decide." Joe sensed an uneasy silence before continuing. "By the way, I almost forgot, but Paul is hosting an engagement party for us at his house Saturday night. It's supposed to be a surprise, so look shocked."

"I'll do my best," she said at last.

* * *

Early that evening, Callie walked with determined steps toward the entrance of the church, then with some hesitation pulled open one of the heavy wooden doors. Pastor Evan Richards greeted her inside the foyer. "Callie, it's good to see you."

"It's good to see you too, Pastor."

"Well, come on in! Let's go sit down and see what it takes to get you and Joe down this aisle." The minister's friendly smile invited her to follow him into the sanctuary where they sat down in one of the front pews. "I'm sorry Joe couldn't come with you. I guess he stays pretty busy."

"Too busy," Callie answered in a dutiful voice. "He . . . wanted to be here, but he had a meeting he couldn't miss."

"Oh, I understand," Richards said thoughtfully. "Just let him know I think having a doctor in the congregation will be a real benefit," he finished with a grin.

She answered with a weak smile.

"And how about you, Callie? What with your work at the hospital and making your wedding plans, I imagine these are busy days for you too."

"Yes, very." Another strained smile crossed her face, her voice barely above a whisper now.

The clergyman sensed her somber spirit. "Callie, is everything all right? Are you feeling a little nervous with all this attention? I know that's never been your style."

She felt like an open book, knowing she had never been good at disguising her feelings. "Just too much to think about right now." "Well, that's understandable, but I want to tell you something, Callie, something I've wanted to tell you for a long time. I really admire you."

Her eyes widened more in dismay than in surprise. "Admire me?" *If he only knew . . .*

"Of course, you! Callie, you've been through more difficulties in your lifetime than most of us will ever even imagine, but the Lord led you through it. You're a walking testimony to what God can do, and I believe He has a mighty plan for your life. And Joe too."

"Thank you for saying so," she said quietly, averting her eyes to her folded hands. "I just hope I'm worthy of that plan." *And was keeping secrets from Joe a part of that plan?*

The minister squeezed her hands. He had long been aware of Callie's struggle with shyness. She would soon be the wife of one of the most prominent and well-known trauma surgeons in the Boston area. Now he could only guess that that rise in prominence might be the cause behind her reticent spirit. "Well, it's not our worthiness that counts, but what Jesus Christ did that really matters. And He's given you a wonderful future, what with your successful heart surgery and Joe to boot, wouldn't you say?" A broad grin covered his face.

With the pastor's words came a barrage of guilt she could no longer hide. Callie's face twisted into a dismayed grimace as she rose to her feet. "I'm . . . I'm sorry, Pastor, we'll have to talk about this some other time." The words were barely out of her mouth when she rose from the pew and ran down the aisle, pushing through the double doors and out into the night.

By the time Richards reached the door, she was nowhere to be seen.

* * *

Joe's day in the OR had been quiet with the exception of a deep knife wound too close to the heart of a teenage boy. He finished the late afternoon emergency repair work and then walked out of the OR suite toward the surgeons' lounge.

Halfway down the corridor, Dr. Marty Stevens caught up with him. "Say, Joe, I've got a problem I was wondering if I could use your help with."

"Sure, Marty, what can I do for you?"

"You know my scrub nurse, Mary Deevers, don't you?" Joe nodded. "Well, she's had a family emergency and left me short-handed for at least a week. Do you suppose you might lend Callie out to me for a little while?"

Joe pushed open the door to the lounge and the two surgeons entered. "Trauma's been a little slow lately," he said with a grin. "Have you talked with her?"

"Not yet. I wanted to clear it with you first." "I'm sure she'd be glad to help you out."

"Great! I'll talk with her, and thanks again, Joe." The surgeons exchanged a friendly handshake before Stevens disappeared down the corridor.

* * *

Joe changed into his street clothes before walking back to his office. He had barely had time to begin sorting through a new accumulation of papers when he heard a quiet knocking on the half-opened door.

He looked up to see the new chairman of the surgical department, Dr. Robert Rainer as he stepped inside. "Dr. Travis, am I intruding, or may I steal a moment of your time?"

Joe rose to his feet. "Dr. Rainer, come in. And it's Joe" he said, extending his hand to the older man.

"And I'm Bob," he returned with a gracious smile. The two men sat down. "I've been looking for Ms. Jordan, but haven't had any luck lately. I was wondering if you might be able to tell me the best time and place to catch her."

"Callie? She's usually in OR with me, but she'll be working with Marty Stevens for the next week. His schedule is a little more routine than mine. Is there something I can do for you?"

"Well, I'm not sure," he said, pulling absently at his thick, graying mustache. "I had asked her to bring me some files from her father's accounting records the night of the reception at Paul's house, but I haven't seen or heard from her since. I assumed with your upcoming wedding, it probably slipped her mind."

Joe tried to stall with a legitimate sounding excuse. "I'm sure that's the reason, and I'm sorry for the delay, Bob. Let me see what I can do. I'll try to get the records to you myself before the end of the week."

They rose simultaneously and shook hands once more. "Thank you, Joe, I'd appreciate it. But don't be too hard on that soon-to-be wife of yours," he said with a grin as they walked across the floor.

"I'll do the best I can," Joe returned before closing the door behind him, but at best, this was just one more cause in his growing concern for Callie.

* * *

The afternoon sun cast long shadows across the polished floor as Paul Martin walked up to the OR nurses' station and spied Callie Jordan working alone behind the counter. He stopped and leaned over the tall desk area. "Hello, Callie."

She looked up from the computer into Paul's kind eyes. "Hello, Paul. I understand we're having a party at your house tomorrow night."

"And you're supposed to remember to look completely surprised."

"I'll remember."

Paul's gray eyes narrowed on the shy smile of the young woman behind the desk. "How have you been, Callie?"

Immediately, she felt a keen sense of nervous tension, intensely aware of the last time they had spoken.

"Paul, if you mean have I 'unburdened' myself to Joe, the answer is *no*," she returned in a hushed voice.

"Callie, I wasn't referring to our conversation in my den."

But the weight of her guilt-ridden conscience was enough for her to misinterpret his innocent question. "Paul, I've thought about this a long time, but I have no intention of telling Joe what I know. I don't see that it would serve any purpose. I *am* sorry that I've placed you in a bad situation by asking you to—" Her words came to a halt as two nurses walked by.

Paul leaned closer to the counter. "Callie, you came to me as an old friend, seeking advice for a very extraordinary situation. I gave you my opinion. But no matter what I think, I *will* honor your wishes."

In spite of his compliant words, she watched the handsome face of the older man tighten with a familiar resistance. "I appreciate that, Paul, but this is a closed issue. I just can't risk what it might do to Joe. I love him too much to tell him."

Again, Paul's eyes narrowed on hers. "Are you sure that's the only reason?"

Without warning, Dr. Marty Stevens approached the desk area and clapped Paul amiably on the back. "Paul, good to see you! Where've you been hiding these days?"

Paul turned and smiled pleasantly at the general surgeon. "Usually buried knee-deep in paperwork, Marty. How about you?"

"Oh, same old thing. Actually, I was looking for Callie here." Callie looked up at the doctor. "Me?"

"Yeah, I've lost my scrub nurse for at least a week, so I had a talk with that old boss man of yours, and he agreed to loan you out to me for the duration, if that's all right with you."

"Why, yes, Dr. Stevens, I'd be happy to help you out."

"Fine." He pulled a crumpled piece of paper from his shirt pocket and passed it to her over the counter. "Here's a copy of my schedule as it stands for the coming week. I'll see you Monday." He clapped Paul on the back once more before turning to leave. "Good seeing you again, Paul."

"You too, Marty. Don't be so shy next time," he called after him.

Paul turned his attention back to Callie once more, but she had promptly returned to her work.

* * *

The gathering at Paul's house the next evening was in full swing by the time Callie and Joe arrived.

"Is this what they call 'fashionably late'?" Paul asked glibly after closing the door behind them.

"I'm afraid it was my fault," Callie apologized. She brushed a hand through her curly blonde locks. "Hair."

Paul laughed good-naturedly as he guided them into the living room. A jovial round of applause hailed the guests of honor as they were caught up in the small crowd.

In due time, Joe found Evan Richards loading a plate of food from the elegantly decorated table in the dining room. "Evan, it's all right to take *two* plates," he quipped in a low voice behind him.

The minister grinned as he set the plate down and turned, reaching for Joe's outstretched hand. "This *is* the second plate. Joe, it's good to see you. I'm sorry I missed you the other night."

"I'm sorry I couldn't get away. Just be sure to show up for my wedding."

The expression on the clergyman's face waned slightly. "Speaking of your wedding . . . is Callie feeling any better?"

Joe looked quizzically at the pastor. "What do you mean?" "She . . . didn't mention anything to you?"

"No, why? Is anything wrong?"

"Well," he began, lowering his voice, "I hope I'm not betraying a trust, but when Callie came to meet with me at the church the other night, she left in tears not long after she got there. I couldn't catch her before she got away to find out what was wrong, and I've been racking my brain trying to figure out if I said something to upset her. I was hoping by now she'd talked to you about it. I want to know if I need to make an apology."

Joe's mouth tightened while a recurrent feeling of apprehension gripped his insides. "I'm sure you don't need to make any apologies, Evan."

"Then do you have any idea what was upsetting her?"

Joe gazed across the small gathering until he spotted Callie in the midst of a group of women. "No, but I think it's about time I found out."

He started to excuse himself when the minister reached for his arm. "Joe, maybe I said too much."

"No, Evan, something's been bothering her for some time now.

It's not doing either of us any good ignoring whatever it is."

Joe made his way across the room in Callie's direction. After being stopped and congratulated several times, he finally caught up with her and quietly ushered her toward the French doors that led outside to the deck.

"Joe, what's this all about?"

"We need to talk," he told her quietly. He opened one of the doors, and they stepped out onto the deck.

The moon was bright, and the air much cooler outside. Joe guided her toward the far end of the multileveled deck where privacy was warranted. Beside the railing, he put his hands around her shoulders and turned her toward him. "Callie, I understand you left the church the other night *in tears*. I want to know why." Unintentionally, his anxiety lent itself to a brusqueness he normally would not have used.

Immediately, she averted her gaze to escape the insightful blue eyes. Muffled sounds filtered from the party, a slight breeze rustled through the trees in the yard, crickets chirped in the grass below them, but from Callie, there was no sound, no spoken words to come to her defense.

Yet her silence was as blatant as a confession and conveyed the one conclusion Joe had begun to fear the most. "Cal . . . you've changed your mind about marrying me, haven't you?"

At once, her eyes rose to meet his. "Joe, you can't believe that—" "I don't *want* to believe that!" he exclaimed in a quiet, urgent voice, his hands tightening around her shoulders. "But why else would you leave *running* from the church? What other reason would you have for being so . . . so distant, so preoccupied lately? What else would you expect me to believe?" His eyes searched hers, waiting for an answer. "Callie, if you don't love me . . . at least *tell me*."

Her heart was breaking. What had she done? She would sacrifice anything before she would hurt him. Tears too close to the surface burned in her eyes. "Joe, no matter what happens . . . *I'll always love you*. You have to believe that!"

Her arms encircled his neck, and he pulled her tightly against his body. He could feel her trembling, and he buried his face in her hair. "Cal, that's all I want, all I've ever wanted. Just love me."

The sound of approaching footsteps quickly separated them, and they turned in time to see Paul coming toward them with two champagne glasses in each hand. "Here you are! Sorry to break up this little prenuptial rendezvous, but we're ready to make a toast." He handed each of them a glass. "It may only be white grape juice, but it's the sentiment that counts."

Joe made a quick apology for their disappearance, and they followed Paul back to the festivities.

Once inside, Joe felt some measure of relief, but for the rest of the evening, he found himself watching Callie more closely than ever, all the while persuading himself that her affirmation of love for him was indeed genuine. Nevertheless, an uneasiness remained with him, for she had yet to explain what had upset her so at the church.

And what could she have possibly meant by the statement, "*No matter what happens*"?

CHAPTER 29

Joe pulled his green scrub shirt over his head, glad that another long week was drawing to a close. The upcoming weekend would allow some respite from the hectic schedule he had endured.

The doors to the OR changing room opened, and Dr. Marty Stevens burst through in his customary boisterous manner.

"Hey, Joe!" he bellowed in an amiable voice. "I don't know how I missed it, but I just heard through the grapevine you're planning to become a married man again. Congratulations!"

With a hearty slap to his bare back, Joe winced unobserved but managed a smile in the direction of his lively colleague. "Thanks, Marty. I feel better knowing you approve." He quickly reached inside his locker for a clean shirt to forestall another painful commendation. "Well, of course, I approve. But how any gal as sweet as that Callie Jordan could get mixed up with a radical like you . . . so who can account for taste?" Stevens laughed affably while rummaging inside his locker. "By the way, I want to thank you for lending her out to me this week, but I have to say I was a little surprised." "What do you mean *surprised?*"

"I guess being in love even with *you* would explain her poor performance in surgery. I suppose when a girl's mind is on marriage—" "Poor performance?" Joe turned toward his colleague while tucking his shirt inside his pants. "What are you talking about?" "Oh, it wasn't anything major. She just didn't seem to have her mind on her work is all."

"That doesn't sound like Callie. She's a pro in the OR," he returned in her defense.

"Well, it wasn't until yesterday I heard about your engagement, and I figured that explained it. Still," Stevens paused, delving deeper into the clutter inside his locker, "the OR is no place to be thinking about anything other than the patient." Finding what he was looking for, he slammed the metal door shut with a tinny clang. "I guess my afternoon on the golf course is shot. It's already starting to rain, and the weatherman is predicting a deluge by tonight, but at least I'm signing out to Sid Morgan for the rest of the day. See you later, Joe." Stevens burst through the door and was gone.

Joe slumped on the bench in front of the lockers. As a result of his own demanding schedule, he had seen little of Callie the entire week. Now Stevens' account regarding her substandard work in the operating room only added to his mounting list of concerns.

He also knew his patience had come to an end.

* * *

Tiny rivulets of rain trickled down the wide glass windows outside Paul Martin's office. Without bothering to knock, Joe walked inside and stood in front of the older man's desk. "Paul, you got a minute?"

Paul looked up from the papers in front of him. "From the look on your face, I'd better have." He gestured to the chair in front of his desk. "Sit down. What's the matter?"

Joe dropped wearily into the chair and looked at his old friend. "I'm worried about Callie. It's been weeks, and I still can't get her to tell me what's wrong. Have you honestly not noticed a change in her yourself?"

"What kind of change?" Paul asked cautiously.

Joe shook his head in frustration before continuing. "She's distant, withdrawn, she won't talk." Then his expression softened into worried anxiety. "The night of the party I even asked her . . . I asked her if she still wanted to marry me."

"Oh, Joe, of course she does! That's absolute nonsense."

"Is it? How do you know?"

Paul slipped his glasses off his face. "What I *know* is that girl loves you. More than you probably realize."

"Then how do you explain her behavior when she met with Evan Richards about the wedding, and he told me she ran, *weeping* from the church? When I confronted her about it, she managed to avoid telling me anything. If that doesn't say something, I don't know what does."

"Joe," Paul began guardedly, "she'll work the problem out her own way. Callie's an intelligent girl. Just don't . . . don't pressure her." Warily, Joe leaned closer to the desk. "Paul, if you know something I *don't*, I want you to tell me *now*."

Paul sighed resignedly. "She'll have to do that."

Joe rose to his feet, knowing it was useless to ask him to break a confidence, a confidence he was certain now that Callie had confided to the older man. "Then that's exactly what she'll do." He turned and walked toward the door.

"Joe," Paul called after him.

He stopped and turned around, his hand on the doorknob. For a moment, it seemed Paul was on the verge of disclosure, but then shook his head and returned to the paperwork in front of him.

* * *

The wind had become a fierce howl and rain was coming down in torrents as Joe rushed from his car toward the veranda of the Jordan house. Soaked to the skin, he rang the doorbell and pounded on the solid oak doors, hoping to be heard above the vicious storm.

Minutes passed, and the doors remained closed. The intensity of the storm was rising, and with survival instinct, he put his hand on one of the doorknobs and turned it. To his surprise, the door flew open, banging hard against the outside wall.

Joe hurried inside and pushed the door shut against the wind. Puddles of water formed on the marble floor as he peeled off his dripping overcoat. He called Callie's name, but there was no answer.

He hung his wet coat over a wooden coat tree and then followed the deep crimson carpet down the long hallway. Through the tall glass windows at the end of the hall, lightening illuminated the courtyard filled with potted summer flowers and hanging ferns.

At last, he came to the den. Finding the doors closed, he abruptly pushed them apart.

Startled, Callie turned and rose from the couch. "Joe . . . what are you doing here?" Her voice intoned more reserve than reception. Joe stood rigid, his hands flat against either side of the double doors. He said nothing as he pulled them together and surveyed the room. Embers from a dwindling fire cast a yellow glow across the hearth, dispelling the cold dampness from the pounding rain outside. "You sound as if I'm no longer welcome," he said at last.

Callie took a step back. "You know that isn't true. Is something wrong?"

"That's what I'd like to know." He walked across the room until he came to where she stood. He pushed wet hair away from his forehead, then reached out to put his hands around her shoulders, but she seemed to shrink from his touch. Her ever-perplexing behavior angered him, causing him to abandon any gentle diplomacy he would ordinarily have employed. "Callie, I want to know what's going on."

"I don't know what you mean."

Exasperated, Joe wanted to shake from her whatever truth there was. His hands tightened around her shoulders. "You know exactly what I mean. I want to know what's been troubling you. And I want to know now."

Nervous eyes met his. "I told you, Joe. Nothing's wrong." "That's not what I'm hearing. Marty Stevens told me your mind wasn't exactly 'on your work' this week. That's not like you, Cal. Something's wrong, and if it involves *us*, I think I have a right to know what it is."

Despite the carefully guarded expression, she could not erase her increasing anxiety. "I . . . I just wasn't concentrating, that's all. I apologized to Dr. Stevens."

The tone of her voice sounded like a child trying to avoid punishment. Joe drew a deep breath and pulled her toward him, cradling her head against his chest. "Cal, come on, it's *me* you're talking with!" he whispered, stroking her hair. "We're going to be married soon! In all the years we've known each other, we've never kept secrets from one another before."

Too close to tears, she pulled herself out of his arms. "Joe, *please*," she pleaded, "please just trust me and leave well enough alone!"

Her baffling words heightened his frustration. "What on earth are you talking about? Leave *what* alone?"

She turned away and walked across the room, unavoidably coming to a stop beside her father's desk. Bright streaks of lightening flashed through the arched window as her fingers moved restlessly across the polished wood.

Joe came up behind her and grasped her shoulders once more. This time, he could feel her trembling. "Cal, I love you! I want to help you."

She knew she had already said too much, and telling him the truth was all that was left. She shook her head. "You can't help me . . . nobody can."

Suddenly, his frustration changed to a longstanding fear. He turned her sharply toward him, but her gaze rested on the floor. "Cal, are you in rejection? Is that it?"

"No . . . no." He stroked her cheek, and she reveled in the comforting touch of his hand, desperate to prolong the tender moment that might have to last her a lifetime once he learned the truth.

Guilt had threaded through every fiber of her being. She knew Paul Martin was right. Come what may, Joe was entitled to the truth. If she truly loved him, how much longer could she withhold what he had a right to know?

With timorous conviction, she looked into the benevolent eyes that reflected the compassion she had loved so long. "Joe, I . . . I never wanted anything to happen to Beth."

He heaved a sigh of relief as at last he thought he understood. "Of course you didn't!" he returned soothingly. Then slipping his hand beneath her chin, he asked, "Cal, do you think you're being disloyal to Beth by marrying me?"

She shook her head. "No . . . it's nothing like that." "Then what is it?"

The dread she felt was overwhelming. Could she persuade him—and herself—that all she really wanted was to protect him from further anguish? Or would the shameless truth be more convincing, that sacrificing her integrity was of less consequence than losing him? "Joe, there's something you don't know—something I'm not sure you'll be able to understand."

"I understand how much I love you," he whispered. Tenderly, he drew her closer and kissed her forehead. "What's so terrible you think I couldn't understand?"

She could not bring herself to look at him. Her breath quickened as she struggled to get the words out. "The night Beth died," she began falteringly, "my father . . . made some . . . some arrangements . . . something he . . . something I know he didn't tell you. I didn't know what he'd done until . . . " Her courage withered with the words that would not come.

His hands tightened around her slumping shoulders. "What sort of arrangements?"

She glanced toward the dying fire, knowing that on this night her dream of becoming his wife could be reduced to nothing more than ashes left after the flame. With a sense of resignation, she slid open the top drawer of her father's desk, withdrew a file and placed it in his hands.

He opened the folder and began to examine the documents. His face revealed little change as he realized he was scanning photocopies of preand postoperative reports of Callie's transplant surgery. He shuffled more pages. Even now, there lingered inside him an uneasiness that her condition had in some way begun to deteriorate, but what would that have to do with her father?

And then, with a spasmodic tightening in his muscles, the mystery began to crystallize.

Beneath the pages of the surgical summary were copies of other medical documents, but these were not Callie's documents. These were lab reports with Beth's name on each one, detailing her blood type and various tissue studies ordered during her final hospitalization. Specific data had been circled and information added for further clarification. Finally, within a paragraph of irrefutable notations and clearly written in Benjamin Jordan's own hand, impossible words leapt out like burning coals: "Based on comparative blood and tissue samples, I believe there is unquestionable compatibility from this donor."

Horror seized him as he glanced at the date of Callie's surgery, realizing it was the same day he had allowed Beth's life support to be discontinued and her organs harvested for donation. Steadying himself against the mantle, he leaned his head against his arm. His hand fell to his side, still clasping the papers, as he struggled to grasp the irrevocable statement. Nothing had prepared him for this, not even the respite from loneliness Callie had brought.

The dreadful days following Beth's accident came rushing back. As the light from the fire shimmered across his face, Joe's stricken mind took him somewhere far past the flames.

* * *

He could still hear the monotonous drone of the respirator and other machines, all that had been responsible for sustaining Beth's life. He had hardly left her side, waiting, hoping, praying for a miracle, but the miracle had never come.

At the end, it was said by many that he had courageously performed the most merciful act possible, considering the extraordinary circumstances, the only compassionate and humanitarian course that remained to be done.

Nevertheless, he had allowed her to die, not only allowed it, but also was the unintentional cause of it.

* * *

A barrage of questions pummeled him. Why had he waited until it was almost too late before allowing Beth's organs to be harvested? Was it because selfishly, he knew that losing her meant life for someone else, that somewhere others were living, breathing, loving because his wife was dead? Had he only been able to sign those release forms because the recipients would never be anything more to him but nameless, faceless individuals, mere strangers?

But Callie Jordan was no stranger, and Dr. Benjamin Jordan—his beloved mentor, father, and friend—had secretly conceived the entire plan.

Seething furor combined with revived guilt consumed him as he turned to look at Callie. "Your father arranged for a direct donation of Beth's heart—*without my consent?*" The words were scalded with anger. "How could he *do* that to me?"

Callie lifted her head from her hands to find the once gentle expression changed to a cold, hard stare. The knuckles of his hand were white as he clutched the papers tightly in his fist. "He told me he'd taken care of everything," she whispered miserably. "But I didn't know what he'd done! *I just didn't know.*"

Joe's face was livid. "Oh, he took care of everything," he said, his voice ominous with rage as the papers slowly crushed in his fist, "everything except *asking me.*"

Savagely, he thrust the crumpled papers into the fire. Wrenching apart the double oak doors, he angrily made his way toward the front entrance and vanished into the tempestuous night while the sudden blaze of testimony turned to ashes.

* * *

Rain poured down in wind-driven sheets, slamming mercilessly against the windshield as Joe's car tore through the dark night. Broken branches and leaves flew wildly about in the air. The wiper blades were almost useless in the blinding deluge.

But Joe was oblivious to the raging tempest as images of Beth rose in the angry storm, engulfing him in a mental struggle from which there was no escape.

In his mind, he saw her lying on a stretcher in the trauma room, remembered the agonizing days and nights he had refused to leave her bedside, numbed to the repetitive drone of the machines that kept her alive. He remembered the endless prayers he had prayed, the faith he had struggled to cling to, the funeral he could hardly recall, the bitter cold of winter that only intensified the finality of his loss, and the grief that had become more disabling than he could have ever imagined.

And tonight, he learned that Benjamin Jordan—his mentor, his friend, the man who had been more of a father to him than his own—had clandestinely arranged for the living heart of his wife to be implanted in his dying daughter! Though he knew nothing could have saved Beth, in his tormented mind, the circumstances did not justify the fact that Jordan had seized upon the untimely opportunity without his acknowledgement or consent.

The tires skidded against the wet pavement as he deliberated this new anger, an anger that would take its place somewhere between his guilt and grief over Benjamin Jordan's death.

He careened around another curve, his hands gripping the steering wheel, his thoughts exploding with the thunder outside. Until tonight, he had not made the connection between Callie's surgery and Beth's death. In his grief, he hardly remembered the circumstances of his own whereabouts. Only now did he actually recall Ben Jordan's unaccountable absence from Beth's funeral.

And what about Callie? He could not forget that she had stood by him, unceasingly extending acceptance and encouragement to him despite his anger with life and rejection of God. He marveled at how she had met with her own difficulties, facing the ordeals of her life not so much with confidence, but with courage.

And now, just when it seemed they had both found some semblance of happiness, she had jeopardized it all for the sake of principle. She could have withheld her father's secret for all eternity, and he might never have known the difference, but she had chosen to hide nothing and, by so doing, had risked everything.

But where did that risk leave him? Could he ever look at Callie Jordan again without remembering the shameless indignity with which her father had treated Beth?

Another flash of lightening fired the night sky with brilliant white, illuminating the perilously swaying trees in the turbulent wind.

As visibility became increasingly difficult, he realized it was not merely the rain obscuring his vision but angry tears in his eyes.

Too late, he saw the odd angle of a swaying tree ahead. With an explosive crack, it snapped and fell, plunging across the road in front of him. Jamming his foot hard against the brakes, he made a desperate attempt to stop before certain collision.

But the slick pavement rendered the effort useless. The car spun, and in one horrifying instant, he was conscious only of a sudden forward thrust, shattering glass, excruciating pain, and then nothing.

CHAPTER 30

Warm rays from the sun filtered through the sheer, white curtains that rustled beside the bed. Outside, Joe could hear the first sounds of spring with the chirping of the robins. He tried to open his eyes, but sleep rested heavily on him. And then he felt the touch of a light hand—Beth's hand—and heard her soothing voice calling his name. He tried again to open his eyes.

Joe's eyes flickered under the glaring lights inside the trauma room. A blur of skilled hands worked over him. He could hear the clatter of instruments in steel trays, blood-soaked bandages dropped into receptacles, the clicking of machines, voices he could neither identify nor comprehend.

His head exploded with pain. He could not voluntarily move any part of his body. His hands felt tied to his sides. The only power he possessed was the power to feel, and feeling was agony.

The pain intensified with every invasive procedure, causing him to moan aloud. He felt as though he was drowning. The taste and odor of blood was overpowering as he struggled for each breath.

His thoughts were disordered between past and present as he tried to gather pieces of memory, for which there was little. Now and then fragments of recall came back, vague memories he could not reconstruct. For mystifying reasons, the words *Beth's heart, Beth'sheart, Beth's heart* pounded rhythmically inside his head.

Brief periods of consciousness came and went, but with consciousness came insufferable pain. He could feel the pulsating of his own heart throbbing in his ears, a tumultuous sound that seemed to increase the pain with every beat. And then, mercifully, consciousness would slip away, only to return moments later with a heightened sense of agony. He longed for insensibility.

"Get another IV going, and keep it wide open. And type and cross-match for at least six more units." Bags of blood and fluids swayed above his head as more IV lines punctured his already battered body.

Muddled words came to him in bits and pieces. "Internal bleeding . . . diminished breath sounds . . . probably a hemo-pneumothorax . . . multiple fractures to the . . . " Hands skated over his exposed and shivering body. Voices faded and grew louder, then faded again. And then he was aware of movement, of lights passing overhead, people on either side of the gurney hurling it with lightning speed down the corridor, squeezing through open elevator doors. More doors opening and closing, more glaring light, more voices giving instruction and returning information. His eyes flickered again.

In the ordered confusion, he tried to piece together his whereabouts until he recognized the distorted features of the operating room.

An array of surgeons, residents, technicians, and nurses—his own colleagues—scrambled to check and recheck the ambu bag, the IVs, the security of the cervical collar that immobilized his neck, every apparatus that connected him with life. In one swift and careful motion, they lifted him from the backboard onto the operating table. He wanted to scream, but nothing would come past the endotracheal tube in his throat.

A masked face hovered over him. He strained to focus on the misty eyes that peered anxiously down at him. *Those eyes . . . he knew those eyes.*

"Joe, you've been in a bad accident, but you're going be all right." The eyes closed, and he listened to Paul Martin's familiar prayer, this time punctuated with strained emotion, "Lord, guide our hands . . . " The pain he felt throughout his body was excruciating. No amount of suffering was worth this. What did it matter if he lived or died? What was there to live for anyway?

Hands held his head and closed his eyelids. Then the voices faded completely.

* * *

Early morning light streaked a cloudless sky, leaving no hint of a storm the night before.

Callie hurried through the front doors of the hospital. Paul Martin's phone call less than an hour earlier had left her stunned. In her worst nightmares, Callie never dreamed telling Joe the truth about her heart transplant would come to this.

She rushed into an open elevator. The miserable scene in her father's den hours earlier comprised her every thought. She could still hear the splintering sound of Joe's car as it tore wildly away from the house. Then there was nothing but the clatter of the rain beating hard against the windows, joined moments later with her own weeping that lasted long into the night. She knew why her father had never told her about Beth. He would not leave it to chance that she would ever connect her friend's death with her own lif-saving surgery. Sometime toward dawn, she had drifted into an exhausted sleep.

But reality had turned her dreams into disconsolate nightmares.

The elevator doors opened, and she stepped into the darkened corridor. Her fists clenched and unclenched as the burden of guilt became more and more overwhelming. Had it been her trial alone to come to terms with the fact that she was alive because of Beth, maybe she could have dealt with it over time, but facing the consequences of what that knowledge had done to Joe was more than she could accept.

The intensive care unit was quiet in the early morning. Joe had been out of recovery little more than an hour. Callie remained outside the door of his room, watching while two of her colleagues, still clad in their surgical scrubs, finished checking the ventilator settings, the chest tube, the nasogastric and vent tubes, the compression boots on his legs and feet. A moment later, the nurses left, each giving her a comforting word and touch she neither heard nor felt.

She stood motionless inside the doorway, her feet refusing to move her forward, her eyes riveted on the pathetic form of a man who, only hours earlier, had been whole and strong.

Now a chest tube protruded from his side, IVs and blood transfusions dripped into both arms. Surgical bandages wrapped the entire midsection of his body while green, blue, and red lights flickered across monitor screens beside the bed. His face—swollen, cut, and bruised—was almost unrecognizable.

She winced when she saw his hands. His left arm hung from an overhead trapeze and external fixtures were wrapped with yellow gauze. Hand splints held out the fingers in a gentle curve.

At last, she made her way to the side of the bed. She reached out and touched his face, brushing aside strands of hair that clung to his feverish forehead. *Could he ever forgive her. Moreover, could she ever forgive herself?* Tears filled her eyes as she leaned over and kissed him. And then covering her face, she openly wept.

But for all her regret, there was no acknowledgement.

* * *

"I should *never* have told him."

Paul Martin had spent most of the night in the operating room, and now he listened in stunned silence while Callie finished telling him the story. He leaned against his desk and watched as she bowed her head into her hands.

"No, Callie, Joe had a right to know," he said at last. "You couldn't spend the rest of your life living in fear that someday he'd find out the truth. Because someday, he would." He sat down beside her on the couch. "Callie, the night Beth died, Joe knew as well as your father that she was beyond any hope. Your father's crime was that he didn't handle the situation objectively because he was acting out of desperation for you."

"But Joe was so angry!" she cried. "He may *never* forgive my father for what he did! And he'll never look at me again without knowing . . . knowing . . . " She looked up at Paul, her eyes wide with anguish. "*What have I done to him?*"

"Callie, this isn't your fault! This is something Joe is going to have to work through himself. Keeping quiet was your father's mistake."

Again she began to weep. "What's going to happen to him?"

"I won't lie to you, Callie. He's in critical condition right now. I'm concerned that he hasn't regained consciousness yet since surgery. But he's young, and he's strong," he added reassuringly.

Callie nodded in doubtful compliance. "What about his hands?" Paul was reluctant before answering. "His left arm was caught between the door and the windshield. We had to reattach both nerves, the artery, and the vein and pin the bones. Only time will tell how much function will return."

* * *

For Joe, all concept of time was gone. He could not distinguish daylight from darkness, dreams from reality.

He drifted in and out of consciousness, groaning fitfully from the pain until it lessened with sleep or narcotics. Now and again, he was aware of a presence in the room, a gentle hand tending to his injuries or soothing his forehead with a cool cloth.

At other times, loud voices filled the room. He could not open his eyes, but he began to recognize some of the voices, the same voices surrounding his bed at all hours of whatever was day or night. But there was another voice, a soft voice, vaguely recognizable, a voice lifted in anxious prayer for him time and again before he would lose consciousness once more.

* * *

Callie dragged herself from the chair she had occupied for three days and stood in front of the window. She quietly raised the blinds. As morning sun flowed into the room, she turned with anticipation toward Joe's bed, but the bright light brought no response. The medication that dripped continuously through the IV lines had finally calmed his painful thrashing. Once more, she prayed that healing would begin in more ways than one.

She lowered the blinds and returned to his bedside. She knelt beside the chair and bowed her head in prayer for him again.

She struggled to her feet and sat down once more. Leaning her head against the back of the chair, she closed her eyes.

There had been a time once when she believed it an impossibility seeing Joe as weak and helpless as he was right now. For too many years, he had been the epitome of strength and self-resilience in her eyes. Undaunted by the demands of his job and indomitable in the stand he took for his patients, she had marveled at his strength of mind and body. To Callie's way of thinking, Joe Travis could supersede any obstacle.

But three years earlier, she had been forced to confront the reality that he was indeed as vulnerable as any human being could be. And until now, she had never felt so frightened for his life as then.

* * *

Joe had been sick for too long. Working beside him every day for the past week and a half convinced Callie that he was only getting worse, in spite of his claims of convalescence.

His persistent, dry cough had settled deeper into his chest. He had been taking antibiotics but still continued to pursue twelve and four-teen-hour days. He would never allow one of his own patients to ignore proper treatment and adequate rest. What made him so stubborn to think he could defy the laws of health when dealing with himself?

Such were Callie's thoughts as she hurried down the corridor toward the emergency department. She rushed past the nurses' station and pushed open the door to one of the treatment rooms. On either side of an exam table, Paul Martin and her father hunkered over their patient.

Paul was pulling a stethoscope away from his ears. "Pressure's low, 92 over 60."

"Heart rate?" Jordan asked.

"One hundred twenty." Paul looked up as Callie approached the table, confirming with a troubled expression what she had overheard moments earlier on the surgical floor. "He collapsed in the corridor about a half hour ago."

Callie glanced down at the exam table. Joe lay motionless except for the labored rising and falling of his chest. His face glistened with feverish perspiration. An IV drip was already in place. An oxygen mask covered his nose and mouth. "How bad is he?" she asked in a quiet, urgent voice. "Bad enough," Jordan asserted while changing the tubing for a respiratory treatment. Rarely had Callie seen her father perform nursing tasks on a patient in the presence of a capable nurse, but to her father, Joe was not just another patient. "He has a fever of nearly 103, and I can almost guarantee he has a full-blown case of lobar pneumonia. He's going to be forced to get off his feet and into a bed. And I mean here, where we can tie him down if necessary."

But somewhere within Benjamin Jordan's commanding voice, Callie recognized a tone of anxious vulnerability where Joe was concerned.

The room was a drone of hurried activity. She watched as her father charted orders, while Paul made arrangements on the phone for an emergency admission. The double doors opened and closed as technicians and nurses carried out test tube samples and pushed machines in and out of the room.

Callie stepped closer to the table. She reached out and brushed aside strands of damp hair that clung to Joe's forehead. She bent toward him and quietly called his name, but there was no response, and his eyes remained closed.

In his increasing delirium, she sensed he was becoming less aware of his surroundings. She desperately wanted him to know she was there. Slowly and deliberately, her hand tightened around his. "Joe?" she whispered close to his ear. "It's Callie. Can you hear me?"

And then she felt the slightest squeeze to her own hand.

He began to cough, and the two doctors hastened to attend to their patient once more. Paul slipped his stethoscope into his ears. Joe continued to cough, his face flushed with fever, until Paul removed the stethoscope. "Joe?" He called his name loudly several times before the young man languidly turned his head in the direction of the voice. He opened his eyes, but the effort seemed too much, and he closed them again.

Callie saw the exchange of worried glances between the two doctors.

Their unspoken concern merely increased her own.

* * *

It was almost midnight when Callie walked unobserved down the corridor toward Joe's room. Light spilled across the floor as she pushed the door open, dispelling the darkness inside.

A sense of relief began to pass through her as she stood beside the bed watching him. Ample doses of antibiotics and much-needed sleep had improved his labored breathing. She picked up a tissue and wiped the perspiration from his face, grateful that his fever was beginning to break. She watched him for another minute before turning to leave the room. Not wanting to awaken him, she crept to the door when she heard a raspy voice. "Is this a clandestine midnight visit, or have I been assigned a private duty nurse?"

A smile he could not see creased her face as she came back to the bedside, then sat down in the chair beside him. "You need a private duty nurse, if for no other reason than to make sure you get some sleep and take a vitamin once in a while."

He looked at her through bleary eyes and grinned. "Are you looking for the position—" But his words dissolved into a fit of coughing. Quickly, she moved to the edge of the bed and pulled him toward her until the spasm passed. Exhausted, he slumped against the pillows and closed his eyes again.

A feeling of dread overcame her seeing him in such feeble condition, such contrast to his usual vitality and indestructible nature. For the first time, he seemed as dependent as one of his own patients, as dependent on someone else's strength as anyone could be.

This was not Joe, for it was she who had always depended on him. He was the strong one; it was his strength she counted on, not the other way around. No, she couldn't bear to see him like this. A single tear slipped down her cheek before she could turn away.

"Hey . . . what's this?" he whispered, stretching a weak hand toward her face. Turning to look at him once more, she found a reassuring smile as he grasped her hand. "Nothing's going to happen to me, Cal. I'm too stubborn to let anything happen. You should know that by now."

She knew how foolish it was to revere him so completely, to depend on him so unquestionably. After all, Joe Travis was only a man—to everyone else, but her. She smiled at him. "Yes, I should know that by now."

But what she knew best was that she only loved him a little more today than yesterday.

* * *

Callie was drifting off to sleep when something caused her to open her eyes. She struggled out of the chair and came to the bedside. Joe had begun to toss and turn once more. She wrung out a damp cloth and began to bathe his face.

As she gently wiped the perspiration away, a terrible sense of anxiety came over her again. She fought back tears as she worked to make him more comfortable, but deep down, she knew there was nothing she could do but prepare herself for more of the same.

* * *

Paul Martin walked into the intensive care unit for the third time that day. As if on cue, the charge nurse gave him an update on Joe Travis's condition. He thanked her and then reviewed the most recent vital signs and test results that had been done during the intervals when he was gone.

As he turned to walk toward Joe's room, he paused while observing a familiar lone figure at the far end of the corridor, slowly pacing from the door to the window and back again.

Callie Jordan stopped when she saw Paul coming toward her. There was no need for any exchange of words as the two embraced in mutual concern. With an encouraging smile, Paul pulled his stethoscope from his coat pocket and walked into Joe's room.

With nervous anticipation, Callie waited outside for the older man to finish his examination. A few minutes later, the door opened. His expression revealed a disappointment equal to her own as he slowly shook his head. "There's still no change, Callie."

The words were merely an echo of her exhaustion and despair as she crumpled into Paul's arms. Her only consolation rested in the dismal fact that Joe was unconscious, a reality that allowed her to do the suffering for both of them.

* * *

Night nurse Jessie Gallagher was making her rounds. As she stepped into Joe's room, she found Callie asleep in the chair beside him. Jessie put her hand on her friend's shoulder. "Callie, go home and get some real rest."

Callie pulled herself up in the chair. "What time is it?"

"It's after two thirty in the morning. You're not going to be in any shape to greet Dr. Travis when he wakes up." Jessie smiled down at her.

Greet him when he wakes up, Callie thought, *if he ever wants to see me again.* "I'm all right, Jess . . . really."

Jessie shook her head. "No, *not* really. You know I'll call you the minute there's any change." She helped Callie out of the chair. As Jessie walked with her to the door, Callie turned to look at Joe one more time. "The *minute* there's any change," Jessie repeated.

CHAPTER 31

The lights . . . the incessant lights.

Joe rolled his head painfully from side to side across the pillow, his eyes squeezed shut against the persistent brightness. He had no idea if it was day or night, if he was awake or asleep. He longed for darkness, where he could lose himself in obscurity. Here, under the merciless exposure of light, he felt he was on display. Yet while everyone watched him, nobody saw.

The tube in his esophagus was gone, leaving his throat dry and sore. His body felt immobilized from the heavy doses of narcotics, his arms and legs pinned to his sides. And then he heard footsteps coming across the floor. He turned his head toward the sound, and a moment later, gentle hands began to change the dressing on his forehead.

With concentrated effort, he opened his eyes. Immediately, the hands stopped working and he saw the distorted form of a young nurse hovering over him. "Dr. Travis? Can you hear me?"

The light was too painful for his eyes, and he closed them. "Yes." He hardly recognized the raspy sound of his own voice. "Where . . . where . . . ?"

"You're in the intensive care unit."

He tried to draw a deep breath, but the brief inhalation only initiated a painful moan. "What time is it?"

"A little after seven o'clock in the morning."

His eyes flickered again. "How long have I been here?"

"Four days," she told him. "Excuse me for a minute, Doctor."

Moments later, the sound of more hurried feet approached him, and then another shadowy face peered down at him. He tried to move but winced in unexpected pain.

"Take it easy, Joe." Paul Martin reached out to steady him. "How are you feeling?"

He closed his eyes once more. "You tell me." Every breath was another experience in pain.

"Well, you've got some broken ribs, a broken arm, a punctured lung, and a pretty bad concussion. You lost a lot of blood. You're also minus one spleen." He knew Joe was far too weak to hear the whole truth yet. Still, he grinned reassuringly. "Your car was totaled, but you weren't."

"I'm not so sure," he said as he drifted into sleep once more.

* * *

Paul Martin and Dr. Clark Sawyer, head of orthopedic surgery, both knew it was a moment that could not be put off.

By that evening, Joe was fully awake. The two doctors stood on either side of the bed and watched with trepidation as he stared at his hands. A wire protruded from each bandaged finger, an endeavor designed to hold the bones straight while they healed. The remainder of both hands were wrapped in tight bandages. Through his drug-induced senses, a frightening reality was slowly dawning on him as he began to comprehend the severity of his injuries. "What about my hands?"

"We don't know yet, Joe," Sawyer told him candidly. "The majority of your hand injuries occurred when the branches of the tree broke through the windshield. They were pinned and crushed between the dashboard and the limbs."

Joe couldn't take his eyes away from the horror in front of him. He wanted to scream but swallowed it. In his mind, he was still a surgeon yet useless without his hands. "What's my prognosis?" Somehow, he didn't want to know. For now, hoping was better thanknowing.

"It's really too early to tell. You'll be out of commission for some time. If all goes well and the fractures heal properly, you'll need plenty of physical therapy afterward." Sawyer tried to sound optimistic.

"And if they don't?"

"Joe, you know as well as I do there's always the possibility of nerve damage."

His head fell back against the pillow and he closed his eyes. "And an even stronger possibility I may never do surgery again."

Sawyer cast an intuitive glance toward Paul before looking at Joe once more. "Let's cross that bridge when and if we get to it. I'll stop by tomorrow."

Paul remained by the bed after Sawyer left the room. "Callie's anxious to see you," he offered readily. "She hardly left this room for three days. Jessie Gallagher finally sent her home last—"

"I don't want Callie here." Joe turned his head to one side. Paul's amiable expression waned as his fear was confirmed. "Joe,

I know it was difficult to accept what she told you."

Joe cast a severe glance at Paul again. "What did Callie tell you?"

The older man hesitated for a moment. "Everything. She told me everything, but blaming her for something she had nothing to do with—"

"I'm not blaming her. I know she had nothing to do with it." "Then why won't you see her?"

He sank deeper into the pillows. A miserable combination of anger, frustration, and confusion seethed within him. "Do you think I could ever look at Callie again and not be reminded of what her father did? Do you honestly expect me to excuse what Ben Jordan conspired to do *behind my back*? Am I supposed to forgive and forget, as if Beth was just so many . . . used parts? She was my *wife!*" The anger spewed forth, but in his weakened condition, the effort proved to be too much, and he closed his eyes as his head rolled to one side of the pillow. The mental torment only added to the constant physical pain that exhausted him.

"I know it may seem that way right now," Paul offered gently, "but Beth was dying, with no hope for recovery. You knew it as well as I did, and so did Ben. You need to remember that Beth literally saved Callie's life. Ben was only an instrument in honoring a decision Beth had made a long time ago."

Joe drew a deep breath. "That doesn't excuse the fact that he took advantage of the situation and didn't even consult with me." His voice shuddered with pain and rage. Never had he felt so exploited and utterly defeated.

Paul understood the resentment but wondered if Joe truly understood the dilemma. "I'll grant what Ben Jordan did he should have done differently. He should have discussed it with you. He should have asked for your explicit permission, but what would you have done if he *had* come to you, asking for Beth's heart? He understood how distraught you were at the time. The man was acting out of desperation! Medically, he knew Beth would be a perfect match for Callie." Paul lowered his gaze on the younger man. "And remember, Joe, Callie had no say in this. The only thing in the world she wants is your love."

Joe looked away. His conflict regarding Callie was more complex than he had been able to admit. In one night, his relationship with her had come to a blinding impasse, leaving in its wake an unspoken shame that weighed on him as heavily as the uselessness of his hands. For Joe believed he had been rendered incapable not only as a surgeon, but also as a man. How could he go from absolute autonomy to total dependence on her? How could he impose on her his debilitating helplessness? He was no longer the same man who had asked her to be his wife.

No, he could not risk having her here only to feel pity for him, pity that could eventually destroy the love. "I have nothing to offer her anymore," he said at last. "I'm useless as a surgeon, useless as a provider and protector. She needs a man who can take care of *her*. A whole man, not an invalid."

"Joe, *you* are no different than you were before the accident. You are *not* your injuries! You're still a doctor, still a surgeon and, most importantly, still the man Callie Jordan wants to marry."

Joe glanced once more at his broken and bandaged hands. The very sight of them was sickening, signaling the end of the only career he had ever wanted. The purpose of his life had been shattered in a matter of moments. "You're wrong, Paul. I'm *not* the same and never will be again."

In frustration, Paul gripped the bedside rail. "So you're willing not only to throw away the *surgeon* Joe Travis, but also the girl who loves a *man* by the same name! Callie loves *you*, not your career, not your status, not your ability to defend or provide for her. It wouldn't matter to her if you *never* walked into that OR again, except for the sake of your own happiness. Knowing all that, can you honestly tell me it's over for you?"

Joe glanced away from his injured hands and looked glaringly at Paul once more. "It was over the minute I read those papers."

* * *

Paul Martin walked down the corridor, staring at the polished floor. Worried and disheartened, he wished only to leave the hospital behind and go home when he looked up and saw Callie coming toward him. He stopped and waited until she caught up. Her face was jubilant.

"Paul, is it true? Joe regained consciousness this morning? I only found out a little while ago."

Paul took her by the arm. "Yes, Callie, he's awake. I was just on my way back to the office. Why don't you walk over with me, and we can talk there?"

"Why? What's wrong?" Her euphoria dwindled as she followed alongside him.

The questions continued as they crossed the parking lot to the medical complex. Paul opened the door to his office and motioned toward the couch. Callie sat down uneasily, never taking her eyes away from him until he sat down beside her. "Paul, he *is* going to be all right, isn't he?"

"Joe's going to be all right, Callie." "Then what's wrong?"

The relief she felt from Paul's reassuring statement began to wane as he explained Joe's reaction to confronting his hand injuries. "It's difficult to project the outcome so soon after surgery. Clark Sawyer tried to be as optimistic as possible, but talking to Joe isn't like talking to another patient. He knows exactly what he's up against."

"Do *you* think he'll ever operate again?"

Paul shook his head. "I'm not sure. Right now, it's his attitude that concerns me. He seems ready to give up hope without even trying. And that's not like Joe."

Callie rose swiftly to her feet. "Paul, I have to go to him. He *needs* me. I *know* he needs me! Please, just tell me what to do!"

Paul dreaded what he had to tell her. He stood up slowly and put his hands around her shoulders. "I'm afraid there's nothing you can do, Callie. He doesn't want to see you." He watched as the expression on her face fell. He longed to give her words of encouragement. "You know how stubborn Joe can be. He . . . he simply hasn't accepted what's happened to him yet."

Tears filled her eyes. "But that's not really why he doesn't want to see me, is it?"

Paul hesitated. "No," he affirmed quietly.

She wiped the tears away from her face. Her voice trembled so badly she could barely get the words out. "I gambled, Paul. I gambled, and I lost. I asked the *impossible* from him! How could I have ever believed he could accept Beth's beating heart inside of me?"

"Callie, Beth saved your life! Joe knows that."

"And I know it too! But . . . why did it have to be *Beth's heart?*"

She began to weep, and Paul drew her against his shoulder. He felt his own heart was breaking, and his fatherly embrace tightened around her. "Callie . . . "

"Oh, Paul, you know as well as I do that he's never gotten over losing her! He loves her as much now as he did when she was alive, and I can't blame him for *that* any more than I can force him to love *me.*"

The older man gently eased her away from him, lifting her chin with a tender hand. "Callie, the finest thing we can offer Joe right now is time. Time and prayer. Both can heal a lot of wounds doctors and nurses can't."

"Time," she observed ruefully as she turned away. "My gift from Beth he'll never understand. Whatever made me think I could fill the void she left?"

CHAPTER 32

Callie Jordan stood at the top of the majestic staircase in her father's house, adorned in her mother's satin and lace wedding gown. The house was scented with an abundance of floral arrangements and soft candlelight flickered from silver candelabras.

Slowly, she descended each step, her gloved hands clutching a bouquet of yellow roses, her eyes riveted on the man who waited for her at thebottom. Joe Travis had never been more handsome, impeccably dressed in a black formal tux with velvet lapels. A yellow rose from her bouquetfashioned his boutonnière. With his hand outstretched to receive hers, she met him with joy on the last step and walked beside him into the drawing room.

Wedding music from the stringed quartet drifted throughout the house. Guests were seated in cushioned chairs on either side of an aisle of white carpet. Callie and Joe joined hands as they took their place in frontof the minister. After years of dreaming and waiting, this day Joe Traviswould take her as his wife . . .until a stranger approached from behind,silently placing a hand on Joe's arm.

Callie turned and saw it was Beth who had touched him. Joe said nothing as his hand slipped away from hers. No sound came from eitheras they turned to walk down the aisle together. No compelling influencehad been employed apart from the love that Joe had never relinquished for his first wife.

Callie watched in anguish as Joe and Beth disappeared from her sight. She turned anxiously to look at the minister, to plead with him what to do, but he merely shook his head.

Only then did she realize it was the disappointed face of her father who was looking back at her.

* * *

Callie sat upright in bed, drenched in a cold sweat. The dream had become a repeated nightmare since Joe's accident, symbolizing every real and imagined defeat in her life—her father's unspoken regret when Joe had not chosen her for his wife, her guilt and grief over Beth, and above all, the liability she took upon herself for the impediment of Joe's career.

She slipped out of the four-poster bed and stood in front of the wide window. Parting the lacy curtains, she stared out at the moonless night. She knew what she had to do. Relentless frustration would drain the very life out of her, if she did not take some action. And the only place to start—and finish—would be with Joe himself.

* * *

Morning sun streamed through the kitchen windows as Maggie McCarran sat down with a hot cup of tea before starting her day.

On her return from caring for her convalescing sister the evening before, she had listened in disbelief as Callie poured out the dreadful events that had taken place during her absence, leaving the housekeeper stunned. *Dr. Joe almost killed in a car wreck, and Callie hadn't sent a single word to her!*

Maggie had tried hard to comfort her, but she knew Callie was blaming herself, perhaps even her father. Yet her dad was only thinking about her. And sooner or later, she had tried to reassure her Dr. Joe was going to understand that too.

She sipped her tea as she glanced at the clock above the stove, wondering why Callie had not come downstairs yet.

* * *

Callie Jordan made her way down the hospital corridor, fearing that if she hesitated even for a second, her courage would fail her completely. Colleagues passed her on either side, nodded and stopped to talk, but she was nearly oblivious to every comforting touch and word. Her sole objective was focused on the last room at the end of the hall.

The days and nights she had spent at Joe's bedside had been agonizing, comparable only to the time she had waited for a heart donor. But then to be told after his regaining consciousness that he didn't want to see her had been worse.

A half hour earlier inside Paul Martin's office, she had listened as the older doctor tried to dissuade her from seeing Joe by putting his dismal state of mind into clinical perspective.

"Are you forbidding me to see him?" Callie had asked.

"No, Callie, I'm not, but you need to be prepared for a very angry and disillusioned young man," Paul warned in a cautionary voice.

As she approached the end of the hall, she could see the door to Joe's private room was partly opened. No sound came from within. A week earlier, he had been transferred out of the ICU. No longer on the critical list, Callie had thanked God for affirming, answered prayers. Now, with tremulous breath and shaking hands, she quietly pushed the door open and stepped inside.

The bed was raised to a partial sitting position. Joe rested languidly against the pillows, his head turned toward the window, his eyes closed. The tubes had been removed. A blanket drawn across his bandaged chest rose and fell with some measure of labored breathing. And then Callie glanced at his hands resting on pillows. Those caring, gentle hands—the skillful hands that had wielded a scalpel with striking dexterity—remained immobilized, the splints and bandages making them appear like something mechanical that lay motionless at his sides.

Though his condition was not the shocking depiction Callie had witnessed several weeks earlier, her heart broke as she realized Joe had become a prisoner in a dreadfully familiar world. He was now helplessly dependent, stripped of his dignity, distinction, and status. At length, he turned his head and saw her. Yet not a trace of emotion crossed his face. Only then did a frightening reality seize her. In place of the angry demeanor, for which she had been warned, was a disturbing look of resignation, and she understood at once that he had abandoned the will to fight.

Before she had a chance to speak, he turned his face again toward the window. "Leave me alone, Callie. Just leave me alone." His voice was calm but wounding nonetheless.

Countless times in the past, she had prayed for courage to overcome her shy nature, but never so much as at this moment. She could not withdraw in cowardice now. She took a step closer to the foot of his bed. "No," she maintained aberrantly, "not until you hear what I came to say."

"There's nothing left to say."

She struggled to steady her trembling voice. "Joe, I want you to know I believe how my father handled . . . what he did . . . was wrong. And I also believe that you never would have been hurt if it . . . if it hadn't been for me." In humble shame, she looked down at the floor, unaware of the surprised glance he cast toward her in light of her declaration of guilt.

She said nothing more, waiting and hoping for some response from him. When there was none, she slowly lifted her head only to encounter the handsome, expressionless face once more. How she ached to put her arms around him, to comfort him, to assure him that everything would be all right. She would gladly care for him the rest of his life, but even more, she hungered to hear him tell her that in spite of everything, he loved *her*, regardless of the truth they both had to accept.

But only silence met with her remorse, and her contrived boldness began to melt into despair. "Joe, what my father did doesn't have to destroy us because . . . *because I love you!* If you only knew how much—"

"*Don't* say anymore, Callie," he snapped in a choleric voice. "It's no use. It's just . . . no use."

She strained to swallow tears that choked her. She was sure he blamed her for what her father had done as well as for the debilitated condition of his life and ruined career. And rightfully so. But still, she pleaded with him. "Joe, please . . . *please* don't do this to me."

He grew more agitated when a cry she could not suppress escaped her lips. He looked away so he would not have to look at her. He wanted her to leave, desperately wanted her to leave before he cried out for her to stay, even if it *was* only in pity.

But his deep-seated anger rekindled his resolve. "There's nothing more to say," he repeated in a slow, measured tone. "Just . . . leave me alone."

Callie was convinced now of what she had wanted so much to reject. By his silence, Joe had made apparent an undeniable testimony. He could no longer pretend to love her as he had loved Beth so effortlessly. The very notion had been a futile delusion from the beginning. The conscious realization brought forth hot, stinging tears, and she turned and fled from the room.

But what she did not see were the tears that came to Joe's eyes after she was gone, tears of loneliness and regret that neither he nor anyone else could take away.

* * *

Maggie heard the front door slam shut and hurried downstairs to the grand foyer. One look at Callie's face confirmed what she had feared most when she discovered Callie had left the house.

The girl fell weeping into her arms. Gently, Maggie guided her into the living room.

"Oh, Maggie, I should never have tried to talk to him!"

Maggie set her down on one of the couches and then sat beside her. "Ya went to see Dr. Joe, didn't ya?"

Admittedly, she nodded her head, and then the bitter account spilled out. Maggie's arm tightened around her shoulders as Callie reached the end of the story. "He told me there was nothing left!" she sobbed.

Maggie drew a deep breath. "Yes, I suppose that's the way he might see it. It was a mighty brave thing ya did, goin' to see him in the state of mind he was in."

Callie wiped her eyes and looked at Maggie. "What do you mean?"

"I mean that given the state of mind Dr. Joe is in right now, your lettin' *him* make a decision for the both of ya was a very brave thing to do."

Callie shook her head in disbelief. "Maggie, you don't understand . . ."

"I think I do." A smile came to the housekeeper's face. "Ya see, right now, Dr. Joe's emotional state could be cause enough for him to say somethin' . . . he doesn't really mean."

"Oh, Maggie," Callie groaned hopelessly, "he meant what he said. But all I wanted to do was tell him I love him!"

"And ya think he doesn't know that? Callie, listen to reason. I know it's hard for ya, but ya need to give him some time to put his life back together again." She pulled the astounded girl closer to her. "Honor the man's wishes. Let him alone for now."

* * *

Paul Martin sighed heavily as he finished reviewing the last of Joe's progress reports. "Poor Dr. Travis," remarked the nurse behind the counter, shaking her head sadly. "We've all tried to encourage him, but he simply refuses to let us help him, and he hasn't eaten hardly a thing for days. I suppose he's just been through too much." "I'll talk to him," Paul offered. "But sometimes, I feel like I'm talking to a head of stone."

Four days had passed since Callie had come to him, imploring him to allow her to see Joe in spite of Joe's pronouncement that he did not want to see her. Though Paul had not had opportunity to speak to her since, he knew his misgivings had proven true as Joe had rejected any conversation that concerned her. Paul admired Callie's courage but knew it was better for now not to broach the subject due to Joe's troubling, and increasing, depression.

He knocked at the door to Joe's room, not surprised when there was no response. He was about to open it when an aide walked out with a tray of untouched food.

Paul closed the door behind her. He stood beside the bed, waiting for some acknowledgement, but there was none, just an idle gaze through listless eyes toward the window. "I hear you're not eating."

Joe continued to stare out the window. "How much appetite would *you* have lying here all day?"

Paul observed the gaunt, impassive face of his friend. He shook his head disapprovingly. "You're a doctor, Joe. You know you have to eat to regain your strength. You'll be starting physical therapy soon unless you're too weak to go."

Despite the obvious derision, there was still no reaction. However, Paul was certain beneath the emotionless façade boiled an anger that, sooner or later, would be unleashed. Though he hated what he was about to do, he knew the time had come to leave the gentle approach behind. Joe was desperately in need of help, and his well-being was of more urgency to Paul than pacifying a treasured friendship.

"I don't think lack of appetite has anything to do with it. I think it's the fact that you've lost of the use of your hands, you can't feed yourself and you can't bring yourself to allow someone else to do it for you. It's too demeaning, too undignified. I think the whole problem has to do with the pride of Dr. Joe Travis."

Joe jerked his head in Paul's direction, the jaded blue eyes turning into rapid anger. "That's ridiculous—"

"Is it?" Paul interjected. "Think about it, Joe. You've treated patients that were in far worse shape than you are. You've had patients you had to tell had lost arms, legs, or their sight and knew their lives would *never* be the same again! I've heard you encourage them to get on with living, to make the most of what they had left, not concentrate on what they'd lost! *You* would never allow them the 'luxury' of wallowing in self-pity because *you* know that self-pity not only annihilates positive thinking, but also impedes healing, and that's exactly what you're doing to yourself!

"I know you've been through a hard time. No one was more frantic than I was the night those paramedics brought you into the emergency room, but I prayed, Joe, harder than I've ever prayed before in my life because *I wanted you to live!* But you have to want that too—want it bad enough to rise above what you've lost and remember what you still have, including what you're throwing away! What does it matter if you have to swallow a little of that 'surgeon's pride' and let these nurses do their job? Let them take care of you until you can take care of yourself! Because if you don't, my friend, you're going to lose a lot more than you've already lost."

The angry speech ended. Grieved at what he had had to do, Paul turned away in an effort to sustain his uncharacteristic pretense. He had preferred to comfort, not confront, the younger man whose camaraderie he cherished.

An awkward silence followed the admonishment. At length, Paul heard a voice, hesitant and uneasy. "You think I'm giving up . . . don't you?"

Paul turned toward Joe again. The outraged expression on the younger man's face had softened. The livid blue eyes had a calm sadness about them. "*Are* you giving up, Joe?"

He looked away without answering. Reluctantly, Paul opened the door and left the room.

For the remainder of the hour, Paul Martin managed to hide the emotional weariness he felt as he accompanied medical students on patient rounds. After rounds, he returned to the nurses' station, curious about the smile on the charge nurse's face.

"I have some good news for a change, Dr. Martin." "I could sure use some."

"Well, you might like to know Dr. Travis ordered a full meal a few minutes ago, and he asked *me* to 'serve' it to him."

Paul sighed with relief as he returned her smile. "Helen, you just made my day."

CHAPTER 33

After her miserable encounter with Joe, Callie's calls to the hospital inquiring about his condition became less frequent. Countless times, she was told that physically he was recovering, but colleagues quietly disclosed that his emotional state remained the same.

Maggie had gone shopping. Alone in the house, Callie wandered into her father's den and sat down in front of the cold hearth. She could think of nothing else but Joe. Paul was right. Joe was a stubborn man, and yet it was that very trait, that refusal to give up, that had enabled him to save the lives of so many patients in the operating room. Why could he not exert the same tenacity toward his own problems? How could he fight so hard for his patients and not do the same for himself?

Callie had resigned from her job and would not return to the hospital. Seeing her colleagues again had proven too awkward, and knowing Joe didn't want to see her at all had been too painful. Nevertheless, she knew she would never love another man as she loved him. Somehow, she had to keep that bitter disappointment from governing the rest of her life.

And this day would prove to be the bitterest disappointment of all. For today would have been their wedding day.

A week after Maggie returned, Callie discovered her mother's gown of satin and lace that had adorned the back of her bedroom door had quietly been removed. She knew the loving and heartbroken housekeeper had been responsible.

How many years had she dreamed of this day! In her mind, she had anticipated the solemn words time and again. *Will you love him, honor him, comfort him, and keep him in sickness and health, forsakingall others, be true to him as long as you both shall live?*

Callie dropped her head onto her folded arms. In the past few weeks, she had cried until she thought she had no tears left. She felt her eyes beginning to fill again when the phone rang. Wiping away the tears with the back of her hand, she rose to her feet and picked up the receiver on the table beside her.

"Callie? This is Stephen."

"*Stephen*?" She brushed aside a few more tears while trying to steady her voice. "Where are you?"

"I'm here, in Boston, at a medical convention. I wanted to know how you were doing. I've hardly heard a word from you since you left." There was a slight pause. "I wanted to be sure you were all right."

Stephen was a perceptive man, but now was not the time to explain her state of affairs. She drew a deep breath. "I'm fine. I'm sorry I didn't keep in touch with you like I promised—"

"I understand. You don't have to explain anything, Callie. But I was wondering, as long as I'm in town . . . " Again, his reserve hindered his purpose. "Would you have dinner with me tonight? I don't know anywhere to go, but it would be my pleasure to leave that up to you."

She brushed aside the remaining tears from her eyes. Stephen didn't need the burden of knowing this was to have been her wedding day. At least now, she had a reason not to be alone. "I can't guarantee how favorable a dinner companion I'll be, but I'd be happy to have dinner with you."

* * *

Dr. Stephen Lewis waited for Callie in the foyer of the popular Italian restaurant. He rose to his feet when she came in a few minutes later. "Callie, you look wonderful."

"Is that medically or personally speaking?" she quipped, her expression merely a pretense of optimism.

"Both," he returned, grinning. Impeccably dressed in a light brown suit, he was younger than Joe and not as tall. His dark blond hair and tanned skin seemed inconsistent with the long hours he spent inside a hospital.

They were seated at a comfortable table beside wide windows that overlooked the city. "So tell me how your practice is doing," Callie fumbled for conversation starters.

"It's getting to be more than I can handle alone," Stephen told her. "You know how busy it can be. In fact, I've been thinking about taking on a partner."

"That's wonderful."

"Well, selfishly, that's one reason I wanted to see you tonight." She felt his hesitation before he continued. "Callie, since your father died, I wondered if you'd given any thought to coming back to Charleston."

She glanced down at the napkin beneath her hand. Again, she would not encumber him with her failed plans. Until a few weeks ago, she thought she knew exactly what she would be doing for the rest of her life.

"I . . . hadn't really thought about it, Stephen. Why do you ask?" His expression revealed some disappointment. "Well, if I do decide to take on a partner, it would mean a lot more patients, and the need for a lot more help. I could really use a good, *experienced* nurse," he finished with a grin.

"I'm flattered. I suppose I could at least consider it."

"Well, at any rate you're not saying *no*," he added, smiling. "I have three more days here. I don't suppose you'd be able to show me a little of Boston before I leave, would you?"

"Well, I owe you, don't I?"

* * *

Stephen's time was limited because of the convention, but he and Callie spent what time they could exploring the historic areas of Beacon Hill, Boston by the sea, the old North Church and Freedom Trail.

Stephen came to a stop their last night out while strolling through the Boston Common. "This is magnificent," he observed. He looked around at the old park. "So what do you know about *this* place? You've been better than a history book and a lot more fun."

She smiled at him. "Well, this is the oldest public park in the nation. In fact, it used to be a cow pasture."

"For real?"

"Oh, yes," she went on. "But now it's mostly famous for demonstrators exercising their freedom of speech because here they don't have to have a permit to do so." She glanced at her watch. "Are you getting hungry?"

"Yeah, I think I am. What do you recommend?" "Quincy Market. It's one of my favorite places." "Then let's go."

* * *

Stephen and Callie walked along the sidewalks in the brightly lit outdoor market place. Among the food stalls, they dined on culinary delights from gourmet soup and frozen yogurt to the finest chocolates and pastries. Stephen wanted to try everything.

"I warned you to come here starving," she reminded him.

He grimaced while rubbing his stomach. "I believe you now." Throughout the perimeter of the market, they enjoyed examining the exquisite crafts and gifts made by the local artisans. Stephen begged Callie to let him get her something, but she politely refused each time.

As they made their way back toward Stephen's hotel, he took her hand and squeezed it. "You know how disappointed I was when you told me you wanted to come back to Boston. I think I understand a little better why you wanted to come home. In fact, I feel like I'm going to have an even harder time now trying to persuade you come back to Charleston."

Callie smiled wanly. The time she had spent with Stephen had been no substitute for her broken heart. Nevertheless, they had been pleasant hours, and she had come to appreciate his gentle nature even more.

"Sometimes, circumstances make it a little easier to leave behind what you thought you couldn't live without."

A bewildered but hopeful expression crossed his face. "Can I take that as a yes?"

Callie smiled at him again. "Let me think about it a little while longer. I won't keep you in suspense for long, I promise."

* * *

Alone in his room, Joe Travis sat in a wheelchair, staring down at his hands while painfully attempting to flex his fingers. Though the wires had been removed, they remained bandaged and swollen, resembling puffy sticks with long, repugnant scars. All he could sense was a pervasive numbness, a definite sign of the nerve damage he had feared the most.

He glanced out the window where the aide had left him after another arduous session in physical therapy. The rehabilitation he had begun a week earlier was more grueling and painful than he had imagined.

Looking down at his hands again, it was difficultto believe that he might one day be able to hold any kind of object once more, much less a scalpel. *A scalpel.* He closed his eyes as he drew a deep breath. What would he do with his life if . . .

No, it was too easy to believe the worst. If he should ever be capable of doing surgery again, if there was ever going to be any *hope* of doing surgery again, he had to determine he would continue with the prescribed course of therapy, however difficult. Though the rest of his plans had come to ruin, regaining the use of his hands would be his only salvation.

Painfully, he attempted to flex his fingers again.

* * *

Stephen sat across the small table from Callie in one of the airport terminal restaurants. His eyes sparkled when he looked at her. "I can't say I've ever enjoyed a medical convention so much." He pushed aside his empty glass. It was only minutes before it would be time for him to board. "I'd really love for you to come back to work with me, Callie. You'll let me know soon, won't you?"

"Of course I will."

"Well, I assumed with your father gone and no brothers or sisters that you had no more real ties here anymore. Do you?"

With Stephen's words came a haunting image of Joe Travis. Like a vision rising before her, Callie remembered them both standing outside her father's house, remembered the joyful anticipation she felt as they had devised plans to make it their home. Now the cold and stoic old mansion would remain just that—empty, lonely, devoid of a family.

"Callie?"

She looked up as her troubled thoughts returned to the present. "No," she said at last, "I really haven't any more ties here."

Stephen glanced at his watch. He took her hand when they stood up. "I want to hear from you soon, okay?"

"Okay," she promised. He kissed her cheek before disappearing into a crowd of people.

As Callie walked back through the airport terminal, her thoughts returned to Joe. His self-imposed isolation, his refusal to see her, his understandable anger, all had left her life in limbo. She had been able to do nothing but hope and pray—and wait.

Throughout the busy terminal, a multitude of people bustled passed her—business executives, families, couples, children, single individuals. All had a purpose, a place to go, someone to meet, something to accomplish. She had only an empty house to return to and nothing to do when she got there, nothing but long for a man she still loved, yet who would never come to the door of that house again. If Joe Travis didn't want her, she would have to find a way to live without him, but she could not allow his rejection of her to isolate one more day of her life.

CHAPTER 34

Joe Travis had lost count of the weeks he had spent in the hospital. His hands remained bandaged, though his broken arm and ribs were healing, and the physical pain was lessening. Every day, he spent time in the adjoining rehab facility, connected with the hospital campus, for physical therapy. Yet his depression concerning his uncertain future worsened, a fact exacerbated by his silence.

He stood beside the window in his room and gazed at the parking lot far below. Though looking, he was not seeing. Today, as every day, his mind was fraught with questions and accusations for which he cursed himself as well as God. Answers had not come easily, or more often, had not come at all.

Whom the Lord loveth, He chastens. His mother had revered the verse from Hebrews and quoted it numerous times in an effort to comfort a young Joe when his drunken father created more trouble for the distressed family, but he had not taken courage from the passage as she had.

As a child, Joe had come to interpret the text to imply that God's punishment, however severe, was something that must be endured for his eventual good. But as an adult, and particularly as a doctor, this interpretation did not answer the inexhaustible question of *why*. Neither did it concur with his mother's concept of a loving heavenly Father.

A quiet knocking caused him to abandon his reverie. He turned and saw Evan Richards standing in the doorway.

"Joe, are you receiving today?" the pastor asked with a cautious smile.

Joe stepped away from the window. "Come in, Evan," he returned in an expressionless voice.

The young pastor closed the door behind him and, without thinking, extended a customary handshake. Immediately, he withdrew the routine gesture when he noticed Joe's bandaged hands. "Joe, I can't tell you how sorry I am for not being able to see you before now. I came several other times but was told you weren't seeing visitors. I understand how you must feel."

"I don't think anyone really knows how I feel, Evan," Joe said in a mildly caustic tone as the two men sat down in chairs near the bed. "How have you been?"

"Well, saddened that some of my more pleasant pastoral duties have been delayed. I was told your wedding has been postponed."

The day of his wedding had dawned with a despair he could not ignore, a fact that had not slipped his mind as he would have preferred that it might. "Not postponed. Canceled. Indefinitely."

"I'm sorry to hear that, Joe. Really sorry."

Evan was disturbed by the lack of emotion on Joe's face, making it more than apparent that the failed marriage plans were something Joe did not wish to discuss, but Evan sensed more than that. He sensed an anger—or was it fear?—that was very near the surface. However, he understood this was not the time or place to probe for reasons for either.

"Is there anything I can do for you, Joe? Anything I can help you with? You must remember that God hasn't abandoned you. He loves you—"

"*He loves me,*" Joe mocked. "And that fact, of course, would explain this?" Joe held up his bandaged hands in front of the young minister.

Evan winced unintentionally, noting with more acuity the distortion of Joe's injuries. "Joe, again, I'm so sorry—"

"Evan, I read something once, something I found at the time to be very insightful, and I contemplated it for a long time." He paused before continuing. "I read that God does indeed discipline us from time to time to improve us, just as a parent would discipline a child. But in the course of that . . . *discipline* . . . His intention is not to bring us down or beat us into submission to accomplish His purpose, but rather to *lift us up to Him*."

The steel blue of Joe's eyes, in addition to the derisive tone of his voice, pierced like daggers into the heart of the minister.

"So tell me, Evan, what have I done to warrant this particular discipline? What have I failed to understand? Just when I thought I'd begun to put my life back together, why did this turmoil come to me? Why would a *loving God* subject me to such a brutal set of circumstances, impose debilitating infirmities on me, take away my career, and then expect me to triumph over that which now holds me prisoner? What good is a God who won't protect me from bad things, but would instead punish me for trying to do what's right?"

Evan Richards looked hard at Joe. During the course of time that he had known him, he had come to admire the doctor's intellect and acute sense of right and wrong. He was asking questions that did not surprise him. Yet they were questions for which he knew the answers would not only be difficult, but would also have to be acceptable to Joe Travis.

"I imagine in your medical practice, you've been asked those very questions from patients and family members, am I right?"

Somewhat taken aback by the younger man's rapid and insightful response, Joe glanced away for a moment before answering. "From some, yes."

"And did you find your answers to be any easier than their questions?" An awkward silence followed when Joe realized he could say nothing. "Of course, you didn't. Joe, we live in a world of unfairness. I can't tell you why God permitted this to happen to you. I think sometimes, He leads us into trials where only our faith will permit us to go. I *can* tell you that I understand your frustration. You're a surgeon. God has blessed you with a pair of skilled hands, and now for some unknown reason, He's allowed you to suffer the loss of that ability for the time being.

"But I believe that what you read was true. Even though you can't see it now, God has chosen to refine you, just like gold tried in the fire. He *does* lift us up to Him, and He *doesn't* do it by beating us down as you feel right now. Eventually, if you'll allow it, you'll see God's mercy at work in your life. And you'll be better for it."

Joe listened to the impassioned words from the young man. In spite of everything, he retained a high regard for Evan Richards, but Evan did not know all the circumstances that he felt justified his anger. And Evan, too, was only a man.

The minister rose to his feet. "Will you let me pray with you, Joe?"

Another awkward silence followed. Unknown to Evan, as the long and tedious days in his hospital room had passed, Joe had ultimately come to a decision: if this was indeed the manner in which God worked, he wanted nothing more to do with Him, for Joe Travis no longer had any clear beliefs.

At length, he looked up at the minister. "Save your prayers, Evan. I've had enough of God's 'mercy' for a while."

* * *

Joe felt a measure of remorse after the minister left. He respected him and almost wished he could have divulged to him his private fears, but anger prevented him from accepting Evan's explanation for God's purpose in his life, and he resolved again that his relationship with a Higher Being had come to an end.

As he stood beside the window once more, he realized he would be discharged soon, and though he savored the luxury of privacy once more, he feared what being alone would mean.

In truth, Joe knew the hospital had become a kind of sanctuary for him. Managing his life away from that support was almost as frightening as the solitude, and this left him feeling ashamed. He was a doctor, a trained physician, a surgeon of the highest caliber, and yet he was afraid. Finding himself on the opposite side of his profession had generated an anxiety he wondered if he had sometimes disregarded in his own patients.

Joe felt an ever-increasing sense of isolation apart from Callie. Yet in spite of his intense loneliness, he could not separate her from her father's reprehensible mishandling of the sacred privilege he had abused, and for that reason, she would remain at an angry distance from his heart.

However, the resulting loneliness was taking a greater toll on him than he realized. For Joe's withdrawal was leading him to retreat from a reality he did not want to face. He found himself dwelling more and more on the world that had existed before his debilitating accident, a world where *he* had had the advantage, fulfilled as a surgeon and a professor of medicine, a world of challenge where preserving life was demanding and stressful yet rewarding nonetheless.

But one glance at his broken and bandaged hands nullified his one-time world of idealism, plunging him miserably into a darker world he had come to despise.

He turned away from the window when Paul Martin and Clark Sawyer, the orthopedic surgeon, walked into the room.

"Joe, your last set of x-rays showed marked improvement," Sawyer announced. "I want to see one more set to be sure, and then I think we can kick you out of here. If we don't let you go soon, we may never get you back. I'll see you downstairs in a few minutes."

Paul cast a pleasing smile at Joe after Sawyer left the room. "I can only imagine what good news that is for you."

Joe nodded, straight-faced. "Yeah . . . good news."

"Joe," Paul began, guessing what was going through the young man's mind, "take it one day at a time. You can't do anything else."

Joe turned toward the window again. "Have you . . . have you seen Callie lately?"

For Paul, the question came as a pleasant surprise. He only wished he had better news. "Well, not for some time now. She resigned from the OR shortly after your accident." Disappointed when there was no further inquiry, Paul continued. "Joe, *you're* the one who needs to see her. You're going to lose that girl for good, if you don't put aside this anger of yours."

"Just like I'm supposed to 'put aside' what her father did?" "What her *father* did has nothing to do with the *girl* who only wants to love you!" Exasperated, Paul thrust his hands into the air. "I can't understand it! You're improving daily, there's a good chance you'll regain the full use of your hands again, and you have a remarkable young woman who loves you, and yet in spite of it all, you're condemning yourself to a living nightmare. Joe, not a day goes by that I don't pray for you."

Joe's eyes snapped to life as he turned abruptly toward Paul. "Forget the prayers," he returned in caustic voice. "What do you suppose God will do to me *next*?"

So that was part of the anger too. Paul shook his head while pointing to the unmade bed. "If that's what you lay there and think about, let me suggest this to you. I believe there are times God has to do some incredibly unusual things to gain our attention. Maybe, just maybe, He put you flat on your back so you'd have *nowhere* to look but *up*."

* * *

An hour later Joe was dressed, standing beside the bed while he reviewed the therapy instructions Sawyer had left with him as he prepared to leave the hospital. He could now slightly move his fingers, but the numbness and swelling still prevented him from picking up objects or making a simple fist.

His conversation with Paul regarding Callie troubled him. Had he not already lost her? Why couldn't he put aside the anger that encumbered him? He glanced at the phone as he had done a hundred times before. Maybe.

Jessie Gallagher appeared in the doorway, standing behind a wheelchair. "Dr. Travis, I have the honor of escorting you downstairs. Dr. Martin is waiting to drive you home."

"I can make it without *that*, thank you," he said, nodding toward the wheelchair.

She shook her head and sighed. "It's true. Doctors *do* make the worst patients. You know the rules, and unfortunately you aren't any exception."

He had always admired Jessie's candor. "I'll take full responsibility."

"Then I guess we won't be using this." She started to pull the wheelchair back into the corridor when Joe glanced one more time at the telephone beside the bed. "Jess, will you help me make a call before I go?"

* * *

Callie Jordan walked through the empty house, listening to the echo of her footsteps against the bare walls. Each room she passed had its own memories, reminders of the only home she had ever known.

Now only a few suitcases sat by the door at the bottom of the grand staircase, and beside them, a small paper bag filled with flower bulbs she had dug from one of the gardens around the house. She had one last obligation to fulfill, a task of love that she wanted to complete before leaving Boston for good.

Callie had released all the part-time workers weeks earlier, but letting Maggie McCarran go had been the hardest of all her unpleasant tasks. Maggie had filled the place of the mother she barely remembered.

She stood beside the large window in her bedroom, remembering how in lonely anticipation she had watched the neighborhood children who had played outside. How she had longed to join those children but had been too restricted because of her heart. Maggie would try hard to cheer her up, playing games with her, reading to her, sewing, crocheting, anything to keep her entertained.

Just when the loneliness seemed intolerable, Beth would arrive. With Beth, the hours had passed like minutes as they played and talked and giggled in this room, sharing everything imaginable— secrets, dreams, special promises made known only to each other.

* * *

"Promise me, Bethie," Callie had whispered to her friend, "promise we'll always take care of each other."

"Always," Beth had replied. "We have promises to keep."

* * *

Callie turned away from the window. For now, it was just another empty room in an empty house, full of treasured memories and haunting nostalgia that was one more thing she had to leave behind.

She walked slowly down the wide staircase. Wearied, she sat on the bottom stair and gazed at the dazzling rays of sunlight shining though the beveled glass on the front doors. As a little girl, she had loved to sit on this same stair on sunny afternoons and watch the pattern of rainbow colors dance across the marble floor.

The years passed in her mind as more memories crowded out the childhood days. She thought about the annual parties that her father had given his students. Shyly, she would stand at a safe distance on the broad staircase to survey the guests as they came to the door. Year after year, she had seen many of the same faces, but Callie would never forget one particular year when a new face had appeared, and from that moment on, nothing had ever been the same for her again.

* * *

The house seemed to get more crowded every year. Extra staff had been hired to serve and work the kitchen duties. Music from the stringed quartet in an alcove of the living room drifted throughout the house. A large ice sculpture beside the punch bowl fountain gradually melted in the warm spring air.

Callie walked down the staircase and stood on the first landing, surveying the residents and spouses who circulated throughout the living and dining rooms, spilling onto the expansive deck outside. Then Maggie brushed past her on her way toward the kitchen, waving an empty silvertray as she passed. "Callie, can ya give me some help?" she asked in an urgent voice.

Without hesitation, Callie followed the tireless woman into the immense kitchen. "Those hor d'oeuvres your father loves so much are going faster than I can make them!" she declared. "Ya know how to prepare them. Will ya make a batch, please?"

"Well, I can't let ya mess up that beautiful dress," Maggie said, slipping a full apron over Callie's head. After tying the white sash behind her, she disappeared through the doorway again. Callie began assembling the appetizers.

Servers hurried back and forth through the kitchen. Callie had almost finished filling one tray in preparation to begin another when the door opened again. "Excuse me, ma'am?"

"Yes?" she answered quickly without turning around.

"Dr. Jordan would like another tray of hor d'oeuvres right away." "Well, I'm sorry, but you tell Dr. Jordan he'll just have to wait

like everybody else," she said brusquely, not wanting to interrupt her concentration.

There was slight hesitation before the smooth male voice spoke again. "I don't think that's a very respectful way to talk about your employer." Together with the mellow voice came an air of polite reprimand.

"My 'employer'?" she asked, turning toward the voice. At once, she realized she did not know the handsome young man standing in the doorway, and neither would she be likely to forget him. As her face reddened, she brushed aside loose strands of hair with the back of her hand. "Tell . . . tell the good doctor it won't be long."

She returned to her work as the door closed behind her. Quickly, she finished the hor d'oeuvres and struggled out of the apron. She bustled through the swinging kitchen door with two loaded trays, meeting Maggie coming toward her. "Oh, Callie, you're a lifesaver!" she said, taking the trays from her hands. "Now get out there and find yourself a doctor husband!"

As she passed through the dining room, she hoped to catch sight of the young man in the crowd, but when she saw him deep in conversation with her father, she was overcame with embarrassment by her brusque mannerism. She came to a stop, looking for a way to retreat, but it was too late. Her father saw her and, raising his hand, gestured for her to join them.

With faltering steps, she walked over to greet them. "Dr. Joseph Travis, I don't believe you've met my daughter, Callie."

The young doctor's blue eyes widened with obvious chagrin. "Ms. Jordan," he acknowledged, his voice full with embarrassment. But as he took her hand, the expiation turned into a broad grin, and the dimples in his cheeks deepened even more. "You might have told me who you were."

"I might have, but I didn't. I apologize."

His stunning smile was infectious and she immediately returned it. "There's no need for that. I'm very glad to meet you—again."

Benjamin Jordan glanced fiercely from one to the other as the exchange came to an end. "What on earth are you two talking about?"

They only grinned as one of the servants stopped to extend a tray of appetizers. "Have an hor d'oeuvre, Dr. Jordan," Joe offered.

* * *

No more, Callie thought as she rose doggedly from the bottom stair. She picked up her suitcases along with the small bag of flower bulbs and set them outside the door. As she pulled it shut and locked it, she determined she would not allow sentimental memories to control the rest of her life.

Neither would she hear the phone ring.

* * *

A heavy, stale air greeted Paul Martin as he opened the door to Joe's long vacant house. "I think the first thing on the agenda is to open some windows and let a little fresh air in," he said as he set down Joe's bags in the foyer.

Joe was silent as he followed the older man inside. In the living room, he stopped to survey the yard through the picture window. The outside appeared as abandoned as within. The lawn was overgrown with tall grass and weeds, the shrubbery thick and unkempt. Dry autumn leaves scattered in the wind across the yard.

Paul emerged from the kitchen after raising some windows. "Looks like we're going to have to do some grocery shopping so you won't starve to death." But there was no response from the younger man who remained fixed beside the window.

Paul stood in the doorway of the kitchen and watched Joe for a moment. His tightly closed lips and creased forehead disclosed a wordless despair. Paul knew there would be a harsh readjustment period ahead for him. He also knew Joe would be forced to adapt to it or give up, and Paul determined the latter would not happen.

Joe heard him pick up his car keys, and the dread that had seized him the moment he walked through the door gripped him even tighter. He would be alone and on his own as soon as Paul was gone. Still gazing out the window, he managed to utter a few barely audible words. "Paul . . . how am I going to get by on my own?"

Paul was actually relieved to hear the plaintive, straightforward question, considering Joe's tacit struggle trying to resign himself to his situation while in the hospital, a silent endeavor Paul was certain masked a fear that Joe had been too ashamed to voice aloud.

The older man put a fatherly hand on his shoulder. "You know, you needed a lot of help those first few weeks you spent in the hospital. You had to accept the fact that you had to learn to cope without the use of your hands. But now you've come to the place in your recovery that having to depend on yourself is also part of the healing process. It's what's going to restore the confidence you've lost." Paul squeezed his shoulder and smiled. "I'm not telling you anything you haven't told your own patients. But if it would make you feel more comfortable, let me arrange for someone to come over a few hours every day to help you out."

Joe continued to stare out the window. No, he could not allow personal fear to dominate his self-respect. "Thanks, Paul, but . . . I guess I need to learn to do for myself, like you say." In the past, he would have asked God for the self-assurance he could not generate on his own, but he could no longer do that. He was alone and on his own now. He swallowed hard. "I guess I'm just a little nervous, that's all."

"It's all right to be afraid," Paul said in a comforting voice. "But you're not alone. There's any number of people only a phone call away, including me. But for now," he said more stridently, "I'm going to go to the store to stock your cabinets with things I promise you'll be able to manage on your own."

Paul was at the front door with the keys rattling in his hand when Joe finally turned around. "Then . . . you'll be back?"

"I'll be back. The food won't be gourmet, but it *will* be nutritious. In the meantime, why don't you unpack and get to know your own home again? I think it's about time."

CHAPTER 35

Stephen Lewis's secretary ushered Callie Jordan into the doctor's private office and closed the door.

While she waited for him to finish with a patient, she admired the beautifully lettered inscription that hung on the wall behind his desk, a line of dialogue from Stephen's favorite childhood film, *The Wizard of Oz*, "Hearts will never be practical until they can be made unbreakable." A smile came to her face as she thought what a suitable passage for a cardiac surgeon.

The door swung open, and Stephen walked in, his face radiant at the sight of his long-anticipated visitor. He reached for her hands. "Callie, it's so good to see you! I didn't think you'd come this soon."

"Did I have a time limit?"

"Of course not," he told her. "But why didn't you tell me you were coming? I could have picked you up at the airport."

"I don't think you have that kind of time," she said, gesturing with a nod toward the packed waiting room.

"Now you can see for yourself why I need a partner and *you* to help me stay on my feet." He squeezed her hands. "I've got so much to tell you. I'll make a reservation at the finest restaurant in Charleston tonight. Where are you staying?"

She relayed the hotel information for him as he walked her to the door. "I'll wait for you in the lobby."

"Perfect. Seven o'clock, and not a minute later," he said in eagerness as he pulled the door open for her.

* * *

Callie had been sitting in the lobby of the hotel almost two hours past the time that Stephen had promised to meet her. She dropped her magazine on the polished table just in time to see him almost running toward her.

He came to a halt in front of her. "Are you terribly mad, or just mad?"

She grinned at the hapless remark. "Have you forgotten how long I've been acquainted with the trials of surgeons, Dr. Lewis? Believe me, I've become more patient than I ever dreamed possible." He released an obvious sigh of relief. "I'm really sorry. I had an emergency and couldn't even get to the phone. Do you know how many potential girlfriends I've lost because of my profession?" "Potential?" she repeated. "I bet you've never even *had* a girlfriend. Too much talent and far too busy."

His tanned face turned a pale shade of pink as he glanced at his watch. "I guess we missed our dinner reservation," he said, genuinely disappointed for ruining their date. "Are you starving?"

"I'm not even hungry. What about you?"

"Not really. Will you at least go for a ride with me?"

"I think I can do that. And I hope you appreciate what a cheap date I am."

* * *

Stephen stopped the car near a scenic park area beside Charleston's famous waterfront battery. The night was warm, and a mild breeze blew across the water as they got out of the car.

"I've always loved this place," he said as they began walking. "I can remember coming here when I was just a kid. I used to watch the boats going up and down the river. I was determined I'd be on one someday. I wanted to be a sailor."

Callie turned to look at him. "A *sailor*? How did you go from sailor to surgeon?"

"My uncle was a surgeon," he explained as they began walking toward the water. "My father convinced him to let me observe surgery one day with hopes of getting me to change my mind. And it worked," he said matter-of-factly. "Instead of fainting, I was fascinated."

"Well, *I'll* always be grateful you became a surgeon."

Stephen came to a stop and looked at her. "It's people like you that's made it all worthwhile." Timidly, his hand slipped into hers. "Callie, I think you know you've come to mean a great deal to me. I asked you to come back to work with me, not only because I knew you were a good nurse, but—" The hesitant words came to an end before they were finished.

"Stephen, I owe you so much—"

"You don't owe me anything. What I did for you was what I was trained to do." He glanced down at the ground before looking at her full in the face. "But I didn't have to be trained to fall in love with you."

Stunned by his unexpected disclosure, she felt his hands tightening around hers as he went on. "Don't look so shocked, Callie," he said, smiling. "I have a good career, two houses, and three cars. But what good is all that if you're only pleasing yourself?"

Callie's gaze shifted from Stephen toward the water. "None whatsoever. Being alone is the cruelest form of punishment." All at once, she realized her voice had taken on a bitterness he could not comprehend. "I'm sorry," she said quietly, looking down. "I understand what you're saying. Really, I do."

"I can only imagine how lonely you've been since your dad died, especially being an only child," he said, presuming she had been alluding to the loss of her father. His hand slipped under her chin. An encouraging smile greeted her uplifted gaze when he added, "But you don't *have* to be alone."

Leave me alone, Callie . . . just leave me alone. Joe's insufferable words came back like a resounding echo in her mind. She had never wanted to be apart from him, but he had given her no choice. He had driven her out of his life, and the merciless command still tore her apart. Anger, she thought, had to be superior to pain; for though she was trying to make her own way, she felt lost without Joe. She could not divulge this to Stephen, not yet, maybe not ever. But he deserved some sort of explanation.

"Stephen, there are certain . . . issues in my life I can't explain to you right now. I only ask that you be patient with me for a while." "On one condition. Will you give me a chance, a chance to prove that I only want you to be happy, here, with me?"

"I think I can do that." He pulled her toward him and folded her into his arms, but he couldn't know that her heart was a thousand miles away.

* * *

Stephen had left nothing to chance as far as Callie was concerned. He helped her settle into his beach house the next day. He had purchased the cottage for the explicit purpose of getting away but had seldom had the chance. His own house was located near the hospital and infrequently used as it was.

Stephen set the remainder of Callie's luggage on the bed before coming back into the living room. "I'd just about forgotten what this place looked like."

"I love it!" she exclaimed, surveying the combination living room, dining room, and kitchen. The bedroom off the living room had a large bay window that faced the ocean. A spiral staircase led to a second floor bedroom and a loft.

Stephen walked into the kitchen and opened the cabinets. "I guess we better go to the store tonight so you don't starve." He closed the cabinet doors and then turned to look at Callie. "I hope you'll be comfortable here."

"It's perfect. How far is it from your office?"

"Well, that's the drawback. It's about a forty-five minute drive in good traffic. But that little car will get you where to need to go," he said, gesturing to his second vehicle parked outside.

"Stephen, you've done too much. You've given me a place a live, provided me with a car . . . what can I do for *you*?"

Though he longed to tell her more of how he felt, he refused to put a burden of conscience on her. Instead, the boyish grin returned. "Show up for work tomorrow?"

* * *

Joe's first week at home proved more difficult than he had imagined.

Tonight, he fumbled miserably with the dirty dishes that had piled up in the kitchen sink. Cups and plates slipped from his feeble grasp; silverware eluded his pathetic endeavor. In exasperation, he finally tossed a towel over the mess just so he wouldn't have to look at another obstacle he could not conquer.

Paul had left him with easily prepared microwave meals that required little effort, but as the days passed, Joe found simple routine tasks all but impossible to accomplish.

The elastic gloves he had to wear continuously to reduce the swelling in his hands prevented him from being able to rinse dishes or grasp them well enough to put into the dishwasher. He could not handle a comb to brush his hair or hold onto a bar of soap. He only managed to get dressed by struggling into his clothes using his elbows and palms of his hands. Depression and frustration became his constant companions for he could see no end to the daily struggles.

There were frequent phone calls from well-meaning colleagues and friends. All offered to do something, but Joe politely, yet stubbornly, refused their help. However, he was grateful for Paul Martin who stopped by as often as possible to assist Joe where he had no choice but to surrender to his own obstinacy.

But Paul had not had an opportunity to visit in almost a week. His responsibilities at the hospital had increased dramatically because of Joe's absence. However, today, he had managed to escape early and met Joe on the front porch. "Say," he said in admiration as he walked through the door, "that's turning into a pretty good looking beard. Is this part of a new image?"

"It's not a new image. I . . . can't hold the razor."

Paul grinned, despite Joe's surly attitude. "Come on. Let's forget that pride of yours and get you looking like a member of the human race again."

They walked into the bathroom where Paul set out shaving lotion and a razor, then filled the sink with warm water. Humbly, Joe submitted his face to the skilled hands of his colleague. "So," Paul said as he tilted the young man's face back, "have you thought anymore about letting me find someone to come over and help you out for a little while?" He made a few strokes with the razor, then swished it back and forth in the water.

"You've suggested that before."

"And I may go right on suggesting it until you decide to give in." He made a few more strokes with the razor. Fine brown hair floated in the soapy water.

"And who gave me the speech about independence and doing for myself again?"

Paul turned Joe's face to one side. "All right, it was me. But I'm talking about a *temporary* situation, as temporary as the condition of your hands right now," he added optimistically.

"We don't know that," Joe returned in a quiet, aggravated tone.

Paul made small talk after that until he finished his task. With a clean towel, he wiped the rest of the soap away from Joe's face.

"Thanks, Paul, and I really mean it," Joe said with genuine gratitude.

"It was my pleasure," he said, hanging the damp towel over the sink. Then he added, "I really wish you'd reconsider letting me find someone to help you out, just for a little while. Will you do that much?"

"I'll think about it," was all he said.

* * *

Joe heard the gentle knocking as he struggled into his robe. It was too early in the morning for Paul to be stopping by. He pulled open the front door and stared in wide-eyed wonder at the visitor on the other side.

Callie Jordan's face carried a pensive, anxious expression. "Joe, I understand you need some help," she began. "I know you don't want to seeme, but you do need some help. I don't want you to send me away again. I just want to help. Please, just let me help you."

There was nothing he wanted more than to feel Callie in his arms once again. He was so tired of being lonely and afraid, and Callie was the only one who could put an end to the miserable existence he was leading. With rapt joy, he eagerly reached out to pull her toward him, but as he reached forward, she slipped away from him. He opened his mouth to callto her, but no words would come.

"Joe, please," she pleaded from a further distance, "please don't send me away! Please let me stay!" He strained to stretch out his hands toward her, but he felt chained to the floor from which he could not move whileshe continued to slip even further beyond his reach, and he could voice nowords to compel her to return.

Again and again, she called out to him, until she faded from his sight, enveloped in an alien fog that kept her at an unreachable distance. Her beseeching words echoed through the mist until he could no longer hear her.

Too late, he found his voice. "Callie, come back! Callie!"

* * *

"Callie!" Joe sat bolt upright in bed. Sweat clung to his body. His heart pounded as he realized the sound of his own voice had awakened him.

He pushed strands of damp hair away from his eyes and then draped his head across his arms.

How could he live with himself after all that had happened? His career was in ruins. He had rejected the one woman who had loved him without condition, and every waking hour was becoming its own living nightmare. Now even his dreams were haunted by his past.

He drew a wearied breath as he lay down once more. Morning light was already streaming through the bedroom windows. He knew he should get up, but if the truth be told, there was really no reason to.

CHAPTER 36

"Callie, I need an EKG on Mr. Somerville in Room Two." Stephen's white lab coat rustled behind him as he brushed past her on his way down the hall to leave phone orders on an emergency hospital admission. Callie barely had time to acknowledge the request before he disappeared into his private office.

Twenty minutes later, she knocked before opening the door. Lifting his head from his arms, he looked up when she entered the room. "You're exhausted," she said, dropping on his desk the little square monitor that would convert the readings of the EKG to Stephen's printer.

Through bleary eyes, he reached for her hands across the desk. "Do you know something?" he said, ignoring her candid observation.

"Occasionally."

He grinned at her wry humor. "It's almost Thanksgiving, and it's been almost one year since your surgery. Let's celebrate tonight. I'll take you anywhere you want to go."

She squeezed his hands in return. "You're going *home* to get your first decent night's sleep in a week. That's how you'll celebrate." She turned away from the desk when he caught her by the hand and pulled her back.

"All right," he conceded, grasping her hand tighter, "but only if you come with me. We'll make something great for dinner."

"Okay, but I'm not going to stay long because—"

"I know . . . I know." A resigned, but boyish grin returned before he let go of her hand.

* * *

Callie lifted the lid from the steaming pot of water and set it on the tile counter of Stephen's spacious kitchen. She opened a box of spaghetti and began adding it a bit at a time to the boiling water. A few minutes later, Stephen opened the kitchen door, refreshed from a hot shower, and paused to watch her. "This isn't exactly the gourmet meal I had in mind," he said, coming up behind her.

"This is as gourmet as it gets when you don't go food shopping for a couple of months."

He turned her toward him and kissed her. "Do you have any idea how happy you've made me?"

"Stephen, whatever I've done hardly seems comparable to what you did for me. You saved my life."

"That's right, I did," he said, as though suddenly remembering. "What's the old Chinese proverb, *He who saves a life is responsible for it forever*? I guess that makes me forever responsible for you."

She returned his broad smile. "And I'll be forever beholden to *you*."

His genial expression slowly vanished as he glanced down at the floor. "I don't want you to be *beholden*," he said quietly, looking at her again. "I hope someday you really *will* let me be responsible for you . . . forever." He grimaced inside. That wasn't the proposal he had rehearsed.

He waited for some response, despite the fact that the tender offer had been a bit vague. But she pulled herself out of his arms and turned back to the stove. "You better let me finish this before *I'm* responsible for a malnourished man."

Disappointed, he watched her for a moment longer while she stirred the spaghetti, then turned and walked away. He paused beside the kitchen door to look at her once more, imagining for the hundredth time what it would be like to have Callie for his wife.

* * *

The dishes were in the dishwasher and the leftovers put away. Callie dropped the dishtowel on the counter, wondering why a half hour had passed since Stephen mysteriously disappeared without volunteering to help her clean the kitchen.

Promised rain had begun to fall outside. Callie pushed the kitchen curtains apart and watched the cold drizzle slide down the windowpanes. For a moment, she imagined the snow that was almost certainly on the ground at home by now.

She walked out of the brightly lit kitchen and found Stephen had turned off the living room lamps. A shimmering light from the fireplace was all that illuminated the room. He had thrown pillows on the floor and pushed the coffee table out of the way so they could sit by the hearth. He held out his hand as she walked toward him. "I wish I could make it snow for you," he said.

"How did you know I was thinking about snow?" She took his hand, smiling at his attentive gesture to make her feel more at home. "In fact, I remember you said the very same thing last year about this time."

He helped her sit down beside him in front of the fire. "But aren't you glad you're not in the hospital this Christmas?"

"Yes, very."

They sat together in front of the fire, sipping sparkling cider from long stemmed glasses. When they had finished, Stephen set the goblets aside, pulling Callie closer to him. She rested comfortably against his shoulder. "This really is nice," she said.

"I was hoping you'd think so." He sighed contentedly, basking in the pleasure he always found being alone with her. "You're such a comfort to me, Callie. I want so much for you to be happy."

He hesitated, gathering his courage before going on. "Callie," he began slowly, "when you first came down here, you told me there were things you couldn't explain to me, and that's all right. I'll wait as long as you want until you're ready to tell me whatever you need to. But I can't wait any longer . . . to ask you to be my wife."

She turned to look at him. In his eyes, there seemed to be a reflection of all the love and sincerity he had saved for this moment, and her heart broke at the thought of hurting him. "Stephen, right now, I don't think I can give you the answer you want."

His disappointment was obvious, yet the tender expression remained unchanged. "You don't have to give me an answer tonight, but I want you to know one thing. I've never felt this way about any woman before. I think I loved you the first time I saw you, and I've only come to love you more since then."

Gently, Stephen's caring arms encircled her. But as Callie laid her head against his chest, words too similar to Stephen's came rushing back. *I loved you then, Cal, and I love you now.*

Like an unflagging presence in her mind, Joe's face, his voice, the words she had longed to hear him say came back clearly, painfully, and unexpectedly. She buried her face in Stephen's shirt and shut her eyes tightly against the memory, but it was not so easily dismissed. Would Joe ever be anything but an aching reminder of what could never be?

But the fact remained that Joseph Ian Travis had left a tremendous chasm in her life. Though she had tried to close the gap by putting the memories behind her, they lingered like an undeviating presence buried deep within her heart, surfacing at the most unexpected moments. She still felt the ache of a tenacious love that had not been abandoned as easily as she had. Even now, it was a powerful influence, and she feared that pain would impede whatever love, if any, she had left to give.

The touch of Stephen's hand caressing her hair quelled the stinging remembrance. "Callie, forgive me if I've been pressing too hard."

She pulled herself out of his arms, hoping the dim light from the fire would veil the tears in her eyes. "You haven't done anything of the kind. I just . . . need some time."

"All right," he said at last. "You have all the time you need."

Once more, he pulled her back into his arms. As he watched the dwindling fire, his yearning to protect her, to provide for her, to love her, grew even stronger.

But Stephen suspected somewhere in Callie's past there lurked a sorrow from which she could not free herself, and until that happened, he feared she could never return the love he longed to share with her.

* * *

Joe Travis had no agenda. No appointments. No place he had to be, no meetings, no schedule. No one demanding his time. No patients who needed him, for that need had been replaced by another. There had been a time when he had believed—understood, rather—that he was an indispensable, vital, extraordinary part of a well-trained team. However, that was no longer the case.

He had been sitting for hours in one of the recliners facing the picture window in the living room. November had stripped away the beauty of October's brilliant weather. Autumn's colors had come and gone, and now the chill of an oncoming winter threatened more months of lonely isolation.

For most of the day, the sun had shimmered through the bare branches of the trees, but as night drew on, oppressive, gray clouds had begun to gather in the sky. The wind turned colder, and as the weather grew bleaker, Joe's thoughts did the same.

He performed his daily ritual of physical therapy exercises with rigid determination, but improvement was so gradual he could not distinguish any significant difference from day to day, even week to week. Now, almost three months after the accident, chronic pain and weakness still held him in a feeble grasp. Yet the pain was secondary compared to his pervasive struggle with depression. Never in his life had he had so little to do or felt so completely useless. Today had been no different, only worse.

Loneliness was an adversary he could not conquer. After Beth died, his salvation had come from increased effort toward his work. The endeavor had been a poor substitute for her loss, but it had kept him occupied and productive, a guard against succumbing to despair that might eventually overwhelm him, and never did he surrender to the thought that the kind of happiness Beth had brought could ever come to him again.

But Callie Jordan had changed that grim scenario. She had brought with her not only a long-standing friendship but a contentment he craved; a love he not only yearned for but desperately wanted to share. Now he was not only without Callie, he was without his work. And without his work, he had nothing.

You have to rise above what you've lost, and remember what you still have, including what you're throwing away. He gripped the arms of the chair a little more tightly as Paul Martin's candid words burned in his mind. Yes, he had thrown Callie away, thrust her from his life, but not so easily from his heart. Maybe, *maybe*, there was still a chance if only he could.

He glanced at the phone on the table beside him. Reaching out, he awkwardly grappled with the receiver, but once in his hand, the frenzied vision of the night Callie had told him the truth about her heart transplant rose like the approaching storm outside. He dropped the receiver. *What was the use?* His unrelenting resentment toward Ben Jordan continued to surpass his deepening depression and longing to see her.

The room had grown dark without his awareness. He got out of the chair and wandered into the bedroom, sprawling across the bed. Hopelessness overwhelmed him tonight. As he stared at his useless hands, a myriad of patients on whom he had operated began to pass like ghosts through his mind.

He thought about Mattie Walker and the special fondness he had held for her. She had been so optimistic and encouraging despite the fact that they both knew his efforts to preserve her life would someday be futile. He remembered the day he had leaned over the side of her bed while she took his once strong hands into her wrinkled ones. *The good Lord has seen fit to give you a set of fine, skillful hands*, she had told him. *You give these hands back to the One who gave 'em to you in the first place, and you'll do all right.*

Yet what had the "good Lord" done for him but take away those fine, skillful hands? And without them, he could not perform surgery, which made his head knowledge worthless. Frustration welled inside him as the same senseless circumstances played out in his mind, and he angrily looked away from his hands.

His eyes came to rest on a bottle of barbiturates he had left on the nightstand. Clark Sawyer had prescribed them for occasional insomnia. Though he typically lay awake for hours at night, he had used them only twice, fully aware of the dependency he could form if he began taking them regularly.

Yet now his hand slid toward the nightstand. He wrestled with the bottle until he was able to grasp it. It was too early in the evening to go to bed, but if he could just sleep, even for a little while, he would be free for a time of the increasingly miserable state of mind he could not escape.

Idly, he stared at the dosage instructions on the label. With painstaking effort, he pushed the cap off and tipped the container to one side, but in his clumsy endeavor, the capsules spilled and scattered across the top of the comforter.

As he attempted to gather the medication into his hand, a strange sensation came over him. Instead of the dismal melancholy, there came a feeling of numbness, indifference, and a sudden weariness—weariness from months of inactivity and tedium, of idleness and despondency. He hated that he had no idea where his life was going, only despair for what had gone before. He had lived life, not merely survived it.

He continued to look at the medication in his hand. *How simple it would be. How many would it take? Eight? Ten? Did it really matter any longer if he lived or died? Why hadn't he died in that accident? He should have.*

He imagined carefully counting out the capsules and lifting each one toward his mouth. *No, what did it really matter.*

A sudden jarring sound broke the intense silence. His hand jerked and the capsules scattered across the comforter again. He pulled himself up and sat on the edge of the bed, cradling his head in his shaking hands. He tried to steady himself as the horrifying reality of what he had almost done became apparent. *How desperate had his emotional state actually become? What was he thinking?*

Suddenly, he realized the ringing of the phone had startled him. With an unsteady hand, he reached for the receiver. "Joe, it's Paul. I was about to hang up. Did I wake you?"

Never had Paul's friendly voice sounded so good. "No, I . . . I wasn't sleeping."

"You all right? You sound a little shaky." "Yeah, I'm . . . I'm all right."

"Well, the reason I called is I'd like you to come by my office tomorrow after your therapy session. I want to discuss something with you. Say, around two?"

Joe took a deep, shuddering breath. "Two will be fine. I'll see you then."

* * *

Joe Travis walked down the corridor toward Paul Martin's office after another arduous session in the physical therapy department. As he drew closer to his own office, he came to a stop in front of the door and looked up at the bronze nameplate. "Joseph I. Travis, M.D."

A gnawing fear gripped him while the same anxious questions burned like fire in his mind. He looked away and quickened his pace down the corridor toward Paul's office.

He knew Paul had hired another physician to cover his medical practice, causing his contact with his work to all but cease. Paul's decision had been unavoidable, but he hated the idea of a stranger managing the practice that had taken him so long to build.

He knocked on the partially opened door and then stepped inside. Paul rose from behind his desk, his usual amiability as infectious as his smile. "Joe, it's good to see you. Sit down."

"Good to see you, too, Paul. Right now, it's good to see anybody." He sat down on the couch as the older man came around to the front of his desk.

"I can only imagine how bored you must be at home by now." Joe shook his head. "I'm not sure you can," he added in a stiff voice, shuddering inwardly as he thought about how close he had come to ending his own life the night before.

"How's the therapy coming?" Paul asked, gesturing toward Joe's hands that rested limply in his lap.

"All right, I suppose. The numbness doesn't seem to be as acute. Either that or I'm just getting used to it. What did you want to see me about?"

"Two things," Paul said in a jaunty voice. "One, I think it's about time you met your temporary replacement, and two, I wanted you to know I took the liberty of suggesting your name for a teaching position at the university." Paul was pleased to see a glimmer of interest in the younger man's blue eyes. "You know, your ability isn't just in your hands but in your head as well."

"Teaching," Joe said thoughtfully. "I never even considered that."

"Well, I did, and when I mentioned your name to Harve Collier, he jumped at the idea. It's not a stressful position, not like surgery of course, but it requires someone with your background for teaching residents. I'll even loan you my secretary to type up your notes. Do you think you're up to it?"

"Well, I still have days I experience a lot of weakness," he admitted, "but doing nothing is driving me insane. And if you're going to be so generous as to loan me your own secretary, I don't see how I can refuse."

"Fine, fine," Paul said. "I'll leave it up to you to contact Harve." "I can do that. As for meeting my replacement . . . " Joe shook his head with trepidation.

"Joe, your position is not up for the taking by any means.

Remember, she's only temporary." "*She?*"

Paul grinned as he slipped on his glasses and reached for a folder on his desk. "Dr. Victoria Keene did her residency in trauma surgery at Boston General, then joined a specialized group practice for five years in the Dallas area. Presently, she's in line for the directorship of the Baylor Traumatology Team but has agreed to come here because of the experience she feels she could gain, *and* thanks largely to the precedence of *your* reputation," he added, closing the folder. Joe's mouth tightened in a wry expression of homage from his superior. "And we were very lucky to get her for the time being." Removing his glasses, he eyed Joe warily. "*The time being only,*" he reassured him.

"I don't know, Paul. I'm not sure I'm ready for *that*—"

A soft knock on the opened door turned both men's heads aside as a slender, dark-haired woman stepped inside. "I hope I'm not interrupting anything, Dr. Martin. You said around two thirty."

"Yes, so I did, and no, you aren't interrupting a thing." Paul took her by the arm and steered her toward Joe, who rose to the occasion. "Dr. Victoria Keene, I'd like you to meet Dr. Joe Travis."

She extended her hand, too late before she recalled Paul's word of warning regarding Joe's hands. With apology, she withdrew. "Dr. Travis, forgive me. Dr. Martin told me about your accident. I'm so sorry." Her voice sounded like a whispering breeze through a forest of pine trees.

He felt bad that she had embarrassed herself. "No need for that.

Progress is slow, but I'm hoping for the best."

"I wish you that too," she returned graciously. Paul invited them all to be seated once more. "I didn't realize how large your practice was until I started going through some of your patient files."

Joe smiled with a small measure of pride. "I understand you were part of a prestigious practice yourself in Dallas, and that you're about to become the director."

"Well, I'm not the director yet. Just hoping. And as far as the prestige goes, it was more like plain, hard work." A set of dazzling white teeth complimented her beautiful smile.

Paul was delighted as the conversation progressed easily. At length, they stood up to leave. "Well, I'm glad you two had the chance to get acquainted," he told them. "Joe, I assume you'll be in touch with Harve?"

"Yes, this week." He turned his attention once more to Dr. Keene. "If there's anything I can help you with, please don't hesitate to call me. I have a few chronic patients you might appreciate some advance warning about." For the first time in months, the dimples in his cheeks deepened with an indisputable smile.

"I'm afraid I've already met some of them," she returned with a grin. "In fact, I was wondering when you might have some time to go over a few files I pulled earlier today."

"Right now, time is all I have."

"But we're going to change that," Paul added, opening the door for them.

As the two surgeons walked toward the elevator, Joe turned around in time to see a smiling Paul Martin close his office door.

* * *

Inside Joe's office, Victoria Keene went straight to the desk and drew a pile of charts toward her. While she sifted through the stack, Joe innocuously inspected his office. Amazingly enough, nothing was out of previous order. He was sure his secretary, Kate, had been responsible for that.

"These are the ones I was hoping you could give me some follow-up on," Dr. Keene said, bringing them with her to where Joe stood. "Kate has been quite helpful. She's very knowledgeable about the workings of your office."

"Kate's been with me since I began my practice. She'll be invaluable to you, especially since she knows the patient histories better than I do sometimes."

They sat down on the couch, going over each file in question until she felt more at ease. Joe was pleased to observe how she made painstaking notations on each patient they discussed. At length, she closed the last chart and leaned comfortably against the back of the couch. "I can't thank you enough for your help, Dr. Travis. I hope you don't consider this to be the only time I'm going to come calling on you."

"Not at all. And please, call me Joe."

She smiled a rapturous smile. "And I'm Vicky. Does your wife feel you're getting under her feet too much during your recuperation?"

The expression on Joe's face waned slightly. "I'm . . . not married."

"Oh, I just took it for granted—"

"My wife died from complications following a car accident a little less than a year ago."

"I'm so sorry," she said, her voice full with compassion. "I didn't realize how difficult things have been for you."

"Are you married?"

"No, I guess you could say I married my career." She looked at him with a pensive expression. "I never wanted to do anything but surgery as long as I can remember. Maybe I've missed out on something. I just never thought combining a home and a career would be a very easy task." She grinned. "I suppose men don't have that problem."

"Don't be so sure," Joe said with retrospection.

CHAPTER 37

For the first time since he had begun private practice, Stephen Lewis was free, at least for a few consecutive days. With the acquisition of his newly acquired partner, he had been able to turn the practice over to him so that he might enjoy a much-needed vacation. Now, two days before Christmas, he and Callie had flown to Denver where they would be spending the holidays with Stephen's family.

Stephen, his father, and several other male relatives were deep into a sporting event in the den, while Callie, Stephen's mother, and two of his aunts finished putting the holiday dinner on the table.

"Callie, I don't know what magic you've worked on that boy, but this is the first time in three years he's been able to come home for Christmas. And the first time in his *life* he's brought a girl home with him!" Stephen's mother was a plump and pleasant mixture of joviality and candor.

"That's very nice of you say, Mrs. Lewis, but I literally owe Stephen my life you know," Callie insisted as she helped set the table. The woman laughed good-naturedly. "It's Maudie. And I don't think that's quite the way Stephen sees it," she said, handing Callie the rest of the good silver. "I've never seen him so happy or relaxed."

"Well, taking on a partner was a great relief to him."

Maudie grinned again. "Oh, I'm sure it was, but if you ask me, I believe he's thinking about *another* kind of partner."

Callie only smiled as she finished setting the table. She loved Stephen's unpretentious family, and they had welcomed her as though they had known her all her life. With Stephen, there were no tragic reminders, no haunting memories of misfortune, no years of longing laid to waste.

Maybe marrying Stephen was the way to put Joe out of her mind forever.

* * *

Joe sat behind the desk in his instructor's office, preparing for his first week of classes.

With trepidation, he reached for a pen inside the desk drawer. He managed to grasp it and, with concentrated effort, focused every ounce of thought on keeping it fixed in his hand as he touched it to the paper.

Seconds later, it slipped from his unsteady grip and rolled across the desktop. Angered, he drew a deep breath before attempting to try once more. But again, the numbness and trembling in his hand prevented him from accomplishing the simple task. In frustration, he thrust the pen and paper aside just as the door opened.

"Well," Paul Martin said, nodding in approval as he glanced about Joe's spacious office, "these accommodations don't seem so bad for a recently instated university professor." His gracious smile began to wane when he suddenly noticed several writing implements scattered across the floor. The aggravated expression on Joe's face explained the rest. Without elaborating, he bent over and picked up the pens, dropping them in the holder on top of the desk "I just stopped by to tell you the ground breaking ceremony for the new wing has been changed to Thursday at noon."

Joe had not relished the idea of attending the ceremony ever since the announcement of the new multimillion dollar wing some weeks earlier. He leaned back in his chair. "That would be . . . *the Jordan Wing?*" he asked with obvious cynicism.

"You know how long we've needed that new surgical wing. No matter *who* the benefactor is, it's the patients that need the consideration," Paul said with some terseness. "Wouldn't you agree that's what's important?"

Joe's dispassionate expression relaxed a little. "Yes, of course. Just don't expect me to be there."

"It's going to be an extensive media-related event; a lot of publicity for the hospital, and you're still a department head, Joe. No matter what your personal feelings are, I expect you to be there, if for no other reason but protocol."

"My presence or absence isn't going to affect the new building one way or the other," he returned listlessly.

Paul's mouth tightened. "Can't you lay aside your anger, even for the sake of the hospital?"

"My 'anger' has nothing to do with the hospital! It's Ben Jordan I don't want any connection with. Not him, his money, his revered memory—"

"His daughter?"

Joe's volley came to a sudden halt. The older man had deliberately struck a vulnerable blow. Slowly, he rose from the chair and leaned over the desk, glaring angrily at his colleague. "Callie got caught in the middle, that's all. If anything, she's the *victim*."

Paul struggled to restrain his temper. "Let me tell you something, Joe. Your anger, including your self-imposed misery, is grounded in nothing more but an unwillingness to forgive. Your keeping Callie at a safe distance only keeps you separated from the problem you refuse to deal with." He walked to the door but turned sharply to look at Joe once more. "But you're right about one thing. Callie *is* the victim," he finished grimly, "a victim of your own choosing."

He yanked open the door and missed colliding into Victoria Keene by a matter of inches. "Dr. Martin, I'm sorry!" she apologized, grappling with an oversized manila envelope that had almost slipped out of her hands. "I was just on my way in to see Joe. How are you today?"

"Fine, until about five minutes ago." He cast an angry glance at Joe once more and then paused to collect his composure. "If you'll excuse me, Vicky, I . . . have other matters I need to attend to."

She stepped back to let him pass, realizing at once there had been a disagreement of some kind between the two doctors for Paul to exhibit such brusque mannerism. She knocked on the open door.

Joe looked up when Vicky approached his desk. One look at his face told her there had been considerably more than a difference of opinion between himself and Paul Martin. "I have the files on Mr. Abernathy you asked for. Kate knew exactly where they were." She laid the large envelope in front of him. "Joe, are you all right?"

"Yeah, I'm okay," he muttered.

She watched him fumble awkwardly with the clasp until he was able to pull some of the papers from the envelope. Then he began to grope inside once more in a miserable attempt to grasp the rest of the material. Without thinking, she reached over and tilted the envelope until all the contents lay in front of him. He stopped struggling when her long, slender fingers settled over his.

"I can only imagine how frustrating this must be for you."

He looked up at her with choleric eyes. "Not quite," he said in an ominous voice, still fuming at Paul Martin's blunt admonishment, but with her rueful expression, he realized how rude he had been in view of her understanding gesture. "I'm sorry, Vicky. My problems have nothing to do with you."

"I know," she said in a soft voice. "I didn't mean to appear condescending."

"I know you didn't. I just . . . I have a lot of things on my mind, that's all."

She turned to leave when something moved her to act with more daring than was typical for her. "Joe, how long since you've had a home-cooked meal?"

He looked at her again and shook his head. "I'm not sure I'd recognize one anymore."

"Well, I'm not so sure either, but I have made several in my time. Would you be willing to risk your stomach on one of mine? Say, seven o'clock at my place?"

He began to relax a little. "Seven o'clock. Shall I bring some bicarbonate just in case?"

"Oh, sure. We can save that for dessert."

* * *

Vicky's apartment was small but meticulously well organized. Joe leaned inside the kitchen doorway and watched her finish tossing a spinach salad. "You handle those tongs almost as well as you handle a scalpel."

She turned her head and smiled at him. "So you've been spying on me from the dome during surgery. That's not very ethical."

"I didn't want to make you nervous. I just wanted to see if you were as good as your reputation."

"And did I pass the test?" she asked as he followed her to the table.

"You're a natural."

"I take that as high praise, coming from you," she said as he pulled out her chair and seated her. "Now would you like to risk starting with some of this salad?"

He grinned. "Yes, please."

She filled a plate and passed it to him. Dinner and conversation flowed easily between them, most of the discussion centering on mutual patients from his practice. Vicky was charming, convivial, and as easy to talk with as she was good at listening. Joe appreciated that she drew no attention to his awkward eating style.

The phone rang, and Vicky rose to answer it. After a brief series of questions, she hung up. "There was a pile up on the expressway. Several people hurt pretty badly. They'll be bringing them into emergency in about fifteen minutes." She watched Joe unconsciously flex his hands. "Sounds like they could use both of us."

"Vicky"—he shook his head—"I don't see how I could—"

"I'd think your years of experience could come in quite handy. Even if you can't *do* everything, expert guidance can go a long way."

She walked to the front door and picked up her purse. With an air of confidence, she added, "Coming, Doctor?"

He rose to his feet and followed her toward the door. "Advice is cheap, you know."

* * *

Joe and Vicky rushed through the doors of the emergency entrance minutes before two wailing ambulances pulled into the ambulance bay. A team of technicians, nurses, interns, and residents were waiting to go to work on the incoming victims.

As the first of the stretchers began to arrive, Vicky followed it into one of the trauma rooms. Joe stood in the corridor while a bevy of medical personnel rushed about him. *What was he even thinking to have placed himself in the middle of such a crisis?* He was still disabled, still hindered by the limited use of his hands. It was absurd that he had let Vicky talk him into this.

The glass doors opened again and another stretcher, pulled by two paramedics, plunged through the ambulance entrance. One held an IV bag over the head of a blood-spattered patient who sat upright against the back of the raised gurney. A nurse directed them into another room. She glanced swiftly at Joe, waiting for him to follow. Unable to shake his feelings of apprehension, he followed the paramedics into the trauma room, knowing it was imperative he put his insecurities out of his mind. He reminded himself he was still a doctor, with or without the use of his hands. What had Paul said?

Your ability isn't just in your hands, but in your head as well.

Once inside the exam room, the paramedics gave a brief account of the injured man. Joe leaned over the stretcher. It was evident the man was in a great deal of discomfort. At once, he noted the bluish discoloration of the skin, a sure sign of a lack of oxygen. "Mr. Moore, I'm Dr. Travis. Can you breathe? Are you in pain?"

"Can't . . . breathe too good," he said with considerable exertion. "Chest hurts too . . . *bad.*" Awkwardly, Joe slipped the stethoscope into his ears and listened to the man's chest sounds. "Doc," he said, anxiety straining in his voice, "am I gonna die?"

"Not on *my* time," Joe returned with a grin, pulling the stethoscope away from his ears. After a visual examination of his head and neck, he watched carefully as the man's chest rose and fell with a measure of rapid, labored breathing. He put the palms of his hands on the man's chest, abdomen, and pelvic bones to make sure they were stable.

At length, he stepped away from the stretcher and turned to one of the nurses. "I need Dr. Simmons to place a chest tube as soon as his chest x-ray confirms the pneumothorax." The nurse left the room to find the senior resident. Joe turned back to the patient. "Jon, do you remember hitting the steering wheel or the dashboard of the car on impact?"

The man nodded. "Yeah . . . hard. Then I . . . I guess I passed out."

"Well, I can't be positive until we get some x-rays, but I believe you have a collapsed lung, but it's nothing we can't handle. You're going to be all right." He squeezed the man's arm and then turned to the nurse who had been assisting him. "We'll need a chest x-ray and an arterial blood gas, stat. Prep him for a chest tube. And call Admitting." He leaned over the patient and explained the procedure that the resident would have to accomplish for him.

* * *

While the x-ray was being done in the trauma room, Joe left to help Vicky. Her patient, a young woman in her early twenties, had been one of the last brought into the emergency room. She appeared distraught on the exam table. "She's seems disoriented," Vicky quietly explained to him when he entered the room. "Her speech is slurred and close to incomprehensible at times. She does respond to painful stimuli, though."

Joe watched as Vicky instructed the patient to follow simple commands and then noted the size and reactivity of both pupils. With effort, the young woman's eyes barely tracked the light that Vicky shown from side to side.

"She'll need a CT scan and a coagulation panel," Joe said. Then he leaned over the woman and carefully examined the deep lacerations on her forehead. He called her name several times, but her response was sluggish. He stood up beside the table. "I suspect a subdural hematoma," he said to Vicky.

"I agree."

He turned to the nurse in the room and verbally left a series of preoperative orders. The nurse quickly obeyed. Half an hour later, the young woman was taken into surgery.

* * *

It was well after midnight when the two doctors walked out of the emergency room together. Between them and the rest of the limited staff, they had successfully treated fourteen patients, from the critically injured to those they had simply treated and released.

Joe ran his hand through his hair as they collapsed into chairs in the doctors' lounge. "That was some stretch. You all right?"

Vicky rested her head against the back of the chair and kicked off her shoes. "Yeah, I'm all right. Sometimes, I wonder why I wanted to go into emergency medicine. Too stressful."

Joe glanced down at his hands. "I never wanted to be anything but a trauma surgeon."

Vicky recognized the dismay in his voice. She leaned forward and reached for his hands. "You'll be a surgeon again." Their eyes met briefly before she let go of them. "I bet they're killing you right now." "You're right, they are." He looked away from his hands back to her. "You did something tonight that I'm not sure you didn't do on purpose."

"You mean you *guessed* I was trying to poison you with dinner so I could take over your job?"

He laughed. "I mean, you insisted I come with you when any number of other doctors could have been called."

"Even though you're teaching, you're still on hospital staff, and you were with me at the time. It seemed like the logical thing to do." Though her voice was full of reasonableness, her eyes carried a hint of culpability. Then she grinned broadly. "All right, I'm guilty. It's just that I knew you could do it. *You* just needed to know it too."

The door to the lounge opened, and one of the emergency room nurses stuck her head inside. "Dr. Travis? Dr. Keene? Just thought you might like to know the young woman with the subdural hematoma just came out of surgery. Word is she's going to be fine."

The two doctors smiled and thanked her. Then she quietly closed the door again.

Joe rose from the chair and pulled Vicky to her feet. "You are a crafty little thing, Dr. Keene. I honestly didn't believe I could manage half of what I did tonight. Thanks to you, I felt really useful for the first time in months."

"I'm glad, Joe. I'm really glad."

With her smile came the sudden realization that she was standing only inches away from him. Her wide, dark eyes penetrated his own. She was so very beautiful. With Vicky, it would be easier to forget, easier to stop dwelling on the emptiness that was still deep inside him. Nevertheless, he would not take advantage of one woman to forget the mistakes he had made with another. He let go of her hands. "We're both exhausted. Let's call it a night."

But before he turned away, he could not help but notice the disappointment in her face.

* * *

Callie had enjoyed spending the holidays with Stephen and his family, but on their return to Charleston, family pictures of her own tucked inside the card from Maggie had sadly reminded her of past holidays in Boston with her father and his annual Christmas parties. She remembered the brisk, cold days, the sparkling white snow, the skaters on the ice covered ponds. Charleston, she thought, was a tropical paradise compared to Boston winters.

The sun was a red ball of flame sinking behind the horizon as Stephen and Callie walked down the beach together. He watched as the cool wind whipped her curly hair in a thousand directions. He suspected her thoughts were bound in the same manner. Wearing only a light jacket, she stopped long enough to pick up another shell. She brushed the sand away and studied it closely, then slipped it into her already bulging pocket.

Stephen pulled his jacket around himself a little tighter as he came up beside her. "You can't keep everything inside, you know."

His smile seemed never ending when he looked at her, his eyes filled with the love he longed to give her.

"I can't seem to let go of any," she told him, patting the stuffed pocket as they began walking again.

"I wasn't really talking about the shells. I was talking about what's inside *you*."

She stopped again, brushing aside wind-swept hair from her face. "I haven't been very fair to you, and I know it."

"You've done nothing of the kind," he said, reaching for her hands. "Besides, let me decide what's fair."

She pulled her hands free with an animosity he could not understand. "Nothing is fair, Stephen," she returned hastily. "After all you've done for me, is it fair that I've never told you I love you?"

Stephen's eyes searched hers. "Are you telling me now?"

As Callie gazed at his beseeching expression, the fusion of anger and disillusion that had crept over her suddenly became overwhelming. His infinite patience in her behalf had not enabled her to surrender a miserable sense of guilt where he was concerned, and she could stand it no longer.

She turned and began to run down the beach. For the first time in all the years she had known Joe Travis, she desperately wished she could escape the love for him that held her captive. It had become nothing more than a curse—a curse that had scarred not only her life but now the life of someone she deeply cared for.

Suddenly, she felt Stephen's hand grasp her arm as he pulled her roughly to a stop. Breathless from the chase, he panted, "Callie, it's time this charade came to an end." She strove to free herself, but he refused to let go. "I want to know if this has anything to do with your heart surgery."

She stopped struggling as her eyes rose to meet his. "How did you know?"

"Because the night I operated on you, I suspected your father had a secret he couldn't trust to tell anybody. I've thought for a long time it's that secret you've been struggling with." Tentatively, he let go of her arm, not sure if letting go of her would necessitate another chase, but she said nothing, only walked in silence beside him until they reached the beach house.

Once inside, Callie sat down on the couch, her demeanor submissive as she watched Stephen close the windows against the cooler night air before sitting down beside her.

"What do you know about that night?" she asked cautiously. "When I talked to your father the night of your surgery, he seemed . . . preoccupied, as if something else was already troubling him. Then when I explained that you were in congestive heart failure, and your only option was a heart transplant, he asked me not to do anything until he called me back.

"Then a short time later, he called to tell me he was sure he could make arrangements for a direct donation, something highly unusual. He told me he knew of a donor in his hospital that he believed would be a perfect match for you, in age, body size, weight, blood type. He instructed me not to ask any questions beyond the medical, and that he would make the arrangements for the transfer himself.

"I knew that he had already called the transplant coordinator and asked her to look at the Registry. I'm sure he wanted to know if there wasn't a listed type in Charleston that was on high alert. He told the Registry that he had a donor heart that he wanted used quickly for a good cause, and he even volunteered to escort the heart himself to the medical center here in Charleston." Stephen looked at her with an intensity she had not seen before now. "Somehow, I knew your father was making a desperate decision for a desperate situation, so I honored his wishes and kept quiet as he had asked me to do."

Callie understood Stephen's position, knowing her life had been at risk that night, but Stephen knew nothing of the ensuing complications that her father's decision had brought since.

She drew a deep breath. "After my father arrived from Boston that night," she began, "he told me he had 'taken care of everything.' It wasn't until after he died that I discovered what he meant." When she looked at him, her eyes were filling with tears. "My father never told me, but my best friend had been involved in an auto accident several weeks before. Beth was brain-dead; the heart was hers."

"You mean the donor . . . was your *friend*?" She could only nod.

"But, Callie, even a dear friend in a condition such as she was in—"

"You don't understand," Callie said, shaking her head. "The circumstances went deeper than that." She struggled to retain her composure. "You see, Beth had married a man by the name of Joe Travis only a few months before. Joe had been a surgical resident under my father and had become very close to our family. As far as my father was concerned, Joe was the son he never had. And Joe and I . . . well, we were always . . . good friends . . . " She hesitated, but not before she could halt the poignant tone in her voice.

But Stephen knew. "It was more than friendship for you, wasn't it?"

She nodded, unable to look at him. "After my father died and I went back to Boston, I saw for myself that Joe had taken Beth's death very hard. Before, he had been the most compassionate man I ever knew, but his entire personality had changed. He wouldn't permit anyone to get close to him, or let himself do the same."

She paused, remembering. "But finally one night, he opened up, and we talked, just like we used to do before he knew Beth. And even though I knew how desperately lonely he was, I was shocked when only a couple of months later . . . he . . . he asked me to marry him." A look of distressing submission came over Stephen's face, and Callie knew there was no need to put in plain words how she had felt toward Joe.

"All our plans were made, the date was set for our wedding, and then *by accident*, I discovered that my father had arranged for Beth's heart to be my transplant. I was terrified to tell Joe what I knew. I knew how much he had loved Beth and the agony he'd gone through after she died. I was afraid if he knew the truth, he might even grow to . . . to hate me for being the one who had received her heart.

"But I couldn't hide the secret. As afraid as I was, I knew he had a right to know. So when I told him . . . " Her voice began to tremble as it became more difficult to continue. "He became very angry. So angry that . . . he was involved in a terrible accident that very night.

He was in a coma. I sat by his bed for days, terrified he was going to die. Then when he finally regained consciousness, I was told he didn't want to see me anymore. And I couldn't blame him.

"After that, I knew I couldn't stay in Boston any longer. It hurt too much to be where he was. So when you asked me to come down here and work with you, I suppose I saw it as an opportunity to escape."

An awkward silence fell between them. Stephen rose to his feet and stood in front of the window, struggling to absorb all that Callie had divulged to him. Finally, he drew a deep breath. "So you used me as your . . . sanctuary."

Stunned, she quickly got up and stood behind him. "No, Stephen, it wasn't like that at all! I wasn't trying to use you! When I agreed to come here, I didn't know how you felt. All I knew was that it was over between Joe and me, and I had nowhere else to go. You have to believe that."

When at last he turned and looked at her, she saw in his face a miserable combination of resentment and resignation. "But in spite of everything, you're still in love with him . . . aren't you?"

Desperately, Callie wanted to refute his all too candid insight. "How I feel about Joe doesn't matter any longer. As lonely as he was, he never really loved *me*. It was Beth he loved . . . *always Beth*." The words dwindled to a guilt-ridden and disenchanted whisper as she glanced away. "Even though she was gone, she was as real a presence between us as if she had never died." She looked up at Stephen once more. "But hurting you was not something I *ever* intended to do."

If nothing else, the passion of truth in her eyes was convincing enough. Stephen put his hands around her shoulders. "I'm ready to forget everything you've told me, Callie. As far as I'm concerned, none of this ever happened. It's over and done with, and the memory of the whole affair doesn't have to concern us because all I care about is *you*! *I love you!* I've loved you enough to wait for you. And no matter how long it takes, I'll keep on waiting until you see for yourself how pointless it is to long for a man who doesn't want you!" His eyes searched hers. "Stay with me, Callie. Stay with me and marry me, and let me love you like he *never* could."

She shook her head slowly. "You're willing to forget, *but I can't!*" Tears streamed down her cheeks. "You deserve someone who can give you a whole heart not just the part that hurts."

He knew then she had made her decision. Just as she had no power to crush the pervasive spirit of the woman who had gone before her, neither had he the influence to affect the love she felt for the man who had unwittingly held her in his power for so long.

He drew the weeping young woman toward him, enfolding her in his arms while he struggled to hold back his own tears. "Sometimes, when you're by yourself and you get lonely for Joe," he whispered, laying her head against his shoulder, *"think about me."*

As he held her in his arms, he could almost feel the beating of her heart, the heart that would always belong to someone else.

CHAPTER 38

Still in her green scrubs, Dr. Victoria Keene hurried to answer the waiting phone call at the desk outside the OR suites. "Yes, I just finished." She spoke softly into the telephone to Joe Travis. "I will, as soon as I change and get upstairs." She handed the phone back to the nurse and gave the woman a wry expression. "I've been here six months, and he thinks I've turned into three people."

The nurse laughed. "No one has envied you taking over Dr. Travis's practice."

"I can understand that now."

The nurse smiled. "We've often wondered if Dr. Travis really had a twin." Then, with a twinkle in her eyes, she added, "That would have made many a nurse up here very happy."

Vicky grinned as she prepared to leave post-op orders. *And I can understand that too,* she mused.

Forty-five minutes later, she walked into Joe's former office and found the man himself working at the desk. "I'm sorry, Joe. It took me longer than I thought to finish up."

Joe waved his hand without looking up. "Been there, done that," he said with a grin as he continued with his work. Then, setting aside his paper, he looked up at her. "But I did want to discuss something with you."

"Sure," she said, seating herself on the couch. "What is it?"

Joe came around to the front of the desk. "While it's true I can't go back into surgery right now, Paul has suggested that we split the work between the two of us until sometime in the spring or early summer. He feels my *easing* back in would be better than *jumping* back in with both feet. My question is, what are your obligations to your former job right now?"

"I'm on professional leave until you or Paul give me the word. I've been hopeful that my work here will have an impact on the directorship I'm hoping for."

"Well, neither Paul nor I want to jeopardize that position. I can understand how important it is to you, but the fact is, by the end of summer, my teaching position will be over unless I choose to continue in the fall. And in all honesty, I'm hoping," he added solemnly, "that by then I'll be back in the OR again."

"I know how much you want to return to surgery."

"I just wanted to make sure you'd be all right with this for a while until I can take over again. You've done a spectacular job. The patients love you."

"Well, as a matter of fact, it would almost be a relief," she said with a sigh. Joe could not help but admire the beautiful, slender legs that gracefully extended beyond the green scrub dress.

"A relief?" he repeated, remembering himself.

"Joe, I don't see how you kept up with it all! You could have enough work for *three* surgeons. Yes, please, help me!"

"All right," he said with a grin, "we can work out all the particulars later. Right now, how about letting me buy you a late breakfast?"

She held out her arm for him to take. "You're on. But I warn you, I'm starving."

*　*　*

An hour later, Joe returned to his office to find Paul Martin talking to the secretary. "Morning, Paul. Were you looking for me?" "Well, I was." The older man followed Joe into his private office.

"Is eating out all you have time for these days?" he asked with a wink. "Well, you can't expect too much from a starving doctor, can you?"

"I suppose not. Where's Vicky?"

"She's checking on some x-rays. She'll be back in a minute. What can I do for you?" He sat down behind the desk as Paul extended a white linen envelope to him. "What's this?"

"Open it."

Joe pulled the tab up and, after some awkward effort, removed an engraved invitation. He mumbled aloud as he half read the beautifully lettered inscription. "Dr. Joseph Travis . . . cordially invited to a dinner party . . . held at the royal home of the chief of staff."

"It doesn't say *royal home*," Paul declared disdainfully.

Joe grinned, waving the engraved invitation in front of him. "Okay, but why all the pageantry? I've been to lots of dinner parties at your house."

"Well, this one is *formal*, tux and tie *not optional*. But don't worry. I'll see to it you have a good time. It will all be catered with only the finest food."

"Oh, I wouldn't miss it."

The door opened with a wide swing, and Vicky stepped inside, unaware that Joe was not alone. "Oh, Joe . . . Dr. Martin . . . I'm sorry, I didn't mean to interrupt anything."

"You're not interrupting," Joe said, rising from his chair. "Paul was just extolling the grand banquet he's *catering* next week."

Paul cast a severe glance in Joe's direction. "*I'm* not catering it; I'm *having* it catered."

Vicky smiled broadly. "Either way, it sounds wonderful. What's the occasion?"

"Some of the more *distinguished* guests," Paul explained, with a bogus glance toward Joe, "will be a few of our physicians who will be retiring soon. As chief of staff, I felt something more than a gold scalpel was in order. You're more than welcome to come, Vicky, even if you aren't highly acquainted with these gentlemen." He looked at his watch. "I have a meeting. I'll see you both later." He ushered himself toward the door when he turned and looked at Joe once more. "And by the way, I expect you not to ignore my *RSVP*." He opened the door and was gone.

Joe dropped the invitation on the desk. With Paul's subtle intimation regarding Vicky's presence at the affair, the casual moment suddenly became awkward.

"Well," Vicky returned quietly, "it sounds like a very nice evening. When is it?"

Joe glanced at the invitation. "Next Thursday night. Would you . . . like to go?"

She smiled. "I'd like that. Thank you."

Joe returned her smile. "Then it's a date," he said but wondered at his unsettled feelings.

* * *

The two beveled glass doors leading into Paul Martin's den were opened wide, allowing the host to glance occasionally past Joe's shoulder at his dinner guests who were entertaining themselves in the main room. Small groups garnered in various places throughout while music from a string quartet flowed smoothly from one classical movement to another.

Inside the den, Paul and Joe stood beside a massive collection of books and journals housed in a floor to ceiling bookcase. Most of their private conversation had centered on patients Joe and Vicky were treating simultaneously. "That was a fine workup you did on Dan Sutherland," Paul remarked with regard to one of their mutual patients. "I know it was a difficult analysis to make. I was impressed with your diagnosis."

A smile crossed Joe's handsome face. "Thank you for the accolade, but Vicky did most of the leg work. She's about as fine a diagnostician as she is a surgeon." He glanced through the open doors where he could see Vicky on the other side of the room conversing with a group of women. Again, it struck him how elegantly her form-fitting black evening gown clung to her slender frame. "It would be a real plus for the hospital if we could convince her to stay on after I'm back on staff full time." Only now did he return his attention to Paul. "Well, it so happens I've been giving that notion a lot of thought," Paul said. "And since you're head of the trauma department, I think you should be the one to bring it up to her. Ask Vicky how she'd feel about accepting a full-time position."

Vicky Keene unconsciously heard her name mentioned and turned her attention toward the muffled conversation inside Paul's den. She politely excused herself to join the two men when she stepped aside to allow another guest to pass. In doing so, she accidentally brushed too close to a large potted dieffenbachia beside the doors. One of the leaves broke off and fell to the floor. Veiled behind the plant, she stooped to pick it up when she caught the remainder of the conversation within.

"A beautiful, remarkable woman. She's helped me more than she'll ever realize. I really don't want to lose her." Vicky broke into a smile when she overheard Joe's complimentary remarks.

"Then why don't you ask her tonight?"

Ask me what? Vicky literally held her breath. *Ask me to . . . why, he's never even kissed me . . .*

"I'm . . .not sure a party is quite the right place."

"Well, I hope you ask her soon. If it was me, I wouldn't wait too long." To Vicky, Paul's statement seemed to carry a slight inflection of urgency.

She rose to her feet. She had not fooled herself into thinking she had not been attracted to the handsome surgeon for some time now, but there had been no noticeable reciprocation from him. He was a very private man and kept much of his personal feelings to himself. Yet tonight he had revealed his most intimate thoughts to his friend, and now she had inadvertently become privy to them.

Through the leaves of the dieffenbachia, she could see Joe shifting his position and stepped back for fear he would see her.

"I'll make my proposal soon, when the right time presents itself," he told Paul.

The conversation ended abruptly when two of the honored guests walked past Vicky, joining Paul and Joe inside the den, but it was with joyous expectation that she turned away and rejoined her original group.

* * *

It was almost midnight when Joe stopped the car in front of Vicky's apartment. He turned to look at her, the dimples in his cheeks deepening with an ever-captivating smile. "Did you have a good time? Or was it just one more dull dinner party?"

"I thoroughly enjoyed myself, but I would have to attribute that to my charming date."

Joe smiled again. "I'm flattered." He got out of the car and managed to open the door for her, longing for the day when he could use his hands once more without ungainly, concentrated effort. He took her open hand and helped her out.

She rose effortlessly in front of him, her stylish poise impeccable, her demeanor elegant beyond description. The full moon cast a faint light across her face, and the delicate aroma of her expensive perfume filled the small space between them. For Joe, it seemed impossible to imagine her in bloody scrubs beside an operating table.

They looked at each other without saying a word. And then with an uncommon boldness, Vicky reached up and touched his face. He offered no resistance when she rose slightly and bent her head toward his. The kiss lasted but a moment, yet the sentiment filled her with a passion she could not have expressed in words.

Joe felt her soft hands glide gently away from his face, and he opened his eyes into hers. An unashamed smile greeted him as her hands tightened around his own. "I really had a lovely time," she whispered. "Thank you for asking me."

"Thank you for going." He returned her smile, though still taken aback by the unexpected kiss.

"Would you like to come in?"

"I . . . wish I could. But you've got a full day tomorrow, and it wouldn't do to keep you out too late." He slowly released her hands, wondering at his own hesitancy in refusing her invitation. "I'll see you tomorrow."

She complied with a disheartened smile. "Tomorrow."

He stood in the misty moonlight, captivated as he watched her walk slowly up the steps in her black satin heels and disappeared behind the front door to her apartment.

* * *

Dazzling streaks of yellow and crimson gradually began to dispel the darkness in the eastern sky, but the first light of day went unnoticed for Joe Travis.

He sat behind his desk, his feet propped up on the window ledge inside his instructor's office. He had been unable to sleep after arriving home from the party and had finally come in before dawn to do some work, but he had not accomplished a single task.

Vicky's impromptu kiss disturbed him. From their first meeting, he knew he had been physically attracted to her. There was no denying what a beautiful, desirable woman she was, but maybe it had not ended there for Vicky. Now he wondered if he had unconsciously allowed something to develop that didn't actually exist, just to quell the loneliness he had been so desperate to escape.

Yet foolishly, he knew he was alone by choice. He had hoped that returning to work would be enough to replace the miserable isolation he had endured since his accident, but longer and longer days at the hospital were failing to compensate for what was really missing.

For while, he yearned to reclaim the conventional life he had once led, it was becoming evident that nothing would ever be the same for him again. He felt as though he had struggled through two separate lifetimes. Events that were part of his past were unquestionably affecting what was happening to him in the present no matter how adept he had become at pushing the past aside. Vicky's kiss had reawakened feelings inside him that had been easier to disregard than to remember.

Because deep in his heart lingered the memory of another— someone who, at the crisis point of his life, had restored his faith and strength of mind; someone who had loved him with a genuine and unconditional love, giving all that she had and asking nothing in return; someone who had given to him not what he thought he deserved, but what he needed.

Callie Jordan was a chapter in his life he still could not close. For Callie had seen him through eyes that only perceived the best in him, through eyes that saw him as he wished he really were.

With a deep sigh, he turned back to his desk and laid his head down on his folded arms, weary of soul as well as body. Someday, in one way or another, he would have to come to terms with the mistakes he had made. Ignoring them would never resolve them, anymore than taking advantage of a beautiful, receptive woman would resolve a past from which he could not hide forever.

* * *

Joe Travis was afraid.

He stood beside the window of his hospital room, glancing anxiously at his bandaged hands. He would be going home today—home toan empty house that offered no companion, no support, no provision forhis disability. The prospect terrified him, and he was ashamed.

His thoughts became more anxious. How could he leave now? How could he possibly manage on his own? How could he do anything . . .

Someone was at the door, and he half turned, expecting to see his nurse behind a wheelchair, ready to escort him downstairs.

"Joe?" He turned and with joy, realizing Callie was standing inside the doorway. Callie had come to take him home.

"Cal . . . " He walked toward her and took her into his arms, holding her closer than he thought he had ever held her before. With his bandaged hands, he lifted her face toward his, reveling in the sweet forgiving smile that accompanied the gentle demeanor he had come to love so much. He put his hand against her cheek, forgetting the frightening absence of sensitivity. Yet her smile was more reassuring than any words she might have spoken.

Never again would he take for granted her gift of love, and never again would he allow another second of lonely time to pass between them.

* * *

Joe awoke with a start, eager to discover reality instead of a dream. He opened his eyes to the full light of the morning sun and then lifted his head. Only then did he notice the loose-fitting scrub dress in front of his desk.

"Good morning, Doctor. Isn't it customary to go *home* to sleep?" Vicky Keene was attractive even in the drab green of her surgical attire. Her smile seemed to compete with the sunlight streaming through the window behind him. "I *know* you went home last night because you're not in your tux."

A weary smile came to Joe's face. "How long have *you* been here?"

"Not long. I saw the light under the door and knocked, but when you didn't answer, I got a little worried and came in. You all right?"

"Yeah, I'm okay. I couldn't sleep, so I figured I could stay awake here as well as at home."

"Well, apparently not," she returned, then smiled again. "You looked just like a little boy asleep at his school desk a minute ago." Joe made a wry face as she leaned across the desk and brushed aside strands of loose hair that fell across his forehead. "I wanted to tell you again how much I enjoyed last night," she added softly.

"I enjoyed it too." He was sincere in his statement but didn't want to deceive her, to lead her into assuming something he was not ready to commit to. He rose to his feet and walked to the other side of the desk, wondering if he was wrong in supposing that her kiss meant more than a simple "thank you for a pleasant evening." He took her hands in his. He had to know, but words eluded him.

Her face was full of wonder as she gazed intently into his eyes. "Is something wrong, Joe?"

Suddenly, he couldn't bring himself to say anything that might expunge the beautiful expression. Maybe he was wrong in his presumptuous thinking. "No . . . nothing that a good breakfast wouldn't cure. Will you join me?"

"I thought you'd never ask."

CHAPTER 39

One week later, Joe Travis fairly ran down the corridor, turning inquisitive heads as he proceeded into Paul Martin's office.

Paul looked up from behind his desk. "Well . . . won't you come in?"

"I *am* in."

"So I see." He gestured toward the matching chairs in front of the desk. "Sit down."

Joe shook his head. "I'm too excited to sit down. Look." He extended both hands in front of Paul, turning them first one way and then another for his superior's inspection. "Decreased numbness and trembling. Improved muscle tone and dexterity. Sawyer tells me it may only be a matter of time now."

Paul rose from his comfortable black leather chair and slipped his glasses on. He reached across the desk and examined Joe's hands for himself. A broad smile began to cover his face. "Joe, that's great news. Great news." The two men sat down. "Does Clark have any idea how long before you might actually perform surgery again?"

Joe's exuberance waned a bit. "It could be as much as six months to a year yet. No guarantees," he said with some disenchantment. "But I *know* with continued therapy and exercises, I'll be back in the OR."

"I know it too, Joe."

Both men turned when they heard a slight knock at the door. Vicky Keene entered unobtrusively at Paul's invitation. "Well, you two certainly look pleased about something."

"Fact is, we were just celebrating," Paul said.

The smile on her face increased. "Celebrating? Celebrating what?"

"A little good news from my orthopedic surgeon," Joe told her. "A *little*?" Paul interjected. "I'd say a *lot*. Clark Sawyer is noting a marked improvement in Joe's hands. He's ready to pick up a scalpel tomorrow," he finished with a grin.

Almost immediately, Vicky became aware of an anxious feeling in the pit of her stomach, and felt the smile on her face beginning to fade. She quickly tidied it before it became obvious. "Joe, that's wonderful," she said with a forced sense of enthusiasm. "I'm so happy for you. It's been a long time coming."

"Too long," Joe finished.

He rose from the chair as Paul's buzzer sounded. He reached for the phone. "Yes, they're both here with me. I'll tell them." He replaced the phone. "Gunshot victim just came into the ER. Unconscious. Lost a lot of blood."

"Let's go," Vicky said, opening the door as she and Joe hurried out of the office together.

* * *

Vicky Keene stripped away the surgical mask from her face and glanced upward toward the observation dome. She knew Joe had been observing the emergency operation, and she gave him a thumbs-up. The gunshot victim they had seen in the trauma room several hours earlier had lost more blood than either of them believed possible for survival. However, the patient had come through better than they had expected. Now Joe returned her high sign with an infectious smile she could almost feel.

As she headed for the changing room, relieved that the stressful operation had been a success, her thoughts returned once again to the gathering she and Joe had attended at Paul Martin's house. For days afterward, she had reprimanded herself for her audacity in initiating the unplanned kiss she had given Joe. Later, she had comforted herself with the delicious secret that Joe was undoubtedly falling in love with her just as she was with him, and by his own words! *Oh, if only he would say them to her!*

But up until now, he had made no mention of the beautiful moment that had passed between them in the moonlight outside her apartment. Since that time, they had shared meals, patients, meetings, engaged in countless conversations, and made numerous diagnoses together. But nothing again had transpired like the events from that night.

She pulled off her surgical cap and fumbled with the gown ties until she had freed herself of the cumbersome attire. Tossing both into a laundry container, she continued to think about her ambiguous, yet alluring relationship with Joe Travis.

Though he did not display the affection she longed for, she still felt there was something undeniable in his attitude toward her. When they were alone together, she sensed something strangely hinted at, something in the way of an allusion she could not define. Consequently, she continued to revel in Joe's cherished remark, *"I don't want to lose her."*

There had been more to the conversation between Joe and Paul she could not explain. What had been so vital that Paul had urged Joe to ask her about? Joe had yet to say anything that even remotely suggested something as imperative as Paul had seemed to imply.

She quickly finished changing into her street clothes and made a beeline for the stairs. She was waylaid twice on the patient floor before pushing open the door to the office. Joe was on the phone but nodded in greeting when she entered. She sat down on the couch as she waited for him to finish.

She watched as he balanced the phone against his ear, then painstakingly wrote something on a piece of paper while still talking. He set down the pen he had been writing with to pull open a draw beside his knee and withdraw a file. He opened it with one hand and began perusing the contents, shuffling the papers within. He pushed aside an empty mug as he began writing again.

Joe was definitely improving. His hands were gaining in dexterity. The agility was measured but returning nonetheless. She could not count how many times in the past two weeks he had happily reminded her how the numbness was receding and his dream of performing surgery again was becoming more of a reality.

So what was preventing her from outwardly sharing his joy? The incident in Paul Martin's office after he had seen the orthopedic surgeon had left her with a most uncomfortable feeling. She felt guilty for not being genuinely happy for him. Now just watching him work behind his own desk was giving her the same uncomfortable feeling all over again. *Why?*

But she knew why. Because her time was running out. Her time *with him* was running out. Her work would be ending because Joe was making a remarkable and progressive recovery. And soon, he would have no need for her services any longer, and maybe no need for her personally if she didn't make her feelings known, and soon.

She rose to her feet as Joe replaced the phone. He came around to the other side of the desk and stood in front of her, putting his hands around her shoulders and squeezing them with affection and admiration. "Hey, lady, you did an excellent job. I really envied you." She gazed into the blue eyes with a sober expression. "I appreciate that," she returned quietly, "but I would have been more at ease if *you'd* been on the other side of the table."

"You didn't need me. You did just fine." His hands tightened around her shoulders. "Now all I have to do is convince you to stay."

A rapturous smile came to her face as she anticipated what she had yearned to hear him say for so long. "You . . . really want me to stay?"

"Would you?"

"Oh, Joe, I love working here. I love working with you! These past few months I've been here, watching you, working beside you . . . ." She quickly put her words in check before she said too much. "It's been wonderful."

"That's funny," he said. "I was thinking the very same thing, only about *you*."

She took a step back, and his hands slipped away. "Do you need me, Joe?"

He smiled at her. "Need you? What kind of question is that? I can't get along *without* you." He leaned easily against the front of the desk. "I know this may sound selfish in lieu of the position you're likely to get in Dallas, but this department *needs* surgeons like you. I don't want to lose you."

As suddenly as the words came, so did the revelation. *I don't want to lose her.* The beguiling words she had overheard him say to Paul Martin the night of the dinner party now struck with painful clarity. *He didn't want to lose her—as a colleague, not as a woman.*

She felt herself biting down hard on her lower lip. "*That's* why you want me to stay on," she said in a quiet voice. She glanced down at her feet. She couldn't risk having him see stinging tears that were too near the surface. Struggling for composure, she finally looked at him again. "Is that . . . is that what Paul wanted you to ask me about?"

He looked at her in stunned silence, a hopeful expression crossing his face. "How did you know Paul wanted me to talk to you about accepting a position here?"

Embarrassment and disappointment tore at her insides. "I . . . I accidentally overheard your conversation with Dr. Martin the night we were at his house."

"Why didn't you say something then?" he asked unknowingly. "I haven't forgotten how important this directorship is to you and what it would undoubtedly do for your career. But would you be willing to even consider it?"

All at once, she realized her feelings for him had become so intense that they had all but overshadowed the once coveted position. Regardless of reputation and prestige, falling in love with Dr. Joe Travis had become the most important thing in her life. Yet she knew now that his being in love with her had never been reality, only idealism.

"Vicky?" he prodded gently. He couldn't be sure, but he thought he saw tears welling in her eyes. "Is it something you'd rather talk about later?"

Whether he knew it or not, he was offering her an out. "No . . . no, it's nothing I need to talk about. Joe, I really have to go." She turned and quickly left the office.

* * *

It was late in the afternoon the following day when Joe walked into Paul Martin's office, casually seating himself in one of the plush chairs across from Paul's desk. The older man seemed engrossed in some paperwork, but he stated his business anyway. "I talked to Vicky yesterday about staying on. Her reaction was a little strange when I mentioned the proposition to her, but with any luck she might consider—"

"Save your breath, Joe." Paul slipped off his glasses and handed him the paper he had been reading.

Joe noticed the disturbed expression on Paul's face as he took the letter from him. "I don't understand," he said after reading the first few lines. "She's leaving. When I talked to her yesterday, I was sure she—"

And then suddenly, he understood. *The kiss, the touch, the tears.* He read to the end of the one page letter, running his hand in frustration through his hair before Paul spoke again.

"Look, I'm as disappointed as you are, but it was a long shot thinking she would accept a position with us instead of taking that directorship she was fighting for. Here, she would merely be a staff surgeon, a far cry from being head of an entire trauma department." Joe drew a deep breath. "I don't think it was entirely the directorship," he returned quietly, not wanting to expound. "Did she give you any other reasons for wanting to leave so soon?"

Paul replaced his glasses. "She told me she feels if she's to become the director of the trauma unit in Dallas, she needs to return as soon as possible. But only because she believes you're ready to take over the department again. Not surgically, but we can work around that for now."

Joe dropped the letter on Paul's desk. He had waited a long time to be fully reinstated, but the circumstances surrounding his return put a damper on the news.

* * *

Joe stopped beside the opened doorway of his former office and watched while Vicky Keene worked behind his soon-to-be vacated desk. Obviously absorbed in her task, he cleared his throat with noticeable intent.

She glanced up. "You aren't here with the eviction notice already, are you?"

He could tell there was a contrived geniality in the midst of her customary good nature. She resumed her work as he walked up to the desk.

"No eviction notice. Fact is, I just came from Paul Martin's office, and he showed me your letter. I understand how important that directorship is to you, but I wonder if you realize what a tremendous asset you've become to this hospital."

She confined her gaze to her work at hand. "That's very kind of you to say."

"I'm not being kind," he returned in a brusque voice, "I'm being honest. You have a remarkable gift for surgery and a wonderful rapport with patients. If you accept that directorship, you're going to waste an extraordinary talent on *paperwork* instead of surgery! Is it really worth that much to you?"

With a gesture of finality, she dropped her pen on the desk top and looked up at him. "Yes, initially it *was* worth that much to me. But my reasons for leaving aren't *quite* the same as they were six months ago—" She stopped, instantly regretting the latter remark.

In spite of the fiery green eyes, Joe's expression grew sympathetic. "Would you mind telling me those reasons?"

Her gaze returned to the papers that rested beneath her hands. *What use was there pretending now?* "Remember in med school the lessons we learned about the importance of patient objectivity? I'm afraid the same is true between professionals. I don't think I can be very objective anymore where you're concerned."

Her candid remark did not take him by surprise. "Vicky, I never meant for you to mistake appreciation for affection."

She rose from behind the desk and came around to the front where he stood. "I know you didn't. But you want to know something?" she began, trying to keep a steady voice. "All my life, I told myself I was going to *be* somebody, *do* something important, *achieve* more than the rest. I'd look at other women and almost feel *sorry* for them because they were trapped in a life of dishes and cooking and endless laundry. But I wasn't going to let that happen to me," she said, shaking her head vehemently. "Oh, no, because I had become so profoundly accomplished I didn't think I needed any of that. I even convinced myself that crying was just something *foolish women did to get attention!*" The last words barely escaped her lips before she thrust her hands over her face and began to weep.

Joe was touched beyond reason as he put his hands around her shoulders and drew her toward him. He held her in his arms for a moment and then gently brushed away a stream of tears that trickled down her cheeks. "These aren't the tears of a foolish woman," he whispered. "They're tears from a very strong woman with an exceptionally tender heart."

At length, she lifted her head and looked at him. "I never thought I cared about anything short of my career until I met you, and all I've really accomplished is making a fool of myself."

"No, no, that's the last thing you've done," he returned adamantly. "You accomplished something you didn't even realize you were doing. You showed me how to stand on my feet again. You gave me confidence after I lost the use of my hands, and out my gratitude came a little . . . confusion. That's a long way from being a fool."

She wiped the tears away from her face. "I knew yesterday I had to make more than just a professional decision." She wavered before gathering enough courage to finish. "I knew that . . . if you couldn't return the same feelings for me, I couldn't stay here. I don't mean to present a problem—"

"Vicky"—he drew a long, lingering breath as he took her hands into his own—"the problem isn't you. It's me."

"I don't believe that," she returned in his defense. "I've watched you. I've worked with you. I know how hard it's been for you since your accident. You've just been through too much!" Her hands tightened around his. "I thought, too, you might still be grieving for your wife."

"I *am* grieving," he told her, "grieving over mistakes I may never be able to rectify. It's going to take me a long time just to learn to live with them. But you," he said, taking her face into the palms of his hands, "you're a beautiful, sensitive, intelligent woman who doesn't need the burden of my problems."

Tears again filled her eyes. "Did it ever occur to you that maybe I can offer you something that you *do* need?"

"It wouldn't be fair, Vicky. Right now, I don't have anything to offer *you*, but I don't want my mistakes to influence the good you can do here. Don't use what's happened between us as an excuse to leave. That would be the worst crime of all."

Slowly, she shook her head. "I'm sorry, Joe. I just can't do it."

He drew her face toward his and kissed her cheek. "I'm sorry too, for a lot of things," he whispered as his hands slipped away.

He was beside the door when she called to him. "Joe?" He turned to look at her once more. A sad smile began to crease her face. "You know where to reach me . . . if you ever change your mind."

The dimples in his cheeks deepened with the smile on his face.

CHAPTER 40

Joe Travis walked across the university campus on the way back to his office. In the distance, he could hear the haunting chimes from the bell tower tolling four o'clock. He glanced upward at the clear blue sky, grateful for the warmth of an early spring afternoon.

His hands had not yet strengthened as he had hoped. Though he was disappointed, he had continued teaching at the university, using the remainder of his time managing his practice to a lesser degree.

Halfway across campus, his pager began to beep inside his shirt pocket. He returned the call and then hurried toward the hospital. Once inside, he ran down the corridor, entering the trauma room shortly after paramedics had transferred their patient from gurney to exam table.

"What happened?" Joe asked, leaning closer to the teenage boy who was moaning in pain, his head rolling from side to side.

"Two car collision on the expressway approximately thirty minutes ago," one of the paramedics began to explain. "Vital signs on transport were stable, BP a little low at one point, but fluids brought it back up. The parents are on the way now. Most of the impact was to the other vehicle."

Joe glanced up. "What about the other driver?" The boy moaned again as the paramedic looked at Joe and shook his head. Joe resumed his examination. After ordering the trauma series, he told one of the attending nurses, "I'll need to talk to the boy's parents as soon as possible. We may have some serious kidney damage here."

"They're already in the corridor," she told him.

Joe stepped outside the trauma room. After explaining the situation to the parents, the mother became especially agitated. "Dr. Travis, Kevin only *has* one kidney. And you say he may have damaged the only one he has left?"

"It's a possibility," Joe told her. "He's going to CT right now, and we'll know more after that. What happened that he only has one kidney?"

"Kidney disease when he was younger," the father explained. "It was thought at the time that both kidneys might have to be removed, but it turned out only one had to go. His mother and I were both tested to see if we would be compatible donors, but neither one of us were."

Joe realized the situation could be potentially more serious than he thought. "What about siblings?"

The mother shook her head. "He's an only child."

Joe began to walk down the corridor with them. "We'll have to wait until all the tests are back before making any decisions. In the meantime, you'll need to go to Admitting and sign some papers while he's in x-ray. I'll meet you in his room when I have all the information. Ms. Walker can show you where you need to go." The nurse accompanied the anxious parents to the elevator.

Joe turned to go back to the trauma room when he saw Dr. Jeff Marcus coming out of the resuscitation room. "Joe, can I see you a minute?" he called. The two doctors walked into the small room behind the nurses' station. "That expressway accident, you're treating the other driver?"

"Yeah, looks like he came through all right except for damage to his left kidney. His *only* kidney."

Marcus shook his head. "The girl wasn't so lucky. Irreversible brain damage. The EEG showed nothing, pupils fixed, and dilated. The parents are with her now."

"Do they know?"

Marcus nodded. "Yes, and they reacted completely opposite to what you'd expect. They wept, but that was all. And they know it was the boy's fault, entirely."

"They're in shock," Joe concluded. "When reality hits them, you'll know it."

* * *

An hour later, Joe came back to the room where Kevin Edison and his parents nervously waited. The boy was more alert now. "I wish I had better news for you," Joe began. "It looks like there is substantial damage to Kevin's remaining kidney."

"What about surgery?" Mrs. Edison asked in earnest.

"I'm afraid surgery wouldn't do any good. There's too much damage to attempt any kind of repair."

"Am I going to die?" The boy's face paled with fear.

"No, we're not going to let that happen." Joe tried to sound reassuring. "But we *are* going to have to find a donor for you."

"A donor!" his mother cried. "That could take weeks, months!"

Joe held up his hand. "Not necessarily. We'll put Kevin's name in the computer and see what happens. In the meantime, we'll keep him stable by way of dialysis. But we need to keep calm and take this one step at a time. Now if you'll excuse me, I'll go see what I can do." The boy's father followed Joe out of the room and pulled the door shut behind him. Joe could see far more alarm in his face than he displayed in front of his wife and son. "Dr. Travis, do whatever it takes. *Please* find a donor for our son." "I'll do everything I can."

As Joe left him standing in the corridor, it suddenly struck him how terribly sorry he felt for them and the innocent girl their son had collided with. Something about their situation was beginning to revive remnants of deep-seated feelings once more.

* * *

Darkness was beginning to settle when Joe heard his name paged over the intercom. It had been a long day, and he was ready for it to end. He picked up the phone at the nurses' station. Paul Martin wanted to see him in his office immediately.

A few minutes later, Joe stood outside Paul's door and knocked, opening it slowly after hearing a muffled command to come in. "Joe, I'd like you meet Mr. and Mrs. Brennan. The Brennans are the parents of the girl who was tragically injured this afternoon on the expressway," Paul explained gently.

It was an awkward moment for Joe as the wearied couple dutifully rose to meet him. He wondered why he had been summoned to a meeting of this nature. "I'm terribly sorry about your daughter." The couple sat down again and allowed Paul to continue. "When the Brennans learned about Kevin Edison's medical condition, I felt it was important for you to be here. Earlier this evening, they asked me if they could meet Kevin and his parents." The request stunned Joe, but he said nothing. "On behalf of their daughter, they feel that to keep her on life support would not be in her best interest. They've agreed to disconnect that support and donate her organs.

And if the tests prove compatible, they'd like to donate one of her kidneys to the boy."

Joe almost did a second take. *Donate her kidney to the boy? To his patient who was responsible for the terminal condition of their daughter?* He looked from one to the other before finding his own words. "I don't understand. Why are you willing to help the boy when he's the one responsible for what happened to your daughter?"

"Doctor," Mrs. Brennan began, "don't think it was an easy decision for us to make. We're Christian people, but we're not immune to the problems and tragedies of this world. It's not up to us to judge, but it is up to us to ask God to help us forgive. There's nothing more we can do for Julie. But if there's something we can do for Kevin— something that might even change the course of his life—we want to do that much. Will you help us or not?"

Joe looked at them in total astonishment. These people were about to lose their daughter, and yet their willingness to forgive astounded him. He looked past them at Paul. In the older man's eyes, he read a message—a very familiar message.

"Doctor?" The voice of Mr. Brennan returned his thoughts to the present.

"I'll order the tests now." Joe rose to his feet and excused himself.

* * *

The next morning Joe received the report from the transplant coordinator. He was amazed at the remarkable compatibility between the donor and the recipient. He picked up the phone to notify Paul Martin when the door opened. "Paul, I was just about to call you," he said, replacing the receiver. He looked carefully at his friend. "You look beat."

Paul dropped wearily into a chair in front of the desk. "I spent most of the night with the Brennans. They're extraordinary people. By the way, have you received any test results yet?"

"That was what I was going to call you about. All of them suggest good compatibility. The boy's being prepped for surgery right now."

"That's wonderful."

Joe lowered his head in thoughtful retrospection as he stared at the test results in his hands. The sacrifice the Brennans were willing to make for his patient had not left his mind since meeting them the day before in Paul's office.

"When I saw the panic in Mr. Edison's face yesterday," he began, "I realized what a parent must go through for the sake of a child. To be willing to do *anything* for the life of that child . . . " When he glanced up, he saw Paul's intuitive gaze bearing down on him. "I guess what I have a harder time understanding is how the Brennans can have so much compassion, so much forgiveness in spite of." He stopped, suddenly realizing the implication of what he was about to say.

Paul said nothing more as he prepared to leave, but the unspoken words caught like daggers in Joe's throat.

* * *

A few hours later, Paul and Joe left the observation dome where they had been observing the transplant surgery. "Looks like the Edison boy is going to be just fine," Paul remarked as they walked down the corridor together.

Joe turned to see his old friend smiling at him. "I think so too."

They said nothing more as they pushed through the double glass doors, walked across the parking lot and into the medical complex. Once inside Joe's office, Paul dropped wearily onto the couch while Joe sat down behind his desk.

Paul guessed what was going through the younger man's mind as he watched him absently flex the fingers of both hands. "Don't be impatient, Joe. You're still a surgeon, and you *will* operate again."

Joe turned his hands over for rueful examination. "Clark Sawyer tells me in spite of all the improvement, it may be months before I regain enough dexterity to go back to surgery."

"You knew going in it was going to take time, a *lot* of time. But you've kept yourself gainfully occupied in medicine. You've kept up with the material just by teaching."

"And I owe that to you. You've saved my life more than once, Paul," he remarked, recalling with undisclosed horror the night he had considered suicide.

"Oh, I don't know about that—"

"It's true," Joe went on. "I had a lot of anger I didn't know how to deal with, and you were the only one who seemed to understand that. You knew I was completely at loose ends when you suggested I teach at the university. Teaching has somehow put things into perspective for me. I needed to feel useful, and you provided a way for me to do that."

"I appreciate your telling me that."

Joe leaned across the desk, still broodingly examining his hands. "I've been doing a lot of thinking."

"Such as?"

He looked at Paul once more. "I haven't been able to stop thinking about the Brennans. When they realized there was nothing that could be done for their daughter, instead of giving in to anger at the miserable injustice that had been done to them, they reached out and helped. That's exactly what Beth counseled the people she dealt with." His voice trailed into a whisper when he added, "She'd be so disappointed in me . . . "

"Don't be too hard on yourself," Paul admonished gently. "We're still human, no matter how hard as doctors we try not to be."

"But it cost them their daughter's life! How can they possibly forgive that boy's carelessness?"

A knowing expression crossed the older man's face. "I don't believe that's something a human being can generate on his own, Joe. I think that kind of forgiveness comes from a willingness of allowing God to take control, and that's the way it is with the Brennans. I believe they would rather choose to forgive than suffer all the justifiable anger that would be perfectly understandable." Paul watched Joe glance down at his hands. He wondered after all this time how justified Joe still believed his own anger to be. "I can't help but think about Ben Jordan. Do you suppose he was . . . just as willing to do anything to save Callie?"

The words struck hard, yet no harder than Joe's caged thoughts had done most of the previous night. "*Yes*," he said at last, drawing a deep breath as he bowed his head over his folded hands. "I know it's over between Callie and me. I'm not fooling myself into thinking she could still love me, not after the way I treated her." His voice grew quiet when he added, "I guess I realized too late how much I really did love her and still do."

Paul Martin shook his head incredulously. "Joe, when are you going to open your eyes and see what's been in front of you the whole time?"

Joe raised his head. "What are you talking about?"

"I'm talking about Callie Jordan. I know I can't speak for her right *now*, but I do know one thing: that girl has been in love with you for years. Even your marriage to Beth didn't change her feelings for you, and I don't think a love that's endured as much as hers has could be swept aside very easily."

Joe sat up, a look of disbelief spreading across his face. "What do you mean, *for years*? Callie and I had always been close, but it was like . . . like *family* between us." He rose to his feet, the disbelief changing to indignation. "Besides, if what you're saying is true, don't you think I would have known it?"

"Oh, Joe, be reasonable!" Paul retorted in exasperation. "She loved you, but *not* like family. Just think about it. She stood on the sideline for years, waiting for you to show even the slightest hint of romantic interest in her. Then when that didn't happen, she watched you marry her best friend! And there was only one way she knew to deal with that kind of disappointment. Did it ever occur to you *why* she left so soon after you got married?"

But Joe didn't answer. Instead, he turned toward the window as memories began to come back to him—the first day he saw her in the OR after he and Beth were married, and then he remembered the rest.

* * *

Callie had been unduly distressed after learning about his marriage to Beth. Alone with her in an empty operating room suite, he had remarked in all innocence, "I don't understand why you're so upset—"

"And you never will!" she had exploded, and then fled from the room.

* * *

Joe stared at the parking lot below as Paul's recollection of the past began to collaborate with the present.

* * *

Days had passed before he had been able to confront her following the episode in the operating room, when he had been told that she was suddenly planning to leave Boston. "I just want you to be sure this is what you really want," he told her.

Callie had hesitated before answering. "It's what I really want . . ."

* * *

Now the truth was all too apparent. Joe drew a deep breath before turning around. "Where is she, Paul?"

"I honestly don't know," he said slowly.

Joe sat down behind his desk, once again bowing his head over his hands, inwardly cursing himself for his abject naivety. "I asked her something shortly after Beth and I were married, when I found out she was planning to leave Boston." Considering Paul's revelation, he cringed as he remembered the innocent question he had put forward to her. "I asked her why she'd never considered getting married and having a family of her own. And she told me . . . the right one had never proposed." He lifted his head. "How was I to know *I* was that one?"

CHAPTER 41

Two days later, Joe stepped out of his car and stood on the familiar veranda outside the Jordan house. Its classic black shutters and white columns rose in bleak contrast against the cold blue of the early spring sky.

His eyes roamed the property for signs of life. All was quiet but for the occasional chirping of birds in the still leafless trees overhead, but signs of spring were evident in the myriad of crocus and daffodil shoots in the gardens and walkways surrounding the great house.

A bitter reminder of the last time he had been here caused him to shudder inwardly. He had come a long way since then—a long way, a long time, a lifetime. As never before, he felt compelled to begin picking up the pieces of his life that had become tangled and shattered. He longed to ask Callie's forgiveness and longed as much to love her as he knew now he had always loved her.

He rang the bell. In his mind, he imagined Callie swinging open the wide door, as she done so often before. He wondered what their first words would be, wondered how he would convince her he still loved her, had always loved her, that he was no longer the hopeless and angry man she had last seen in the hospital that day so long ago. Disappointment overcame him after several minutes of waiting.

Slowly, he turned away when he heard the door open behind him. In anticipation he looked back, only to see a friendly, dark-haired stranger standing inside the doorway. "I'm sorry. I was upstairs and didn't hear the bell. I'm not used to such a large place yet."

He came back to the door. "I'm . . . I'm sorry to bother you, ma'am. I was looking for Callie Jordan."

The woman's expression became inquisitive as she considered the name. "Jordan," she repeated. "I'm afraid I don't know anyone by that name."

Taken aback by her startling remark, Joe glanced around the grounds as if expecting all that had once been familiar to suddenly materialize. "I don't understand. The Jordans have lived here for years."

"Oh, of course!" the woman said at last. "*Dr.* Jordan. I'm sorry I didn't understand. I work for the Van Pelts who own the estate now."

"Own it?"

"Yes, they bought it from Dr. Jordan's daughter. Is…that who you're looking for?"

Joe looked at her with expectation. "Yes. Do you have any idea where she is?"

The woman shook her head. "Oh, that I wouldn't know., but I'd be more than happy to ask Mr. Van Pelt if he has any information about her."

Joe scrawled a phone number on a piece of paper and handed it to her. "If you would, please." He mumbled his thanks and hurriedly made his way down the steps again.

* * *

Working late in his office that evening, Joe finished compiling lecture notes for his morning class. A knock on the door interrupted his concentration. "Burning the midnight oil, Doctor?" Paul Martin poked his head inside before inviting himself in.

"I was just finishing some lecture notes," Joe told him. "What can I do for you?"

"Well, I came by to ask if you'd consider taking my place at the surgical conference in Phoenix next week. My schedule won't let me go, but I hate to lose the reservations. Besides, escaping a cold Boston spring for a few days might do you a lot of good."

Joe looked at his hands. "You seem to have more faith in me than I have in myself right now."

"Joe, you've never been one to quit. No matter what the outcome may be, God has a plan for your life. Whether that plan includes doing surgery or something entirely different, remember He's the One who knows what's best for you."

Joe leaned against the back of the chair. "I know. It's just . . . " He hesitated. "As much as I've enjoyed teaching and gradually returning to my practice, I can't imagine never doing surgery again." He shook his head in an effort to purge himself of the maudlin feeling. "I'll go to the convention. Maybe it *will* do me some good."

"I know it will. I'll have Debbie bring the itinerary to you in the morning." He pulled the door shut behind him.

Joe finished his lecture notes and then slipped into his jacket. He was almost to the door when the phone rang. He was tired and tempted to ignore it, but remembered he had not yet turned it over to the answering service. He reached for the receiver.

"Dr. Travis?"

"This is Dr. Travis."

"My name is Henry Van Pelt. I'm sorry to call you so late, but I understand you were at my house looking for someone this afternoon."

Joe sat down behind his desk again. "Yes, I was looking for Callie Jordan. I didn't realize she had sold the house."

"My wife and I purchased the estate through a private sale. I never met Ms. Jordan personally. All of our communication was done by way of mail."

"Would it be possible to tell me from where?"

The man seemed agreeable enough without asking questions. "I may have something in the desk drawer here, if you can wait a moment."

"Yes, of course." In his mind, Joe visualized Benjamin Jordan's study where he pictured the man sitting. It was difficult to imagine the familiar house occupied with strangers. It was as though his last connection had been severed, the last kinship from the past removed and taken away from him.

Van Pelt returned to the phone. "Ms. Jordan's correspondence was from Charleston, South Carolina. One of the letterheads says *Dr. Stephen Lewis, Cardiology*."

Joe made a note of the information only as fast as his weakened hand would allow. "Thank you, Mr. Van Pelt. You've been very helpful."

* * *

The next day, Joe stuffed his notes and student papers into his briefcase following his last class and headed back to his office. His concentration since the night before centered on calling the office of Dr. Stephen Lewis.

"I'm sorry, Dr. Travis, Dr. Lewis is out of town right now. Is this in regard to a patient?" Joe listened disappointedly to the prim voice of the secretary.

"No," he said at last, "I'm looking for Callie Jordan."

"Ms. Jordan no longer works here. She resigned her position some time ago. We were all sorry when she left."

"Do you happen to know where she went?"

"No, I don't. I suppose Dr. Lewis might know where she is. Would you like him in get in touch with you when he comes back?"

"Yes, please."

* * *

Joe's thoughts tumbled restlessly on the plane to Phoenix three days later. Throughout his hospitalization and prolonged recuperation, he had carried the burden of his broken relationship with Callie.

Vividly, he recalled them together in her father's den, while the fire had burned and the cold rain pounded against the house. On that night, he had no doubt his lonely world had at last come to an end. Callie would be his wife, and he looked forward to loving and protecting her as he had loved and protected Beth.

And then she had told him about her father's exploit. He remembered her cheeks streaked with tears, the anxious expression on her stricken face. He remembered his disbelief, then anger, and finally rage, while he struggled to absorb what must have taken every ounce of her courage to confess. He closed his eyes to escape the bitter remembrance, but images of that night were scarred into his memory as well as his hands.

He thought about his devastating accident and being told of Callie's unrelenting vigil beside his bed as he lingered between life and death. He remembered after regaining consciousness when she had come to see him in the hospital, despite his warning that he didn't want to see her. With rare boldness, she had come anyway, trying to persuade him that nothing else mattered but how much she loved him.

If only he had put his anger aside and told her then how much he still loved her! But instead, he had shut himself away from her and everyone else in an impossible attempt to barricade himself from pain.

But he had merely succeeded in creating more. Once again, he cursed himself for what he had done, not only to her, but ultimately to himself. He hungered to make things right with her, ached to take her into his arms again.

But she was no longer there, and no longer a part of his life.

* * *

The stylish lobby of the hotel was thronged with people making their way to selected sessions of the surgical conference. Joe walked down a richly carpeted hallway with a schedule clutched loosely in his hand. As he compared his agenda with the program titles beside each conference room, the name of a presenter suddenly caught his attention: *Dr. Stephen Lewis.*

A line of doctors was already beginning to file through the door. Foregoing his own agenda, he decided to stay and listen to the cardiologist, hoping for a chance to speak to him after the session.

Throughout the presentation, Joe was increasingly impressed with the young man behind the podium. It was obvious he was highly trained and on the cutting edge of his profession, despite his youthful appearance. In a candid and congenial manner, the young surgeon unpretentiously presented case studies of extreme surgical risk patients he had successfully treated.

The session ended, and Joe waited until the room had emptied before approaching the podium. "Dr. Lewis?"

The doctor closed the lid to his laptop as he turned toward the voice. "Yes?" he answered, smiling at the stranger in front of him.

"I was very impressed with your presentation," Joe complimented him.

"Thank you very much."

Lewis extended his hand in a sociable fashion as Joe introduced himself. "My name is Joe Travis, trauma surgery."

The amiable expression on the cardiologist's face quickly sobered as his hand slipped out of Joe's grasp. "Joe Travis," he repeated the name in a derisory tone. "You don't practice in Boston, do you?"

A bewildered expression crossed Joe's face. "As a matter of fact, I do. I was wondering if there might be some place we could talk privately?"

Lewis shoved his computer into the carrying case and stepped down from the platform. "I don't believe we have anything to discuss, Dr. Travis." He started to walk away. Then with an apparent pang of conscience, he stopped and turned around. "I have a room here at the hotel. We can talk there."

Joe could not understand the doctor's sudden defensive manner but followed him in silence into the elevator to the ninth floor. Inside Lewis's tastefully furnished suite, Joe sat down uninvited on the sofa, still perplexed by the younger man's brusque behavior.

"I assume this has something to do with Callie Jordan," Lewis said at last, seating himself in a chair.

At the mention of Callie's name, the doctor's puzzling conduct was becoming clearer. "Yes, it does. Doctor, I apologize if I've offended you for some reason. I had no intention of—"

"I'll come right to the point, Dr. Travis," he interjected hastily. "I'm not sure what your intentions *are*, but I *am* sure you aren't going to hurt Callie Jordan again. Ever."

At once, Joe felt threatened, his mistakes regarding Callie an open book in front of a stranger. "That's the *last* thing I intend to do," he retorted. "I happen to care a great deal about Callie."

Lewis gave him a calculating look. "And so do I."

Joe could feel his frustration mounting as he got to his feet and looked at Lewis. "I was told Callie used to work for you. Your secretary informed me that you might know where she is. I see no need to explain my situation to you, but all I want to know is where she is."

Lewis shook his head. "I don't know where she is. But even if I did, I don't think I'd tell you."

"*Why?*" Joe demanded, his blue eyes glinting with aggravation. "What do you know about Callie that I don't?"

Stephen's own temper was on the rise now. He would not allow this man to hurt Callie any further, in spite of the fact that she had rejected him just as Travis had rejected her. He rose cautiously and stood beside the chair. "I know you refused to have anything more to do with her after you found out it was your wife's heart that saved her life! She didn't *have* to tell you that. She could have borne that secret to her grave, but she chose not to."

The appalling disclosure from a stranger regarding his private ignominy was humiliating. Unable to deny the truth, he lashed out at the young surgeon. "What made it any of your business for her to divulge information like that to you?"

Stephen narrowed his eyes on his challenger. "Because I was the surgeon who performed the transplant."

Stunned, Joe looked at him in disbelief. "You?"

"Yes," Stephen declared triumphantly, "and instead of accepting the fact that the surgery *saved* her life, you *blamed* her because it was your wife's heart and not one from a total stranger! If you have to have a scapegoat, blame her father because all Callie was left with was a guilty and grieving conscience. Your wife was her friend, Doctor. She loved her. And whether you choose to believe it or not, she was heartbroken."

Joe sank down on the couch. "Callie thinks I *blame* her because she was the receiver of Beth's heart?" The thought had never entered his mind.

"What else would you expect her to think? How can you possibly hold her responsible for something she had no control over?"

"I *don't* hold her responsible!" Joe exploded. "The fact that her heart transplant came from Beth had *nothing* to do with—" His words fell short.

"Had nothing to do with what?" Stephen demanded.

With a deep and shuddering sigh, he looked away. "My anger wasn't with Callie."

"Then why else would you leave her?"

Joe dropped his head into his hands. He ran his fingers through fine brown strands of hair, mortified, self-conscious, stalling while he tried to compose himself. "I had no idea how severe Callie's condition had become the night my wife died. Obviously, you were the one who alerted her father. But at the same time, Benjamin Jordan also knew the critical condition of my wife and subsequently made all the arrangements for the transplant, with the exception of *telling me*." He closed his eyes as the nightmarish memories flooded his mind like a raging river. "I suppose he thought at the time maybe I . . . I couldn't have handled the decision. I don't know. Maybe I couldn't have."

He shook his head in retrospect. "For many years, there was no one I admired more than Benjamin Jordan. When Callie told me the truth about her transplant, I couldn't understand how he could do such a thing to me. I felt . . . exploited by a man who had not only been my mentor, but more of a father to me than my own had been." His voice grew softer. "And even though I still loved Callie, I drove her out of my life because of my anger and disillusionment toward her father. I was afraid I could never look at her again without being . . . reminded."

Stephen's antipathy began to lessen when he watched Joe slowly turn his hands over. For the first time, he saw the distinct outline of scarring in both of them and remembered the story Callie had related about his accident.

"Because of my anger, my hands were crippled so badly in an accident I may never hold a scalpel again. I couldn't imagine Callie spending the rest of her life having to care for me like some sort of invalid. The one I'm blaming is myself, not Callie. I was a fool to let her go. All I want is to find her, to ask her forgiveness, *not* cause her any more pain than I already have."

Stephen was amazed at the revelation of humility he was witnessing. No longer was he looking at his contrived image of a man fortified against pain and sensitivity, but at a very vulnerable man—a man admittedly as lonely without Callie Jordan as he was.

Stephen eased himself into the chair. "There's something else I think you have a right to know," he began in a subdued voice. "It's apparent to me that Callie misinterpreted your anger, but she did understand how betrayed you felt because of her father. She understood, too, how much you loved your wife, and she didn't believe you could ever love her in the same way. But she never blamed you for either," Now the words came harder, "because she's never loved anyone but *you.*"

Slowly, Joe lifted his head and looked at Stephen. Through the absence of animosity in the younger man's face, he recognized a comparative sadness and realized he was not alone in his love for Callie. "I can't be sure," Stephen continued, "but my guess is she went back to Boston . . . to be near you."

The two men rose simultaneously. Joe extended his hand in a gesture of gratitude and contrition. "I want to apologize for misjudging you, and I'm not sure how to thank you."

With some lingering uncertainty, Stephen reached out and grasped Joe's hand. "It was I who misjudged you. And all I can ask is that you love her enough . . . for both of us."

CHAPTER 42

Paul Martin dropped his fork on the empty plate. His gray eyes turned toward the large window beside him in the hospital cafeteria where he had been enjoying a late lunch with Joe. Now he contemplated the younger man's story of his ironic meeting with Stephen Lewis and the mystery surrounding Callie Jordan's whereabouts.

"Well, what you're telling me doesn't really come as a surprise," Paul remarked pensively. "I thought for a long time Callie had been considering leaving Boston, but she never said a word to me. Yet you say this fellow has no idea where she's gone since she left Charleston?"
"No. He only guessed she'd come back to Boston to . . . to

be near me." The last words were tinged with self-repugnance. He looked up at his colleague, a thousand unanswered questions in his eyes. "After the way I treated her, why would she want to be *anywhere* near me? It doesn't make sense."

The fine lines on Paul's face crinkled into a broad smile. "It doesn't have to make sense, Joe. Love is a powerful thing. Love can overcome obstacles all the scientific knowledge in the world can't conquer or attempt to explain." He narrowed his eyes on the younger man. "And don't forget, Joe, love can *forgive* anything too."

"After everything that's happened, do you honestly believe Callie could *ever* forgive me?"

"Yes, I do."

Joe looked away, shaking his head. "I wish I could believe that." Oh, how he wished he could believe that! *She's never loved anyone but you.* He clung to the disclosure of Stephen Lewis's words, his solitary thread of hope.

Paul tossed his napkin aside. "Even if she *never* forgave you, don't you think it's about time you forgave yourself? Because if you can't put the past behind you, you won't have room for anyone in the future."

Joe looked at Paul again. "I'm not sure I can do that. I feel like I've reached the end of my resources. And I don't know where to go from here."

The older man's face filled with tender sympathy. "And that's exactly where God wants you, Joe. I think sometimes He waits to answer our petitions until we've reached the end of own ropes because only *then* have we come to the place where we'll allow Him to step in and do what He's *wanted* to do all along. Can you understand what I'm saying?"

Joe's eyes rose to meet those of his colleague. "I wouldn't have a few months ago."

"A few months ago, you were still trying to do it all yourself, relying on your own strength to solve your problems. But maybe that's not the case any longer." Paul rose to his feet and smiled down at the younger man. "You know, it's been said that the greatest distance in the world lies somewhere between the head and the heart. I think you've just taken a giant step toward lessening that gap."

* * *

Joe lay awake that night, his hands clasped behind his head. Through the window, shimmering light from a full moon traversed the bare branches of the trees, creating shadows that played against the walls and ceiling.

He glanced at the digital clock on the nightstand. It would be dawn in another hour. He had become so immersed in his thoughts that he had not realized most of the night was gone.

He contemplated his impromptu meeting with Stephen Lewis and the words that had given him some reason for hope. *She's never loved anyone but you*, and Paul's remarks at lunch the day before.

Could love really forgive anything? Was it indeed time to forgive himself? Could he honestly allow God to step into his life and trust Him again? All these occurrences could have been the result of coincidence, or had they been divinely sent?

He pulled himself out of bed and walked toward the large window on the other side of the room. A thick fog had settled outside, creating ghostly silhouettes in the cold moonlight.

Pushing the drapes farther apart, he leaned against the window. Somehow, he knew he had come to a turning point. The intense anger he had once felt so keenly had succumbed to a mental weariness from which he could not break away. For what had he gained by his anger? Who had he ultimately hurt but himself and Callie?

Callie . . . if only he could find her. But even if he did, how could he prove to her that he still loved her? All he had proven to himself was how weak he really was. Callie had proven to be the strong one.

He took a deep and shuttering breath, trying to elude the wave of emotion that wanted to overtake him. He was weary from a long night of no sleep, but even more so from months of loneliness, the kind of loneliness that came from trying to achieve contentment on his own.

He turned away from the window. Without realizing it, he dropped to his knees beside the bed and buried his face in his hands. *"Dear God, forgive me,"* he whispered. "Forgive me for trying to do it all on my own, for thinking I could be satisfied with a life without You. I may never understand why You allowed the trials to come into my life, but let Your purpose for all of it be fulfilled. Help me, refine me, let me be gold tried in the fire.

"If it's in Your will, please let me find Callie. Just give me the opportunity to ask her for forgiveness and to accept that, that's all I may ever have from her. And even more than that," He felt the tears on his face now. "please enable *me* to forgive."

Streaks of crimson had begun to lighten the eastern sky when Joe rose from his knees.

* * *

Wisps of clouds floated on their way to nowhere through a late afternoon sky. Trees stood bare against the brilliant blue while patches of snow slowly melted in the shadows of the branches. Cardinals and chickadees chirped unseen as robins went in search of insects venturing into the early spring sunshine.

Joe Travis wandered slowly among the headstones, pausing now and then to read an epitaph designed to comfort the living and remember the dead, but all he wanted was to forget, for he would never find solace here.

At length, he came to a stop in front of a marble stone. Crouching on one knee in front of it, he mourned the brevity of the life that had passed. He had come down a long and difficult road since leaving Beth here.

Apart from the funeral, he had not returned once to her grave, an unspoken testament of shattered promises and unanswered prayers. The physician's oath he had taken years earlier had resulted in a sense of failure that had never completely left him. How unjust life was to be unable to fulfill that vow to the one person he had loved more than anyone else.

Weary from his sleepless night, he was not sure what had prompted him to come back here. What difference would his coming back make now? Had he returned for more self-punishment, to do more penance for that which he had never been able to forgive himself?

With keen awareness, he felt the weight of guilt and abandonment as he knelt beside Beth's grave. "I wanted to save you, *but I couldn't.* You'd be alive today if I just hadn't called you out that night." Steadying himself with one hand against the cold stone, the bitter confession ended in a strained whisper as he added, "I only hope you knew how much I loved you."

Memories of the night Beth died rushed into his mind. He remembered running, running, running, as far away from the hospital as he could get. Too late, he had discovered he was only running toward a future as dark and cold as the night through which he had come and all because of his anger with God.

But there would be no more running. Escaping had not resolved his struggle. Attempting to shield himself from pain had procured no victory.

Still crouching beside the headstone, his hand passed lightly over each letter of Beth's name, as if in so doing he might be granted some semblance of self-forgiveness. He brushed aside the snow from the base of the stone to expose the rest of the epitaph when something unexpected caught his attention.

Tiny green shoots of spring daffodils were beginning to push their way through the iron hard ground. *Someone had purposefully planted the bulbs of Beth's favorite flower over her grave. Who else but he would have remembered her love for daffodils?* He touched the tender leaves, marveling at their power of strength and survival in spite of the severe limitations of the cold. It was a miracle how anything so fragile could endure so much hardship.

Let him take hold of My strength, that he may make peace with Me…

The text from Isaiah came to him without warning. He looked away from the gravestone and glanced at the patches of snow melting in the warmth of the sun. He knew he had allowed the brutal events in his life to weaken and destroy his faith. And then, in a dismal effort to protect himself against further pain, like the snow, he had permitted himself to grow cold and impassive. To escape his own grief, he had succumbed to the very disease he had determined early in his career never to fall victim to—the disease of indifference.

Again, he touched the tender life emerging from the frozen ground. In spite of the cruel and unrelenting winter, the fragile daffodils still persevered.

He had been wrong to blame God for the trials that had taken place in his life, when all along it had been *he* who had made the choices that had brought him thus far. But could it be that, by linking his own weakness to God's strength, he might be able to put the past behind him and find the peace that had eluded him for so long?

And would that peace enable him to forgive?

He remembered the night Cory Robinson had received his kidney. Though he was grateful for his patient's life-saving surgery, Joe had felt tremendous indignation toward the drunken driver who had killed the young donor. And then he remembered something Beth had said. *"Sooner or later, you're going to have to find forgiveness because if you don't, the anger will ruin the rest of your life."* He bowed his head in shame as the relevance of her words expressed the very essence of his own intolerance.

He thought about Kevin Edison and the willingness of the Brennans to save his life, in spite of the fact that Kevin was the one responsible for the loss of their child. Through that experience had come a genuine understanding of what Ben Jordan must have been willing to forfeit for Callie, even if the penalty had meant risking the love and respect of someone he cared for as deeply as he had cared for Joe.

Slowly, he rose to his feet. Gazing down at the marble stone, he suddenly understood what had brought him to the grave.

Though he would never forget the love for the woman who had gone before, he felt a measure of peace he had never had until now. He reached out and touched the stone for the last time. "Good-bye, Beth," he whispered.

* * *

Benjamin Jordan's grave was on the other side of the cemetery. As Joe climbed the hill toward the tall, granite pillar in the distance, he thought how fitting that a hundred-year-old oak tree overshadowing the grave should rise like a tower of strength, just as Jordan had been to him.

Reaching the top of the hill, he came to a stop in front of the monument. Ben Jordan had encompassed his entire world during the stressful years of his surgical residency, and beyond that had become more of a father and a friend until the revered relationship had come to a devastating end.

Joe looked down at his hands. His anger had come with a price. The years of training he had spent with Benjamin Jordan had been recklessly thrown away in one night of rage—one night that had cost him not only his career, but a lifetime with a girl who had loved him far longer and with greater forbearance than he had ever realized. His anger seemed inconsequential considering what he had lost. Regret was little consolation.

He stood before the grave of his former mentor, suddenly realizing that memories, more than anger, were filling his mind.

Though tough and exacting, Jordan had another side to him of which few were aware. On one night in particular, Joe had seen through the rough façade more clearly than ever before.

* * *

Joe sat listening to his former mentor retell a similar story about the loss of a woman he had once loved. In an extraordinary transformation of character, he had pleaded with Joe to stop punishing himself for losing Beth and urged him to find forgiveness. With tears in his eyes, Jordan had uttered a mystifying statement. "And if you can find it in yourself . . . forgive me."

* * *

For months, Joe had mulled the baffling admission over and over in his mind, and yet had never reached an understanding.

Until now. With sudden realization, Joe understood exactly what Jordan had been trying to tell him. He understood for the first time that, in his own awkward way, Benjamin Jordan must have been asking him to forgive him for his secrecy.

Joe looked up at the bright blue of the sky and breathed in the cold, fresh air. He knew he would not spend the rest of his life in anger and resentment. *He could forgive Benjamin Jordan* and live in gratitude to a God who had not forsaken him but who had been leading him every step of the way. For whatever reason, known only to God, Beth's life had been cut short and, in a very real sense, given to Callie.

Callie . . . of course. On impulse, Joe knelt and brushed aside the snow from the base of the tombstone. The same tender, green shoots were coming up through the snow. An image rose in his mind of the hundreds of colorful crocuses and daffodils that had surrounded the Jordan estate every spring. Callie would have known those flowers had been her father's favorite, just as she knew they had been favorites of Beth. Only Callie could have planted them.

Joe rose slowly to his feet, his eyes still on the promise of spring that was making its way through the frozen earth. A startling parallel between the snow and the gentle perseverance of the flowers had miraculously unfolded before him.

Flowers in the snow, an impossible combination. Yet with God, all things were possible.

CHAPTER 43

Nightfall had long settled as Joe labored to complete the mound of paperwork in front of him, his office lit with only the brass lamp on his desk.

He had hoped by the end of the summer, he could resign his teaching position and return to surgery, but by autumn, his hands still lacked the necessary measure of strength and agility. However, he remained grateful that teaching had given him purpose and incentive to go on.

Though his life was returning to normal, he still felt a lingering sense of emptiness, a loneliness that long hours of work did not satisfy. Throughout the long days of summer and into the cooler days of fall, his quest to find Callie had yet to become a realization. Daily, he asked God to help him, to give him strength to endure whatever trials He saw fit to send, even if it meant spending the rest of his life without her.

The memory of the daffodils he had found in the cemetery earlier that spring continued to give rise to his hope that he would find her again. But with that same hope had come the more realistic notion that maybe she did not *want* to be found. It was yet another bitter pill for him to swallow.

A knock on the door broke his concentration. He leaned against the back of the chair and rubbed his eyes with his hand. Who would be looking for him at this hour?

"Who is it?" he called wearily.

"It's Maggie, Dr. Joe. Maggie McCarran."

He rose to his feet as Benjamin Jordan's former housekeeper entered the office. The smile on her face grew as she took a long look at him. "Dr. Joe, ya look great," she said in her quiet Irish brogue.

He stepped around his desk and wrapped her in a tight hug. "Maggie, you're a sight for these tired old eyes. How did you know where to find me?"

They sat down on the couch together. "It was the good Dr. Martin that told me where you were and whatcha been doin' with yourself."

"And what about you? What have you been doing with *yourself*?" "Well, I'm not about to retire yet, even though I could, easily, on the generous bequest Dr. J. left to me, bless his soul. I don't require much, ya know, but I found I just had too much time on me hands! So I hooked meself up with an old widowed Irishman named Brannigan, a retired banker nonetheless. I cook and clean for him three, sometimes four days a week. I figure if he's got any sense a'tol, he'll ask me to marry him sooner or later, and we can simply combine bank accounts."

Joe laughed. "He'd be a fool not to want you, rich *or* poor." Then his dimpled smile changed to reflect his restless query. "Do you . . . do you ever hear anything from Callie?"

She cleared her throat nervously. "Well, as a matter of fact, that's the reason I'm here."

Joe's eyes grew fearful. "Maggie, has something happened? Is she all right? Do you know where she is?"

"Dr. Joe, one question at a time!" Maggie insisted, holding up one hand. "Physically, she's doin' just fine. She's takes a bucket o' pills every day, but so far she's had no trouble." Joe nodded in relieved understanding. Then she hesitated, glancing down at the purse she clutched tightly in her hands. "But she's not happy. No matter what she says, I know she's not happy." She shook her head sadly. "Ya know I raised that girl like she was my own for more years than I care to remember. So I know what I'm talkin' about."

Joe drew a deep, anxious breath. "Do you know *why* she isn't happy?"

"Of *course* I know why she isn't happy!" Maggie affirmed quickly with a bold air. "She's been without the only man she's ever loved for too long." She took pleasure in Joe's wide-eyed expression. "She needs ya, Dr. Joe, just as much as I suspect ya need her."

Maggie's statement was more than he ever expected to hear. "I *do* need her, Maggie. I've been trying to find her for months." Maggie's eyes brightened. "You've been tryin' to find her?" "Yes! I found out she'd sold the estate and gone to work for her cardiologist in South Carolina, but by the time I discovered that much, she was no longer there. I've just been coming to dead ends . . . until last spring when I found daffodils growing in front of Beth's grave and more at Dr. Jordan's. I knew only Callie could have planted them."

Maggie nodded in agreement. "That she did. She wanted to do somethin' for the memory of Bethie, somethin' that would continue to give life, just as Bethie had given life to her."

Joe reached for Maggie's hands. "Please tell me where to find her, Maggie."

"Ya still love her, do ya?" "Yes, very much."

Maggie smiled. "Well, I only see her from time to time anymore. She's livin' in a little place away on the outskirts of the city, a far cry from that grandiose mansion she was raised in. She isn't workin'—doesn't even *need* to—so speakin' of time on your hands, she's another one with far too much of it right now." She opened her purse, pulled out a piece of paper, and placed it firmly in Joe's hand. When he unfolded it, he understood the real purpose for her visit.

"Ya know, in our conversations since she came back from Charleston, your name has rather conspicuously *not* come up. So I decided to leave well enough alone until I just couldn't stand it any longer."

Maggie rose to her feet, and Joe followed her to the door. She turned and looked at him one more time, a broad grin across her face. "You're still a handsome, charmin' man, Dr. Joe. Go to her. And use everything ya got!"

* * *

Dry October leaves scattered in all directions behind Joe's car as the city faded from sight in his rear-view mirror. The breathy autumn wind chased the leaves across the narrow, two-lane road ahead of him. To Joe, it seemed almost like a game.

The long drive allowed him a rare, but welcome, opportunity—an opportunity of uninterrupted thought to reconsider the events that had so significantly altered his life.

It seemed like an eternity past, but not so long ago Joe Travis had been at peace with his life. Had she lived, he knew Beth would still be at his side, just as he knew he would have continued to love her more with every passing day. Perhaps by now, there would have been a child between them.

But that idyllic life had ended in unexplained tragedy. As a result, the faith he had come to live by had been destroyed. The promises he once embraced had been replaced with a dark sense of foreboding. His compassion and optimism had gradually been exchanged for indifference and doubt, and the ensuing loneliness had threatened to drive him over the edge.

Until Callie Jordan reentered his life in a most unexpected way. He thought of all the years they had known each other, still marveling at how blind he had been to every sign, every hint, that she had been in love with him, solely and without condition. Through the difficult years of his surgical residency, through a myriad of trials and triumphs as he endeavored to begin his practice, Callie had been there for him, and it was she who had ultimately become the stabilizing presence in his life after he lost Beth, a time when he thought he had no life left in him.

Even though he had taken Beth for his wife, Callie had remained his cherished friend. Thus for weeks Stephen Lewis's remark had weighed heavily on his mind. *Callie knew that you could never love her in the same way.*

And to a great extent, the words were true. He had fallen helplessly in love with Beth, and had loved her with a pure and passionate love, unlike anything he had ever experienced before. They had become as one, in every facet of their lives. Thus, when she died, devastating him with unimaginable grief, he had coped with the loneliness and despair in the only way he knew how, by burying his love with her.

But Callie had seen through the façade. Where others had merely seen an angry man, he could not hide his guilt and grief from her. And once again, her friendship had come to his rescue, giving him reason to accept life again with all the risk and potential, joy, and pain that went with it. Unlike Beth, his love for Callie had grown in a quiet, imperceptible way. And though he loved her for different reasons, he loved her all the same.

And so miracles *did* happen—miracles at God's direction, not his. Yet what he had done with that beautiful miracle was inexcusable. His conversation with Maggie the night before had not ceased to worry him because she believed Callie wasn't happy. *She needs ya, Dr. Joe, just as much as I suspect ya need her*, Maggie had asserted. And he did need her and wanted her.

But could he convince her of that? Would carefully rehearsed words be enough to prove he still loved her and always had? Would she even allow him the opportunity to tell her?

The changing colors of the trees, with their varying shades of reds and greens and yellows, glistened in the late afternoon sun. Lengthy shadows fell across the narrow road as he rounded another curve.

For all his anxious thoughts, one light of encouragement seemed to penetrate the sadness. *All things work together for good*. He remembered the verse from Romans his mother had so often quoted. It would be difficult to embrace that promise, but he would try.

Lord, keep leading, he prayed silently, *just don't let me get ahead of You again.*

The dense forest seemed to enclose the road until at last he spotted a small frame house sitting all to itself not far ahead. He glanced again at the directions Maggie had placed in his hand the night before and then slowed and turned into the driveway.

Great trees rose like pyramids of gold, swaying listlessly in the last warm breezes of autumn as he brought the car to a stop. He opened the door and stepped out while gazing about the quaint surroundings.

The small house almost resembled a fairy tale cottage hidden away in the woods. Chrysanthemums of every color ornamented either side of a pebbled walkway that led to the front door. Behind the house, a stream tumbled gracefully over a bed of smooth stones, winding its way between banks overgrown with fading wild flowers. But he saw no one. He made his way to the front door, knocked once, and waited. Before he could knock again, the sound of footsteps coming toward the house caused him to turn.

And then he saw her. Callie walked up the hill behind the house, a muddy garden spade in her hand. An oversized hat perched atop her disheveled hair, the once bouncy curls reverted to strands of limp blond once more.

"Is there something I can do—?" Only now did she glance up while pushing the hat away. Her eyes widened as a small gasp escaped her lips. The hat fell to the ground behind her; the spade dropped from her hand.

For an interminable moment, they stood only yards apart, neither one moving. In her eyes, Joe imagined a combination of resentment and reservation, and he could only speculate with understandable reason what must be going through her mind.

He ventured a cautious step toward her. "Callie, I . . . I don't blame you for never wanting to see me again." The long rehearsed words began to elude him as an autumn breeze brushed lightly at his hair. When she said nothing, he stumbled on. "Cal, I was angry, but I was never angry with you. I was angry with your father. And not because he arranged for *you* to be the receiver of Beth's heart, but because . . . *because I loved him.*"

Long months of bitterness brought the admission to a momentary halt. "Your father meant everything to me," he said at last. "But that night when you told me what he'd done, all I could believe was that he'd betrayed our relationship. I assumed he thought the only way he could save you was by misleading *me*, and I just couldn't handle that kind of deception from someone I trusted as much as I trusted him." He unconsciously flexed his hands. "My anger cost more than anyone can ever realize. It took me a long time, but I finally came to understand that what your father did wasn't out of disloyalty to me, but out of a great love for you." He hesitated, silently praying for the right words. "Cal, there are a lot of people I need forgiveness from, but I need it from you most of all."

She glanced nervously at his hands. "You want me . . . to forgive *you?*"

"Callie, *please—*"

"But I was the one responsible for your accident!"

The memory of her determined visit to see him in the hospital and her confession of supposed guilt swept through his mind like wildfire. For by his angry silence, he knew he had allowed her to hold herself accountable.

He took a tenuous step closer. "Because you had the courage to tell me the truth about your surgery?" He shook his head incredulously, aching to take her in his arms. "You weren't responsible for my accident. *I was.*" He looked at her with beseeching eyes, unguarded, vulnerable, resigned to whatever consequences would come. "I had no right to let you take the blame," he continued hastily, "any more than I have the right to tell you . . . *I still love you . . . and always have.*"

Her eyes widened at the indisputable revelation. She stumbled toward him, and with inexpressible joy, he caught her up in his arms as months of loneliness without her came to an end. "Oh, Cal, I was afraid I'd never see you again!" he murmured, clinging to her as though afraid to let go.

She buried her face in his shirt. "I know Dad must have hated what he had to do, but he loved you, Joe. He loved you like you were his own son."

"I know . . . I know." He held her tighter. "Cal, I've hurt you so badly, but I've hurt myself most of all. Yet God allowed my own trials to lead me in ways I never dreamed possible. And He's led me all the way back to you."

She gently eased herself out of his arms. "But . . . how did you know I was here?"

"I went to the cemetery last spring and found the daffodils. I knew then you'd come back." He wiped tears away from her astonished face. "Last night, Maggie came to see me and told me where you were. I was afraid you wouldn't let me see you if you knew I was coming. But I had to come."

A smile edged at the corners of her mouth. "I was afraid you *wouldn't* come."

He pulled her into his arms. "I lost you once, I'll never let that happen again." He could feel her body trembling next to his own. "I love you, Callie, and I want to marry you more than anything in this world. Will you still have me?"

This time, there was no hesitation, no uncertainty now about his love for her. "Yes . . . oh, yes!" Cupping her chin in his hand, he kissed her long and lovingly. The Joe she knew had come home, the one she had lost, but who had come so far to find her.

As she rested safely inside his arms once more, the candor of a gentle voice came to her mind, *When you get lonely for Joe, think about me.* Stephen had helped her through a trial in which she could never have come through alone. Yet she had been unable to give him the love she knew he wanted so badly. That love had been given away years before and could not be divided.

She closed her hands over his, caressing the still visible scars. "Joe, your hands . . . "

"No one knows for sure," he said ruefully, "but I won't give up until I have to."

* * *

The elation Joe felt as their wedding day grew nearer stayed with him. Two weeks later, he and Callie exchanged vows in front of Evan Richards, surrounded by friends and colleagues in Paul Martin's candlelit living room.

Following the ceremony, the house—crowded with guests—was growing warmer by the minute. Paul slipped unobserved through the wide French doors to enjoy the cooler night air on the deck when, to his surprise, he discovered he was not alone.

Joe was leaning against the railing, gazing across the moonlit lawn. "A splendid night for a splendid occasion," Paul remarked as he joined his friend. "Are you . . . alone out here on your wedding night for any particular reason?"

Joe smiled pensively. "No, I was just thinking," he returned, continuing to gaze across the lawn. "A year ago, I never imagined I could be as happy as I am right now. Only God knows how many times I've thanked Him for bringing Callie into my life again." He turned and looked at Paul. "I'm not the same man I was, and I don't ever want to be that fiercely independent man again."

"You've come down a long road, Joe. You dealt with a lot of hard lessons."

"And in spite of myself, God was leading me through every one of them." He shook his head thoughtfully. "I thought God was beating me down in order to affect a change in my life, but I see now that's not how He operates at all. After I allowed Him to *open my eyes*, I saw He was actually lifting me up the whole time."

Paul smiled. "That's exactly right, my friend. God has a way of working things out in our lives, if we'll only let Him. He doesn't need our help. He could do it all with or without us. It's for *our* good that He chooses to use us, and only the Lord can make a way out of what seems an impossibility."

"I believe that now. And, Paul, you're another one I owe a great deal to."

The older man grinned and squeezed Joe's shoulder. "You don't owe anyone but Callie a lifetime of joy, and I'm happy for you both," he said, embracing the younger man with a fatherly hug.

Afterward, Paul leaned against the railing. Through the polished glass of the French doors, he could see Callie in her mother's satin bridal gown, surrounded by friends in the dining room. The small, unpretentious celebration was enough. Paul had been greatly pleased when she and Joe had accepted his offer to have their wedding in his home.

"You know, Joe, there's one quality for which you really have to admire Callie," Paul remarked.

"Only one?"

"Well, one that seems to stand out more than the others." Even in the dim light of the moon, Joe recognized the mischievous gleam in the older man's eyes. "And that is?"

"The girl has demonstrated a tremendous ability for patience. I hope you appreciate the advantages of that attribute."

Joe grinned sheepishly, the dimples in his cheeks deepening along with the color in his face. "I think I've come to appreciate that, and I won't let it go unrewarded." The two men laughed as they pulled open the doors and returned to the reception.

Maggie McCarran handed Joe a plate of food as he joined his bride at the beautifully decorated table. "Where were you?" Callie whispered. "They're waiting for us to cut the cake. You weren't trying to slip away without me, were you?"

"Of course not," he said seriously. "I was on the deck having a few minutes of thoughtful meditation."

"Then you *aren't* trying to get away from me."

"Mrs. Travis, rest assured it will be a dull day in the ER before *that* happens." He set the plate on the table and pulled her into her arms, thoroughly enjoying the amusing round of applause as he passionately kissed her.

Later, as they drove away toward their mountain honeymoon, with Callie's head resting comfortably on his shoulder, Joe breathed a silent prayer. *Dear God, thank you for the suffering, and thank you for the miracle of healing love.*

* * *

The hands of the surgeon trembled unnoticed as he called for the scalpel. For a moment, he looked upward past the giant lights and into the expectant faces of residents, medical students, and colleagues in the observation gallery above him. Then, with a prayer on his lips, he took the gleaming instrument, steadied his hands and began to make the incision.

After surgery, Dr. Joe Travis walked through the operating room doors and found Paul Martin waiting for him. "A beautiful job, Joe. Excellent work."

"Thanks, Paul, but I wasn't exactly alone in there," he said with a grin, glancing heavenward as they walked to the elevator at the end of the corridor. Then he looked at his watch. "Oh no, am I too late?"

"Not if you hurry."

The two men got off the elevator and quietly stepped through the door of the conference room. They stood against the back wall, listening as the speaker drew the seminar to a close.

"Organ donation means life, but it's more than a second chance. For most, it's the *only* chance. I know. Because I wouldn't be standing in front of you today if"—Callie Travis paused, collecting her words as well as her emotions—"if someone had not signed a donor card. The heart I received was a gift of life, a precious gift that came from a precious friend. My best friend."

Some gasps, and then a hush fell among the listeners, followed moments later by a standing ovation as Callie stepped away from the podium.

But no tribute for her touching speech rendered as much enthusiasm as that which came from her husband.

ABOUT THE AUTHOR

Bobbi Blanzy always dreamed of becoming a writer. In high school, she started a school newspaper and wrote short stories for friends. But when real life got in the way, she took a more practical route and went into education. Currently she teaches grades 1 - 4 in a multigrade classroom in addition to high school English at a small, Seventh-day Adventist Christian school in Elkins, West Virginia. She loves music, sings with a mixed quartet, and particularly enjoys entertaining (aka teaching) her students with her lively (sometimes bizarre) sense of humor. She lives with her husband and two spoiled dogs, and is the mother of three grown children.